The Child Daredevil Hero

A Fictionalized Account of a True Story
For ages 9 to 99

Illustrated
By the Author

By

Sal Kapunan
Ph.D., Ed.D.

authorHOUSE™

1663 LIBERTY DRIVE, SUITE 200
BLOOMINGTON, INDIANA 47403
(800) 839-8640
WWW.AUTHORHOUSE.COM

© 2004 Sal Kapunan.
All Rights Reserved.

No part of this book may be reproduced, stored in a retrieval system, or transmitted by any means without the written permission of the author.

First published by AuthorHouse 11/30/04

ISBN: 1-4208-0563-0 (sc)

Printed in the United States of America
Bloomington, Indiana

This book is printed on acid-free paper.

Dedication

I dedicate this book to *Victor Kapunan*, my forgotten youngest brother. Because he saw light only after the Big War, I forgot to include him in my Memoirs. I wrongly thought that because I wrote about my life during the war, it didn't include him. However, when I wrote it, he was already a big part of my life. I'm truly sorry for the omission!

I also dedicate it to all children who have suffered from the insanity of wars of all kinds. Finally, I dedicate it to all mothers, but especially to my late mother, *Catalina Castaneda*. To me, good mothering is essentially heroic! My mother was the greatest hero I ever knew! She raised ten children who became successful professionals.

Acknowledgments

I thank my wife, Ruthe, for encouraging me to write a special book for children. I thank my friends who encouraged me to write for their children and grand children.

Thanks also to Nora Percival and Professor Tom Hearron for helping me with the original manuscript.

I want to extend my heartfelt gratitude to the High Country Writers of North Carolina for critiquing some chapters of my manuscript. From their suggestions and criticicism, I learned significant lessons that I applied to my other manuscripts.

My special thanks to my brothers and sisters both in the USA and in the Philippines for their encouragement and support. Growing up with them provided me both the physical and moral support needed for my professional success!

Thanks to my loving family and especially my grandchildren. They inspired me to write this book so that they and other children might read it and learn about the heroism of an ordinary child!

My special thanks also goes to my long time friend, David Anderson, for his interesting design of the front cover of the book. It captured the essence of the story! David was skillful in manipulating a simple photograph of a canoe on the computer and turned it into something profound, mysterious and beautiful! It was truly amazing and admirable!

Table of Contents

Dedication v

Acknowledgments... vi

Preface.. ix

Chapter One. Burning and Massacre!... 1

Chapter Two. The Displaced Lopez Clan 9

Chapter Three. Diaz, The Angel of Mercy.. 16

Chapter Four. In the Gullet of the Enemy... 23

Chapter Five. The Raid of Ibizan.. 32

Chapter Six. Pangga, the Outrigger Sailboat 41

Chapter Seven. The Skipper Who Couldn't Sail 50

Chapter Eight. The Impossible Voyage! 55

Chapter Nine. The Swamps 67

Chapter Ten. A Special Assignment.. 80

Chapter Eleven. Survival Obstacles.. 90

Chapter Twelve. Survival Schemes 98

Chapter Thirteen. Depression! 106

Chapter Fourteen. Renaissance!.. 111

Chapter Fifteen. A Hermit by Choice 118

Chapter Sixteen. Playing Russian Roulette 125

Chapter Seventeen. The Tides and Fishing....................................... 128

Chapter Eighteen. A Hermit's Social Life... 133

Chapter Nineteen. Digging a Well 141

Chapter Twenty. New Ways of Fishing.. 144

Chapter Twenty One. Important Insights about Nature 148

Chapter Twenty Two. The Good Happy Life................................... 150

Chapter Twenty Three.   Famine! 154

Chapter Twenty Four.   The Treacherous Rivers 164

Chapter Twenty Five.   Selecting the Food Hunters 170

Chapter Twenty Six.   The First Food Hunting 175

Chapter Twenty Seven.   The Vicissitudes of Food Hunting 197

Chapter Twenty Eight.   The Liberation of Manila 206

Chapter Twenty Nine.   The Guerrilla Fighters 211

Chapter Thirty.   Daredevils and Heroes 214

Chapter Thirty One.   The Last Days of the War 227

Chapter Thirty Two.   At the Edge of a Breakdown 232

Chapter Thirty Three.   New Beginnings, Lucky Endings 237

Epilogue 241

Preface

The author had already told the basic story of *The Child Daredevil Hero* in his memoirs, *Surviving WWII As A Child Swamp Hermit* (1stbooks Library, 2002). But, the extraordinary daring and heroic aspects of the story failed to stand out for two reasons. In the first place, telling the story in the *first person* put too much constraints on his memory. He could mention only the details that he could still remember. Since the events occurred almost sixty years ago, the details were too hazy and fuzzy!

Secondly, the life of the swamp hermit greatly overshadowed the daring heroism of the boy because the latter was explained only in passing. Because of the title of the book, he had to put greater emphasis on the life of the child hermit. Hence, the reader focused more on the hermitic life of the child and less on his heroic deeds.

When he was planning to write his memoirs, he could not decide what to underscore. There were too many aspects to focus on. He kept shifting between the life of the hermit, the heroism of the child, how the illiterate thirteen-year-old overcame illiteracy and ignorance of the medium of instruction, how he overtook those ahead of him in class and his academic and professional successes.

His final decision was to underscore primarily the life of the child hermit. His decision was based on the fact that a child hermit was unheard of. Rightly or wrongly, he assumed that the potential readers would like to read about the unusual child hermit. The partiality for the hermitic life logically determined the title of the book.

By making that choice, however, he put less emphasis on the heroic adventures of the child in eluding the Japanese guards. Moreover, he omitted many interesting scenes, events and details that dealt with the obstacles he encountered in his journeys with his mother.

For instance, he didn't develop the natural ferocity and inherent dangers of the Rivers. Because they were set in a deep, rocky canyon, the Rivers naturally created dramatic and awesome whirlpools and rapids! They were awesome, although not as frightening as the Colorado River! The canyon vertically dropped the riverbeds to at least one hundred feet below the rim, in most areas. The drop left precipices on the riverbanks that made climbing out of the Rivers very difficult or impossible in the dark. Since any use of light would call Japanese attention to their presence, they had to travel in the dark! Navigating a small wooden canoe at night through whirlpools and rapids was not only daring but was always heroic!

The tropical rains caused constant *flooding* during the rainy season that made the Rivers almost impossible to navigate! The rainy season lasted between six to eight months a year. To minimize starvation among family members and relatives, they often steered their ten-foot long canoe in partly flooded waters!

Some rocky bends in the Rivers created deadly *whirlpools* that sucked canoes and people into their bowels! The *rapids* were so swift that they had to pull the canoe with long ropes from both sides of the riverbank!

The constant nightmare, however, was the *darkness*! In order to elude the Japanese guards, they paddled their boat through the Japanese occupied territories only at night. Maneuvering the small canoe through the whirlpools and the rapids in the dark was always a horrible experience!

But, what they were most afraid of were the *crocodiles!* The upper regions of the Rivers were infested with vicious crocodiles! When hungry, they attacked and ate even humans. The mature reptiles were wider and longer than their canoe. They could easily overturn the small craft and attack the riders!

There were other factors that overshadowed the heroic story of the boy. After the war, for example, his problems with *illiteracy* and *ignorance of the medium of instruction* consumed his entire life! These academic obstacles completely ruined his school life!

His repeated academic failures at every grading period led to severe *depression* and *despair*! He *attempted suicide*, which fortunately failed! Still, the attempt itself became the *turning point* of his life! An *instructive dream* taught him how to gain literacy and learn the foreign medium of instruction, without help from anyone.

On his own, he crept from the bottom to the top of his class. The *academic and professional successes* that followed later on became more important in the whole story!

For these reasons, after his memoirs, 'Surviving WWII As A Child Swamp Hermit,' was published in 2002, he felt unhappy with the fact that the child's heroism was merely a small part of the whole story. In fact, the weekly trips to obtain food for the family and relatives were essential to their daily survival. Their near death missions once a week were central to their lives! Without the food, they would have starved! But the cost of obtaining food could be their lives! Every trip was a life or death situation!

And yet, most of the feedback from the readers dealt with the child's hermitage and why his father chose him to do a he-man's job.

Consequently, he wrote this book in order *to emphasize specifically the extreme daring and heroism of the child*! Hence, he limited the story only to the boy's childhood during the war. The title, **The Child Daredevil Hero** would put the proper emphasis on the child's heroic deeds and the circumstances of his accomplishments!

In order to give a full picture of his childhood, however, the author had to retell his hermetic life in an abridged form. Even though he went out every week to obtain food, he was basically a hermit because he continued to live alone in a mangrove forest. Besides, his contact with people was brief and superficial. When he was at the village to prepare for their trips, he purposely remained uncommunicative to show his anger to his father and his teenage brothers!

To give himself greater freedom to tell the heroic stories, he chose to tell the tale in the *third person.* This technique would allow him to *fictionalize the story.* It also allowed him to change the names of the characters, including his own. The fictional element gave his imagination a greater freedom to add more interesting *details* and *dialogues.*

Still, the story is at least 95% factual.

He wrote this story primarily for young children from *age nine to ninety-nine.* He selected *age nine* because that was how old he was when the war started. He believes, however, that younger children may also benefit from reading it.

He also wrote for *older readers* because the adults were basically responsible for his life as a child. More importantly, the greater hero in this story was his frail mother, **Catalina**, who was then in her early thirties. She was the one who turned both of them into *daredevils* so that they could accomplish their deadly missions of obtaining food for twenty-five starving refugees. Hence, this book also celebrates the heroism of women!

He also wanted children to live, vicariously, through the heroic life of a boy when he was between the ages of nine and thirteen. This was the period when he formulated his own *philosophy of life* while living in a swamp. This was also the time in his life when he performed his heroic acts every week, for three years!

To enhance the interest in the narrative, he used dialogues extensively wherever and whenever he could. Dialogues allow the reader to listen directly to the voices of the different characters.

He tried to simplify the stories and the language. Hence, he changed every word that younger children might not understand.

However, when necessary, he retained certain uncommon words when he couldn't find a simpler substitute.

Moreover, he purposely retained certain *vernacular words* to give a *Filipino flavor* to the story. After all, it happened in the *Philippines to a Filipino boy*. More importantly, he wanted the reader to learn some *Filipino words* in the process of reading the story. The vernacular words will constantly remind the reader about the foreign setting of the story.

Yet, the story should not be alien to many children. American children can have a first hand experience about coastal swamps in the tropics by visiting some of the coastal swamp regions in Florida, eastern Texas or western California. They will have an idea of a canyon, whirlpools and rapids by visiting the Grand Canyon and the Colorado River.

They can have a firsthand experience with whirlpools and rapids by taking a rubber raft down the Colorado River! The front cover of the book tries to portray the awesome whirlpools and rapids!

Even though the story happened during World War Two, there are many small children today, in war ravaged countries, who have performed greater heroism than what the author has narrated in this story. The story is basically about the *human condition* and the *tragedies* and *near tragedies* that happen to some children anywhere in the world!

The author is a living witness to what can happen to some children. While some don't survive to tell their stories, there are others who are lucky to survive and tell their unique stories of uncommon heroism!

Chapter One
Burning and Massacre!

On May 6, 1942, after the fall of Bataan and Corregidor, in the Manila Bay area, General Jonathan Wainwright surrendered the Philippine Commonwealth to the Japanese Empire, through the Japanese General, Masahara Homma.

A collective shiver hit every Filipino home as if a blast of arctic air had swept through the torrid archipelago of over seven thousand islands! The Filipinos knew about the Japanese atrocities perpetrated against the Chinese in Manchuria and other Cities in mainland China!

Junior heard the order from his father that the family would immediately evacuate to the air raid shelter just three kilometers away. Salvador, senior, (Badong) predicted that the Japanese forces would arrive in the town of Mambusao in a day or so.

Badong and his brother-in-law, Rafael (Paing), had dug up the shelter about a kilometer above the base of the Mambusao Mountain. It was situated in a forested hollow of the Mountain. Both the Lopez and the Castaneda families were supposed to use the shelter in case the Japanese air force bombed the town.

The Mambusao Mountain

The air raid shelter was not suited for comfortable living. It was hot, humid and suffocating! The twenty-five evacuees spent their time outside the shelter where there was shade and mountain breeze. Both families decided to sleep around the grounds. At night, sleeping bodies were strewn around like corpses.

Suddenly, life was purposeless, strange and alien! Nobody knew what to do. There was an almost complete silence! Everyone was preoccupied with his or her own jumbled thoughts!

Two days after the two families had moved to the air raid shelter, at around eight in the evening, everyone heard two rifle shots, "Bang! Bang!"

"What was that, Badong?" Taling asked her husband. "It sounded so close; it can't be more than a kilometer away!"

"Obviously, they were gun shots. I guess they didn't come from Japanese guns. I would expect a lot more shooting if the Japanese were involved. The Japons would have bigger guns than just two pistols. I expect bigger weapons, like machine guns from the occupiers.

"Keep listening, Taling. I expect to hear more gun shots!"

He was right. Suddenly, everyone heard machine guns firing from the same general direction. Badong kept nodding his head, indicating to his wife that those were the Japanese guns shooting. The shooting lasted for at least ten minutes. Then, there was an eerie silence for at least forty-five minutes!

While waiting for more hostilities to happen, Badong said, "I'm sure that the last shooters were the Japanese. I have a strange feeling that they're marching towards the town!

"Let us go down to the meadows where we can have a clear view of the *poblacion* (population center). I expect something to happen there soon! I don't know exactly what."

Every body walked down the slope and looked for a good spot to view what might happen. Some sat down on the *cogon* grass; others remained standing and gazed at the sky and the cloud formations. There was a crescent that lighted the sky and the night. Junior saw the anguished expressions on everyone's faces!

Mabini, the oldest son, moved further down and climbed a small tree for a better view. Suddenly, he yelled, "I see a smoke rising into the sky! Look! Over to the right side of the town! I also see something burning!"

Paing yelled back, "Yes! Ah also see smoke and fire! Ah see more dan half a dozen at da center of da town!"

"*Dios mio!*" (My God!) Taling exclaimed. "I see several balls of fire shooting up into the sky! Look at how quickly the smoke is rising to the heavens!"

"Susmariajoseph!" (Jesus, Mary and Joseph) Dolor, Paing's wife, prayerfully muttered. "Da Japons are destroying the whole town!"

"Fire is now all over the town!" Badong remarked. "*Maldito! Que barbaridad*! (Curse words in Spanish) Those bastards are purposely burning the whole town! They have torched every street and every block!"

Both Taling and Dolor started to cry! They couldn't bear the sight of their beloved town going up in smoke!

"What will happen to us, now, that we are losing our homes?" Taling murmured, as bullet-sized tears dripped down her face.

"Where are we going to go?" Dolor asked, as if someone omnipotent could hear and respond to her question. "We can no longer stay here. We're too close to our enemies and our potential murderers! Dey'll kill us if we don't move away!"

All of a sudden, everyone heard machine guns firing in the burning town!

"*Susmariajosef!*" Dolor again exclaimed in a prayer. "Dey're killing da civilians!"

"Yes, Dolor," Badong remarked. "They must be killing those who had remained in town! I'm sure they're massacring the innocent people! They're evil barbarians and we should run away from them! We won't surrender to their authority!"

"Poor *tia Kikay*!" Taling murmured tearfully. "Oh! That poor woman! She refused to evacuate! She didn't care if she lived or died. I'm so sorry for all our relatives who had remained in town. I hope they'll find a way to escape!"

"Dis is a terrible day for Mambusao!" Paing wailed, full of sorrow. "On dis wretched night, we're losing our town and many of our relatives!"

"*Susmariajosef!*" Dolor cried out again in a prayer. "Ah feel like a lonely orphan, without family, home, town and relatives! Now, we have not'ing left! We might as well be dead!"

"Look, everyone!" Paing yelled. "Da fire is burning a tall building! I t'ink dat is our Sta. Catalina Church! *Carajo*! *Walang hiya*! (Curse words in Filipino) Dey are burning even holy places. Dat building next to da church is da *convento* (rectory)! Dat is where da parish priests live. Dey might be killing our priests too!"

"Paing, the assistant priest is our first cousin, Benjamin," Taling reminded him. "He was ordained only two years ago. That is a real shame! He is a great loss to our family!"

Columns of smoke rose and darkened the skies. Some fingers of fires pointed sideways, without any certain directions. They pointed to the right, left, up, down and every where else. Some flames couldn't decide where to go.

As the dazzling columns of fire and smoke rose to the sky, they took a variety of colors. The multicolored smoke saturated the clouds, forming a radiant spectacle!

The cumulative effects of the flames and the heavy smoke gave the clouds a reddish cast. The skies looked angry because the plundering invaders were burning down an innocent town!

The massacre and burning of the town of Mambusao

In a period of an hour, fire was exploding all over the community. The whole *poblacion* became a three-kilometer-square of a violent bonfire! It heated up even the empty spaces kilometers away! People's faces on the mountain slope glowed in the radiant heat!

Badong could no longer control the flood of tears cascading down his cheeks. After an hour of silence, he morosely confessed, "I feel so violated, helpless and in utter despair! I worked so hard for everything we owned! Now, they are going up in smoke literally!"

"Yes, Badong. I feel the same way!" Taling commiserated with her husband. "I'm heartsick, powerless and helpless!"

"That is true, Taling. We are losing everything! To make matters worse, this is just the beginning of the war. We're beginning with nothing. So, we can't lose anything more except our lives. We're still fortunate to be alive! All the members of our immediate family are all with us. We have to stick together and survive whatever the cost!"

"Badong, where shall we go now?" Taling asked. "We can no longer stay here because the shelter is no longer safe! We are too close to the *Japons*. I'm very nervous right now because we're within shooting distance!"

"Yes, darling. I'm thinking of the same thing. Honestly, I don't know where to go.

"Paing, do you have any suggestion where we can go from here?"

"*Manong*, if you remember, ah had suggested before to go to barrio Libo-o. You own a large farm dere. It has everything: food supplies and other necessities."

"To a certain extent, I agree with you. But, I have some problems with living in the barrio.

"In the first place, I'm not sure whether it is safe to walk along the highway to get there. The Japanese are deploying their forces all over the island. They'll be using the highway and overtake us because they use trucks and other vehicles."

"I think Badong is right," Taling interjected. "The *Japons* got here by using the highway system. If we use the same highway, they'll probably pass by us and kill us!"

"Ah see your point, *nang Taling*," Paing responded. "Ah just wonder if we can get to da barrio by some oder route."

"If there are other routes," Badong pointed out, "we don't know their existence. Hence, we're forced to take the highway, which would be foolish to do."

"So, what is our alternative?" Taling asked.

"Why don't we just climb da Mountain?" Dolor asked. "We're already almost a quarter of da distance to da top from here. Climbing da Mountain will give us a safer distance from da *Japons*."

Taling raised her hand and said, "I vote for Dolor's suggestion."

Paing also raised his hand and said, "We don't have any oder choice at dis time."

"Before finalizing the decision," Badong said, "I want to discuss what other benefits are there for climbing the Mountain? More importantly, is there a possible disadvantage in taking this route?"

"The oder advantage," Dolor pointed out, "is da possibility of discovering hiding places, like forests or caves."

"That is a good point, Dolor," Badong conceded. "But, can anybody think of something negative?"

"One negative factor," Taling pointed out, "is that the mountain is not likely going to provide us food supplies. Everyone knows that Filipinos don't normally farm the mountains. Except in the *Ifugao* regions of Mountain Province where ancient farmers had created those marvelous *rice terraces*, there is usually no water up there. I have seen some pictures of the rice terraces. Some of the stone walls of the terraces are over one hundred feet high. I believe, those rice terraces are the *eighth wonder of the world*!

The Ifugao Rice Terraces in Mountain Province

"In contrast, our modern Mambusao farmers don't have that kind of creativity. If some farmers have cultivated certain areas of the mountains, it would be in a small scale. We need constant food supplies to feed twenty-five people. And, remember, it has to be for the duration of the war!"

"Taling, you've also mentioned other negative factors, which are the lack of water and food," Badong repeated.

"Nang Taling is right," Paing conceded. "Filipinos farm primarily da flat low lands. By building dikes in rectangular shapes, dey catch and store rain water. Da water in da dikes allow da young rice plants to grow faster and taller. Da yield in wet farming is at least four times more dan dry farming."

"Even if we don't find any food or water in the mountain," Badong explained, "we can still find them in the lowlands nearby. The mountain range is not far from the low lands."

"Dat is right," Dolor chimed in. "We can hide in da caves or whatever we find up dere and still survive. But, only if we can obtain food and water supplies from da farmers in the low lands."

"Dat is true, Dolor," Paing said. "In dat case, dere is no real objection to your proposal to climb da Mountain."

"In effect, that is true," Badong said. "So, let us climb the Mountain, then. Let us leave as soon as we can, but no later than midnight."

"That is soon enough," Taling said. "I'll get the kids ready."

"Taling, Paing and Dolor walk closer to me," Badong began. "While we're climbing this mountain, I want to discuss some other topics. … What if we find nothing useful up in the Mountain? What do we do next? Where shall we go?"

"*Manong* Badong, when we made business trips to Aklan, before da war," Paing responded, "do you remember da large coastal swamps in the Ibajay and Makato regions?"

"Of course, I'll never forget them."

"You told me, at dat time, dat da swamps were excellent places to hide, in case da *Japons* invaded da Philippines."

"Yes, Paing. I still believe that the swamps are excellent places to hide."

"Ah suggest den dat we proceed to Sapian, if we find not'ing in da mountain. Let us explore da possibility of sailing to da swamp regions. We can rent a sailboat and hire sailors from Sapian. Dey can take us eder to Ibajay or to Makato."

"Of course, I vote to go to Makato!" Dolor interrupted excitedly. "Dat is where I was born. I was actually born at da seashore, in a small fishing village called Punta Oeste."

"Dolor, Makato is as good as Ibajay," Badong consented. "The problem is that it is much farther away than Ibajay. Furthermore, we don't know what the safety situation might be. Let us wait until we get to Sapian and decide what our best course of action will be."

"Dat is fine," Dolor said. "Just don't rule out Makato."

"I'm not ruling out anything, Dolor. Let us just wait until we reach Sapian."

"We're now on da top of da mountain," Paing said. "Ah don't see any trees here. What happened to the trees, manong Badong?"

"They were cut down by loggers years ago. My father had told me that this mountain used to be covered by a dense rain forest. But an influential politician in Manila had acquired logging rights from the American Governor Howard Taft, who was then the governor of the islands.

"The logging went on for years until all the trees had been cut down. Now, the cogon grass has taken over."

"Indeed, the cogon grass is every where!" Taling said. "I can see cogon grass as far as my eyes can see."

"If Taft had given logging rights to someone, does it mean dat da government owns dis mountain?" Paing asked.

"I suppose so," Badong answered. "When I was growing up, I always assumed that this mountain belonged to the town of Mambusao. Honestly Paing, I don't know who owns this mountain."

"Right now, the Japanese government owns this mountain and every other mountain in the Archipelago," Taling said sadly.

"Dat is true," Dolor said. "But, America will take it back from dem!"

"Just being on top of this mountain answers some of our questions," Badong observed. "Now we know that there is no forest up here that we can use for hiding. This means that we must keep on walking until we get to Sapian."

"Obviously, we have no other choice," Taling said. "Let us resume our hike while we still have some energy left!"

Chapter Two
The Displaced Lopez Clan

Mambusao was an idyllic community of about a thousand Spanish mestizo inhabitants. Spanish colonists in the 17th century had laid out, on a ten-block grid, the *town-center*, which is normally called the *poblacion* or population center.

The residents were relatively affluent landlords who had partly descended from the Spanish colonists. Because of intermarriages with the brown Malay natives, and later on with some Chinese immigrants, the predominant population was *mestizo* (mixed races).

There stood, at the center of the *poblacion*, a large town square, called the *plaza*. At the north end of the plaza stood the colonial church, dedicated to the patron Saint, Sta. Catalina. Next to the church was the rectory, called the *convento*, where the priests resided.

At the south side of the plaza were the municipal building and the municipal services, such as the police department, jails, courthouse and a post office.

Along the eastern and western streets that enclosed the plaza, were the residences of prominent families that anchored the community.

At the southeastern corner of the plaza was the residence of Don Hermogenes Lopez, affectionately known simply as *Don Mones*.

At one time, he was the richest and most powerful man in the community. He had been the town mayor for three consecutive times, until the provincial governor appointed him as district judge for life. His judicial jurisdiction covered several communities.

Don was an honorific title bestowed by the community to some persons regarded as extraordinary and famous!

Mambusao was a rural town on the bank of the swift but navigable Mambusao River. Before there were roads to the town, the River provided the people in the barrios, access to the commercial, religious, political, social and cultural centers of the whole municipality. The town was the commercial hub to the larger population centers of Capiz City in the north, Iloilo City in the southeast, Buenavista City in the southwest and Kalibo City in the northwest.

The Don Mones house was the most prestigious address in the town! It was situated right on the west bank of the River.

Sal Kapunan

Dona Leona and Don Mones

At the same time, it was located at the corner of the town plaza where people tended to congregate. The plaza was the social center of the town.

Don Mones and his family had immediate access to the River and all its commercial, social, religious and recreational amenities at all times.

He also had easy access to the social, political, religious and cultural activities that occurred in the *town plaza.*

From his front balcony, he could carry on a conversation with the prominent community members, as they passed by on their way to the church, the municipal building, the post office or to socialize in the plaza.

The plaza was where the young converged to play different games, to converse, gossip and flirt. Romances started and bloomed there.

And, in the late afternoons, the social elite took their promenade along the plaza and showed off their latest fashions. The men dressed formally in their stiff *Barong Tagalog shirt*, embroidered with fancy designs. And, the women wore their Maria Clara style dresses and the latest fashions from Europe and the United States.

From his balcony, Don Mones conversed with people who walked near his house precisely to talk to him. He was the prominent town mayor and later a judge, to whom they paid their respects.

Some times, he walked down to the front door to shake hands with the other residents. They carried on a lively discussion about politics, the events of the week or about their families.

From the balcony, he could see some devout people enter the Sta. Catalina church to make a short visit to pray for their sick or dying relatives. He could also see the maids gather around the artesian well in the plaza. They took turns in filling their containers with drinking water for different households. The artesian well was the chief source of potable water, long before plumbing was available to any home.

The Maria Clara dress

In the early evening, as the sun began to set, the church bell rang six consecutive times. It was six o'clock. Everyone stopped whatever they were doing to pray the *angelus*, which marked the end of the day and the start of the evening. While the bell tolled, some women knelt down on the ground to pray in silence. The men, by custom, remained standing but bowed their heads in silent prayer.

After the *angelus*, Don Mones raised his eyes to admire the beauty of the setting sun to his left. He looked at the silhouette of the church,

Sal Kapunan

the rectory and the townhouses on the plaza. He looked up to the golden Mambusao Mountain behind the town, covered by the gold *cogon* grasses that gave it its golden glow.

With heightened interest, he was delighted with the view of the Mountain that lazily meandered across the horizon. It served as the scenic background of his beloved town.

He gazed at the serpentine gorges of the mountain twisting down the slopes like monstrous emerald serpents. They accentuated the auriferous sierra.

Mambusao was a rural town in the province of Capiz, in the Island of Panay. It was the largest island in the Visayan region. The Visayan Islands, together with Luzon and Mindanao comprised the whole Commonwealth of the Philippines. It was still a colony of the United States but was preparing for its independence.

America colonized the Philippines in 1898 after Spain lost it in the Spanish-American war.

The Philippine Archipelago had over 7000 habitable islands.

Don Mones had nine children. He had three sons and a daughter from his marriage to Dona Leona Lozada, who died quite young. Then, he had three more boys and two girls from his marriage to Dona Aurelia Lozada, Leona's younger sister.

Don Mones left a rich legacy to his children and descendants. Without any formal education, he became also a balladeer, music composer, author, dramatist and playwright. By the time he died of natural causes, he had built a sterling reputation that beamed brightly on the pathways of his children and all his descendants!

His own children made him proud of their achievements.

Barong shirt

The Child Daredevil Hero

Putenciano, the oldest, became a renowned superintendent of schools. His second son, Salvador, was a successful businessman, farmer, politician, sailor and a roving entrepreneur. Jose was a famous mining engineer who discovered gold in several mountain mines. Felicidad became an outstanding school teacher.

His younger children became military men, bankers and teachers.

Don Mones was the paternal grandfather of Junior, who will emerge as the *unknown child hero of World War Two*. He was the fourth son of Salvador, the second son of Don Mones.

When the 'Big War' broke out, all the descendants of Don Mones were scattered in the different barrios in Mambusao. The family of Salvador, however, remained in town. After the burning of the town, the family was forced to wander far and wide!

When the war started, Badong and his wife, Taling, had also nine children. They were Mabini, Paterno, Hermogenes III, Junior, Leona, Trinidad, Ruperto, Diadema and Juliet. The tenth child, Victor, would be born after the war.

Before the war, Badong and Taling had enjoyed a business bonanza for at least seven years. They had a successful rice and corn wholesale business, a variety store and rice and corn milling businesses. Badong became an exclusive rice and corn distributor in the whole Aklan region of Capiz.

Catalina and Salvador, the parents of Junior

Their children went to elite schools, designed primarily for the children of landlords. They enjoyed an aristocratic culture inherited from Spanish colonists.

They spoke a vernacular called *Ilongo*, which was really *chabacano* (a vulgar form of Spanish). Unlike the Spanish colonies in the Americas where they taught Spanish to the natives, the Filipinos were forbidden from learning the language. The Filipinos who worked for the colonists on menial jobs, learned the language by hearing. Slowly, Spanish heavily influenced the native languages.

Sal Kapunan

The Filipinos speak eighty-seven different languages, which the colonists downgraded to dialects. In fact, they were distinct languages.

Every dialect, including Tagalog (the national language since 1946), is heavily mixed with Spanish. For example, every noun that refers to imported goods from Europe, America and other Spanish colonies is invariably in Spanish. For instance, the utensils are commonly called *cuchara* (spoon), *tenedor* (fork), *cuchillo* (knife), *plato* (plate) and so on. Filipinos use non-conjugated Spanish verbs extensively and weave them into the fabric of the vernacular. For example, the common greeting is, "Comosta ka?" (How are you?) This commonly used greeting comes from two Spanish words: *Como* and *esta*. However, *ka* is a Filipino pronoun, which means 'you.'

The ten children of Salvador and Catalina: Mabini, Paterno, Hermogenes, Junior, Leona, Trinidad, Ruperto, Diadema, Juliet and Victor.

The Filipinos use many Spanish nouns and adjectives but only in the masculine form. Because they learned their Spanish by hearing, many of the words are misspelled and even truncated. For example, *ahijado* (godson) becomes hijado and *aretes* (earings) becomes aretos

In truth, the Philippine dialects have become Spanish patois.

On December 7, 1941, America declared war on Japan after the aggressor country had treacherously bombed Pearl Harbor! As a colony of the United States, the Philippines, ipso facto, was at war with Japan.

Within hours of the bombing of Pearl Harbor, Japanese planes destroyed American bases around Manila and the neighboring provinces. They virtually wiped out the US Air Force and Navy in the Philippines.

It wasn't until May 10th 1942, however, when the Japanese forces torched the town of Mambusao, that the Lopez clan dispersed in the winds! Salvador's and Catalina's family just kept on moving from one village to another until they felt safe for the time being! Fear of Japanese raids kept them on the edge and ready to move to a safer hideaway! Their future was completely in a limbo!

Chapter Three
Diaz, The Angel of Mercy

They kept hiking for days, without any relief from the sun! Luckily, they were walking down hill most of the time, which made the trek less strenuous. Still, after eighteen days of walking, they felt worn out and were running out of food!

When they were about five kilometers from the beach community of Sapian, they saw a small hut in the middle of a wide meadow. It was on stilts and its windows were propped open. The hikers were sure the house was inhabited.

Badong yelled out loud, "Hello! Is anybody home? We are civilian refugees from Mambusao. Hello! Anybody home?"

A middle-aged man looked out of a window and said, "*Comosta ka*? Welcome to Sapian. Just a minute; I'll have to put on my slippers. I'll go down to meet you. ..."

He went down in his abaca slippers and introduced himself.

"I'm Juan Diaz. I own this hunting lodge. Where are you folks from?"

"We're from Mambusao. We're running away from the *Japons*. My name is Badong Lopez."

Taling, Paing and Dolor also introduced themselves. The children moved under the shade of the hut and sat down to rest and fan themselves with their hats.

"From Mambusao!" Juan repeated the town. "That is quite far away. I assume you hiked across the mountain."

"Yes. We did," Taling said.

"Only few people have done that! Where are you going?"

"We want to reach Sapian before it gets dark," Badong answered. "We're looking for some sailors who will take us to Ibajay or Makato."

"I'm afraid you can't get there from here, for many reasons. First of all, nobody lives in Sapian right now. The civilians had left the town days before the *Japons* arrived."

"Are da *Japons* here too?" Dolor asked.

"Of course, they are! They arrived here at least fifteen days ago. In fact, the soldiers are now marching towards Aklan.

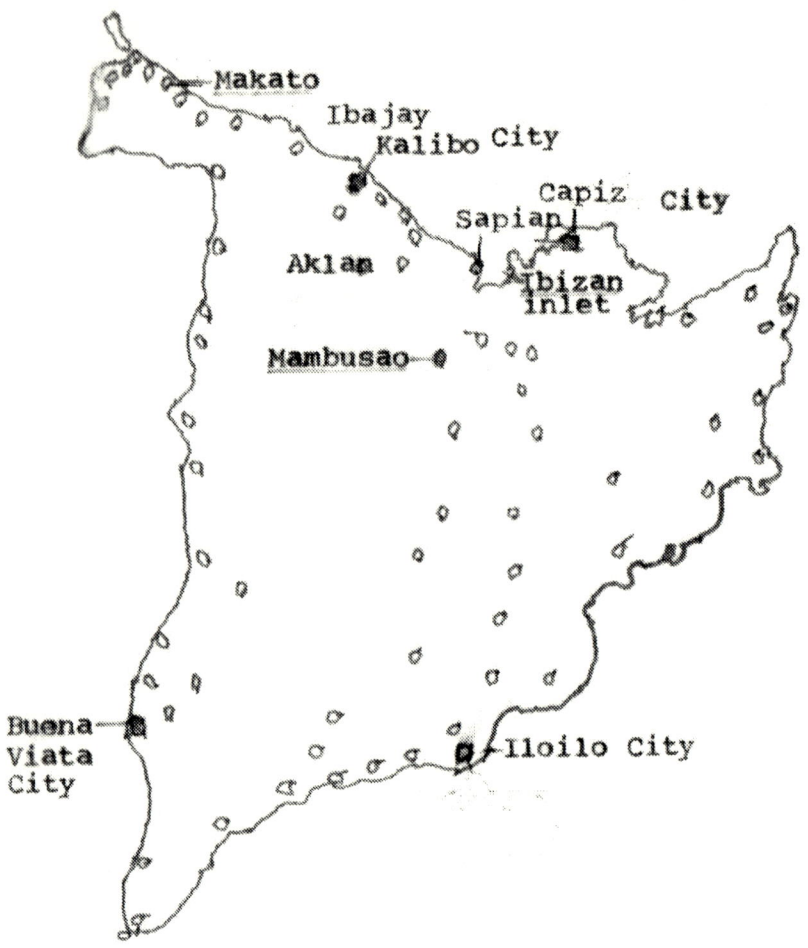

Map of Panay Island. Capiz Province was the northern portion of the island. After the war, the western portion became a new province of Aklan. Mambusao is at the center of the province of Capiz.

"They are deploying soldiers from Capiz City to Kalibo and other Aklan towns. The highway is full of Japanese soldiers."

"Have dey been deploying soldiers here since dey arrived in Capiz City?" Paing asked.

"Yes, they have. I don't know how long the deployment will last. I expect it to stop in a few days."

"With the *Japons* all over the land and the highways, I assume we can't get to Ibajay or Makato by land," Taling remarked.

The Child Daredevil Hero

"Yes, that is right," Juan said. "But, I don't think you can get there by sea, either. You might not know it, but the Japanese Navy has blockaded the shipping channels through out the islands. Every civilian sailboat at sea has been either destroyed or confiscated."

"I guess, we arrived too late!" Badong observed.

"Too late for what?" Juan asked.

"To go to Ibajay or Makato," Badong responded. "This new situation calls for new plans.

"Juan, can you recommend a place where we can hide from the occupiers?"

"Yes! Ibizan! It is a small fishing village just across the Sapian Bay. On a clear day, you can see it from the Sapian beach."

"Can you get there by land?" Taling asked.

"Were it not for the Japanese using the roads, you can easily walk to the village from here. Of course, it will take you at least four days. Because of the Japanese presence, however, you can get there only by sea."

"I thought you said earlier that the *Japons* had already confiscated all civilian boats," Badong objected. "Is the sea route to Ibizan outside the big shipping lanes?"

"Fortunately, yes. The Sapian Bay is not in the shipping channel. Moreover, you should cross the Bay only at night when the Japanese patrol boats are not on duty. During the day, there is a chance that the patrol boats might see the canoes from a distance. They can chase and arrest the boaters."

"Thank God for dat information," Paing said. "At least, we have a place to go to without being arrested or killed."

"How long will it take to cross the Bay?" Taling asked.

"I think four to seven hours, depending on the skills of the boaters."

"Juan, please tell us something more about this village you're recommending to us," Badong asked.

"I know Ibizan very well! I have been going there since I was a child.

"My family has resided in Sapian since colonial times. My parents owned a very large fishpond there, which I have inherited. The village is small; it has no more than one hundred people."

"Do you think we will be safe there for the duration of war?" Taling inquired.

"Taling, to be perfectly honest with you, I don't know of any place where anyone can really be safe. Still, my answer is that you will be safe there.

"First of all, my family lives there now and I'll be crossing the Bay as soon as the *Japons* are out of the highway. I have a man observing the Japanese deployment now and he'll tell me when it is over.

"The primary reason why I think it is safe is because the village is very small and insignificant to the Japanese. It has no strategic, economic or military value to them. The people are poor and there is no reason why the *Japons* will invade it."

"I want to ask a 'what if' type of question, Juan," Taling said. "What if the soldiers should invade the village? Is there a place to hide from them?"

"Of course, Taling. There are large boulders on the side of the hill, just past the coconut grove. They are ideal for hiding. The boulders will protect you even from canons."

"Where can we rent canoes for crossing the Bay?" Badong asked.

"Badong, you came to the right man. I have several *single outrigger canoes* hidden in the bushes for the purpose of helping stranded people like you. I have enough of them to accommodate all the twenty-five of your group."

"What are outrigger canoes, Juan?" Badong asked.

"They are *bancas* that have floats on the side for more stability. You can have two or just one float. My *bancas* have only one float."

Single Outrigger Canoe

"Juan, you're truly an angel of mercy!" Taling exclaimed and hugged him tightly out of sincere gratitude. "We are so lucky to have found you!"

"Think nothing of it, Taling. It gives me pleasure to help those in need.

"While we're waiting for the ideal time to cross the Sapian Bay, I'm inviting all of you to share my hunting lodge. Let us wait patiently until the *Japons* have vacated the roads. Then, we'll cross the highway to the beach and paddle across the Bay together. I'll let you know when my scout tells me it is safe to cross the highway.

"Meanwhile, I'm inviting all of you to share whatever I have. I have a lot of rice and vegetables from my garden. I have some fresh meat I brought in myself by hunting. Come up and rest your aching feet!

"Of course, I have a lot of water to drink."

"Juan, between you and me, why are you still here in Sapian while your family is already in Ibizan?" Badong asked.

"I came here to hunt some deer, wild pigs and large iguanas. However, I also miscalculated the arrival of the *Japons* and what they might do militarily.

"I got stranded here. However, I knew I could easily escape to Ibizan any night I decide to go. In fact, I had planned to leave for Ibizan last week. I changed my mind only after seeing a large iguana that got away. I set up some traps that I check every day. The big reptile has eluded me for several days now. I know, it is just a matter of time."

"Juan, I really appreciate your generosity! I intend to make it up to you if and when we survive this war."

"Badong, it is my pleasure to help those who have been victimized by the ambitions and greed of the Japanese emperor. If we survive this war, I'll send the bill to him as part of war reparations."

"Without your help, Juan, I don't know where we'd end up. We didn't even know the *Japons* were marching down here too. We can easily fall into their barbaric hands."

"Badong, I know we are the same kind of people. I noticed that you're also a Spanish mestizo, like me. I'm sure you'd do the same for me if I were in the same situation."

"Juan, can you give me some pointers about crossing the Bay? I don't know anything about navigating a canoe across an ocean."

"You came from Mambusao, Badong. I assume you're not used to large waves, ocean currents and winds. I'll try to wait for the ideal night to cross the Bay. Still, there are conditions that nobody can predict. For example, the wind might suddenly gather a lot of strength; it happens quite frequently. Then, the waves may begin to swell larger and higher and spill into your canoe. Don't panic! You can easily survive such a situation.

"Make sure every *banca* has a bailer, whose only job is to scoop the water out of the boat. Every boat is provided with two buckets for bailing. When necessary, put another person on the job. Unless you bail out the water, the craft will become waterlogged. Then, it may capsize and even sink!"

"You're right Juan. I wouldn't know how to handle these situations."

"Does Paing know anything about canoe navigation?"

"He is as bad as I am."

"Don't worry Badong. I have experienced men who will navigate the *bancas* for you."

"I'm so glad to hear that. I'd feel more comfortable if your men handle the boats for us."

"All right, then. I'll instruct my men to take charge of each boat. All your men need to do is help paddle the vessels and bail out the water.

"I'll let you know, Badong, when I think the conditions for crossing the Bay are right."

"Thank you again, Juan. I'll repay your kindness and hospitality by doing the same favor to others! As my wife had said earlier, 'You're an angel of mercy!' I'll add that you're also a model of charity and goodness!"

"I'm happy to be in the position to help you, Badong!"

Chapter Four
In the Gullet of the Enemy

"Don Ambrosio, my name is Salvador Lopez. My friends call me, Badong. I know about you from my new neighbors. They suggested that I see you about some of my questions."

"Am happy to *uh* ... meet ya, Badong. Since ya already know ma name, ah ... won't give it to ya again. But, just coll me Ambros. Please, don't coll me *don*. *Dat* is too formal and high for me. Am just an ord'nary fisherman."

"Ambros, you might know already that I'm a new refugee in Ibizan."

"Yes, Badong. Ah hear ... 'bout ya; dat ya arrived from Mambusao. For *mi communidad* (for my community*)*, may ah ... say, 'Bienvenido' (welcome) to ya for ma humble village."

"Thank you for your hospitality. Ambros, you have the reputation of knowing a lot of things about this village and about life in general. Some people even refer to you as the *village philosopher.* I hope, you don't mind my asking you some questions."

"Not at all. But, ... ah warn ya dat some of what ya hear 'bout me are exaggerated.

"For me, admire a person like ya. Ya seen many wonderful thangs dat ... ah only dream 'bout. Ya come from ... a bigger world dan me. Yet, ... ya're 'umble enough to ask a simple man like me."

"You're far from simple, Ambros. Everyone here thinks very highly of you."

"Maybe so. But, Badong, ... am an ignorant man. Like *los indigenos* (the natives) in this village, am ... uneducated. In fact, *ah* can't even write ma name.

"We're ... simple fish'men. But, dere are *thangs* we know somethang 'bout. For exemple, ... ah know somethang 'bout fish, sailboats, how to mend ma nets and ... how to get 'long with ma neighbors."

"Ambros, I'm sure you know the answers to my questions. I suspect that many of them might seem too simple to you; but very complicated to me."

"Don't fool ya'self, Badong. Everythang ... outside ma world is complicated!"

"But, I'll be asking you only about your world. Let me start with a question about navigating boats and ships."

"*Aha*! Ah know somethang about dem."

Sal Kapunan

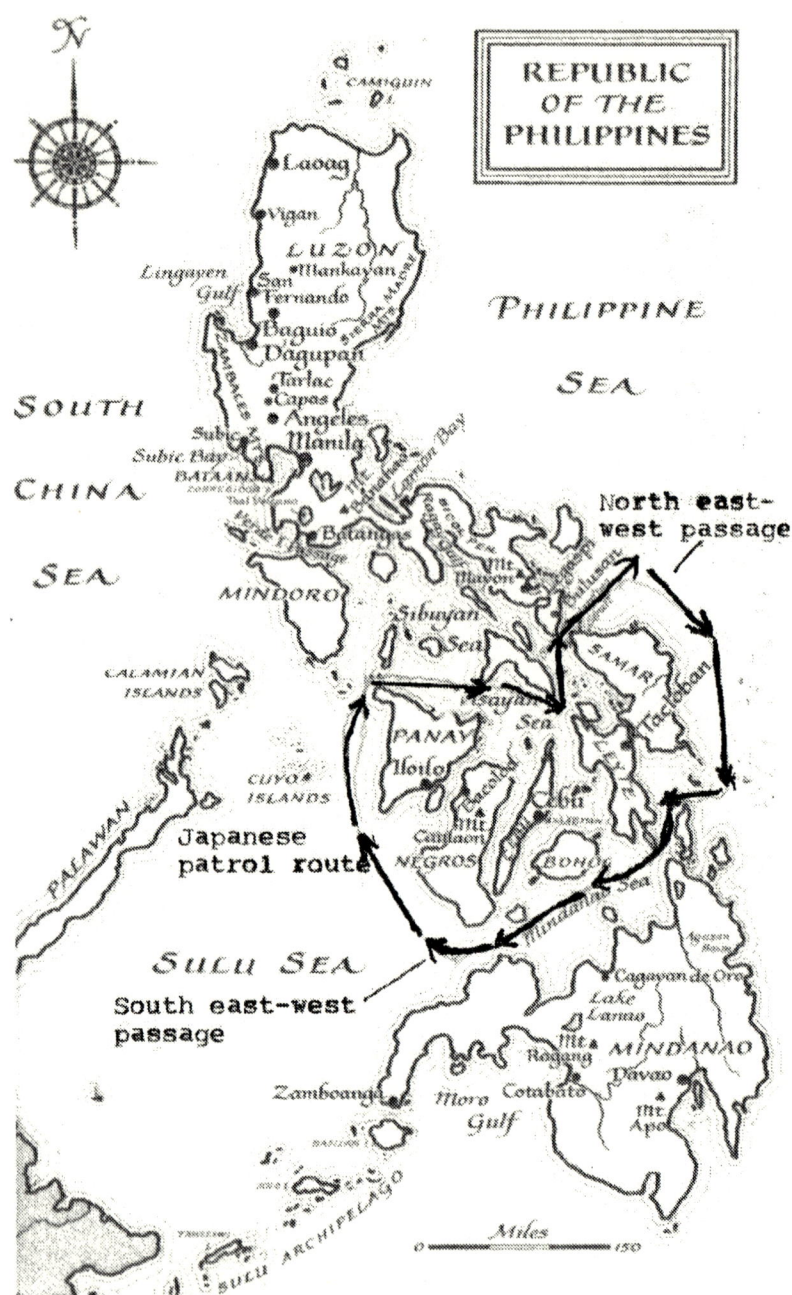

Map showing the route used by the Japanese Navy when it blockaded the shipping channels during the war.

The Child Daredevil Hero

"I've observed that the Japanese patrol boats sail only eastward. Occasionally, they also patrol westward. I'm also curious why do they use only the same routes every day?"

"Ah thank ya asked me tre questions, Badong. Dey are simple questions, yes! But, ... da answers are not. It might take me da ... whole day to answer dem."

"Ambros, take your time. I'm not going anywhere."

"Badong, am a ... simple man and ... ah say what comes to ma mind. So, ... let me 'splain to ya as well as ah can."

"Ambros, answer my questions as you feel like answering. If you don't want to answer them, that is fine with me too."

"T'ank ya for being considerate, Badong. No one ever asked me des questions before.

"Try to understand dat ... *da* big ships are much heavier dan sailboats. Dey sink in deeper into da water. What ah mean is ... dat dey need deeper waters in order to ... sail shrough.

"Da problem is dat ... da waters between many of da islands look wide but ... dey are shallow. Da big ships can't ... sail shrough dose waters.

"For a long time, ... fisher men and navigators studied des waters. Dey ... recorded da channels where da waters are deeper. Deir findings were ... put in ... a fancy word colled ... *nautical maps.* Da maps inform da sailors of ... where da deeper channels are.

"Badong, ah've never looked at ... nautical maps. Ah wouldn't know ... how to read 'em. And, nobody 'round here has one. But, people told me dat ... da waters right in front of us is part of a long deep channel. Des waters are ... good for deep sea navigation.

"Dere are very narrow channels dat are colled *uh ... straits ,*like da *San Bernardino Strait.* Dey look more like wide rivers dan oceans."

"Where is the San Bernardino Strait?"

"It is between da Bicol Peninsula and the island of Samar."

"That is not too far from here. Samar is already part of the Visayan islands."

"Y'are right, Badong. In fact, San Bernardino is part of da chain of channels in da Visayan islands."

"Well, then, tell me the whole chain of channels."

"O.K., den. Starting from da west and going east, da deep channels start ... south of Mindoro Island. Den, dey go north of Panay Island. Den, dey go along da Visayan and Sibuyan Seas. What dey coll *seas* mean ... wide bodies of salt water. Da Visayan and Sibuyan Seas are part of da Pacific Ocean.

Sal Kapunan

"As da ships go furder towards da east, dey enter da *uh ... San Bernardino Strait.* Past San Bernardino is already da Gulf of Leyte, which is also part of da Pacific Ocean."

"So, Ambros, what you have just described to me is the whole *east-west passage* for large ships across the Visayan Islands."

"Dat is right, Badong. Ya 'splained everythang ah said in just few words. Ya have to be *uh* ... a very intelligent man!"

"Thank you for your compliments, Ambros."

"Now, let me point out somethang ... interesting for all of us who live here in Ibizan.

"Because we live right here along da nordern rim of da Island of Panay, we ... see da Japanese patrol boats every day. As ya said earlier, ... dey navigate eider eastward or westward, along da deep sea channels."

"*Caramba! Carajo!* (Curse words in Spanish) Ambros! Are you telling me that we live right along the *shipping lanes* completely controlled by the *Japons*?"

"Sorry to inform ya, ... yes! We live right along ... da naval corridor!"

"Does this mean that any Japanese boat that we see out there patrolling can literally invade our little village?"

"Yes, Badong. Look out der, right now, ... Do ya see about ... twenty Japanese ships sailing toward da east?"

"Yes, I see them. But, I see maybe even more than thirty-five ships."

"Yes! It doesn't matter how many. Every one of dos ships can anchor ... within a kilometer of our village!

"Even worse, Badong. Da Japanese soldiers don't even have to come to da shore. Dey can just ... point deir canons at our village and shoot! Dey can reduce Ibizan into a pulp or even to nothang!"

"*Que lastima!* (What a shame!) I brought my family right into the gullet of the enemy! I can't believe I did that!"

"In effect, yes! If, tomorrow, da American navy and deir allies decide to engage da Japanese navy in a ... naval battle in des waters, we'll 'ave front seats right 'ere! Ha! Ha! Ha! We can watch ... da whole naval battle from where we sit. Da battle ships will be shooting at each oder ... right in front of us!"

"Ambros, I assume that we will be in the line of fire! And, we might be accidentally hit by their shells and canons."

"Of course, ... it is possible. Dey will be shelling at each oder and ... most of da ammunitions will land around deir targets. But, some of da canon balls ... might land right at us! We're dat close ... to da action! Ha! Ha! Ha!"

The Child Daredevil Hero

"Ambros, why are you laughing? This is not funny! This is like waking up from a terrible nightmare! I'm sweating right now from shock and fear!"

"Badong, ah didn't realize dat our location was dat bad. In fact, ah tot … we're privileged to be where we are."

"I simply don't understand why you're excited about our vulnerable location. I expect you to be horrified and afraid! We are terribly open to attacks and raids by the *Japons*!"

"Forgive me for … not reacting as ya want me to. Ah live all mi life here … in dis unexciting sleepy village. Suddenly, because of da war, … ah expect to see some naval battles right where ah can see dem!"

"Ambros, if you're not afraid for yourself, aren't you concerned for the life and safety of your family, relatives and people?"

"Not really! Even do we're vulnerable, as ya said, am sure dat we and … our village are not directly affected by da war. We're just insignificant civilians! Dey have no reason to attack us!"

"But we can be in a line of fire!"

"Not exactly. Stray bullets? Some times. And … canon balls? Dat would be occasional and harmless!"

"Tell me the truth, Ambros! Are you a frustrated navy man or soldier? Are you one of those people who love extreme danger?"

"Yes! Ah admit it. If not for my age and poor health, ah would be a guerrilla fighter right now. In fact, … two of my grown sons, Jose and Roberto, are now in da hills fighting as guerrillas. Ah hate des invaders! Ah'll kill any *Japon* when ah have da chance!

"Let me tell ya my fantasy, Badong. Ah picture miself … watching a naval battle in which … da American Navy is hitting and sinking every Japanese ship! Da battle is so one-sided in favor of da Americans, so dat da last remaining Japanese battle ship …raises a white flag and surrenders! And, Japan is completely defeated and surrenders without any conditions! Dat would be da ending of dis world war!"

"Ambros, I see where we clearly differ. You live in a fantasy world; while I live in a nightmare!"

"Perhaps, one oder way of saying it is dat … am optimistic; but ya're pessimistic."

"No, Ambros. I'm not pessimistic; I'm realistic. In contrast, you're idealistic."

"Badong, ah don't understand what idealistic means. So, it does not matter to me and ah don't want to know."

"Ambros, let me ask another question. Honestly, I'm scared now to ask you any more questions! I'm afraid that your answers will reveal more bad news for me and my family!"

"Go ahead. Ask yar question."

"As I said earlier, most of the Japanese ships that I see out there are moving eastward. Why do the last patrol boats just disappear into the right horizon?"

"Aha! Ya have been very observant, Badong. Da simple answer is ... da fact dat da naval headquarters of da *Japons* is only about ten kilometers north of us at Capiz City. So, da ships dat ya see in da late afternoon are only going home to deir port."

"Is that really true?"

"Yes, Badong! If ya climb da hill behind us, ... ya'll see some of da ships, including carriers loaded with airplanes, tied up in da port.

"Ya can see everythang with ya'r naked eyes. Am sure some of ya'r children 'ave ... already seen da port of Capiz. Am not kidding ya, Badong. Ya can see da Japanese naval port from ... da top of da hill or from da seashore below da hill. Ah keep going up dere miself ... to observe what da *Japons* are doing."

"Ambros, the facts you have just told me make this place even a worse nightmare than a few minutes ago! No wonder I felt scared to ask you more questions!"

"In my opinion, Badong, it is better for ya to know all da facts. Den, figure out what to do 'bout dem."

"I agree with you about that point. Still, what I have just realized is that when the allies come back to retake the Philippine archipelago, we will be in real trouble! Among the ports that the Americans will bomb will be the port of Capiz!

"Our closeness to the port puts us all in serious danger. Stray bombs can easily fall over us!"

"Again, ... we differ in our assessment of danger. Ah see da danger as quite remote. Da distance between ... da Port of Capiz and Ibizan is at least ten kilometers. It is not like ... being next door!"

"Of course, you're entitled to your opinion. But, to me, ten kilometers is very close!"

"Yes, of course. Ah know dis war will be more interesting when ... ah see some naval battles going on right here!"

"Ambros, when the Japanese ships navigate eastward, after they get out of the San Bernardino Strait, where do they go?"

"Da ships dat go eastward, ... normally come from da port of Manila, which is ... in da west coast of Luzon. After dey get shrough da *east-west* channels, dey go out to da Gulf of Leyte. Da ships may den go to … Japan, China, Australia, Guam, … da Hawaiian Islands, to various ports in America and anywhere in da Pacific.

"Ah swear, Badong, am just repeating what people tell me. Ah have no idea where dos places are."

"Ambros, give me another missing but important information. Are there other east-west passages between the islands anywhere?"

"Yes! Der is only one oder passage. It is in da soudern islands. If ah can remember it correctly, da route, going from west to east, from da Sulu Sea, is … across da Mindanao Sea. Den, shrough da … *Surigao Strait*. Dat narrow passage is just … nort of da big island of Mindanao.

"Da Surigao Strait is very narrow. Ah had traveled shrough der a couple of times. Da ship has to pass south of da islands of *uh* … Leyte and Samar but nort of Dinagat Island."

"Ambros, I'm really impressed by your knowledge of these islands and the secret passages between them!

"Still, I must ask you this very important question! Is it possible that the Japanese patrol boats that go eastward, continue moving to the south through the Gulf of Leyte? Then, they enter the Surigao Strait and go westward, out into the Sulu Sea? Then, they go north on the west side of Panay Island and turn right and enter the northern east-west passage? Are all these movements possible?"

"Yes, dey are all possible because da Japanese control all des channels. Dere is … nothang dat would prevent dem from doing so."

"In that case, they might just go round and round along the two east-west channels until the end of day."

"Dat routine dat ya suggest is probable!"

"Yes! This circular patrol routine along the channels would explain why the last patrol ships, late in the afternoon, just disappeared on the right horizon."

"Yes, Badong. Ah had already 'splained dat da ships return to da naval port in Capiz City. Derfore, after dey make deir last round of patrolling, dey … anchor deir ships in da port. Dat 'splains why ya don't see dem again until da next day."

"That makes complete sense, Ambros! Do you realize that we have just figured out what the Japanese patrol boats do when they are out patrolling? This information is valuable to the allies. Do you realize that the allied navy can trap and annihilate the whole Japanese navy because of this information?"

"Ah certainly do, Badong! Da allies don't have to trap dem. Dey can just wait at da end of each strait and sink dem as dey come out slowly! Da narrow straits forces da ships to slow down!"

"Dis is a valuable information! Ah'll share it with my guerrilla boys. Perhaps, dey can relay it to General MacArthur."

"That is a wonderful idea, Ambros. This is an important insight on our part!"

"Badong, an important idea just came to me! Don't … share dis information with anyone! My guerrilla boys suspect dat der are Filipino spies in our village! Dey suspect at least three spies. If da spies know dat ya have dis valuable knowledge, … da *Japons* might kidnap and kill ya!"

"What about you? Are you safe?"

"No! Both of us are … in danger! We must never discuss it with anyone! Our lives are seriously in danger! But, … ah'll still tell ma boys because dey are family."

"I promise you I won't even tell my wife and children. There is always a chance that they might secretly reveal it to others."

"Ah'll tell my boys not to tell anyone where dey got da information!"

"Ambros, this conversation has been very informative to me. Much of the information, however, is disturbing! By knowing our precise location, in relation to the Japanese forces, I've realized that I've made some bad judgments.

"For example, I'm really bothered by the knowledge that my family has been running away from the Japanese since we escaped from Mambusao. But, instead of distancing ourselves from them, we went right into the mouth of the monster!"

"Badong, ah understand why … ya feel terrible about ya're situation. Ya must feel like … ya have betrayed ya'r family!"

"Exactly! But they'll understand that we didn't know where we were going. What do I do now, Ambros? What do you suggest?"

"Listen, Badong. Ya're going shrough *uh* … a reexamination of yar strategy. Ah had to do da same thang … at da beginning of da war. Knowing how close we were to da occupiers, naturally, … ma tendency was to run away … as far as possible.

"Ma family helped me to examine carefully … where we could go to be safe from da Japanese. After at least a month of discussion, … we arrived at da same conclusion. We realized … dat we were as safe here as anywhere else."

"How did you figure that out?"

"First of all, ... every place we knew was close to da ocean. It meant dat wherever we went, ... we were still vulnerable to da *Japons*. Ah said earlier dat we are as safe here as anywhere else. Our safety is based on da fact dat we don't matter to da *Japons*. We're just insignificant civilians.

"Da *Japons* know dat we live here. If dey needed to invade us, ... dey would have done so several times already. In fact, dey ... have not attempted to raid our village at any time.

"Take my word, Badong. Da Japanese commanders ... had already decided to leave us alone. So, enjoy yar stay here in Ibizan ... until da war is over. Ah consider ya lucky for choosing to live here!"

"Ambros, can you think of any reason whatsoever why the *Japons* might decide to invade this village?"

"Ah can't thank of any. So, let yar mind relax! Ah assure ya, ... ya have nothang to worry about!"

"Thank you again, Don Ambrosio. Now I know why the village folks think of you as the resident philosopher!"

Chapter Five
The Raid of Ibizan

Don Ambrosio was right. The Japanese navy knew the existence of the civilians in Ibizan but they regarded them as harmless and left them alone.

When the happy month of May came around, Taling started a celebration of Flores de Mayo (The Flowers of May) in honor of the Virgin Mary. She assumed that the *Japons* would not even suspect that the Filipinos in Ibizan were celebrating a religious festival during war time.

Beds of flowers with Mayon Vulcano in the background

Some volunteers built a little chapel and decorated it with artificial and fresh flowers. Someone lent a large statue of the Virgin Mary. Taling installed it at the center of the altar. Some people found some old candles and lit them in the early evening, while the faithful sang devotional songs to the Virgin Mary. Then, Taling led the communal praying of the rosary.

The Child Daredevil Hero

After the religious devotions were over, young men and women sang folk songs, accompanied by two guitars, a ukulele, a violin and two banjos. Someone started to dance and others followed. Some folk dancers performed popular numbers like the *Tinikling, Fandango sa Ilaw, Sakutin* and others. Everyone was having a good time and forgot all about the war. Every night, the festivities went longer and longer until around midnight.

The dancing couple tiptoe and jump in time to miss the banging bamboo poles. Their attempts to avoid being hit by the bamboo poles unwittingly made them imitate the movements of the tikling bird (heron). For this reason, the dance is called Tinikling.

One night, however, a Filipino soldier, in uniform and fully armed, showed up to join the festival. Nobody paid much attention to him. However, Junior overheard the whispers that he was a soldier, who was unofficially on leave. Others were surprised why he was not in hiding in the hills or in a cave.

Early the next morning, at around five o'clock, Taling saw seven Japanese launches moored right on the beach. The soldiers disembarked with drawn swords.

She yelled, in a controlled voice, "Wake up, everyone! The Japanese soldiers are raiding our village! Wake Up!"

Badong immediately ordered, "Everyone! Run up to the hills and hide! Don't carry anything! Go! Go! Don't look back! Run! Hurry up!"

Taling picked up her two-month old son and ran as fast as she could! She heard the soldiers chasing her and she ran even faster! Suddenly, she stumbled and fell on her child!

The soldiers passed by her and left her unharmed. They were rushing to the house, where the Filipino soldier had stayed. They kicked the door open but nobody was in. They searched the whole house for some evidence.

Then, they fanned out into the neighboring homes and interrogated everyone. They routinely tortured the men to extract military information! They bayoneted six of them and left them for dead!

The commanding officer was unhappy with the information. He ordered a civilian shot to death to intimidate the other civilians to cooperate! He ordered the arrest, interrogation and torture of more men!

Still, the terrified civilians insisted they knew nothing. They told a consistent account. *Yes, they saw a Filipino soldier but he and his hosts had left the village the night before. The hosts were refugees in the community and they knew little about them. They came from the town of Sapian.*

By three in the afternoon, the launches left the village but only after they had tortured half of the men, wounded six and killed one. The raiders had completely intimidated the entire population!

The commander issued an ominous warning, "I return and kirr arr if invite Firipino sordier to fiesta!"

Of course, the civilians knew that the Japanese raiders could return for whatever reason. They might return just to harass the poor civilians. They might return any time because they have *Filipino spies* working for them. They found out about the Filipino soldier enjoying a wholesome festival because of a Filipino spy or spies who acted as observers for the occupiers.

The disturbing thought was that there might be several spies living in the village. Everyone was asking, "Who might be a spy?"

Because of the suspicion that spies might be every where, people became secretive and even anti-social. They didn't want to say anything that might be interpreted as anti-Japanese.

The villagers became suspicious especially of the refugees who came from some other villages or towns. Consequently, the Lopez family became objects of suspicion. Badong had a younger brother who was a Philippine Constabulary.

Captain Edwardo Lopez, with the other officers and members of the Constabulary, had surrendered to the Japanese forces on May 6, 1942. The Japanese command forced them to take arms as new auxiliaries of the Japanese forces. In effect, the Japanese forces had annexed the Constabularies and coerced them to work and fight for them.

Edwardo retained his rank of captain and lived in Capiz City with the Japanese forces. Suddenly, there was a rumor that he might be the person who sent the Japanese soldiers to raid the village. The hostility against the refugee population became obvious just from the hostile gazes of the natives.

Two days after the Japanese invasion, Taling's infant son died in his sleep. She was inconsolable because she felt guilty for the death of her baby! She couldn't stop crying and couldn't sleep! After a week of grieving, Badong became alarmed that his wife might become ill or suffer a nervous breakdown!

"Paing, your sister has not been able to sleep for several nights," Badong said to his brother-in-law. "She hasn't eaten a meal in a week. She just drank some broth every now and then. She said she has no appetite."

"Ahm saddened to know 'bout her situation. It's understandable why she grieves for her lost son. What do ya t'ink we can do to help her?"

"She wants to leave this village, as soon as possible! She is sure the *Japons* will come back and kill all of us!"

"Dolor too has been having nightmares after da raid! What can we do to help da women?"

"The women are not the only ones who have problems. I've been losing a lot of sleep over Taling's condition! She has been losing a lot of weight. If she continues to refuse sleep or take any food, she'll become sick and die!"

"What alternatives have ya considered until now?"

"My mind has been working overtime! Still, I have not been able to come up with any good solution.

"I'd like to take her out of this village and bring her to some place that is safer like Makato. With this war raging viciously, however, I can't think of anything that makes sense."

"*Manong* Badong, ah suggest dat we go through every possibility. Let us just rule out anything dat is far out and impractical. Perhaps, we can narrow down our possibilities."

"We can do it that way or *um* … start with what we really want to do. For instance, what I want to do is to learn how to sail. Then, I'd like to buy a big sailboat and escape from here to Makato!"

"Dat is a better suggestion dan mine. But, how can we learn how to sail when we can't take out any boat? Everyone is afraid of being arrested by da *Japons*. Fishermen have not taken out their fishing boats to deep waters. Dey are afraid dat da *Japons* might kill dem and confiscate deir property."

"Then, maybe we ought to learn how to sail without taking any sailboat out."

"How do ya propose to do dat? I don't tink dat ya can learn how to sail without practicing on real boats."

"We will observe the sailors carefully as they sail. They're still using their small sailboats but keep them close to the shore. Perhaps, later on, they might allow us to practice on their boats."

"But, ya can keep on observing and still not know how to sail. Ah think we must practice on real sailboats to get da feel of sailing."

"Paing, that would be the normal procedure in peacetime. But, there is a big war going on and we can do only what is possible!"

"I think I have a better idea! Why don't we look for a cargo boat that we can buy and actually practice on it!"

"Why a cargo boat? Ah don't even know what dat is."

"There are twenty-five of us. We need to load various types of food and drink. We have to take with us some small animals like chickens, pigs and goats. Then, we have clothes and some small furniture. We need a big boat that can carry everything we want to bring with us."

"Tell me first, what is a cargo boat? How does it differ from da sailboats dat we see around?"

"Don Ambrosio Tolentino had explained to me why we might need a cargo boat. The sailboats we see around are too small. I think he called them *passenger* sailboats. They are fast and their primary purpose is to take passengers and some cargo from one port to another.

"Ambros explained that cargo boats are larger, wider and slower. Their primary purpose is to carry cargo from one commercial port to another."

"Now, ah see why dere are no cargo boats here. Dis is not a commercial port. But, where can we find a cargo boat to buy?"

"Don Ambrosio knows one cargo boat being hidden in a *sangja* (fish pond). A refugee from Sapian, Esteban Jaramillo, owns it. He had used it to transport rice, corn, dried fish and other cargoes from Sapian to Capiz City during peacetime.

"On his return trip, he loaded his boat with luxury goods that came from America and other countries. He had made a killing on the luxury goods because his customers were the rich families in Sapian.

"After the Philippine surrender, he transported his entire family from Sapian to Ibizan. Then, he kept it hidden in the swamp."

The Child Daredevil Hero

"In dat case, we should go and see senior Jaramillo and find out if he is interested in selling it."

"Exactly, Paing. Let us go and visit him. He owns the two-story house near the fish pond; the one with aluminum roofing."

"Ah know which one dat is. Da man must be very rich! His house is da biggest and da most beautiful in da village."

"Before we see him, however, I'd like to have a conversation with Don Ambrosio, the village philosopher. I'd like to use him as an intermediary.

"I'd like to find out, through him, whether Esteban might consider selling his boat and for how much? I want the village wise man to soften him up by recommending us to him."

"Dat is a wise idea. Due to Ambrosio's influence, we might be able to buy it for a reasonable price."

"Don Ambrosio, I know you're a friend of senior Jaramillo, who owns a cargo boat. My brother-in-law, Paing, and I are interested in making an offer to buy it. But, I want him to know that we have hardly any cash. The *Japons* had burnt down our homes and businesses and we had lost almost everything.

"As you might have heard, my wife is having severe physical and psychological problems. The Japanese raid and the death of her infant son have traumatized her! I must take her and the rest of the group to Makato, where she might be able to recuperate.

"Don Ambros, may I ask you a great favor? Please find out if Esteban might sell his cargo sailboat to us?"

"Badong and Paing, am sorry to hear dat ... ya're planning to leave da village. Ah know ya came from a landlocked community of Mambusao, *uh* ... which means ya know nothing about sailing. Both of ya are mature people and ah shouldn't treat ya like children.

"However, when it comes to sailing, ya're worse dan children! Honestly, the children of Ibizan ... know more about sailing dan ya do!

"As da oldest member of dis community, ah feel ah must tell ya dat, ... in ma expert opinion, yar plan to escape by sailing is impossible!

"But, ya asked me to do ya a favor to see Esteban. Ah will still comply with yar request. Give me ... a couple of days and ah'll tell ya what ah find out."

"Don Ambrosio, we're all ears," Badong said to the wise man five days later. "We're eager to find out what Esteban told you."

"Badong and Paing, ... we have our own special way of doing thangs in dis village. We never ... directly bring up da purpose of our visit. Dat would be regarded as rude!

"Ah brought a little gift and ... talked about his family and mine. Den, we drank a few glasses of *tuba* and ... talked about pleasant thangs.

"At some point, ... ah talked about yar families and where ya came from. Den, ah told him ... what wonderful persons both of ya are.

"And, den finally ah told him ... how wonderful his cargo boat was. By dat time, he knew da purpose of my visit."

"That was polite and clever of you to approach him that way. But, I'm not as diplomatic as you are, Don Ambrosio. I have a sick wife and a sister-in-law who also has problems with her sleep. I want to learn how to sail as soon as I can. Would it be rude of me to ask you now what he told you?"

"Yes, Badong. Ah consider it rude, indeed, because y'are pressuring me! But ah forgive ya because of da illness of yar wife.

"All right. Ah'll tell ya what he said. He doesn't want to sell it to ya 'cause ya don't know how to sail."

"I was afraid he might say that. Don Ambrosio, would you allow us to see him and explain our special case directly to him?"

"Of course, ... ya can see him on yar own. But, ... ah don't thank he'll change his mind. He loves dat boat and he doesn't want to sell it to ya or to anybody else. Above all, ... he wouldn't want to sell it to someone ... who might lose it at sea."

"Don Ambrosio, let me thank you, from the bottom of my heart, for trying to convince Esteban for us.

"I don't pretend to be a better negotiator than you are. I'm just more desperate and terribly in a hurry!"

"Yar welcome, Badong. Ah wish ya better luck!"

"Don Jaramillo, may I introduce myself, if I may. My name is Salvador Lopez and I'm a refugee here from Mambusao. I knew about you from Don Ambrosio Tolentino."

"Welcome, Senior Lopez. Don Ambrosio did mention you and Paing, your brother-in-law, to me. I assume that you received my message."

"Yes, senior. That is why we are here to plead our case directly to you. I want to apologize for my rudeness of approaching you directly. I bring you no gifts because the war has reduced me to poverty.

"I would like also to apologize in advance for by-passing our usual Filipino formalities. I'm direct because I'm under duress!

"My wife, senior Jaramillo, is now gravely sick because she lost her infant son recently after the Japanese raid of Ibizan. She hasn't slept nor eaten for almost three weeks now! I must take her away from this village. I intend to take her and the rest of the group to Makato. If I don't take her away from here, she'll die!

"Senior Jaramillo, I'm asking for your consideration and pity for the sake of my wife and family! I promise you I'll meet every condition you impose upon me in order to buy your sailboat!"

"Senior Lopez, I can feel your pain and concern for your wife. But, my boat is not for sale! It is my primary business asset. I'll need it when I resume my wholesale business after the war is over.

"My business, before the war, was that of a *middleman* for the local fishermen in Sapian and the neighboring communities. I bought fish and other marine products from them. After I had accumulated a certain amount to fill my sailboat, I took my products to commercial ports, like Iloilo, Capiz City and even to Manila."

"That is very interesting to know, senior Jaramillo! I was also a *middleman*! But, I dealt with rice, corn and other commodities that the local farmers sold to my store to create cash. Every week, they bought medicine, can goods and other commodities they needed for their families.

"I also sold my goods wholesale to small retail stores throughout the Aklan region."

"So, you were also a middleman! Let me shake your hand again, Senior Lopez. We are in the same business; we understand each other's language! From now on, just call me Esteban."

"And, just call me, Badong. I'm glad to talk to you directly because we're both business people!"

"Badong, even though I don't want to sell my boat, I'll negotiate a reasonable price for you to help you out of your situation! However, I'll sell only on the condition that you learn everything that you need to know in order to navigate it properly. I want you to respect and love that vessel!

"I had that boat custom-made; and I had even done some of the work on the hull. Moreover, I designed the sails myself. I really love that boat!

"I'll teach you everything I know. When you're ready, I'll take you out and practice with the boat at night, when the Japanese patrol boats are not out to get us."

"Esteban, I'll learn everything you can teach me so that I can take good care of the boat. I'll take good care of it and love it because it will be our *salva vida* (life saver)!"

"Dat is right," Paing added. "Da sailboat will be our life saver. It will save my sister's life and will give us a new life in Makato!"

"Badong and Paing, let us drink some *tuba* and eat some marinated *bangus* for *ante pasto*. I invite both of you to stay for supper. You'll honor me and my family with your company and friendship!"

"We accept your invitation with gladness!" Badong responded. "Let us raise our glasses of *tuba* and drink to our safety, to the end of the war and to the happiness of our families!"

"I'll drink to that," Esteban said.

"I drink to dat," Paing said.

"I'll rename the boat *Pangga* for my beloved wife. As you know, *pangga* means beloved in *Ilongo*. To me, the name refers both to the sailboat and to my wife, Taling."

"That is an appropriate name for the sailboat, Badong. Now, I feel better about losing it because I know you'll take good care of it! I'll always remember the elegance and grace of that vessel. I have owned it for only ten years; now, it will be yours.

"Have a good and safe trip on the beautiful sailboat named *Pangga*!"

"Thank you so much Esteban. I can't thank you enough! And, my wife thanks you so much! Pangga will take her to Makato and save her life!"

"Tank ya very much Esteban," Paing said. "Ah assure ya, ah'll help in caring and maintaining da boat for as long we can!"

"Now, come and join me and my family for supper!"

Chapter Six
Pangga, the Outrigger Sailboat

What Badong and Paing bought in a hurry was a single-masted sloop outrigger, with a triangular mainsail. It was a fifty-foot hand-made cargo sailboat with hand-painted sails.

Outrigger Sailboats

Nine-year old Junior asked, "*Tatay*, are those decorations and *uh* ... bright colors on the sails dangerous? Will they *uh* ... attract the *Japons*, who might then arrest us?"

"I agree, son. The sails would be better if they were just plain or even black. They will better blend with the surroundings. However, there is no time to make the changes. We will go ahead and sail away, even with the loud decorations."

"The hull of the boat is also *uh* ... attractive, with three different colors. Will those bright colors *uh* ... also call attention to the boat?"

"I agree; they will. But you must understand that Filipino sailboat owners are proud people. They hire artists to paint and decorate their vessels. Sailboats are status symbols for some people."

"What is a status symbol, *tatay*?"

"It is a valuable piece of property that some people own to tell others they have money."

"Does it mean they're rich?"

"Not necessarily. They just pretend to be rich in order to impress other people."

"*Tatay*, I noticed that this boat *uh* ... looks different from all the other boats around. It is much longer and larger. But, it is not as wide as the *uh* ... fishing boats I have seen around here."

"You're very observant, son. This boat is different because it is a *cargo outrigger*."

"What is an outrigger? And, why is it called a uh ... cargo boat, *tatay*?"

"Junior, you have always been a pest because you ask too many questions."

"I'm sorry, *tatay*. I didn't mean to annoy you. I just wanted to know *uh* ... what an outrigger means."

"I'm sorry, son, for sounding annoyed. I'm nervous and afraid that one of these days, you might ask questions I don't know how to answer. Then, I would feel embarrassed."

"No, *tatay*. That will never happen because *uh* ... you already know everything!"

"Son, you'll never know how much pressure you're placing on me, until you become a father yourself. For now, I'll answer your questions while I still know the answers.

"An outrigger means that the boat has a special framework that extends outward from the body of the boat, to several feet on each side. Floats, made of bamboo logs or other suitable materials, are attached to the end of the framework. The floats stabilize the vessel.

"Look at those three long arms extending more than twenty-five feet from each side of our new boat, named *Pangga*. Notice how they are tied to the giant bamboo floats, which also look like long tiny boats. The use of outriggers makes the boat much wider and therefore more stable."

"That is a very clever invention, *tatay*. You said that the floats are *uh* ... like long small boats. You said that they help the boat to become more stable.

"Are there sailboats where *uh* ... the floats are real boats but are very narrow?"

"Why would anyone make them into real boats, son? This time, I'm asking you to answer my question, for a change."

"Yes, *tatay*. If they are real boats, then *uh* ... little kids like me can ride in them. And, *uh* ... there will be more room for people to ride."

"Ha. Ha. Ha. Son, you make me laugh! One of these days, you may invent a three-boat sailboat for the purpose of drowning brats like you."

"I'll think about that, *tatay*. It might be fun uh ... making the floats into real thin long boats."

"Son, let me tell you why it wouldn't work. When the sails of the boat are fully loaded with the wind, the float touching the water bears the load of the sail. What happens then is that the float is forced down under water. The float might sink for about four to six inches in water.

"If the float were a real boat, it would be filled with water. So, the float boat would then sink and the sailboat would fall over and capsize."

"If I'm the inventor, *tatay*, uh ... I'll make the 'float boats' big and high so they don't go under water."

"That is clever thinking, son! I've never seen a three-boat sailboat before. Still, it is theoretically possible."

"I think children, like me, uh ... would like to ride in the *float boats*. It would be a more exciting ride. The children will not get wet *uh* ... because the riders will ride only in the float that is up in the air."

"It is an interesting idea, I admit. But, it wouldn't work! The large float boats would make the boat heavier and slower. But, part of why it is fun to ride a sailboat is because it is fast."

"Right, *tatay*. It would be slower. But, uh ... I will make the sails bigger and wider! That would make the boat sail even faster!"

"Son, I didn't know you have such an active imagination to create such weird inventions! Perhaps, you can even imagine sailboats that swallow other boats. You can even imagine sailboats that catch sharks on their own. Can you, son?"

"No, *tatay*. But, I can imagine *uh* ... my three-boat sailboat with children riding in the float. It would be exciting to ride in a boat float *uh* ... while it is up there in the air. Also, those riding there *uh* ... will put added weight against the wind. Therefore, I can make the mainsail uh ... even wider and taller, if I want to."

"Son, you've made your sailboat even more weird! But answer this question. Those kids who are riding in a float boat up in the air, what happens when the same float goes down to the water? Don't you think that they will then get wet?"

"When that happens, *uh* ... the boat changes its position, like when it is tacking. Well, the riders then *uh* ... will transfer to the other float. There, they also provide *uh* ... added weight against the sail. And, they will remain dry because uh ... the float is up in the air again."

"Son, you have just invented a new type of sailboat. If we survive this war, I hope you invent and produce it. Then, you can sell your new invention to millionaires and make us rich."

"Do you think I can really invent anything, *tatay*?"

"Of course, you can. You just did it."

"No, *tatay*. That was not inventing. I was just playing in my mind."

"I know, son. But that is how you get started."

"And, why is it called a cargo boat, *tatay*?"

"Junior, I thought you were finished asking your questions today! You should pay me for answering so many questions every day. Do you also ask other people many questions, son?"

"No, *tatay*. I ask only those uh ... who know and are nice about explaining their answers.

"*Tatay*, is it bad to ask questions? Some people don't like to answer them."

"Son, it is good to ask questions. It is a good way to learn from others. But, there are people who are not sure about their answers. They can get annoyed especially when they don't know the correct answers.

"You are wise, son, to ask only those who like to answer your questions. I have to admit that you can be very annoying!

"What was your original question, again?"

"Uh ... What are cargo boats?"

"They are usually large boats used primarily to carry loads of merchandise, like rice, corn, fish and others, to large ports. Before you ask me about ports, they are towns, villages and cities on water, where boats load and unload merchandise."

"What are passenger boats, *tatay*?"

"Where did you learn about passenger boats? I didn't use that word to you earlier."

"I learned it from my friend, Santiago. He said that *uh* ... his *tatay* has a passenger sailboat. But, he didn't know *uh* ... why it is called that."

"For some strange reason, I thought you might ask me that question when I was talking about cargo boats.

"Any way, some boats are called passenger because they are used for transporting people from one port to another."

"I still don't understand why *uh* ... it is called passenger boat."

"Son, the people who ride boats, buses, trains and other vehicles are called passengers."

"But why are they called passengers?"

"Son, I'm not a linguist. I think people are called passengers when a boat, bus or airplane gives them passage or a ride."

"What is a linguist, tatay?"

"Oh, my goodness! Junior, once again, you get me tied up to answering your endless questions. I won't get anything done if you keep this up! I have to get this boat ready for our departure!"

"I'm sorry, *tatay*. I only ask questions *uh* ... when you use big words that I don't know."

"So, it is really my fault that you don't know the meaning of some of the words I use?"

"No, *tatay*. It is my fault for asking the questions. Next time, *uh* ... I won't ask you anything when you're busy."

"Sorry, son. I'm only mildly upset with you because I'm preparing this boat for a long voyage. Because your mother is sick, I have not been able to sleep properly. I become irritable when I lack sleep. I don't want you to stop asking questions. Please, ask me some other time."

"Yes, *tatay*. Can I ask just one last question?"

"Go ahead. Ask me."

"Are sailboats in other places, like America, the same as our sailboats here?"

"According to Don Ambrosio, who knows a lot about boats, the outrigger boats make the Pacific Ocean sailboats different from those in the Western world. That means that the sailboats in America or in Europe don't use the outriggers."

"In that case, sailboats in America must look weird!"

"Weird to you? Perhaps. But, they won't look weird to Americans."

"Thank you *tatay* for *uh* ... informing me about sailboats. I know more *uh* ... about them today than yesterday.

"I'll join my friends now at the promontory. We'll eat oysters that growing on the boulders. They are so delicious!"

"See you later, son."

"Bye, *tatay*!"

"Ambros, I'm sure you know now that I bought Senior Jaramillo's cargo boat."

"Yes, ah've heard it. In dis little village, ... ya hear about everything dat happens to everyone.

"Badong, if yar coming to me ... to ask my approval of yar plans to leave Ibizan, yar mistaken. Ah honestly believe dat ... da escape yar attempting is not possible! No one among yar group ... really knows how to handle a sailboat, especially one dat big."

"You're right about that, Ambros. The only boats Paing and I are familiar with are small *bancas* that we occasionally paddled down the Mambusao River. We have more experience using bamboo rafts than with canoes."

"Badong, *ignorance* is a tricky thang! Ya have no realistic idea of how much ...ya don't know. Ignorance makes ya as simple as a little child.

"Navigating even a small sailboat in da Pacific Ocean ... needs an extensive body of knowledge and experience. Ah have experienced sailing for ... at least fifty years. Yet, dere are times when ah still make mistakes.

"Badong, ya need to know ... about prevailing winds, ocean currents and ocean swells dat can look like mountains. Ya must know ... actual weader conditions dat are always unpredictable.

"Da navigator needs to know da ... peculiar characteristics of da sailboat and ... its specific responses to different sails. Dere are different shapes and sizes of sails dat ... need to be understood. Ya need extensive experience in ... controlling and guiding yar boat under unpredictable conditions."

"You're right, Ambros, I have no realistic understanding of my own ignorance about sailboats and sailing.

"However, I'm here not to ask your permission to make the voyage. I've already made that decision!

"I'm here to ask you about the most basic knowledge and skills for sailing. Please, Ambros, give me just the bare essentials!"

"No, Badong. Ah can't give ya da basic knowledge of anythang. Ah would not know what da bare essentials are as ya coll them. Dere is simply ... too much to know about navigation. Am not informed enough to know ... what is basic and what is not. To me, everythang ah know is basic.

"Da only thang dat ah can help ya is ... share some of da most important lessons dat ah have learned over da years."

"That is excellent, Ambros. That is exactly what I want to learn!"

"Ma heart aches to thank dat ... whatever ah teach ya will never be enough. Still, let me answer yar request in a very general way."

"General explanation would be sufficient, Ambros."

"Da first thang ah want to tell ya is dat Filipino sailboats are extremely light and sensitive. Dat is ... because da upper portions of da hull are made of light materials. Some boats even use ... thin bamboo matting dat dey paint over. Dey are as thin as cardboard.

"Da shape of the boat is ... very narrow, especially at da bow and the stern. Dis design makes dem very unstable. Moreover, Filipino boat designers purposely ... designed oversized sails. Dis technique makes dem ... top heavy and da boat may capsize easily!"

"Why were they designed with such irrational proportions?"

"Supposedly, to make dem extremely fast. In da past, ... pirates, who probably designed dem, needed to get away fast with deir loot. Piracy had been ... a profitable occupation especially by da *Moros* in Mindanao.

The Child Daredevil Hero

Even today, dere are still rumors about Moro pirates. Da *Moros* ... often committed piracy against da Christians in da Visayan Islands."

"If the large sails make the sailboat so unstable, what do sailors do to stabilize their sailboats?"

"Filipino sailors have practiced, for centuries, a ...very risky acrobatic maneuver on da ... narrow platform of da middle outrigger. Ten to twenty crewmen ... may stand on a platform. Deir purpose is ... to counterbalance da extra wind load on da sail. Hence, dey always stand on da ... opposite side of da loaded sail.

"For safety, ... dey hold on to diagonal ropes. Da ropes come down from da mast and ... are tied to da middle outrigger."

"Ambros, do the men on the middle outrigger just stand there to provide the weight?"

"Oh, no! What da crewmen do is both a science and a delicate art."

"In what sense is it a science? And, in what sense is it a delicate art, as you put it?"

"Badong, y'are ... touching on da most mysterious part of sailing. It is mysterious because ... almost every sailor has a personal explanation. Some will tell ya dat ... dey have a spiritual union with da ... wind, sail, waves, rudder and da mind of da captain.

"Oders will even tell ya dat ... God makes dem behave in a manner dey don't understand.

"Frankly, it boils down to ... understanding what yar supposed to do. After doing it a number of times, ... da balancing process becomes instinctive."

"Ambros, your explanation was far from clear to me. That was not your fault. As you said earlier, I have a profound ignorance of sailing.

"Let me break it down so that I might understand it. When you talked about 'understanding what you are supposed to do,' I suppose that is the science part of it. In other words, the crewman must know all the rules that he must follow."

"Ya can say dat. But, da rules are not clear because ... da understanding is more instinctive."

"Is the artistic part also instinctive?"

"Badong, as ah understand it, ... da artistic part follows from da instinctive knowledge of what needs to be done."

"Are you telling me that you have to be born into the sailing life and culture and instinctively absorb what you need to do?"

"Ah assume, dat is exactly what happened to me. Ah know what to do but ... ah don't know how to splain it. As ya see, Badong, dere was never a time in ma life when … ah didn't know how to sail. As far as ah can remember, … ah always knew how to sail."

"Come to think of it, Ambros, I have observed what those men do on the platform. They seem to be moving all the time. But, they seem to do everything in unison."

"Yes. Dat is true. What ya see on da platform, from da outside, are … da daredevils moving togeder to da right or da left as dey thank is necessary. Somehow, … dey can *feel* what to do … based on deir refined knowledge of da … wind, da speed of da boat and da amount of wind being caught in da sails.

"Dis instinctive feeling is … not easy to splain to anyone. But, if yar a crewman, … ya simply know what to do.

"Ah don't know if ya really understood what … ah was trying to splain to ya. It is very complicated and difficult to … understand in a short period of time."

"Honestly, Ambros, I didn't understand most of what you explained to me. However, I hope to get the feel of this balancing act on the platform as I learn more about sailing."

"Ah admire yar honesty, Badong."

"Ambros, tell me something that might be a guarded secret among sailors. Those crewmen who are standing on the platform outside of the boat, do some of the big, high waves knock them down accidentally into the sea?"

"Oh, yes indeed! It is not a secret; it is common knowledge! Many crewmen have … accidentally fallen from dis narrow perch on a platform. Some large waves have swept dem away.

"By da time a helmsman … can maneuver da boat to … search for a fallen broder, he would have already drowned! Or … some sharks and oder predators may have already attacked him. Da possibility of death is a … necessary part of da Filipino style of sailing."

"I guess that standing out on a narrow platform to counterbalance the wind on a sail has to be among the most dangerous activities in the life of any sailor. Are the crewmen aware of these dangers when they take the job?"

"Of course, dey do. In fact, some of dem seek out dis job because … dey find da danger fascinating and exciting!"

"That is quite a scary picture you have shown me, Ambros! Fortunately, what I just bought is a cargo boat, which is really not made for speed. As you had informed me earlier, they are heavier and wider than the ordinary cruise sailboats."

"Dat is true, Badong. Still, you must master da fine art of trimming da sails and … carefully maneuvering da rudder at precise angles.

"A sudden gust of wind or … a wrong turn of da rudder could capsize da boat. An abrupt turn of da rudder, especially when tacking, could … tilt da boat on its side and turn it upside down.

"Badong, da science and da art of navigating a Filipino sailboat takes … many years to master. Dis is why am worried about ya. Ya simply lack both da … science and da art of navigation!"

Chapter Seven
The Skipper Who Couldn't Sail

Badong was the oldest of the group, at thirty-five, and the *de facto* leader. He was the self-appointed helmsman. Yet, he didn't know how to sail an outrigger sailboat. He didn't even know what a squall was. And, in the beginning, he didn't even know what outrigger meant.

Paing, his right hand man and head of the crew of two adults and six children, was as ignorant about sailing as the captain was. He didn't know the difference between a passenger and a cargo sailboat. And, he thought that a jib sail was a baby's bib or apron.

The extent of the skipper's sailing information was what the previous owner, Esteban Jaramillo, had shared with him over a period of about eight hours. There was no manual that came with the handmade sailboat. There was no literature for navigating any sailboat available around.

However, he spoke to a lot of fishermen about sailing. After he had purchased a cargo outrigger sailboat, however, he became more focused about sailing a cargo boat.

His navigational skills were whatever he had acquired from a two-hour practice, done in the open ocean. The practice sailing occurred only at night to avoid the Japanese patrol boats.

His sailing crew were Paing who was thirty, Jose a nineteen-year old servant, and six children, including Junior, who was not yet ten. No one among the crewmen knew anything about sailing either. Badong gave his crew only a brief instruction about their duties because he didn't know what to tell them.

Paing, the crew master, was supposed to tell the crewmen what to do in every situation. Yet, his primary duty was to help the helmsman trim the sails. He was the most confused man on board!

When Paing was not around, the crew just guessed what to do. Chaos often prevailed! The older children didn't know any better.

Everything was disorganized! Junior was sure that the voyage would not succeed and that he would die at sea!

Badong's primary concern was how to keep the boat balanced and afloat. As Don Ambrosio had pointed out, the important tool for keeping the boat in balance and afloat was the *collective weight* of the crewmen on the balancing platform. For this reason, Badong gave his crew some pointers on how to move on the platform.

The Child Daredevil Hero

Nine-year old Junior

He announced awkwardly, "Go as far out as you can on the platform, when the wind is really blowing. However, don't go out too far or you might fall off.

"When the boat is tacking, change sides quickly from the starboard side to the port side or vice-versa. Stand ready to move as far out when necessary. Try to use your weight to counter-balance the force of the wind on the sails. Therefore, the whole crew must move to the right or left together. Make two or three steps in either direction, as you feel necessary.

"Listen to Paing at all times! He will tell you when to step to the right or to the left."

His instructions lacked true knowledge and conviction. They hardly made any sense to any one. He was trying to teach them general principles. But, he failed to demonstrate how to execute those principles. He sounded as if he was just repeating what Jaramillo or Don Ambrosio had told him.

The crew had no practical idea of when to move in any direction. The knowledge and skills necessary for counter-balancing the force of the wind on the sail were extremely complex. It was more of an art than a science.

Almost every seasoned sailor ridiculed Dadong's plans to sail a fifty-foot cargo sailboat. Among the vocal critics was Roque Maldonado. He was a new neighbor from Sapian who claimed to be a master sailor with many years of experience. One day, Paing became critical of Roque, in an attempt to bolster Badong's confidence.

"Manong Badong, dis fellow Roque is an amusing Country Club type of gentleman. He is only about yar age, but he brags about being a master sailor for over twenty-five years. Does he really know what he is talking about?"

"Roque is like a square peg in a round hole in Ibizan. He claims to have abandoned an eighty-foot yacht and a mansion across the Bay in Sapian for a *nipa* hut and safety in Ibizan.

"He probably exaggerates his social status and capabilities somewhat. But, to me, he has all the trappings of a rich man. He always wears expensive clothes. And, he acts as if he is still living in an exclusive Country Club setting.

"Next to the humble and poor fishermen in the village, who are practically naked, he is always overdressed and appears ridiculous!"

"How about his sailing skills? Do ya think dat he is as good a sailor as he brags about?"

"Granted that he is an arrogant aristocrat, I think he is sincere in his assessments of our chances of survival. His wishes are heartfelt and well intentioned.

"Paing, I don't mind constructive criticisms. It is one good way of learning from others. If he were mean-spirited, then I would feel differently."

"Yar probably right. Sometimes, we learn even from our enemies."

Just before *Pangga* set sail, Roque said to Badong, "I know it's not really my business. But, I like you and your family. I feel very sad to think that all of you will likely die at sea! I wish I had never met you so I wouldn't feel so badly!

"Theoretically, however, your planned escape by using a large sailboat is foolish and doomed to fail! The prevailing wind right now is blowing as fast as twenty to twenty-five kilometers per hour. That means you can't sail slowly because you have to go with the wind. That also means that you'll be sailing at about eighteen kilometers an hour. That's too fast for an absolute beginner!"

"I appreciate your concern for us, Roque," Badong responded. "I know I have no experience about sailing I can brag about. But, I feel confident I can do this. I have no time to practice and acquire the proper skills. Just wish me luck!"

"That's your decision to make, Badong. Still, I'll stay around when you leave. I predict that you'll capsize shortly after you load your sails or within a period of ten minutes!

"Everyone will watch you leave, so we can rescue everyone as soon as disaster happens! I'm especially concerned for the children and the women. Our sailboats and *bancas* will be ready to help you."

The Child Daredevil Hero

"That's not necessary, Roque. If I were not confident I can handle this boat, I wouldn't do it. I'm concerned about the safety of my family and relatives, not to mention my own life.

"From my point of view, I'm leaving the village because I think the Japanese soldiers will make our lives more miserable! They might even massacre everyone! I'm not wishing evil for the community. But, my fear of what the Japanese might do to this village is one big reason why I'm taking this major risk!

"As I see it, we can choose to die here or at sea. I have chosen the latter because I'm still convinced that we'll make it to our destination."

"Badong, this is wartime and we don't know what will happen to us. I do hope and pray that you and your family survive this impossible voyage!"

"Thank you for your good wishes, Roque."

Another neighbor, Ramon Rodriguez, was concerned about the fact that the group was traveling during the beginning of the typhoon season.

"Badong, I just want to remind you that you're making this trip in the middle of May. I assume you know that this is already in the typhoon season. You may possibly encounter small and large storms during your journey. I suggest that you stay close to the shore so you can seek shelter, if necessary. I wish you the best of luck!"

"I thank you for your advice and your best wishes, Ramon."

Ramon was also a refugee from Sapian. He was among the few, who did not openly criticize Badong's plan to escape. However, he was also an experienced sailor and may have doubted Badong's chances of making it safely to Makato.

Junior heard many critical remarks from the fishermen who were trying to stop Badong from making the trip. The most credible critic was the venerable fisherman named Don Ambrosio Tolentino. Badong had lengthy discussions with him about different subjects.

He was a rugged-looking fisherman in his sixties. He had deep wrinkles on his forehead and face. He was dark brown from a daily exposure to the sun. He was the undisputed leader of the village and commanded great respect for his fishing skills and worldly wisdom. The whole village regarded him as 'The Resident Philosopher!'

Tolentino had already lectured Badong and Paing on the impossibility of their voyage. He had communicated to them almost all his objections. Still, he was sending his final parting message.

"Badong, be on da lookout for squalls," he advised him. "Dey are unpredictable and can be disastrous."

"What are squalls, Ambros?" Badong asked.

"Dey are sudden violent gusts of wind dat blow without any warning. Da wind is usually accompanied by a ... heavy nasty rain dat falls diagonally and sometimes horizontally!"

"That sounds extremely dangerous! What can I do to prevent the boat from capsizing if I encounter one, Ambros?"

"If ya see it coming or ... suspect it from various weader conditions such as ... heavy rain, make da sailboat face da wind by throwing an anchor from the bow. Bring down da mainsail, if ya have time. Throw more anchors from each side of the boat and da stern. Dose moves might stabilize da boat."

"Thank you, Ambros. I'll try to remember those lessons."

"Badong, ya know ... ah had already expressed ma negative views about yar trip. Ah told ya dat ... in ma opinion it is foolish and suicidal.

"Ya have already established ... yar residence in dis village for nearly a year. Yar family should stay here ... for da remainder of da war.

"Still, it's yar decision and ... ah can't prevent ya from doing it. If ya're ma son, however, ... ah'd forbid ya from leaving. Just da same, ah wish ya luck!"

"Ambros, I'm thankful for your advice and your concern for our safety."

"Badong, ah have many reasons ... for ma pessimism about yar voyage. Dere are many ... unknown weader and sailing conditions dat ... a novice skipper like ya had never experienced before. Ma guess is dat ... ya wouldn't know how to deal with dem. Ah'll say it again, dis voyage is like a group suicide! Ah plead to ya not to leave!"

"Don't be too worried, Don Ambrosio. I'm determined to prove to all of you that you're wrong!"

The reason why Badong was so confident that he could survive all his obstacles was because he had spoken to as many seasoned sailors as he could find. He concluded that there was one *secret key* to safety: *sail slowly by limiting the wind load on the sails.*

He had decided that he would not load his sails more than *fifty percent*. If he could stick to his plan, he might survive being a novice sailor sailing a monstrously oversized cargo sailboat and live to tell his heroic story!

Chapter Eight
The Impossible Voyage!

Badong and Paing carefully observed the routines of the Japanese patrol boats. They stayed awake for two nights in a row to observe if there was any naval activity on the waters. They confirmed the common knowledge that the Japanese navy didn't patrol at night.

Based on this meager but important information, they carefully planned an escape that entailed sailing only at night and hiding in safe harbors during the day.

Still his biggest problems remained. His primary problem was how to acquire the basic knowledge and skills to navigate the sailboat and keep it afloat. His other problem was how to deal with a prevailing wind that was stronger than he knew what to do with. His resolve to lessen the load on the sails to no more than fifty-percent would be tested soon.

If he had any doubt about his capacity to sail the boat, he didn't show it. He would employ the most primitive method of teaching himself, which was 'learning by doing.' This method entailed great risks. But, he was determined to learn everything that he needed to know. He was also determined to overcome all the obstacles that his harsh critics had pointed out to him!

The departing group informed all their neighbors about the time and date of their daring escape! They would embark at about eight in the evening, on the fifteenth of May 1942. Almost the whole village was there to see them off. Some continued to discourage their trip.

Some fishermen helped by pushing off the stern of the boat against the surf. With the help of Paing, Badong started to load the mainsail and then the jib. He straightened out his rudder.

The crewmen stood nervously on the middle platform at the port side of the boat. The navigator excitedly adjusted the rudder as he trimmed the sails more refinely. The sailboat slowly and smoothly glided forward!

Some villagers clapped wildly and yelled their parting wishes! Some were crying because they would never see each other again, even if the voyage succeeded! Taling, Dolor and the girls were also crying uncontrollably!

Initially, the skipper maneuvered the boat slowly and carefully as the wind allowed him. The strong Pacific Ocean winds forced him to sail about twelve kilometers an hour. It was faster than he wanted but he had no choice. Still, the boat cruised slower than Roque had predicted.

After the voyage had survived the first ten minutes, Badong felt that he had already proven Roque Maldonado wrong! He might really prove that all the nay-sayers were mistaken in their assessments of his chances of surviving the voyage!

Junior had watched his father do many things without any training. He marveled at his capacity to accomplish them. He shouldn't have been able to do them, but he did. For example, he built their home in Mambusao and a complex of buildings for milling rice and corn. He also built a couple of warehouses. Yet, he had never built a house before or worked in a construction job. He made himself the architect, builder, general contractor and foreman. He could do every facet of the construction.

He was a natural at whatever he tried to accomplish. In a mysterious way, he had the superb confidence and daring that he could do whatever he decided to do.

He was sailing a monstrous outrigger sailboat, which he shouldn't be able to sail. Junior suspected that Don Mones, his grandfather, possessed the same unusual trait as his father. Don Mones must have passed on genetically this rare trait to his dad, his brothers and sisters and perhaps to himself. He suspected that the other members of his clan must have also inherited the same remarkable trait.

To a nine-year-old like Junior, his dad's performance as an inexperienced navigator was incredible and almost miraculous! Badong trimmed the sails and adjusted his rudder as if he had been doing them all his life.

During the first stopover in an inlet, Junior said to his father, "*Tatay*, I'm afraid *uh* ... I don't know what I'm doing on the balancing platform. Nobody seems to know either."

"Son, I don't know what to tell you. But, keep trying to learn how to move to the correct direction. Don Ambros told me that the crew members will *instinctively learn what to do*. I really don't know what that means.

"As I understand it, pay attention to the *force of the wind* and how it affects especially the mainsail. When the sails push the boat down with their weight, you will naturally move to the opposite direction to provide a counterbalancing weight. And, when the sails slacken, it means that the wind is not blowing as hard. That is when you move towards the mast at the center of the boat and apply less weight against the sail."

"I'll try *uh* ...to pay more attention to the force of the wind on the sail, *tatay*, as you suggested."

"Keep learning, son, until you understand what you're doing."

Paing also registered a complaint. "What really concerns me is dat we don't know da weather conditions. As Ramon Rodriguez had warned us, we might experience a storm at any time. I wish I know when it is coming!"

"Paing, even though we are unfamiliar with many things in this part of Panay Island, we are still in the Philippines. Therefore, we must continue to use the same knowledge and skills that we had already acquired in Mambusao to forecast and predict events.

"You know what the weather conditions are by looking around and especially by examining the different types of clouds. When you see rain clouds hovering above and they appear to be moving downwards, you can predict that it is going to rain soon. Is that not so, Paing?"

"Yes. Ah suppose so. Maybe da ocean is so unfamiliar to me and dat is why I feel insecure and afraid!"

"Still, I repeat, use the knowledge you already have! For example, when the winds pick up velocity and start moving in circles, you should suspect that a storm might be forming. Isn't that so?"

"Yes, *manong* Badong. You're right."

"So, stop whining about not knowing the weather conditions! Use what you already know!"

"*Manong* Badong, I don't mean to be disrespectful, in any way. But, dere is one factor dat we have overlooked. Da crewmen are supposed to be mature strong men. Our crewmen, however, are not men; dey are lightweight inexperienced children."

"Paing, that was obvious right from the start. Ideally, what we needed were twenty mature burly men who could counterbalance the oversized sails. Since six of the eight crewmen are children, I realized all along that our boat was seriously undermanned!

"I knew that we didn't have even the minimum of manpower to undertake this voyage. Yet, we had to sail just the same, with the few people we actually had. We had no other alternative, except to remain and die in Ibizan!

"Paing, settle down! We're already underway and we're learning as we sail. I feel I'm learning every moment that we are sailing. Let us hope that our collective efforts will take us safely to Makato."

"*Manong* Badong, as you know, every experienced sailor we met in Ibizan was really predicting disaster! I suppose, being severely undermanned was among da reasons why dey were pessimistic about our trip. I noticed in Ibizan dat even small sailboats had at least six adult men as crew members.

"But deir criticism was primarily about your lack of experience in navigation."

"I suppose that was the most obvious weakness, Paing. The skipper is primarily responsible for the whole sailing operation. Frankly, I understood their concerns. We are a makeshift group, headed by an absolute novice navigator."

"*Manong*, I brought up da problem about da shortage of crew men because I realized dat I was doing too many things at the same time. For example, you ordered me to help you trim da sails. But, at da same time, you also ordered me to be with da crewmen and to train dem."

"I'm sorry for my contradictory orders, Paing. But, they weren't intended to be contradictory. What I meant was for you to help me with the sails until I had gotten setup on my course. I found out that I couldn't adjust the sails properly, while, at the same time, trying to control the rudder.

"After that, I wanted you to join the crew and provide the leadership especially to the children."

"Thank you for clarifying dat. Dis first day of da voyage was very hectic for me! I felt pulled into different directions. Of course, my primary problem was inexperience."

"Paing, I want you to know that I have already made adjustments to compensate for the lack of manpower. I placed much less load on the sails especially when the wind was blowing hard. In fact, the lack of manpower was among my biggest problems!"

When he was not with the captain, Paing himself rarely told anyone what to do. He was more bewildered about the science and the art of counterbalancing on the platform than any of his crew.

The captain's instructions were definitely insufficient and inadequate. However, it was enough to start with. The crewmen, in fact, learned on the job as they slowly figured out what to do.

In the beginning, the crewmen were simply inept and confused! They had no idea of what to do. Because Paing was more often with the skipper, Mabini, as the oldest child, assumed that he had to lead. He barked such orders as, "One step to the right!" as everyone was actually stepping to the left. He shouted, "Two steps to the left!" as the other crewmen made one step to the right. After a while, the subordinate crewmen became insubordinate. They just ignored his commands.

Chaos was the normal order of operation especially in the beginning!

Again, Junior complained to his dad, "*Tatay*, I'm really scared *uh* ... about sailing across the ocean. Even though we are sailing close to the coastline, *uh* ... the ocean is still unfamiliar to me."

The Child Daredevil Hero

"That is understandable, son. This ocean is so big, you don't know what large fish and monsters live here. It is also unfamiliar to me. I'm just as scared as you are."

Paing also joined the conversation and said, "Dat is true, Junior. I'm also scared of da sea animals. I don't know anything about dem. I have heard a lot about sharks. Just da idea of seeing a big one makes me shiver!"

"Tay Paing, *uh* … why are you so scared of sharks?" Junior asked. "They have not done *uh* … anything bad to you."

"Yes. But, dey are so big dat dey can actually attack our boat and eat us."

"Paing, where did you get your ideas about sharks?" Badong asked. "Did you get them from books, magazines, stories or movies?"

"I got dem from stories I heard from different people."

"That is your trouble, Paing. Your source of information is faulty. Some people talk about things they don't know anything about. Because they're really ignorant, they manufacture imaginary beings, facts and actions out of their imagination. Hence, you should always find out the sources of your information. Figure out whether you can believe them."

"One of my sources was *manong* Beting, who is my cousin. After he came home from the seashore, in Iloilo, he told me unbelievable stories about sharks."

"Beting is a good example of an inaccurate and even a false source of information. Beting is not necessarily a liar. He tells stories for amusement. He likes to tell jokes to make people laugh.

"So, he manufactures incidents and tells them as if he had actually witnessed them. For example, when he said he just came back from the seashore, I found out from his wife, Maria, that he had never been to an ocean.

"In fact, he returned from Iloilo City, after visiting a relative there. Maria told me that when he was in Iloilo, he spent his time gambling on fighting cocks."

"So, all his stories about sharks dat attacked his *banca* weren't true?"

"Yes, Paing. He just made them all up to draw laughter and amazement He is a comedian, not a historian or a marine biologist."

"So, what should I believe about sharks and other sea monsters?"

"Don't believe in anything unless you have proof of their existence. And, don't believe in any fantastic exploits of people and monsters. Normally, they are just the products of people's imagination and fantasies.

"I suggest that you read books about sharks and learn about their characteristics, personalities, psychology and everything about them. You'll find out that they're not as scary and evil as you had imagined them."

"I'll do dat as soon as da war is over. After da town library is rebuilt, I will borrow some books on sharks."

"Do that Paing. Meanwhile, start observing real sharks in the ocean and learn directly from them."

"*Manong* Badong, now dat we have completed our first three days of sailing and we are still doing well, da negative predictions by people were simply wrong."

"Yes! Now I can laugh at Roque Maldonado who predicted an immediate disaster!

"Maldonado was simply wrong! If we survive the next two to three more days, I think we will settle into a definite routine. I was never scared that we would capsize as Roque had predicted.

"Still, for the most part, we have been lucky. The weather has been ideal. And, there has been no storm to complicate our voyage."

"Dat is right, *manong* Badong. In fact, I'm beginning to enjoy our trip. Da children who are helping me, as crewmen, are also learning fast. In fact, dey seem to understand what to do faster dan me."

"I have observed that to be the case, from where I sit at the helm. Junior came to me after the first day. He said that he had no idea what to do on the platform. He had no idea when or where to step.

"After I explained to him what he should do, he seemed to pick up the skills naturally. He is definitely improving and seems to enjoy what he is doing.

"However, I'm a little concerned about Mabini. He wants to lead but his brothers don't seem to respect him."

"Paing, it is difficult to be the oldest. On the one hand, he assumes he should lead. On the other hand, he must first know what to do and lead by his skills; not by his words."

"I'm glad dat we are learning a lot every day. I'm becoming more optimistic dat we will reach our destination."

"As you well know, I was optimistic right from the beginning!"

"I knew dat, manong Badong. Am very glad dat ya had such confidence dat we could sail safely and complete our journey!"

"Paing, we will achieve our goal!"

If Badong experienced any difficulty in navigation, it was in choosing the right harbor for hiding from the patrol boats. Because of his lack of familiarity with the coastline, he couldn't be certain if an inlet had the right shape for hiding his boat.

Of course, there were no maps of the coastline available to him. He was just going by the natural contours of the island of Panay.

A couple of times, Badong decided to pull out into the sea and look for a better harbor. Those were very risky decisions! The boat was still sailing when it should be in hiding!

One time, Junior spotted a squadron of Japanese naval ships at a distance. The sight sent shivers down his spine! He figured out that if he could see them, then they could also see the flamboyant sails, especially since they used binoculars. The skipper hurriedly headed for the nearest inlet and yelled, "Crewmen! Grab a paddle or an oar and help me navigate this boat to safety!"

After the boat had gotten into the inlet, Badong brought down the mainsail and the jib. He looked terrified! He assumed that the *Japons* had spotted the sailboat!

Everyone waited in fear and trembling, expecting the patrol boats to arrest and kill them!

The ships were still at a good distance and they couldn't hear the engines. But soon, they heard the humming of the motors. The sounds grew louder and louder! Finally, the noise reached a crescendo! Everyone's mouth was wide open and their eyes were bulging from their sockets!

Junior watched his parent's expressions. They were holding their breath for as long as they could!

All of a sudden, the noise of the boat engines decreased slightly in volume! They were moving away! His parents exhaled loudly and raised their hands to the heavens and said, "Alleluia! Alleluia! We are safe for today!"

That was a close call that scared Badong and taught him to seek harbor much sooner.

The risks Badong was taking were also taking their toll on Taling's health. She had been weakened by weeks of sleepless nights and insufficient nutrition. She was continually suffering from seasickness and couldn't keep any food in her stomach.

One day, she just collapsed from exhaustion and slept for ten straight days! Junior suspected that she was actually in a comma. Dolor continually checked her breathing and her pulse. She poured broth down her throat several times a day.

When Taling finally woke up, she was dizzy and weak. But, she had started to recover. She ate on her own and slept soundly at night. Slowly, she was putting on more weight and a healthier complexion!

Everyone felt relieved and happy to see her return to her old self again. Thus far, the voyage was definitely successful! Badong had made the right decision to take his wife away from Ibizan. She was, without doubt, recovering her health!

The voyage experienced few minor problems during the second week. One night the dreaded squall that Don Tolentino had warned them about hit the boat and it nearly capsized! Because it was dark, no one saw it coming. Some crewmen ran to the outrigger platform to counterbalance the tilting boat in a blinding rain! There were some panic and crying among the children! But, the boat stabilized!

However, the captain noticed a three-foot long rip on the top of the mainsail. Taling and Dolor mended it in the dark and under very wet conditions. The near overturn of the boat was very scary especially to the small children!

The captain ordered a body count of the crew and the passengers. Everyone was safe and unharmed. He also asked the crew to check the animals and food supplies. The total losses were two pigs, four chickens and two sacks of rice.

At another time, the starboard side float became detached from the front outrigger. The skipper slowed down the boat, almost to a stop, so repairs could be made. However, some people had seen earlier a large fish that could have been a shark. Paing and Jose, the only adult crew members, dreaded the chore of fixing the damage. They acted as if it were not their responsibility.

The skipper brought the boat to a complete stop, by making the bow face the wind. He ordered that an anchor be thrown down from the bow to maintain the boat position.

Then, he drew his knife from its scabbard and said, "Rafael and you, Jose, get rattan strips and go down to re-attach the float. Don't make me repeat my order!"

The skipper was a master of *arnes*, an oriental martial art. He didn't have to repeat his command. He meant no harm; he was just giving a martial emphasis to his authority as the ship captain.

For an inexperienced navigator, Badong had a remarkable control of the sailboat. He also turned out to be a good captain in managing his inept crewmen. They were still learning the rudiments of sailing. They were also learning by 'trial and error.'

The Child Daredevil Hero

By the third week of the voyage, Junior felt that he had improved a great deal in his skills as a crewman. He was enjoying certain routines. His father's advice to watch for the force of the wind on the sails was extremely helpful.

What he enjoyed the most was perching on the balancing platform. Perhaps, he enjoyed it because it was very dangerous. His joy might have been perverse, but it didn't matter to him. In his opinion, the joy was the natural reward of performing a job well!

When he first looked down at the large waves, he felt terribly afraid at the thought of falling off from the narrow platform. In his effort to control his fear, he decided to fix his gaze at the horizon instead of the water. He also concentrated only on positive thoughts. The technique worked perfectly and he ceased being afraid!

He became attuned to the movements of the boat and the force of the wind on the sails. Instinctively, he knew when to move to the left or the right and when to take two or three steps in either direction. He could sense when the boat was in perfect balance. At that precise moment, he felt in harmony with the boat, the sea and the wind. For him, the experience was exhilarating! He had never experienced something so magnificent! He felt proud of being a good crewman even though he was just a child!

Fortunately, night was often not totally dark. As Junior's eyes became used to the darkness, he could observe the ocean at least faintly. He saw the impressions of the flying fish and several dolphins that liked to accompany the boat. He could also make out the outlines of larger fish with prominent dorsal fins. Badong was sure that they were sharks.

Junior could easily make out the uneven shapes of the coastlines. The boat stayed close to land so they could seek harbor as soon as they observed the faint traces of dawn.

When the moon started to appear as a sliver, Junior became very excited and happy! He knew that every night, as the moon grew bigger and brighter, his vision of the horizon and the surroundings would become clearer.

When the full moon was over them, it felt almost like day. The kids moved around with confidence because of the moon light to exercise their muscles and joints. Everyone stared at the moon as if they had never seen it before. Perhaps, they stared at it so it wouldn't go away. They were afraid of the dark dreary nights!

Watching the dawn break silently over the coastline was like watching a miracle unfold before Junior's eyes! Slowly, light squeezed out the darkness and painted the vegetation light green, the ocean blue and the sky bluish white. Light also painted some feathery clouds all over the sky.

Then, the sun appeared dressed in luminescent orange, with touches of yellow, red, blue and the other colors of the rainbow. The magnificent sun rose on the horizon like a flaming eye of a god, staring knowingly at him!

Sunset was equally majestic! Slowly, darkness pressed out the colors of the vegetation and darkened the sky. The setting sun came down in dazzling shades of burning orange, with streaks of yellow, blue, red and the other wonderful colors of the sunset. It looked like the god of the day was descending majestically to a deep cave to sleep for the night.

In his wake, he painted the sky and saturated the clouds with flaming hues of orange, yellow, purple and the other marvelous colors in his palette.

For a long while, the sky was ablaze in a colorful abstract painting that awed and mesmerized him! The sun was a great painter whose daily artwork was always unique, original and worth framing!

Everyone was developing a weird routine of staying awake all night and sleeping most of the day. It was amazing how human nature could adapt to an artificial regimen imposed upon it. After a few days of this new schedule, however, Junior was perfectly adapted to it. It was an inversion of the natural order.

He wondered whether he could continue following the new habit when they reached Makato. He felt he could live with such a strange pattern, if necessary.

After they had enough sleep, some went fishing from the side of the boat. Others went swimming. But the maids went to gather firewood for cooking and just relaxed before it was time to cook a meal.

Mabini and Paterno were resourceful. First, they hooked some fish for crab bait. Then, they tied the baits with strings, which they fastened to bamboo poles. They made a very crude net from an old shirt to capture the crabs safely and avoid the fury of their sharp claws.

When a crab was feeding on a bait, it tried to carry it to its lair and eat it there undisturbed. As the crustacean pulled the bait, the string became taut, which was the signal for action to an eager crab catcher.

Junior pulled the string gently and most crabs foolishly left the safety of the sandy bottom. He pulled the crab almost to the water surface. Then, he gently placed the net under the crab and lifted it to captivity. They ate crabs everyday.

As they sailed further west, they saw fewer Japanese patrol boats. Those they saw were navigating further north where the channels were deeper. Every day, they distanced themselves further from the enemy. Still, the captain decided to navigate only at night for continued safety.

The Child Daredevil Hero

After at least three weeks of sailing at night and covering at least three-hundred-fifty kilometers, Dolor spotted the mouth of the confluent two Rivers, Rio Oeste and Rio Este. The six-hundred-foot wide mouth of the Rivers was aptly called Boca Grande (Big Mouth).

She told the captain to enter the Boca Grande and to proceed to the wharf behind the right village called Punta Oeste (West Point). Across the Boca Grande was another village called Punta Este (East Point).

Badong ordered the crewmen to use paddles and oars to help him propel the boat to its final destination. He had already lowered the mainsail but left the jib to do some work. It was almost morning.

By the time they anchored at the wharf, the villagers had come down to welcome the refugees. Among those who came down to welcome them were the surprised parents of Dolor!

She was born and raised in Punta Oeste until she was eighteen. Then, she migrated and lived in Mambusao, where she met and married Raphael, Taling's younger brother. She had left as a single woman and suddenly arrived with a husband and six small children. The unexpected reunion was deliriously delightful!

The gigantic sailboat dwarfed the little canoes tied to the same wharf. The banged up old canoes looked like they had been fighting each other all night long. Because of the wake created by the big sailboat, the little canoes kept bobbing up and down like members of a polite and proper welcoming party.

Junior could not believe that the impossible voyage became a reality! From his childish point of view, he thought that they were permanently trapped in Ibizan and were at the complete mercy of the Japanese occupiers.

The Japanese navy had completely blockaded the straits and channels and they totally controlled the roads.

Badong and Paing, however, discovered a weakness, which they exploited: the blockade was in place only during the day. By navigating only at night, they eluded and nullified the purpose of the blockade.

Badong's determination and daring to escape from Ibizan so Taling could recover from the trauma of the raid and the loss of a son were *heroic*. He accomplished the feat because of his natural ability to acquire the skills to control and navigate an oversized sailboat!

This was an incredible escape because it was carried out by a very small group of adults and children who didn't know how to sail!

They succeeded because of human inventiveness, fierce courage to overcome obstacles and the intuitive confidence that some 'impossible' goals could be accomplished! This was how some heroes were made! The *true hero* was Don Salvador Lopez!

Chapter Nine
The Swamps

Upon arriving at the fishing village, called Punta Oeste, Badong and Paing decided to forego their preveious plan to live in the swamps. Everyone told them that the mangrove forest was not suited for human life. Moreover, the fishing village was relatively safe from the Japanese invasion. In order to make life at the shore completely safe, however, it was necessary to have an evacuation hut in the swamps.

Since the Japanese raid of the village may occur at any time, building a hideout was very urgent! The residents of both Punta Este and Punta Oeste had already built their escape shacks deep in a vast swamp forest a year earlier.

The new refugees must choose a specific location for the construction of their hut near the existing hideouts, about five kilometers away.

The escape huts were part of the *defensive strategy* formulated by the village leaders. Their plan of defense was to assign village sentries twenty-four hours a day. On a three-hour rotating shifts, the lone male guard rode a horse and watched the only pathway leading to the village, which was three kilometers away.

As soon as he had ascertained the approach of the Japanese soldiers, he galloped to notify the villagers. He rang the village bell and yelled, "Evacuate immediately! The *Japons* are coming!"

Boarding their fast canoes, they disappeared in the swamp wilderness in a few minutes. The evacuation huts would, therefore, insure their survival throughout the war.

Almost every adult male volunteered to harvest bamboo logs, coconut fronds, nipa palms and rattan vines. In only two weeks, the crew built a twenty-by-twenty-foot shack on a gigantic crayfish mound. The harvesting of the materials took about a week and the actual building of the hut took another week.

After finishing the hideout, however, Badong was still worried by some unanswered questions that could immediately cause serious problems.

Was it safe to leave their valuables and extra food in a hut that anyone with a canoe could ransack? Would the cabin floor stay dry when the highest tides occurred during full moon? Would the flimsy shack withstand the violent storms, especially since the area was in a typhoon alley? If a monstrous typhoon directly hit the area, would the storm surge that usually followed, flood the cabin?

As the leader of his refugee group, Badong decided that the best way to answer at least some of these questions was to assign someone he trusted to live there temporarily and observe the events as they occurred. His immediate concern was the *flooding* of the cabin floor at the first high tide, which would occur during the first full moon. The moon would be full in two to three weeks or sooner. Flooding would make the hut unusable for evacuation. They would have to build a new one with a higher floor elevation.

The leader of the volunteer group of workers was Juan Capistrano. He became Badong's instant friend. Badong asked Juan's enlightened opinion.

"Juan, do you think this floor is high enough to prevent flooding, especially at full moon?"

"Honestly, Badong, *um* ... Ah can't be sure. Unfortunately, after da workmen had leveled da top of da mound, da floor seemed to go down much lower dan ah had expected. Hence, it is possible dat da floor might be inundated."

"That is exactly what I'm afraid of. If the floor gets wet, the few things that I have salvaged from my businesses and my house in Mambusao are too valuable to lose."

"So, what do ya have in mind?"

"It might be a good idea to assign someone to observe the tides, especially at full moon."

"Dat is a good idea, Badong. Leave *um* ... one of yar servants here for two or three weeks and observe what happens."

"Frankly, Juan, my servants are too valuable to my family to stay here. They do the gathering of firewood, the cooking as well as washing clothes. I'd rather assign one of my boys."

"Whom do ya have in mind?"

"Will you please pick up Junior from the village for me? He is probably swimming in the ocean or just playing some games on the beach."

"Certainly, Badong. Ah'll leave right now *uh* ... before da sun gets too low on da horizon. Ah should be back in less dan an hour."

"Thank you, Juan. I appreciate the favor."

"Think not'ing of it, Badong."

Junior was in a middle of a good volley ball game, which his team was winning. He was annoyed to be distracted from the game for unknown reasons.

He tried to ignore the summons until Juan yelled, with obvious annoyance, "Yar fader wants ya in da swamp right now! Leave da game immediately and come with me. ..."

"Uncle Juan, *uh* ... what does my father want me to do in the swamp?"

"Let him 'splain it to ya. Yar assignment is more complicated dan ah know how to 'splain."

Peasant children of Malay ancestry. Notice their dark brown complexion and black hair.

Juan was a Punta Oeste native and the *de facto* head of the village. He was only about thirty-five-years old but he looked like at least sixty to Junior. Without shoes, he stood at five feet four inches tall and weighed about two hundred ninety kilos. Deep wrinkles furrowed his face and his complexion was dark brown from over exposure to the sun. He had a full head of dark hair that he wore short above his ears.

His features were similar to the dark brown peasant farmers who were of Malay ancestry.

His eyes were big, round and dark that seemed to twinkle. He wore short pants and was bare-chested. He looked like a typical wiry rugged fisherman.

He was one of the three villagers who owned his own boat and a long fishing net. His two-story bungalow house was the largest and the most attractive in the village. His neighbors regarded him as well off. Juan was the natural leader of the community.

He handed Junior a wooden paddle and said, "Sit at da bow of da *banca*. Ah'll navigate da boat but ya'll help me paddle. Tell me, do ya know how to paddle, son?"

"Yes, sir. I know a little bit."

"Dis is a good chance for ya to learn not just to paddle, but how to pilot a *banca*. Ya need dese skills around here."

From Punta Oeste, they steered the canoe across the swift six-hundred-foot wide *Boca Grande*. Then, they entered the *Rio Este* and fought the swift tidal current for about two kilometers. Then, Juan steered the boat to the left bank of the *Rio Este* and stayed close to the bank as they paddled against the swift current.

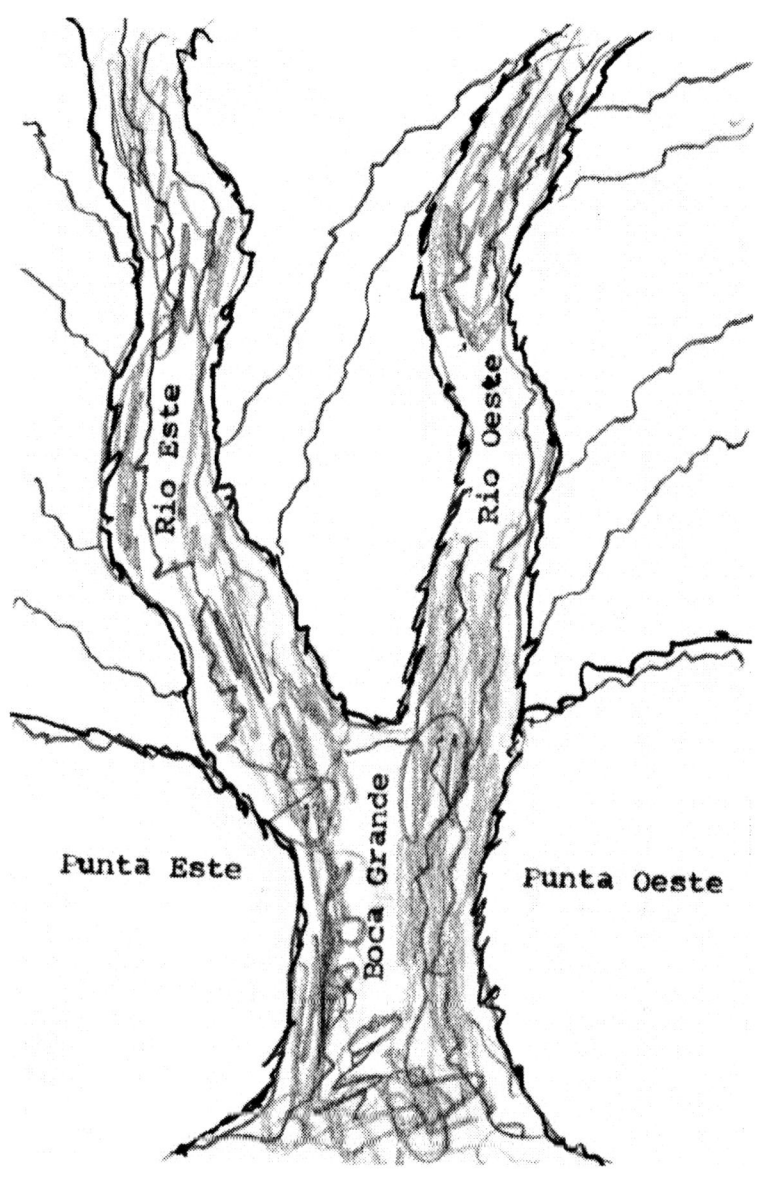

The configuration of the three Rivers: Rio Este, Rio Oeste and Boca Grande. On each side of the Boca Grande were the two fishing villages: Punta Este and Punta Oeste. The refugees from Mambusao lived in Punta Oeste.

"Uncle Juan, have you lived here all your life?"
"Yes, all my life."

"I don't mean to be critical uh ... but these Rivers are *uh* ... very confusing and very dangerous. There are three Rivers that are *uh* ... connected to each other. I have never seen three Rivers *uh* ... flowing into each other before."

"Ya're right about dem. For people who are new to the area, the three Rivers are confusing. However, ya can see dat da Rivers are distinct. Da two main Rivers are ... *Rio Este* and *Rio Oeste*. As dey both approach da ocean, dey come togeder and *uh* ... become one big River, which is what we call *Boca Grande*.

"Boca Grande is a very wide River, as ya can see. It is dangerous, as ya said, because da tidal water is very fast and strong!"

"Do people drown in these Rivers, uncle?"

"Every year, several people drown in them but especially in da *Boca Grande*. Da boats dat capsize *um* ... easily lose deir passengers to da ocean. In a few short minutes, *um* ... da big ocean sucks out both da boats and deir riders."

"That is very scary, uncle Juan! Are there big fish that *uh* ... attack those who are in the water?"

"Unfortunately, yes. Dere are always sharks around waiting for accidents to happen! Dey have learned from experience *um* ... dat all kinds of food come out of da *Boca Grande* and dat includes humans."

"I don't mean to be disrespectful, but *uh* ... why would you live near the *Boca Grande* when you know ... that you might drown any day?"

"Junior, we have been asking da same question for several generations. Da simple answer is da fact dat *um* ... food is most plentiful in da *Boca Grande*.

"When we were still in the *Boca Grande*, did ya see dose poles all over da River dat were in a line formation? Dey were actually in a shape of a big letter V, like this?"

"Yes, I saw them. What were they?"

"Dey were all *net traps* to catch anything dat comes down with da current. At da end of da V-shaped structure are ... long nets, which start as a six-foot round opening. Da nets are about thirty feet long and taper gradually to about ten inch openings. The openings are tied shot by a heavy string to catch anything dat gets into da net. Da current is so strong dat da fish trapped in it can't escape.

"Everyday, tons of fish are caught in it with little effort from da fishermen. During rainy season, tons of eels are caught in it everyday!"

"How do the fishermen *uh* ... harvest the fish from the net?"

"It is very simple. Dey take deir canoe to da end of da net. Den, dey lift about five to ten feet of da end of da net into da canoe. Dey untie da string and empty da contents into big bamboo baskets in deir boat. It is dat simple and easy!"

"What is the purpose of the uh ... two rows of pilings that form the V shape?"

"Da tidal current shakes da pilings and scares da fish towards da hatch of da net. Da shape is like a funnel. Local fishermen believe dat da pilings funnel da fish and eel into da net. All ah know is dat it works!"

"Now, I understand *uh* ... why you live close to the mouth of the River. Still, it is a *uh* ... very dangerous way to make a living."

"We know it; but we're used to it! Dis is why our families have lived here for generations."

Tall, dense red mangroves covered the riverbank, which was flooded by the high tide in many areas. They passed by the wide entrances of several tributary streams that added water and tidal force to the Rivers. The mouths of each stream varied in width from fifty to two-hundred-feet. Obviously, the swamps were made of *a network of many branching smaller streams.*

The Kingfisher

Junior saw many predatory birds like the kingfishers, egrets, white and blue herons. The herons and egrets waded through shallow waters. However, the kingfishers perched on low tree branches, waiting for some fish to come up to the surface to breathe. He noticed that the birds were graceful divers and efficient predators.

As they approached the two-hundred-foot wide mouth of the tenth stream, Juan said, "Listen carefully, Junior! Take note of da features of dis entrance. Look for special identifying markers, like a dead tree or low branches dat touch da water. Dose features will allow ya to remember da entrance."

"Why is it important to *uh* ... remember the entrance, uncle?"

"Just in case ya have to pilot a canoe yarself. Am sure, ya have to go to yar swamp hideout some time. Dis is da *only entrance* to yar hut. From dis stream, we'll branch out to smaller streams. We keep branching out until we reach a *shallow creek*. Dat is where yar new cabin is located."

"How many *uh* ... kilometers would the cabin be from here?"

"It is quite close now. Ah estimate roughly about three kilometers."

"Uncle, how many times will we *uh* ... branch out to smaller streams during this trip?"

"Approximately *um* ... twelve times."

Blue Heron

"That would mean that *uh* … there are at least twelve separate but inter-connected streams in this area of the swamp. Am I right?"

"At least, dere are dat many. Dis is why ah suggested dat ya make some kind of mental notes every time we branch off into smaller streams. Dat way, ya'll find yar way around da swamps."

"Uncle, I find it very difficult *uh* ... to distinguish one stream from another. Right now, they all look the same to me. They differ only in the uh ... sizes of the openings."

"Junior, dat is normal. It is like going to a market place and seeing hundreds of people at once. In da beginning, dey are just people with no specific faces. Ya can't distinguish one person from anoder.

"But, when ya want to buy something, ya talk to a sales woman. As ya ask questions about prices and negotiate da cost, ya look at her eyes. Without really intending to, ya notice her pretty nose, cute lips, long silky hair and sexy voice. By da time ya leave her stall, ya know enough about her. Da next time ya pass by her business, ya recognize her.

"It is da same way with dese streams. When ya look at dem more carefully, ya will see dat dey have distinct personalities."

"That is so true, uncle Juan. It is a matter of *uh* ... knowing more about them. I'm sure that if I become the navigator of this *banca*, *uh* ... I'll pay more attention to certain features of the stream. If I don't do that, *uh* ... I won't know my way back."

"Now, ya're getting da right idea, son."

"Uncle, tell me, *uh* ... something about all these areas on each side of the streams and Rivers. Are they all part of the swamps?"

"Yes, dey certainly are. We call dem coastal swamps 'cause der are oder types of swamps. Dey have been dat way for millions of years."

"How large is this *uh coastal* swamp area?"

"Oh, ah don't really know. Ah guess *uh* ... it is about twenty-five to thirty kilometers deep into da mainland. And perhaps, it is about ninety to one hundred kilometers along da coast areas."

"Wow! That's *uh* ... really a big swamp! I noticed that there are several creeks and streams that flow out of the swamps. Is it like that as you go up the *uh* ... *Rio Este* and *Rio Oeste*?"

"No. Da feeder streams are deeper and wider close to da ocean. Da strong tidal currents created dese swamps, streams and creeks.

"Da farder ya go up da Rivers, da weaker da currents become. So, da streams and creeks also become smaller and shallower."

"That's really fascinating. I hope to *uh* ... explore those streams when I have the chance."

"Do dat, Junior. Ya'll find it worthwhile but it will be a hard work. Ya don't have to see da whole swamplands because dey are so vast.

The Child Daredevil Hero

"Just going into some of da streams will give ya some idea of what a coastal swamp is."

"Uncle, do these two Rivers come from the same source?"

"No. Dey don't. Dey have different starting points in some mountains far in-land. However, as ah had already explained, dey came togeder and formed da *Boca Grande*, which empties into da Pacific Ocean."

"Uncle, I have heard people talk about the *estero* (estuary). Will you please explain what it means?"

"Da *estero* is da lower parts of da Rivers where the fresh water meets da tidal sea water.

"In oder words, *Boca Grande* is both da mouth of da Rivers and a part of da *estero*. It includes da lower regions of da two Rivers."

"How do you determine *uh* ... where the *estero* ends?"

"Da boundaries are not set definitely. But, we go by da salt infiltration. Since da sea water enters da swamp areas, strictly speaking da whole swamp regions are parts of da *estero*. But, we talk as if da swamps are separate from the estero. In practice, we refer to da lower parts of the two main Rivers and the *Boca Grande* as the estero."

"It is interesting uh ... that the existence of the Rivers allowed the sea to flood the swamp regions during high tides."

"Yes, Junior. All of dese three Rivers are responsible for turning all dese areas into swamps. Without these Rivers, the swamp areas would be farmlands today.

"It happened millions of years ago, when da ocean first flooded da land."

"I have to think more about *uh* ... all the information you have given me today. And, it might take me a long time to recognize each of these streams."

"Ah tell ya, Junior, dat it won't take too long. As ya said before, when ya become da pilot of yar boat, ya'll remember where ya're going."

"I'm grateful for all these information, uncle Juan."

"Believe me, ya'll need to know much more thangs about dis wet wilderness dan ah have told ya. It would be necessary to know dem if ya're going to find yar evacuation cottage more easily."

"You're probably right. But, I'll learn just few things at a time. I don't want to clog my brain with too much information in one setting."

"Uncle, who decided *uh* ... to use the swamp for evacuation?"

"Da two village communities had decided to put da huts deep in da wilderness so dat da *Japons* don't find dem."

"I think it was clever of you *uh* ... to use the swamp wilderness to hide from the invaders."

"Thank ya. But, to us it was an obvious decision especially because we all knew da nature and composition of the swamp!"
"Before the war, did you know the swamps very well?"
"Yes. We used to go into da swamps to catch crayfish."
"What are they uncle?"
"Dey are like lobsters, only smaller."
"I'm sorry, I don't know what lobsters are either."
"Let me say dat dey belong to da same family as crabs."
"I do know crabs. They are among my favorite foods."

Common Crayfish

After so much interesting information from Juan, Junior stayed silent because he had so many things to think about and new things to observe and enjoy. He observed many types of birds and trees. He also saw many kinds of fishes.

But, the most fascinating were the jumping mullets. Perhaps, they were jumping to escape from their predators. He suspected that they were also afraid of their paddles, which made a banging noise as it hit the side of the canoe. Four medium sized mullets mistakenly jumped into their boat. Juan said that his wife would cook them for supper.

As they approached the new hut deep in the swamp, Junior noticed that the area was very dark. The mangrove trees were very tall and thick. Even the creek leading to the cabin was partly covered with trees and the dangling prop roots of red mangroves.

He examined the squat-looking building on a very large crayfish mound. His eyes weren't used to the darkness and he strained to make out its shape and proportions. What he saw wasn't pretty. It was just a functional building but better than nothing. He hoped he would never have to use it for whatever reason.

It was high tide when they arrived. The water was only about two feet below the dirt floor of the shack. Brackish water flooded the whole swamp area. Junior noticed that the high water mark on the barks of the mangrove trees was just about two feet higher than the water level. He wondered whether some high tides might flood the cabin floor.

Chapter Ten
A Special Assignment

"Jun, welcome to our new evacuation shelter. Isn't it big and wide?" his father asked him.

"Yes, tatay. This can accommodate *uh* ... both the Lopez and the Castaneda families in case they have to hide from the Japanese raiders."

"I think it is big enough for twenty-five evacuees. I guess some people might have to sleep on the grounds outside. Some of the boys might have to do that.

"We will solve that problem if and when we have to live here for whatever reason. If the Japons raid our village, I hope it will be for a very short period of time."

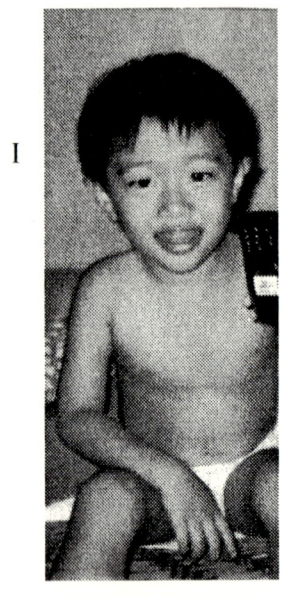

"Tatay, why did you send uncle Juan to bring me here?"

"Jun, I'm sorry for interrupting your game at the shore. I asked you to come here because I want you to help me solve a problem. This cabin floor is at least a foot too low. The volunteers leveled the floor lower than I had planned. There is a good possibility that the high tides might flood the floor. If that happens, all this construction will have to be redone."

"Why, *tatay*? Will the high tide uproot *uh* ... the shack?"

"No. But, the water will soak the floor and everything that we store in here. I intend to keep any extra food and family valuables in this hut.

"Listen, son, I want you to stay in the hut just until the full moon. The tides will be at their highest level then. I want you to check if the floor gets flooded. Flooding would make the hut useless for evacuation. No one will be able to sleep on a wet floor.

"If you observe that the shack gets wet, you must tell me right away! I'll have to build another one immediately. It must have a higher floor elevation."

Junior as a young child

The Child Daredevil Hero

Badong appeared aggravated and angry! Junior, on the other hand, was absolutely shocked! This assignment was completely unexpected! He didn't even know that a hideout was being built in the swamp.

He also resented the assignment because there were others who should have been assigned the job, such as his teenage brothers, Mabini or Paterno. He also thought of their male servant, Jose, who was nineteen-years-old.

Badong was thirty-five-years old and stood five-feet eight inches, without shoes. Because of dandruff problems, he wore his hair very short, like a round brush. He had broad shoulders and an athletic build. He was a master of an oriental martial art called *arnes*, which had some similarities with *karate* and *tai chi*.

He had muscular arms, thick thighs and legs. His complexion was light brown. Because he was a Spanish *mestizo*, he had a high well-shaped nose, piercing dark eyes, bushy eyebrows and an evenly shaped mouth with fairly thin lips. Because he was disturbed, he pursed his lips and looked stern and intimidating!

Junior had never disobeyed him before. Yet, he felt that his father was not fair to him. He dared to challenge his father's decision.

With trembling voice, he asked, "Why *uh* ... did you choose me? I just turned *uh* ... ten and I'm small for my age. I really want *uh* ... to play with the other kids at the seashore. I'm too scared to stay here in this *uh* ... dark and smelly place! Wild animals will *uh* ... attack and eat me here! Honestly, *tatay*, *uh* ... this place is too wild and *uh* ... isolated for any human being to live!"

"It does look wild and hidden; but there are other people living here. Juan told me there are many others who live here. They are also guarding their own huts. Therefore, ... you won't be living here alone."

"But, *tatay*, why not pick *uh* ... Mabini? Or, *uh* Paterno? They're older and bigger. They can guard the hut and *uh* ... take better care of themselves here."

"Let me explain, Junior," he said sounding irritated. "I can't assign Leona. She is a girl. Hermogenes is sickly. Trinidad or Ruperto are too young. Your Uncle Paing's children are also too young. Mabini and Paterno are already teenagers. They're too independent and hard to control. As you see, you're my only choice!"

This was a more serious responsibility than he had ever done before. It was a very dangerous and scary assignment. He suspected that his father might be abandoning him in the swamp forest because he was the runt of the litter! He understood his terrible fate. His own father was abandoning him so that wild animals could eat him!

His father said the assignment was only until the full moon. However, Junior suspected that he wouldn't live that long. This was a wilderness where many wild predators lived! They could attack and devour him in minutes or just hours! To him, the assignment was a life or death situation! He must figure out how he could excuse himself and survive!

Even if he survived, living in the swamp would completely isolate him from his family and other people. What kind of life would he lead? How would he deal with loneliness?

He felt confused, scared and angry! How could his parents leave him alone in a wilderness? He just turned ten!

He kept regurgitating his father's words. He said that there were other people living there. Junior doubted the truth of that statement because he didn't see any hut nearby. He and Juan didn't see any other cabin on their way there. Everything was so quiet; there couldn't be a community existing there!

Still, Junior couldn't call his father a liar to his face. He was scared of him but also loved and respected him. This was the first time he ever doubted his father's words! He was very skeptical because he was facing a life or death situation! He wanted to survive! He was desperately trying to wiggle his way out of this responsibility!

Instinctively, he felt inclined to reject the assignment. However, he didn't have the courage to do it. He knew his dad could physically force him to stay there! He was just a small child and an open defiance of his father's authority was out of the question!

Since he couldn't see any way out, he felt resigned to his virtual abandonment!

He looked around to survey his potential graveyard. Every where he looked, he saw the same water-filled wilderness, with weird-looking mangrove trees. The swamp was damp, dark and smelly. The odor was fishy, salty and really strange. He had never smelled this awful scent before!

He was sure he would die soon! The spiders and the lizards might be poisonous. He had heard of some marine animals that were poisonous and could kill him instantly! Some shellfish were known to carry venom. There were even small jellyfish that had killed people. He couldn't distinguish one poisonous food from another. He was doomed to die!

Even if he didn't die, he had no real life in a wet forest. The swamp was meant for mangrove trees, fish and predatory wild animals. His father was leaving him in exile, which was a fate worse than death!

The assignment was definitely unfair because his father was denying him his childhood! He had the natural right to play like his other brothers,

The Child Daredevil Hero

sisters and other kids. As a child, he could, in theory, choose to do nothing.

Instead, his father was giving him a serious responsibility of observing many natural occurrences. That assignment demanded mature judgment about the tides, floods and storms. This assignment should be the responsibility of an adult!

He kept thinking of different possible situations. What if the cabin really got flooded? Was it his obligation to move everything to higher grounds? But, there were no higher grounds except on top of some mounds. Did his father really expect him to carry those boxes and packages that looked too heavy for him to carry? He wouldn't know what to do if a real catastrophe happened!

On the other hand, he realized, this was wartime and many things didn't make sense! He knew that children everywhere were being maimed, abandoned and killed! The assignment wasn't fair to him. But, he also knew that there were many things that weren't fair during the war. War itself wasn't fair. War was destructive of properties, lives, art, culture and countries!

He admitted to himself that his father couldn't assign anybody else other than the two teenagers or Jose, the male servant. Moreover, his father had acknowledged that he was powerless in controlling the teenagers. And, the servants were needed to do things for the family. He couldn't argue convincingly against his father. His case was closed!

He also realized that it was his cruel fate to be sandwiched between a sickly older brother and a little sister. As far as he could remember, his parents imposed upon him greater responsibilities than on anyone else. This horrible assignment was another example of a responsibility imposed only on him. It was always his unfortunate duty to do what nobody else would do! And yet, he was just a small child!

He cried like a captive sea turtle, with beads of tears cascading down his face. He realized he couldn't get out of the assignment. He felt completely defeated and depressed! He could feel life itself oozing out of his body!

Noticing that he was deeply discouraged and dispirited, Badong put his fatherly arm around his son's narrow shoulders and tried to console him.

"Junior, I'm not treating you as a servant. I've chosen you because I can depend on you. I know you're just ten but you were a responsible kid even when you were younger. I know you can do this. It's just until the full moon. Will you please do it for me and the family?"

"Yes, father," he answered very softly, as an act of obedience. Still, he kept crying out of self-pity!

He also concluded that he was a victim of favoritism. His father chose him to do the awful and dangerous job to protect his older brothers from physical danger and menial responsibility. There was also a question of higher natural rights that belonged to the older children. He was very young and he had to admit that he had the least rights among the older children.

Because of his lowly position, what suddenly worried him was that he might be fated to *take on even greater responsibilities in the near future!* He shuddered to think of the other assignments waiting for him! He tried to guess what terrible jobs were waiting for him, if he survived the present assignment. Nothing came to his mind but he was sure they would come!

He was the least valuable member of the family because of his young age. Someone had to do the thankless jobs. It was his dad's responsibility to sacrifice the most dispensable member of the family. By making the small boy dispensable, Badong was saving and protecting the rest of the family.

This strategy seemed unfair to Junior. But, this was wartime and horrible things were happening everywhere! As the head of his family, Badong had to make decisions based on the resources available to him.

Junior had just learned how to play chess. He thought of himself as a mere pawn at the middle of the board. All the important personages were hidden and protected behind the lines. The formidable towers, the holy bishops, the valiant knights and the powerful horses surrounded the Queen and the King.

The pawns, however, were lined up at the front lines ready to sacrifice their beings! Or, they waited for the players to exchange them for other useless pawns. He admitted that he was just an insignificant pawn in the real chess game of life! *Asi es la vida*! (Such is life!)

Badong suddenly prepared to return to the shore. The day was fast changing into darkness. He was in a hurry to leave since the swamps can be very treacherous. He could get lost in the woods. Traveling through a maze of streams in the dark would be impossible!

"Junior, I want you to pay attention to my instructions," he began. The child shook his head to wake himself up from his deep reverie!

"The volunteers cut some firewood for you so you can cook simple meals. You'll have to continue cutting and gathering your own firewood. Here's a *bolo* (machete) for cutting and splitting wood and many other chores. It's a very handy and versatile tool.

"They also built a nice fire for you. It can keep on burning if you feed it with more firewood. Keep it burning or you'll have to start your own fire. Without it, you'll have to eat raw food. Do you know how to start a fire, son?"

"I think so, *tatay*. Someone *uh* ... had shown me once. But, I didn't *uh* ... pay much attention. I didn't see the need for it. Still, *uh* ... I have a general idea of how it is done."

"To make sure you know how to do it, I'll teach you how to make fire next time I'm here."

"Yes, *tatay*, *uh* ... I'm eager to learn it now! For the time being, *uh* ... I'll just nurse the fire you're *uh* ... leaving me."

"I suggest you feed it with bigger pieces of wood. Some embers will stay burning even when you're asleep. In the morning, the embers will allow you to build a new fire so you can cook breakfast."

"Yes, *tatay*. I'll try to keep it *uh* ... burning for as long as I can."

"I'm leaving you a small sack of rice and some dried fish. I know your mother had taught you how to boil rice. Just broil some fish on live coals and you'll have something very simple to eat."

"Thanks, *tatay*. I think I can do that."

"I'm leaving you some rainwater to drink and to cook with. You'll have to catch and conserve rainwater on your own. It won't be easy. Rainwater will be your most difficult item to get here. It's scarce even at the seashore village."

"What will I do if *uh* ... I run out of water? What can I *uh* ... use to drink?"

"That's a very good question, son. I really don't know what the answer is. You can't dig a well here. Even if there is a well, the water would be too salty; it would be impossible to drink. I guess I'll send one of your brothers to bring you more drinking and cooking water.

"I'm leaving you a couple of small buckets. Use them for catching and storing rainwater."

"*Tatay*, do you think I should *uh* ... ration my daily use of water?"

"That's a good idea. Limit your drinking until you have saved enough rainwater.

"Do you have more questions, son? I should really be leaving now. It's getting quite late."

"Yes, *uh* ... I had many questions in my head. But, I can't remember them now. Well, *uh* ... how long do you think I'll be staying here?"

"I don't know for sure. It might be a week or two weeks. Definitely, it won't be more than a month."

"If I gather the information you want, *uh* ... how will I report to you? I don't have a canoe."

"I'll send someone here every week. Just send your messages through your brothers when they come. Goodbye, son, I know you'll be all right."

Badong hugged his son affectionately! Junior hugged him in return but he was crying like a baby. He felt so sad, so alone and so forsaken!

Junior was resentful and angry, but not necessarily with his father. He was a victim, but he didn't know whom to blame. Yes, of course, he blamed the Japanese invaders for starting the war and causing all his troubles! The Japanese Emperor and his imperialistic military generals were the real causes of his misery!

After Badong had left, the boy stood outside the hut. He stared at the flimsy cottage he was supposed to guard. He could see through the thin walls made of one layer of coconut fronds. The walls couldn't possibly protect him from wild animals. He looked at the door opening and realized that there was no door to close it. He shook his head in desperation and yelled at the top of his lungs in frustration! He couldn't believe how badly the workers had built the rickety hut.

If a python or a crocodile should come to attack him, he wouldn't know what to do or where to hide and escape. His flimsy hut was good for nothing except to shelter him from the rain. He felt like a helpless lamb about to be slaughtered!

He entered the hut and examined the burning fire in the middle of the room. He was looking for a way to defend himself more effectively. He looked at some of the branches burning. He realized that he could use the burning pieces of firewood as weapons. He could pull out a flaming piece of wood and roast a predator's eyes or burn its tongue!

He knew he wouldn't be a match against large monsters. However, he could force some predators to risk dying for their meal.

He decided to use everything available to him: machete, burning firewood, teeth, fingers, nails, feet and everything in his disposal! He resolved to fight to his death because he refused to be an easy prey! In the process, he might gouge their eyeballs, roast their tongues or kill and eat them for lunch or supper!

He raised his machete in the air and yelled, "Beware, you predators in the wild! A mighty boy will slay and cut you to pieces! I'll roast and devour you for my meals! I'll fight and kill anyone who comes near me!"

His bravado felt good! He was determined to defend himself and survive! This was the first time he realized that he was a fighter and a

The Child Daredevil Hero

survivor! He was willing to do anything and everything to protect himself and remain alive!

He realized that he was most vulnerable when he was asleep. With an open door, predators could easily sneak in and attack him. He thought of making some kind of warning system. He figured out that if he tied pieces of rope or string around the lower level of the cabin, especially across the doorway, and hanged pans, silverware and empty cans along, they'd serve as a warning and wake him up. If an intruder touched any part of the rope, the hanging things would automatically ring like bells!

To make sure that he heard the noise and felt the presence of the intruder, he'd connect the strings to his big toes before he went to sleep. He'd keep his machete next to him when asleep.

His first night was the loneliest and scariest he had ever experienced in his life! He was so primed to fight he didn't want to eat anything. He reasoned that eating had no purpose since he was going to die anyway! He expected the predators to start showing up as soon as it got dark!

He watched every movement on the water and on land. However, he couldn't see anything. The darkness was so intense it was blinding. He couldn't see his hands at an inch distance from his eyes. He felt like he was deep in a large cave. Apart from the little fire at the middle of the room, the entire swamp was a total darkness!

He heard the leaves drop in the water. He heard the jumping mullets, which made him feel very tense. Sometimes, the mullet noise instantaneously made him raise his machete in the air ready to strike! He was certain he was under siege!

He listened carefully to every noise. Several insects made familiar sounds. However, there were unfamiliar insect sounds that made him shiver with fear! He listened to the accompanying sounds caused by the rustling of the leaves.

Suddenly, he heard a weird mysterious moaning sound in the background! He imagined hearing a loud fiery breathing of a green Chinese dragon! His hair felt like they were quills standing to protect him from the predator! A whiff of cold air seemed to rush through his spine and on his face! He felt like running away to hide, but he had nowhere to go! He was stranded on a crayfish mound, surrounded by swamp water.

He analyzed the mysterious sound more carefully. But he couldn't figure it out. When the sound didn't move any closer, he finally decided it couldn't be that dangerous. The sound seemed to come at regular intervals. He concluded that it was neither a human nor an animal sound.

He guessed that tree trunks or branches were rubbing against each other and caused the scary noise. After a while, the sound ceased to scare him.

Nevertheless, every unfamiliar sound was a call to arms! He had raised his machete in the air at least ten times that night!

Dawn and day came sooner than he had expected. He didn't sleep at all. And, he didn't make any armed contact that evening and felt disappointed. With daylight saturating the swamp, he relaxed his watch. He could see, smell or hear the intruders quite easily.

By noontime, however, he felt tired, dizzy and hungry. He boiled a big pot of white rice and broiled a large *bangus* (milkfish). He ate like a hungry pig. He drank two glasses of water and felt relaxed.

Without planning it, he fell asleep on the bare dirt floor. Since he didn't have any memory of preparing to go to sleep, he suspected he might have passed out from exhaustion! He slept throughout the afternoon and into the night.

Sometime at night, the ringing of the pans, silverware and empty cans rudely awakened him! He frantically disconnected the strings from his big toes, picked up his machete and ran to the fire to pick up a burning piece of firewood! He turned around, ready to fight the intruder! His hands were shaking like leaves! He looked everywhere for the trespasser but found no one.

After a while, he figured out that it was just a false alarm. He suspected he might have triggered the alarm himself by unconsciously moving his own feet. He didn't realize he had the strings tied to his toes when he fell asleep. Still, he felt happy that his alarm system worked.

He couldn't return to sleep. His heartbeat was still racing and his blood pressure must be elevated. He also felt rested and wide-awake. So, he spent the rest of the night watching in solid darkness. He listened to everything happening in his wet world. The rest of the night was uneventful.

After a week of high alert but encountered no predators, he suspected that their numbers might not be as large as he had assumed. Against his will, he automatically relaxed his guard. He could not maintain his fighting spirit.

Still, he continued to be watchful. But, he no longer felt he had to be on high alert all day long. Nevertheless, his weapons were at easy reach when needed.

With so much time at his disposal, he couldn't help but reflect on his lonely life in the jungle. He couldn't help thinking of the helpless kittens and puppies that his father had chosen as runts of the litter in the past few years. The runts were killed so the rest could grow strong and mature more quickly. With one or two less mouths to feed, the lucky ones had less competition.

He wondered seriously whether he was also the reject of his family. His actual exile seemed to prove that he was the disposable runt. His father sacrificed him so his brothers and sisters could enjoy their lives.

He remembered the times when his dad had asked him to get rid of the weakest and the smallest puppy or kitten in a litter. They had several dogs and cats when they were living in their farm in barrio Libo-o.

His father said, "Go and get rid of this runt. It will die anyway. The mother will even refuse to feed it. Watch how the bigger pups purposely dislodge the smaller fellows from a nipple. The smallest and the weakest are naturally doomed to die. Even if the runt survived, it would have a miserable life anyway. He or she would never be a top dog or cat anywhere."

Junior kept wondering how he would grow up if he survived the war. Would he be at the bottom of the totem pole? He was already the fourth boy and had been everyone's servant or factotum. As the fourth child, he was sure he would not get anywhere. He realized that even before the war, his self-esteem was already low.

His dad had said something he'd never forget because he suspected that it applied to him, "Remember, son, there's always a runt in a large litter. You can easily pick out the reject because it is the smallest and the weakest."

What he had said sounded personally threatening to Junior. He was the lowly fourth son and was smaller than average. It was more than probable that he was indeed the reject of his family!

He hated to consider the possibility that he might be the runt! Still, the way events were turning out, being the reject explained why he had been abandoned! By being left alone in a swamp, his parents had in fact rejected him. The realization made him extremely sad and he cried endlessly!

Chapter Eleven
Survival Obstacles

Fortunately, Junior realized that he was not as helpless as the puppies or the kittens that he had abandoned to die. He reasoned that as a ten-year-old human being, it was possible for him to survive his abandonment!

He made the resolve to survive his exile by using every possible means! He decided to plan out carefully his own survival. If he succeeded, then it would prove to his parents that he was a resourceful survivor! Perhaps his parents would then decide that he was worth keeping, at least for a while.

However, he had serious misgivings! Even if he survived, he realized that his feelings of self-worth had gone down considerably. Thinking of himself as the abandoned runt was more than enough to convince him of his own worthlessness! The war itself had already destroyed his self-esteem and he may never recover the loss!

The indiscriminate killing of innocent civilians had cheapened life considerably! The Japanese soldiers put no value to Filipino lives and put little value even to their own. It was commonly known that they committed *hara-kiri* for very superficial reasons.

The war had cheapened life in general and Junior's life in particular. Consequently, he no longer really cared whether he lived or died. At the time, he preferred life over death. Still, if he died, he was not a loss to any one else, other than his family.

In a global warfare, lives became disposable and reduced to mere numbers. The bottom line was the ratio of survivors to dead soldiers. The company or regiment that lost fewer lives won the battle. It didn't really matter who lived or died. Even the officers were dispensable!

In spite of his mental inertia, he looked around to take stock of what he had to deal with in his struggle for survival. His first reaction was *discouragement and despair*! All the things he observed around him were *barriers* to his survival!

His first obstacle was *forced idleness*! There was simply nothing to do! For the first time in his life, *idleness* became a serious issue because it made him feel guilty! It also made him feel strange because he knew it was not natural just to do nothing. He was also afraid that idleness might lead to boredom!

He looked around further and saw that there was absolutely nothing he could do for amusement. When the tide was high, he became stranded in his cabin like a prisoner. And, there was nothing in the hut that he could do to amuse himself.

Low tides weren't any better. The water in the streams was low, about ankle deep, but he couldn't think of anything to do there either.

The prop roots of the red mangroves

Walking in a swamp was very difficult, if not impossible to do. The arching and interlacing prop roots of the red mangroves blocked his progress at every turn. The red mangroves were the weirdest trees he had ever seen. Over and above the existing roots that were buried in the ground, supplemental roots miraculously grew anywhere on the trunks and branches, to provide additional support.

There were prop roots that started as high as forty feet above. In the beginning, the roots just dangled from the underside of the branches. Soon, the dangling roots branched out and subdivided further like new branches that pointed downwards. By the time they reached the ground, the initial root had at least a dozen branching tentacles that buried themselves in the ground. No wonder, some people called the red mangroves 'walking trees.' They had the power to extend their branches indefinitely because of their capacity to send down more roots to assist their travel.

Apart from the dangling prop roots of the red mangroves, the black and the white mangroves sent up from the ground four to eight inch pointed shoots, which could easily puncture any bare foot. Those vicious 'daggers,' as Junior called them, matted the ground like carpeting.

He was puzzled how he could survive living there without doing anything. He was simply out of his natural elements. He was just existing as a breathing creature, like a fish out of water. He knew that a fish, out of water, would shortly dry up, become rigid and die!

If he did absolutely nothing for a while, he wondered whether it would make him bored, lazy, crazy or depressed! He was curious how he might act when he became depressed or crazy.

He had seen some depressed people in town squares who looked extremely sad and lonely. They appeared eager to die but didn't bother anyone. He was more concerned about going crazy. He had seen crazy people who did shameful and embarrassing behaviors, like eating their own feces. He preferred being depressed to going crazy.

Still, becoming depressed or going crazy was nothing compared to what he had already predicted would likely happen. He was sure wild animals would kill and eat him any time soon! There must be all kinds of meat-eating predators living in the swamp area, looking for an easy meal.

Moreover, he became painfully aware that he wasn't only forced to be idle, he was also *forced to think*! Being awake, with nothing to do, left him no other alternative except to think.

As a young child, he didn't know how to think productively. He didn't know the creative powers of the thinking brain.

As far as he was concerned, the only thing worth thinking about was his problem of being forced to think. It was idleness that forced him to think. If he had some things to do, he would not even think that he had any problem with thinking. And, thinking about thinking wasn't leading him to anything meaningful or productive except to do more useless thinking!

The constant numbing bouts with thinking was frustrating because he couldn't get out of the rut! He had a most sophisticated mental tool (thinking) at his disposal but he didn't know how to use it.

He compared himself to a rice mill that his father had owned. He had observed the mill working, without anything to grind, while the engine was still warming up.

He was just like a rice mill that was continually running, day after day, with no grains to grind. It was just wasting fuel. The wasted operation would eventually wear out the engine and the various parts of the milling mechanism. Both the engine and the milling apparatus would inevitably breakdown and disposed of as junk!

Just to fill his mind with something, he recalled his one time experience in a forest when he was seven-years old. He had accompanied his father and a dozen men to a forest where they were logging for timber.

A Python

One day, he saw a python slowly gliding down a tree. Then, he realized that it was stalking a wild pig. He could feel his hair all over his skin, especially at the back of his neck, standing in fear! The young pig looked so innocent and he wanted to warn it of the impending danger. He yelled out but no sound came out of his throat. He wanted to throw a stone or a stick at it. To his surprise, he had become frozen out of fear and couldn't move!

The python struck and bit the pig at the neck. Then, it wound its body around it until it was dead.

The twenty-foot python started to swallow its prey, beginning with the head. It forced the corpse through its elastic jaws. He watched the whole process like watching a magic trick being performed before him. He watched it happen, but he couldn't believe his own eyes.

The snake looked so grotesque. It looked like it might choke to death. Unbelievably, however, it swallowed the whole pig into its bulging belly.

It was a gross behavior even for a snake. It couldn't possibly be savoring and enjoying its food. It had such a barbaric eating habit!

He imagined himself swallowing a whole uncooked chicken, with all its feathers still in place. The image was simply disgusting!

He also saw large lizards that looked like the Chinese mythical dragons. There were giant *orangutangs*, which had reddish fur. They were larger and heavier than humans. The *orangutang* behaviors, apart from language, were human like! Some Indonesians believe that they are wild humans. *Urangutang* means 'man of the forest.'

There were different species of monkeys and wild hogs with curved tusks, as long as ten inches. There were deer and various types of snakes. The forest was populated with wild animals of different kinds, from small ticks and leeches to thirty-foot-long boa constrictors.

He compared his recollection of the dry forest to the swamp he found himself in. He realized that the swamp was also a wild forest. But, it had an added feature of being flooded once or twice a day with ocean water. Therefore, he reasoned, a swamp would have more wild life than a dry forest. The wild animals in the swamp would come from both the dry lands and the deep seas. Hence, he expected more than twice as many predators there, as he had observed in the forest in Mambusao!

The Asian Orangutan is regarded by primatologists as the smartest among the great apes. They are dangerous in the wild!

He was certain pythons, dragon-like lizards and crocodiles lived in the swamp. There should also be alligators, octopuses, giant squids and monstrous slugs. He was sure all those predators would be preying on him very soon. He became paralyzed with fear because his chances of survival was almost zero!

Still, he was determined to fight with all his might and survive!

While standing in his cabin, ready to slay his first predator, he thought of the good times his siblings were having at the beach. Anyone else would have a better time than he was having. He was naturally envious of their leisure and pleasures!

He envied them for being carefree! They could play all kinds of games with the other kids. They could be making new friends and learning new games. They were learning how to speak *Aklanon*, the local language.

The islands had eighty-seven different languages that the Spanish colonists had downgraded to the status of *dialects*. To them, there was only one language, i.e., Spanish. According to them, what the natives spoke were indistinguishable barbaric *grunts* called dialects.

Junior would have liked to learn how the Aklan natives grunted to each other. He had already picked up few grunts since he arrived in the area.

The natives of Makato spoke with a staccato accent. They sounded like children struggling with certain vowels or consonants. It was tempting to imitate their manner of speaking.

His brothers and sisters could harvest edible sea weeds and fish roe that fish had deposited in the weeds. They were both delicious to eat raw. They could harvest different kinds of shellfish. Junior had become familiar with at least twenty different kinds of shellfish and at least forty different types of seashells.

Over 21,000 of the 100,000 shellfish species known worldwide are found in the Philippines

Seashells were also edible and their empty shells were a joy to play with. Some seashells were so naturally colorful and beautiful. Women used them as ornaments by stringing them into colorful necklaces and bracelets. They also mounted the larger ones into pendants, rings and earrings.

Conch shells were big and delicious to eat. The larger specimens could weigh as much as a pound.

There were small shells with yellowish enamel patina, that had commercial value. The Pacific Islanders called them *money shells* because, at one time, they used the delicate marine jewels for that purpose. For that reason, Junior collected them as if they were gold nuggets.

His siblings and cousins could sail to the barrier islands, like Boracay Island, where shells were even more plentiful. One could just turn a rock over and gawk at the live shells clinging to the rock surfaces. They could choose only the most beautiful jewels.

They could use goggles to examine and observe the multicolored live corals and other marine creatures under water. In their natural habitat, corals were among the most spectacular marine animals one could ever behold.

The Child Daredevil Hero

A closeup of some seashells

The *coral polyps* that inhabited the hard beautiful coral structures appeared like soft exotic flowers, with a variety of designs and an infinite color patterns and combinations. The gentle movements of the waves made them sway as if a genial wind caressed them. The bigger waves, however, scared them to withdraw into their ports and disappear!

A few moments later, the polyps slowly came out again to display their fineries and to forage for food that flowed in with the currents.

When Junior first saw the corals, he thought he had died and went to heaven! He kept staring at the enchanting marine wonders until his parents forced him to leave and go home.

There were village festivals that his family could attend, such as the shrimp festival, the *Flores de Mayo* (Flowers of May) and the patron saint's day. There were all kinds of religious festivals like the St. John the Baptist's day when lay people carried his statue along the river. The devotees doused the statue and each other with buckets of water. They pretended to baptize each other as the Apostle John baptized Christ.

There was a feast for every occasion, including the blessing of animals.

They could help fishermen pull in their nets and receive a portion of the catch. They could swim in the ocean and fight the dangerous surf. They could learn how to tame the waves like pets.

They had so many interesting things to do. They were growing and developing various new skills. They were very happy and contented with their lives!

In contrast, Junior was just vegetating, stagnating and wasting away in fear, sorrow and misery! Life wasn't fair to him! However, it was wartime and the troubled world was unfair to a lot of children!

These feelings of envy, frustration and self-pitty created a damper on his resolve to survive by becoming a fierce defender against predators. He must find a way to reverse the situation. If his negative attitude continued much longer, he might get caught in an emotional whirlpool and drown in a catastrophic depression!

Chapter Twelve
Survival Schemes

Dwelling on his miseries wasn't helping his fighting spirit against predators and monsters. Instead, he must strengthen his courage and become a brave warrior! In order to survive against predators, he must cultivate his killer instinct and kill every predator that shows its ugly face! He must never show any mercy to any potential attacker!

Before he could actually slaughter any predator, he thought he could cultivate his bravery simply by *fantasizing* about various battles and encounters with different adversaries. *Fantasies* were useful tools for cheering himself up and for enhancing his courage!

Using his vivid imagination, he fantasized taking different key roles in which he excelled and felt good about himself!

For example, he fantasized swimming in the big wide Pacific Ocean where the waves were as tall as mountains. This type of fantasy made him feel like a fearless giant!

He needed to escape, at least mentally, the covered gloomy swamp and bask in the full sun! Most of all, he wanted the necessary courage and the freedom to travel, mentally, anywhere in the wide expanse of the Pacific Ocean.

Hence, he enjoyed fantasizing how he could tame the giant surfs generated by the Big Ocean.

In the previous seashore village, called Ibizan, where his family had lived for less than a year, he learned how to tame the waves skillfully. He suffered lumps, bruises and sprained neck in the process! Nevertheless, he gained valuable skills in dealing with the giant waves. The new skills he had acquired not only prevented him from getting hurt again, but he learned to enjoy his mastery over the vicious surf!

He had learned, for instance, that if the top of the wave didn't break, it was fun to jump over it. It gave him the feeling of power and supremacy over a tremendous natural force. It was exciting because he had learned to control the waves that were unpredictable, awesome and extremely dangerous!

In his fantasy, he didn't just jump over the waves; he jumped three feet above, while clinching his fists in majestic triumph! After he came down to earth, he yelled to the retreating wave, "I won! I won! You're powerless over me because I'm strong and smarter than you are!"

However, when the waves were large, between five to fifteen feet high, and the top of the surf was breaking, the only safe course of action was to *dive under* them. As he crouched on the sand, he felt the jaws of the big Pacific Ocean trying to swallow him.

He felt the giant waves violently churning over him but powerless to hurt him! This moment was what he called, 'taming the waves!' He was, in fact, deflecting their natural power and reducing their potential to harm him! Again, he took great pleasure in overcoming a very powerful force that could hurt or kill him!

In his *fantasy*, he taunted the waves to hit him with their strongest weapons. He was fearless because he knew how to neutralize their lethal force!

"Come waves!" he mocked the on-coming serpentine monsters. "Hit me with your giant fists! I know how to parry your blows and turn each of you into my pet serpents."

Unfortunately, he had his share of wrong judgments when he jumped over breaking waves. A wave, between five to eight feet, might appear small. But, it may suddenly rise to its full height and strength. After he had made the wrong decision and started to jump, it was too late to change his action to avoid being hurt. He had to suffer the terrible consequences of his mistake!

The mean surf grappled him, threw him down and shoved him hard to the sandy bottom! It churned him around mercilessly like a helpless jellyfish! It mangled him and he ached for several days after the encounter!

Still, such rare incidents didn't stop him. He got up, flexed his muscles and clinched his fists in defiance! He said to the victorious wave, "You're lucky that time, Lucifer, because you had deceived me. You looked small but then you suddenly changed into a devilish monster!

"You smashed my face to the sand and twisted my neck like a piece of rope, only because I made a mistake in my judgment. That wasn't nice of you. But mark my word. I won't allow you to become lucky again! My skills are far superior to your luck. Come back here and I'll show you I'm smarter than you are!"

The angry waves seemed to regroup and teamed up with the arriving surf! They looked much larger, more ferocious and completely merciless! They intended to call his bluff!

With great courage and superhuman confidence, however, he confronted the next array of battering and writhing serpents! He was becoming more skillful at recognizing the true size of the surf. He was more careful in choosing his proper course of action. He made sure the stupid surf was never lucky again!

Dealing with the surf was like being in a hand-to-hand combat! He had to outsmart the adversary because he won only if he was more clever and intelligent. He knew that he would never be stronger than the opponent.

To fight and win over a much superior enemy entailed tremendous courage and determination not just to survive but to be victorious!

The most dangerous moment in the battle against the giant waves was entering the water from land! Because the waves severely pounded the shore in rapid succession, the only effective way to neutralize its power was to single out a smaller wave and dive through it (not under or above it).

The timing had to be perfect. He jumped in only after the wave had just pounded the sand. This way, he avoided the full brunt of its fury! He also gained enough time to prepare and face the next wave. Errors in timing could get him injured.

In his *fantasy*, however, all his entries were flawless! He could go in and out of water with great ease, without any fear of being hurt. He strutted out like William, the Conqueror, because he was the master of the surf, the tamer of the ferocious waves!

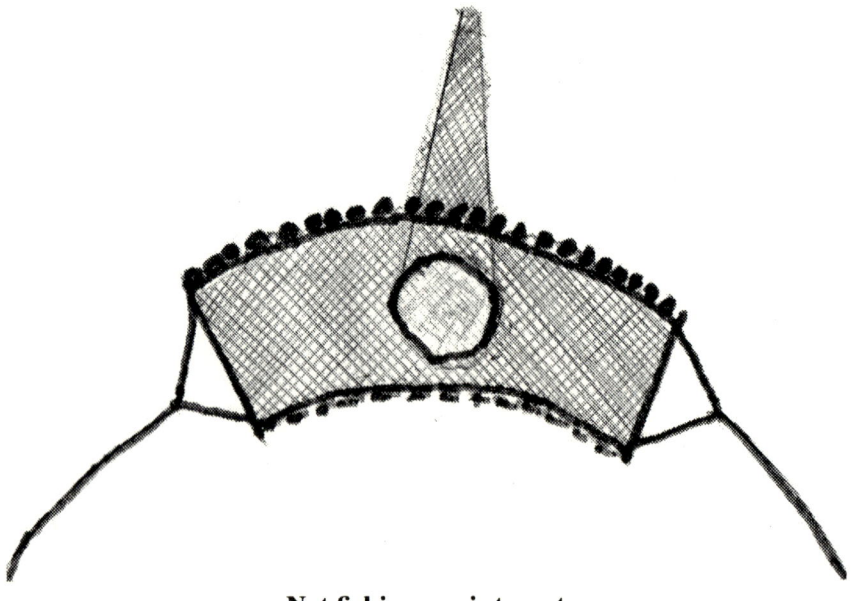

Net fishing equiptment

The Child Daredevil Hero

Among his most *favorite fantasies* was about a difficult and sophisticated type of *net fishing*. It required at least forty people in a cooperative endeavor.

Two fishermen in a large long boat dropped their long net from about thirty feet away from the shore. As they dropped portions of the net in a linear sequence, they paddled at least three kilometers out into the ocean. They spread the entire net in a semi-circle, facing the beach.

The net and the long ropes that extended at both ends were about four kilometers long but only twenty feet wide. The net stood vertically in the water because of a chain of buoyant cork balls that kept the top edge afloat. The bottom side sank under water because of a series of lead weights attached to the bottom of the net.

The top and bottom ropes that threaded through the net were tied together at about five feet beyond the net, so that the workers pulled only one rope at each end. The act of pulling each end of the rope moved both the top and bottom of the net simultaneously. Fishermen helpers slowly but steadily pulled each end of the net to the shore.

As if playing the game of tug-of-war, the fishermen pulled with their hands and walked backwards. The helpers increased their leverage by tying a small rope around their waists and then tied it to the big rope. This technique allowed them to use their entire body. Moreover, they could rest their hands, periodically, while still pulling with their bodies.

The first man who reached the top of the shoreline released his grip, detached his rope from the main rope, walked down to the waterline and started all over again. Each man performed the same routine until they hauled the whole net to the shore. This way, the pulling was continuous and smooth. The trapped fish remained calm and unsuspecting of their true fate, until it was too late to escape!

As the net became shorter, the two groups pulling the net at opposite ends gradually moved closer towards each other. After they hauled in the whole net, the groups merged.

Encircling an area of the ocean with a long net, theoretically, trapped a large number of marine life in the net. Since the net was only twenty feet wide, some fish were smart enough to swim below and escaped. Some mullets, for example, simply jumped over the net. Hence, it was predictable that a large percentage of the encircled fish would escape. They could see the net and had plenty of time to avoid the trap.

However, the percentage of the fish actually trapped and harvested was more than enough incentive to use the complicated technology. Even if only ten percent of the fish encircled were caught, the catch was still substantial.

Sal Kapunan

A large factor in the success of net trapping consisted in the *deceptive use* of a *trailing cylindrical sack of netting*. The net designer cut out a circular hole, three feet in diameter, from the center of the net. The large hole appeared to the fish as if it were a natural escape hatch.

In fact, the net designer had sewn to the rim of the hole a cylindrical sack, which was thirty feet long. The sack gradually tapered to ten inches. The fisherman/owner tied the end with a cord during the fishing operation.

In their attempt to escape, some fish naturally ventured into the sack and became trapped. As the net moved closer to the shore, more fish became frantic and 'escaped' into the trap.

The fisherman/owner remained in his boat to monitor the amount of fish filling the sack. Periodically, he lifted and opened the sack and poured its contents into large bamboo baskets. The fisherman hauled in at least sixty percent of the catch this way.

When the net reached shallow waters so that the bottom touched the sand, all the trapped fish were doomed! The fisherman and some helpers scooped out most of the catch, with small nets, into large bamboo baskets. Then, they hauled in the rest of the net to the shore.

By this time, most of the villagers came down to check out the catch. Some were there to buy fish; the others were there just for the entertainment value! They enjoyed looking at the catch because they saw abundant food coming from the ocean. It was reassuring to look at live food and fantasize what delicious dishes they could make out of them.

Socializing became festive during this period! The head fisherman's wife served glasses of *tuba* to the thirsty crew. As they were resting and waiting for their portion of the catch, some storytellers told funny or interesting stories. Those who could carry a tune sang their favorite folk songs.

After the head fisherman had emptied the whole catch on a big, wide bamboo mat, he divided it as fairly as possible between the owner and the helpers.

The simple formula for dividing the catch was: the sum of all the helpers plus ten. Ten portions went to the owner and each helper received one.

A portion could be large enough to feed a family for several days. If a family had three or four other helpers, their take home portions could be substantial!

At this time, only the head fisherman was working. He was dividing the catch into the right and fair portions.

The Child Daredevil Hero

Everyone, including the bystanders, tried to help the fisherman equalize the portions. Trying to divide fairly the varied sizes, shapes and weights of the fish was a very hard and tricky job! Everyone was in a good mood to banter and make suggestions to favor certain portions that they were eyeing for themselves. Every helper was free to choose his or her portion after the owner had announced that the time for choosing was up.

The whole process was a cooperative endeavor and was very festive! Laughter constantly filled the air!

The whole fishing endeavor took three to four hours, depending on the number of helpers. Because this type of fishing was labor-intensive and long, a fisherman would normally spread his net just once a day. Before dropping his net again, normally he needed to do some mending.

Some of the bigger fish, like sharks and dolphins, just swam through the net as if it were nothing more than a flimsy cobweb, leaving big holes in the process. If the damage was considerable, the fisherman may not spread his net again for a couple of days.

This technique of fishing was more advanced than most of the other methods used in the islands.

The work of net trapping was very hard, tedious and long. However, the fisherman and his helpers were all from the same village and knew each other very well. In fact, they were all related in some convoluted way.

They were very glad to help each other. The owner of the net needed the helpers and the helpers needed a capitalist who owned a long net and a big boat. Conversation, storytelling, singing and wholesome laughter made the whole process less tedious and more jovial.

Because Junior *fantasized* himself as a superman, he made himself a super fisherman. He imagined being bigger than his real self and being the best fisherman in the whole world! He pulled the rope more vigorously than the other helpers. He started pulling the rope ten feet below the waterline and more often than anyone did. He pulled the rope further away than anyone did. He was more enthusiastic about fishing than the others! And, he sang more loudly than anyone did!

When he received his portion, it was much larger than the others. It weighed at least a ton. He received baskets of groupers, snappers, yellow tails, mullets, flying fish, thousands of amber jacks and several baskets of shrimps, squids and octopuses.

The fisherman was proud of the catch saying, "This is the most I've ever caught in my life. Junior is the best and the luckiest helper I've ever had. He is a true super fisherman!"

Sal Kapunan

There was another type of fishing Junior also *fantasized* doing. For three months of the year, the ocean would become bright under water at night. Tiny shrimps carrying phosphorus in their bodies brightened the ocean as if there were billions of fireflies swimming underwater. This was the famous phenomenon called 'bioluminescence.'

Standing from the shore, Junior could see several kilometers of the ocean shining brightly! The water twinkled more brightly and intensely than the sky above! He felt awed by the magnitude of the marine life and their collective power to brighten the vast darkness! The abundance of life in the sea overwhelmed him!

The fishermen used finely woven nets because the shining shrimps were small. They were only about half an inch long and about the size of a toothpick. The fishermen dropped the rectangular nets into the water vertically, then lifted them horizontally by using long poles and a complicated pulley system. The net filled with shrimp and sea water was very heavy to lift. To hoist and pour the catch into large baskets or vats needed the assistance of supermen; and Junior was the right man! Fortunately, the shrimp boats were purposely outfitted with tall masts for hoisting the catch.

Folk dancers performed at fiestas (festivals)

The shrimp season was very festive! As soon as the shrimp boats pulled in early in the morning, by ancient custom, the villagers scooped shrimps with their bare hands and ate them raw. They could eat as much as they wanted before the captain divided the catch into portions. Of course, they washed down the shrimp with several glasses of *tuba*, the lightly fermented coconut wine.

Junior *fantasized* being a *shrimp fisherman* in the biggest shrimp boat! He was the foreman who ordered his subordinates to push or pull as he commanded them to do. The crewmen ground the pulleys as he dictated the cadence.

The workmen emptied the nets into large vats where they ground the shrimps with their bare feet. They salted some and stored them in large barrels. They ground the rest into a paste and stored them in big tanks and drums.

The reddish shrimp paste is the popular Filipino delicacy called *bago-ong*. Since it is heavily salted, it is often used in place of salt. Most Filipino homes kept a jar of *bago-ong* on their dining tables, since it was a necessary part of every meal.

In his *fantasy*, Junior joined the shrimp festival with his men as *local celebrities.* They participated wholeheartedly in the singing and folk dancing. The women of the village cooked and served shrimp in a hundred ways! *Bibingca, puto, suman, ibos* and other local delicacies were in abundance. Male attendants poured jugs of *tuba* freely like water. The party participants laughed and caroused into the wee hours of the morning!

They were happy because life was good and they were successful fishermen! The luminous shrimps, once again, brought new light, hope, comfort, food and a modicum of joy to their simple lives!

For at least four weeks, Junior's vivid fantasies kept his courage and determination at a maximum level! At least, they served as his only form of entertainment! He felt good for his imaginary achievements! He could always use the same or similar fantasies to rekindle his bravery in the future. He needed those fantasies to help him survive his exile in the swamp!

Part of his fantasy was imagining the beautiful female performers who sang and danced at the fiestas! They were always very entertaining!

Chapter Thirteen
Depression!

When the predators he had expected didn't show up, Junior found it difficult to maintain his fighting spirit. The *uncertainty* of the combats with the animals naturally drained his intensity! He could not maintain his fantasy life for more than a month.

Slowly, he was going back to reality, which was quite miserable and depressing! Willy-nilly, it was time to face the facts of life, however grim they might be!

He felt sorry for himself again because he didn't know what to do with his time. He felt so lonely and homesick! There were no books, magazines or any reading materials whatsoever. In fact, he never saw a printed page during the whole time he lived in the swamp.

There were no toys to play with and no playgrounds because the entire area was covered with water. The only dry ground were the floor of the hut and the top of some crayfish mounds. But, the mounds were not suitable for any practical use. Years of erosion had naturally turned the top of the mounds into inverted pointed cones. Besides, they were too steep to climb.

He felt so worthless again like a spare coin with very little value. His dad had given him the lonely assignment because he could spare him. No one in the family would even miss him. No matter how he looked at his situation, he couldn't escape the conclusion that he was nothing more than a lowly dispensable member of his family!

His father was unfair and exempted his teen-aged brothers and the adults from taking the same risks of boredom, tedium, frustration, loneliness, depression and even suicide that he was taking! As a small child, he deserved and needed more care, protection and consideration!

If his father thought that he shouldn't assign Paterno or Mabini the job, then he should have assigned a servant to do it. Servants in the islands were very easy and cheap to acquire.

It hurt Junior very much to think that his father preferred servants over him. This was another proof of his lowly status in the family. His status was even lower than that of a servant!

He figured out why his father didn't assign any servant to replace him. He needed them to do work for the entire family. If he had assigned their servant, Jose, in his place, then the teenagers and the other children might have to do some hard work. Looking for dry firewood for cooking, for example, could be tedious, backbreaking and time-consuming. Once again, his father left him with the short end of the stick!

To make his situation even worse, *fate had condemned him* to serve those older than him. That was the preordained fate of every fourth child in any family, especially in the Philippines. The unfortunate late comer became the convenient servant of the older brothers and sisters. His older brothers, especially Mabini, forced him to drop whatever he was doing to attend to their needs. They treated him as their convenient personal servant.

Mabini had simply assumed that it was his divine right to treat Junior in any way he wanted. From his point of view, as the firstborn, he had the natural right to demand service from his younger brothers and sisters. For instance, he had singled out Junior to scratch his back especially at night.

"Hey you, come here," he would call him at around seven. "My back is itching. Do you know what that means?"

He took off his undershirt, glared at him and ordered him to scratch his back immediately. Mabini did suffer from heat rashes. Junior only wished that he was more diplomatic and nice about his demands. It would have been nicer to ask, rather than demand the service.

When he wasn't busy, Junior went ahead and obeyed him before he became ugly or abusive! Still, he hated the chore and hated Mabini for turning him into his special servant. It was humiliating and degrading!

The war had nothing to do with Mabini's flagrant abuse of his birthright. He treated the younger children abusively before the war. For some reason, he was angry with his parents and took his anger on the other children.

The next time he or Paterno picked on Junior to do things for them was after classes in the afternoon. If Junior stayed around to do a homework or some personal project, he would likely hear Mabini yell, "Junior, get me a pack of cigarettes and a box of matches from the store." He was a chain-smoker and was often running out of cigarettes.

Paterno might chime in saying, "While you're getting cigarettes for Mabini, get me some bananas and a glass of water."

However, what Junior truly detested was when they used him as a personal courier. Because they had no telephones then, they often sent him to deliver messages to their friends, classmates and girl friends. Sometimes, Junior had to walk ten blocks to deliver a message. He had to wait for an answer, which could take sometime. There were times when he had to wait for hours before a response was ready.

Then, he walked another ten blocks to get home. Walking twenty blocks under a tropical sun could have given him a heat stroke!

Since he resented their daily impositions, he always registered a complaint, which never did him any good. He would say, "I'm busy. Get them yourself!" Or, he'd say, "I can't deliver your message because I have personal things to do."

In his childish way of thinking, it was necessary to make excuses to escape the imposed chores. However, his brothers interpreted the excuses as indications of bad attitude and acts of disobedience. Mabini always scolded and threatened him with some form of violence!

"What did you say?" he asked in a threatening voice. "Are you asking for a beating? Go! Do the things I told you to do or I'll beat you with a stick!"

He obeyed their commands while he whined about being turned into a slave. He knew his whining didn't change their behavior. However, it made him feel better to express his anger and frustration!

His usual strategy for coping with the unwanted chores was to avoid his older brothers as much as he could. He went swimming with his friends in several secret sections of the Mambusao River where they couldn't find him. However, this strategy worked only for a short time.

Mysteriously, the older brothers often figured out where his new hiding places were. Junior suspected that there were informers among his circle of friends. For a few centavos, some friends became traitors!

Life for him became a constant scheme of evasion and escape, which he knew was not healthy!

Just thinking about his lowly status and being treated like a servant made Junior feel depressed! Remembering the times when Mabini beat him with a bamboo stick also made him feel angry and depressed!

Given the unfair treatment he had endured for years, he became delighted when he suddenly realized that his unpleasant swamp assignment allowed him to avoid his older brothers permanently! They could no longer boss him around!

For the first time in his life, he was his own boss. He alone would decide what to do or not do. He decided to do only what was interesting to him, regardless of their value or meaning.

The new freedom was definitely a gift from heaven! It was a chance to grow independently from the older boys. He imagined himself growing like a proud acacia tree, alone in an open meadow!

Finally, without really working for it, he was free from the encroaching shadows of the bigger trees! He could grow more quickly and more symmetrically, without any harmful interference from his older brothers!

Unfortunately, more immediate troubles awaited him before he could take advantage of his newly found freedom. *Boredom* quickly set in sooner than he had expected!

The swamp atmosphere was very weird and gloomy. The mangrove trees blocked the sun almost completely. There was something mysteriously depressing about the absence of the sun, especially to someone who was so used to it. The arching forest canopy felt like he was living in a cavern, in almost *total darkness*!

Just the idea of living alone in a swamp, even for a short time, was depressing and scary! The pervasive *foul smell* caused by layers of *decaying leaves* constantly reminded him of death and decay! The darkness, gloom and foul smell of the watery wilderness were suffocating!

He expected all kinds of monsters coming in with the tides. After the high tides had crested, he waited in fear for some *sea monsters* with a thousand tentacles to reel him into their cavernous hungry mouths!

Without realizing it then, those were already the thoughts of a depressed scared child!

The awaited full moon finally arrived and the cabin floor stayed dry! He immediately reported his positive observations to his father, through his younger brother, Trinidad. He expected his dad to order him to return and live with the family at the seashore. For reasons he does not understand even today, his father didn't change his assignment! (He can't ask his parents for clarification today because they had been dead for a while.)

Understandably, Junior became concerned that his exile in the woods might become permanent! This fact alone confirmed his suspicion that, indeed, his father had abandoned him to die!

After four weeks of doing nothing and fearing that his assignment might be permanent, a *full-blown depression* suddenly seized his psyche! He felt very sad and lacked the energy to get up! He cried uncontrollably and lost his appetite. His chest started to hurt and his heart felt very heavy!

Then, he experienced something very scary! He had *anxiety attacks* that prevented him from sleeping or resting! The anxiety heightened his fear of dying and his breathing became labored! He felt panicky because he thought he was suffocating! He was shaking constantly!

The strong foul odor of the decaying vegetation bothered him even more intensely. The darkness made him feel he was in a tomb in a cemetery. The absolute silence made him imagine he was dead! He felt closed in and couldn't breathe properly. Suddenly, he also had *asthma attacks*!

He was asthmatic when he was only five but it disappeared by the time he was eight. His depression must have triggered off his new asthmatic illness!

His head just naturally hanged down and he couldn't lift it, even when he wanted to. The constant bending of the neck made his neck ache! Everything in the swamp seemed to push him down into the bogs!

For hours and days, he sat there on the dirt floor, with his head bowed down, crying and feeling like a zombie! Sometimes, he felt like a wet rag rotting and dripping with tears in a dark corner of the room. He was in absolute despair! He just wanted to disappear or evaporate in the air! He really wanted to die so he would be free from *extreme pain*!

The depression must have lasted for at least a month. He was powerless to change his condition. Although he wanted to die, he didn't know how to do it. Mysteriously, he was not motivated enough to try anything that would terminate his own life. Since he was not eating anything, he expected to die from starvation at some point!

However, a *psychological change* happened that he didn't expect! He felt that he was getting used to the depression; it became his natural state. He stopped feeling bad about being depressed. After a while, depression didn't feel so bad any more!

He wondered whether his depression had bottomed out!

Chapter Fourteen
Renaissance!

Miraculously, one night, the emaciated boy had a very long deep sleep! He had *a wonderful dream* that taught him an important lesson!

He was a small child crawling into a tiny cave. From the cave, he saw various scenes of the swamp where everything was alive! The mangrove trees were waving their branches as they welcomed him! Even the crabs and fishes were excited and jumped with joy! The oysters and clams opened and closed their valves excitedly as they clapped their shells like castanets!

Junior was no longer afraid of the swamp creatures and felt happy to live among them. They welcomed him as the head of their community.

When he woke up, he realized he didn't feel depressed anymore! He was no longer afraid of the dark swamp. With the depression over, he felt happier to live in the woods. It was a surprising change from night to day!

The meaning of the dream was quite clear to him. He was the crawling child and the cave was his humble cabin. The swamp was alive because living creatures inhabited the land and sea. The mangrove trees were waving to him because they were also alive.

His subconscious mind was telling him, through the dream, that the swamp was safe, friendly and welcoming. The trees, birds and fishes were inviting him to become the head of their community.

Inspired by the dream, he wanted to explore his environment more actively. An aggressive exploration of the swamp would make him more familiar with his environment and feel much better about his life in exile.

If he could only make a raft out of bamboo logs or whatever suitable materials he could find, he intended to float around and discover the features and the treasures of the swamp.

Unfortunately, he didn't find bamboo logs anywhere. He cut down some of the dead branches of mangrove trees and lashed them into a raft. But the wood was soft and quickly absorbed water. When he rode on it, it virtually sank. He jumped off and swam to his cabin for safety.

As a last resort, he went to the storage corner of the room to look for anything he could use for flotation. He peeled off layers of unfamiliar and unusable things. However, at the bottom of the heap, he found a large *wooden wash basin* that might serve his purpose.

The wooden basin that became a canoe. In the background are giant crayfish mounds, which the residents of the shore used as the foundation of their hideouts.

Since they had escaped hurriedly from a burning town, with only the clothes they were wearing, their maids no longer needed the basin for washing clothes. Hence, the basin was just sitting there, doing nothing.

It was thirty-six inches across, round and hewn in one piece from a large mahogany tree. It was about ten inches high.

He floated it at high tide and rode on it. To his surprise, it carried him and still left a freeboard of about five inches! He couldn't believe his luck!

He became overjoyed with this discovery! It was the *turning point* of his life!

This was his *moment of liberation* from being stranded in his hut for hours! Fate was finally working in his favor!

Immediately, he decided to use the basin as a canoe. It would give him the mobility he needed. He could finally use it to visit the other shacks in the swamp village. He'd introduce himself to his neighbors, if anyone else actually lived there.

Meanwhile, he nursed himself back to health. He had lost weight but he didn't know how much. He ate as much rice and fish as he wanted. But what really nursed him back to normalcy were frequent visits to his favorite food: the succulent abalone! He ate as much as he could.

Within a three-week period, he felt he had completely recuperated! His energy level was back to normal and depression was just a bad memory!

In the beginning, he just floated around wherever the tidal current might take him. He was just randomly discovering the various features of the watery woods. He was just enjoying his newly found freedom of flotation and navigation. And, a deep sense of gratitude overwhelmed him for his relief from depression! Above all, he felt healthy and happy once more!

He realized, once again, that the streams branched out into little streams; and the little ones also branched out into even smaller creeks. Swamps, he concluded, were *networks of branching streams and creeks*. Just where they ended was something he wanted to find out as quickly as possible.

For this reason, he wanted to be more methodical in his exploration of the streams. He planned to follow some of the waterways and find out where they ended.

He wanted to know everything about the swamps: how they came into being? Why the tides occurred? Why were the mangrove trees salt-tolerant? What marine and land creatures existed there? What marine organisms lived there that he could harvest for food?

Those were difficult and important questions. Still, he was determined to learn everything directly from the natural source of knowledge. The swamp itself would be his primary textbook and teacher. He would allow the watery jungle to teach him and reveal to him her innermost secrets.

Apart from the tides, which fascinated him immensely, his constant obsession were the *mangrove trees*. Everywhere he paddled with his bare hands, he saw mangroves of different kinds. He decided to find out how many kinds of mangroves existed there.

Since he also wanted to find out where the streams ended, he combined the two investigations. By studying the largest stream and all its ramifications, he could also study the mangrove trees growing on each bank.

He started his primitive research by examining the small stream where his hut was situated. He noticed that some mangroves had darker bark. Some of the older and bigger trees even had black coverings on them. So, he called them *black mangroves*.

As he steered his basin to deeper waters, he noticed that most of the mangrove trees had prop roots and reddish new leaves. So, he called the trees *red mangroves*.

Since he wanted to find out where the streams and creeks ended, he navigated towards the smaller streams. Then, he detoured into the first branch. After following it for a while, he detoured again at the first smaller branch. He kept entering the smaller creeks. Finally, he remained in one small creek and followed it until it ended. To his great surprise, the creek ended on *dry land*!

That was an important *discovery*! This new information gave him the hope of digging a *well* that might provide him drinkable water later on.

To confirm his new discovery, he followed another stream and made the necessary detours, until he reached land again. This time, he wanted to know and compare what the dry land was like in relation to the swamp.

He tied his canoe and walked on dry land. He walked for about half a kilometer in various directions to get some idea of the lay of the land, the vegetation and especially the mangrove trees.

He estimated that the dry land was no more than two feet above sea level. The dry land was not mountainous; it was just higher than the land covered by the brackish water.

He saw certain areas that were either wet or moist. It was obvious to him that some high tides, probably during the full moon, flooded the dry land. He guessed that some tides were higher during summer months. He also guessed that the same flat areas were covered with sea water during storms.

He concluded that the flat dry land itself was saturated by salt. Therefore, he assumed that all the vegetation he found on the dry land had to be salt-tolerant.

Most of the dry land surfaces had few vegetation. The sparse vegetation was limited to shrubs, bushes, and low types of grasses. He saw some vines that were succulent. He wondered why the vegetation in the dry land was very sparse.

He remembered that in Mambusao, every inch of the farmlands was covered with vegetation. If a farmer removed the grass or weeds from any land area, within a month the bald area would be covered with young vegetation. Hence, there had to be a reason why vegetation did not grow on the dry ground. He guessed that the salt content of the ground was very high and that high salt contents prevented the growth of plants.

There were few trees that he suspected were mangroves. Most of the trees had white bark and he called them *white mangroves*. The white mangroves were smaller and shorter than the black or red mangroves. Their trunks grew straight and in clusters. He noticed that most of the trees in the dry land or in very shallow waters were of the white variety.

He also saw some black mangroves whose bark ranged from gray to black. But, there were very few of them on the dry land. The few that thrived grew tall, with a wide canopy, as much as sixty feet wide. He had observed that in deeper waters, the black mangroves were dominant.

Since he wanted to dig a well, he intended to explore other dry lands with higher elevation. If he found an elevation, which was at least five feet above sea level, he intended to dig a well as soon as possible and test the water quality.

Then, he turned his attention to the shrubs. He assumed that they were also mangroves. They didn't turn into trees because of the high salt contents of the ground. Later on, he found out that, indeed, the shrubs were also mangroves and were called buttonwood. The tallest buttonwood mangrove shrubs he encountered was about ten feet tall.

As he paddled back to his lean-to, he observed the mangrove trees more carefully. He discovered that the white mangroves stopped growing where the water was more than one foot deep. Beyond that point, the black mangroves predominated. As he paddled towards deeper waters, he noticed that the red mangroves almost monopolized the territories.

The most *distinctive features* of the red mangroves were the *prop roots* that grew out of the branches and trunks of the trees. Some of the roots were dangling patiently in the air. They were waiting for the time when the tips touched the ground so they could burrow deeply into the soil. The older prop roots had already established their foothold in the ground. They provided the needed support for the growing trunks or the extended branches.

Based on the actual roots already established, he tried to figure out why the red mangroves propagated prop roots. He concluded that each prop root was a necessary support. He suspected that the trees somehow 'sensed' the need and decided to grow those roots when needed.

He also examined the new roots dangling from the branches. He could see the reason why they were growing. For example, where a branch was crowded and shaded by another tree, the victim tree grew prop roots in the same area to support a new growth that would move it away from the encroaching neighbor. In every case, the new roots were needed to support growth that would maximize its exposure to the sun. For this reason, the trunks and branches of the red mangroves were never straight.

He also noticed areas where the red and black mangroves coexisted. Those areas were where the water was relatively shallow. In deeper waters, only the reds thrived in the environment. They could continue to grow even in deep waters because of their prop roots. The adventurous roots could crawl down into the bottom of a stream, river or shore and establish some kind of foothold. He discovered that every prop root in deep waters had been firmly anchored to the soil. They were truly marvelous and amazing trees!

His next mission was to find out if he had actual neighbors in the swamp. From the beginning, he was skeptical about anyone else living there. He could finally verify his initial assumption that nobody else lived there with him. He was pretty sure that nobody else live there because he hadn't seen anyone canoeing around during the three months he had lived there.

He *theorized*, based on his meager knowledge of the mangrove habitat, that the evacuation huts could be found close to shallow streams. He knew that one criterion for choosing a hideout was inaccessibility by the Japanese launches. However, the shallow waters must also allow the small native canoes to get through.

He *theorized* that the shallow streams where the huts could be found were situated in areas where the *black* and the *red mangrove trees* shared the land. He had discovered earlier that the *black mangroves* naturally prevented the reds from completely choking the waterway with their prop roots. In effect, the black mangroves allowed small canoes to have access to the huts.

He was surprised to discover that, like animals, the trees also controlled each other. He had discovered that each type of mangroves dominated a specific territory and virtually excluded all the others.

He finally set a day to look for the other cabins. Using his hands as paddles, he went out to search methodically for the other huts. He followed the shallow creeks and navigated for at least a kilometer on each direction. His speculation about the location of the huts was accurate.

He quickly discovered that the evacuation huts were scattered around at various distances. In a couple of cases, the cabins were at least two kilometers away from his cabin. Some of the huts formed a cluster of three or four.

It actually took him a whole week of searching before he was certain that he had found all the dwellings. He stopped looking only after two days of fruitless searches.

As he had strongly suspected, *no one answered his knocking, banging and yelling*! Some cabins were simply padlocked. Others were not even locked and their doors were wide open. Like his hut, some cabins didn't even have doors.

Finally, he was certain that nobody else lived there. *He was the whole community*!

Even though he had a strong suspicion that nobody else lived in the swamp, the actual confirmation of his suspicion shocked him more than he had anticipated! To know for sure that he had lived as a recluse for three long months shocked him like a bolt of lightning!

He suddenly became terrified in knowing that he had nobody to go to if he got sick or injured. He had no medication of any kind in his cabin. Out of fear, he immediately made the resolve to be more careful and to avoid getting hurt or sick!

He wondered whether his parents knew he was living as a hermit all along. Even though he was suspicious that they might have known it, he didn't want to confront them with his evidence. He was afraid that the evidence would force them to finally require him to live in the village. Such a decision would force him to end his life as a hermit, which he had learned to enjoy! The thought of ending his hermitic life was shocking and unbearable!

Just the thought of Mabini harassing him and making irrational demands on him gave him nightmares! Hence, he decided to keep quiet and never brought up the subject, even after the war was over.

After Japan had formally surrendered, nothing was ever said about their war experiences. The memories were too painful to recall! For almost sixty years, Junior had successfully repressed his memories about his hermitic life in the swamp!

Chapter Fifteen
A Hermit by Choice

On his own, Junior found out that he had been living as a hermit without intending to. Thenceforth, he decided to live as a hermit out of his own volition! He knew he could put up with the hardships and the isolation because there were *sufficient benefits* in living alone.

Living alone was rewarding for him because he freed himself from the authority of his parents and his older brothers. Freedom from the control of Mabini was, in itself, sufficient reason to continue living as a recluse.

However, becoming a hermit, by *choice*, became *possible* only after he had reflected hard on the advantages of living alone.

He decided to become a hermit only after he had converted the wooden basin into a canoe. Shortly after his discovery of the basin, he found many sources of food in the swamp.

He could freely indulge in several enjoyable activities like harvesting the succulent abalone, bait-fishing during the peaks of high tides, finding clams with his bare feet, catching crabs with his bare hands and many other fishing adventures. He had discovered so many enjoyable activities that he could pursue leisurely on his own.

Moreover, as he will discuss in chapter eighteen, he would form a *swamp society* that consisted of trees, birds, fish, shellfish and other marine animals. He would bond with the members of his society by giving them names and conversing with them on a daily basis.

However, becoming a hermit became a *meaningful life style* only after he had formed a **philosophy of life** that conformed to the natural processes of the material world. *Formulating a personal philosophy at a young age was the most gratifying achievement of his entire life*! It served as the essence and guide of his life even today.

He expects some people to doubt whether a child, his age, could form a philosophy of life on his own. They'll argue that philosophy is specialized, abstract and difficult even for adults to understand, let alone to create one.

He admits, as a formally trained philosopher, that most adults never form a philosophy of their own. Most of the people he has met know very little formal philosophy. Even those who have college education remember very little about the subject beyond remembering the course number and some popular philosophers like Socrates, Plato, Aristotle, Descartes and some Existentialists.

The Child Daredevil Hero

Nevertheless, as a philosopher with advanced degrees in the field, he knows that everyone is capable of forming his or her own philosophy, even at a very young age. He is certain of this point because he formed his own personal philosophy when he was between the ages of ten and thirteen.

Philosophy is not only *simple*, it is *necessary* for life even for children. When children start to ask questions at around the age of two, they're looking for explanations, reasons, causes and meanings of things. That is precisely what philosophy means. It is a *natural search* for the *meanings* and *causes* of things. Among the questions a child often asks is, "Why?"

The great Greek philosopher, Socrates, was often quoted for saying, "An unexamined life is not worth living." Interestingly, when children start to ask questions, they're examining their lives. In the process, they're becoming philosophers.

The children want to understand the different things that happen to them and around them. They want to know who they are and why they exist. They're looking for explanations that may enable them to understand the meaning of their own lives. They're examining every facet of their beings.

Everyone is, in fact, a philosopher!

In time, many children become *religious philosophers* because the explanations given to them by their religious parents, teachers and ministers are religious explanations. A religious faith may become 'hereditary' in the sense that the same beliefs are passed on from one generation to another. In the same way, a religious philosophy maybe passed from one generation to another.

For this reason, few individuals form personal philosophies independently of the *ready-made religious philosophies* that already prevail in their culture.

For example, when John Walker Lindh, the American Taliban, turned his back from Catholicism, he didn't go far to experiment on Buddhism, which his own mother had also investigated and dabbled in.

From Buddhism, he inquired into Islam, while he was still living in California. His interest in Islam led him to Yemen, Pakistan and finally to Afghanistan where he ended up as a Taliban fighter.

In the Western World, most babies are born into Judeo-Christian families. Still, some are born into the Muslim faith and other small pockets of religious beliefs.

There are also those who are not raised in any faith at all because their parents are atheists or agnostics. Those are the ones who will develop their own personal philosophies because they need it to survive in any world. The philosophy that they will form will allow them to make sense of whatever world they live in.

In the Middle East, many babies are born into Muslim, Jewish or Bahai religions. Of course, there are also many other faiths in such a vast region, including the followers of Zoroaster.

In the Far East, many babies are born into Taoist, Shinto, Hindu, Muslim, Buddhist and, to some degree, the Christian faith. The Philippines, for example, is at least 80% Christian, most of whom are Catholics.

There are, in fact, many indigenous religions, which maybe classified as variant forms of animism. They're based on the veneration of ancestral spirits and different kinds of spirits they presume to dwell in inanimate objects and in plants and animals.

Each religion, to which a set of parents belongs, is a religious philosophy. Parents naturally impart their own beliefs to their children in the course of parenting. Hence, it's not surprising why Catholics emerge from Catholic families and Muslims come from Muslim families.

Contrary to erroneous assumptions, children generally don't choose their own religions. Most believers *inherit* their beliefs almost as naturally as they inherit their parents' skin color.

In contrast, Junior had to form his own philosophy of life because it was necessary for his survival in the swamp. What he formed, over a three-year period, was a *naturalistic philosophy* because his religious philosophy was too ill defined and inadequate to guide his life in the woods. This was due to lack of formal religious education and his young age.

What he did was to form a system of basic rules for the guidance of his daily life. The rules he formed were suggested by the natural laws he observed in his daily routine, such as the rising and setting of the sun and the ebb and flow of the tides. Some rules he formulated had been derived from the teachings of his own parents. But, he adapted them only to the extent that they conformed to the laws of nature as he knew it.

Since he lived in a *primitive state in nature*, formulating rules based on natural processes was *easy* and *natural*.

It was *easy* because they arose from the life he was already living. It was *natural* because his life already conformed to the rhythms and cycles that existed in the natural world. (He is using the terms 'cycles' and 'rhythms' almost synonymously.)

Because the earth, sun, moon, planets and other celestial bodies are circular and because they revolve in circular orbits, people normally observe *recurring* movements that produce *repeated occurrences*. Take for example, the occurrences of *days and nights, the seasonal changes, the cycles of the moon, the tidal flows, the circadian rhythm of the human biological system* and many other natural phenomena.

Based on these natural cycles, Junior formulated certain rules such as: *follow the commands of nature as expressed or implied by the cycle of day and night*. What the rule meant was that he stayed awake and worked during the day and, apart from *siesta*, he limited his sleep and rest during the night. He observed that the birds and other animals followed the day-night cycle like him. They limited their feeding, drinking, defecating, mating and so on during the day. At night, they also went to sleep.

The rule didn't change anything in what he was already doing. It merely forced him to accept the fact that his waking and sleeping routines were directly tied up with the movements of the sun around the earth as he observed it. (Of course, he would learn later on that it was really the earth that revolved around the sun.)

He scheduled his *meals* based on the day-night cycles. Hence, he ate breakfast after waking up to energize his body for work in the morning. He ate lunch at noontime, to energize his body for the afternoon work. He ate supper at night and relaxed to prepare himself for sleep.

From the first day of his life in the swamp, he felt he had to formulate some *practical principles* just to survive from day to day. His immediate environment was almost completely unknown and hostile to him. He knew that he could die from bites of fish, snakes, spiders and other organisms. He could die instantly from eating all kinds of poisonous food.

In order to survive, he formulated *practical rules* that *respected the noxious nature of the environment*. He reasoned that poison was part of nature.

Consequently, he formulated specific *prohibitions,* such as: *Don't eat anything unfamiliar; don't touch anything that might bite or secret poison; and, stay away from unknown and dangerous-looking surroundings.*

Since his knowledge of what were familiar and safe had been acquired from his previous life outside the swamp, the range of his 'safe' actions and daily activities was extremely limited. Nevertheless, these survival strategies worked very well for him. They explain why he survived in a hostile environment where thousands would have perished!

After his basic survival was relatively assured, he formulated some other simple principles intended to *improve the quality of his life*. One of the principles stated: *Accept whatever nature offers and adjust your conduct to conform to the natural conditions.*

In practice, what it meant was: if the day was sunny, he enjoyed the sun. If it was rainy, he sought shelter or took the opportunity to take a bath. If a typhoon was raging, he took shelter in his cabin or hid behind a large mound. These were just common sense applications.

Above all, he followed *two major principles* religiously: *Avoid extremes and follow the middle of the road.*

He believed that he had already learned the first principle from his own upbringing. His parents were always telling him to eat, drink, run, walk, talk or play in moderation. *Moderation* became the touchstone of his daily life.

He also realized that *his own body naturally dictated* that he should follow the rule of moderation. His own stomach told him when he had eaten or drank enough.

He noticed that his own body, as an organism, followed a certain rhythm that conformed to the rhythms of nature. The natural rhythm has been called *circadian*, which literally means in Latin 'around a day.'

Following the middle of the road is the essence of every *virtue*. There is a saying in Latin, *En medio stat virtus* (Virtue stands in the middle.) This rule was central in his formulation of a balanced happy life.

He combined these two principles because there were areas where they overlapped. In many ways, they prescribed the same things. In other words, he simplified both principles by stating that *moderation is the essence of virtue.*

Even before he started living in the swamp, he was always intrigued by *opposites such as: high-low, right-left, above-below, early-late, hot-cold, bright-dark, day-night, strong-weak, solid-liquid, active-passive, male-female, old-young, life-death, wise-ignorant, long-short, wide-narrow, far-near, fast-slow, rain-shine, wet-dry* and many more.

Strong oppositions that led to new creations and realities especially intrigued him. Among the opposites that first fascinated him was *hot-cold*. He had observed how a blacksmith heated a piece of iron and molded it into various shapes. When the metal became cold, the new shapes became permanent. The *opposite qualities* seemed responsible for allowing things to take new forms.

The *day-night* opposition occurred every twenty-four hours. However, they never occurred in the same way. Some conditions were almost always different. There were always many natural forces that changed the natural conditions such as the wind, clouds, rains, temperature, humidity, altitude, air quality and others.

Interestingly, the regular occurrence of day and night allowed people to plan their days ahead. The creation of the Gregorian calendar even allowed people to plan their lives months or even years in advance.

The *work-rest* cycles that conformed to the day-night sequence were not only natural, they allowed people to lead more productive and happier lives. Daytime was conducive to work and nightime was naturally suited to sleep and rest.

He analyzed every *natural opposition* he could think of and found them to be **categories of reality**. Every opposition seemed to represent two categories that opposed each other. Hence, 'hot' was a category of reality and 'cold' was another category.

However, he discovered that some oppositions were *false*, i.e., the two apparent categories represented only one category. For example, *'far-near'* are relative *categories of space*. Both represent a small continuum in the same category of space. In other words, *far* is not a true opposite of *near*.

Still, others represent only a category and the opposite represents its absence. For example, the *day and night* opposition represents only the category of sunlight. Night is the absence of light.

The *strong-weak* opposition is a *continuum* within the same category of *force*. The *short-long, wide-narrow and above-below* are relative categories of *space*. Slow-fast are relative categories of *velocity*. *Early-late and young-old* are relative categories of *time*. The categories of *wise and ignorant* are the extremes in a continuum of *knowledge*. An ignorant person has some knowledge.

Active-passive and *work-rest* are categories of *action*. *Male* and *female* are reproductive categories. And the *life-death* opposition really refers only to the category of *life*; death is the end of life.

He concluded that *reality* is made up of different opposites. A given reality is in opposition to another reality to which it is related. As the examples above show, however, some oppositions are not true because the categories may differ only in degrees but not in kind.

However, there are **true opposites**, like *positive-negative and hot-cold*, in which the categories interact and may even cause natural catastrophes.

For example, from *positive and negative ion interactions* come thunder and lightning. From *hot and cold air* come condensation, wind, clouds, rains, cyclones, typhoons, monsoons, hurricanes and tornadoes!

He concluded that *the interaction of true opposites create movement, change, evolution, revolution, cataclysms, catastrophes, growth, birth, death and other natural phenomena.*

He took it as a given that there were existing realities in nature that he couldn't and shouldn't change. Therefore, he started from a set of given realities as the springboards of his activities and creativity. He yielded to higher forces and bent his will to follow the will of nature. He religiously refrained from imposing his will over the natural order.

These principles constituted the essence of the philosophy he had formed as a hermit. Every meaningful thing he did as a hermit served to formulate, confirm, stabilize and systematize his philosophy of life. It is still his personal philosophy as an adult today!

Chapter Sixteen
Playing Russian Roulette

Before the war, Junior knew nothing about any coastal swamp, its geography, configuration, inhabitants and resources. He didn't even have a dictionary definition of what a coastal swamp meant. Yet suddenly, he found himself living in one. It was like suddenly finding himself living in Mars or Venus. He didn't know how to survive in it.

Without the basic information, everything was virtually unknown. As a defensive strategy, he had to put the swamp in the enemy column. It belonged to the same category as monsters, predators and serial killers! He could die any time from poison, radiation, bacteria and viruses coming from various sources in the swamp environment.

Yet, he was forced to live in it and was not at liberty to run away. His assignment was for at least three weeks, which became extended to months and later on to years.

Under normal conditions, he would survive as a child by being nurtured by his parents, relatives and the community where he lived. His community would have provided him a continuous wealth of knowledge and expertise from which he acquired information and training through observation, imitation, participation and other social programs and devices.

His family would be the social agent in his upbringing for the society to which he belonged. His parents were going to be his teachers, trainers, models and watchdogs in the transmission of social traditions, knowledge and know-how. He wasn't growing up in a vacuum but in the context of a specific society.

Therefore, if he grew up in a *swamp community*, he would have learned how to gather and catch food from his parents, older siblings, elders and community members from age one to seven or eight. By age ten, he would be knowledgeable about the geography of the swamp and the specific characteristics of each nook and cranny of the wetlands. He would be adept at distinguishing the edible from the poisonous creatures. He would be skillful in catching and harvesting all types of food in the swamp.

As a matter of fact, however, there were *no human swamp communities anywhere in the world.* It is almost impossible to survive in a swamp, unless you happen to be a small fish, an oyster or a crab. His parents and relatives actually lived in a landlocked community at least fifty kilometers from the nearest coastal swamp. They knew nothing about coastal swamps and about the poisonous inhabitants of the streams, rivers, estuaries and the sea. Nobody in Junior's family could help him live safely and comfortably in a swamp.

This explains why his father's instructions for his daily living were very brief. The instructions were more suited for a normal life on dry land. He couldn't teach his son what he didn't know.

As events actually unfolded, at age ten, he was suddenly left to find out for himself *what were edible, what could make him sick and what could kill him instantly* in his swamp environment. Theoretically, this was an *impossible task* for a child. Normally, it took several generations for a *primitive civilization* to achieve these refined but necessary distinctions in order to survive.

Many lives were lost, through trial and error, before a tribe could distinguish, with certainty, what was edible from what was not. Random experiments, using trial and error, were crude and dangerous instruments. Many people had to die in the process.

Even today, many people still die from eating poisonous mushrooms because ordinary people still cannot distinguish, with certitude, between poisonous and non-poisonous mushrooms!

Nevertheless, there he was as a small boy, completely outside his elements, trying to survive in an unknown and strange environment. He had no medication whatsoever. He didn't know how to medicate himself from the flora and fauna around him. Even if he had some medication, they would probably be the wrong ones for whatever illness he might contract.

He lived in solitude and any poison could quickly kill him! Because he didn't know his way in the swamp, he was taking *mortal risks* every time he placed his hands under water to grope for food! A poisonous snake could bite him or a poisonous fish could sting him and he'd be dead! Every day, he was playing Russian roulette with his life!

To minimize his risks, he needed a crash course on the plants and animals of the swamps. He needed to know everything about his surroundings. Some knowledge about the different land and marine inhabitants of the swamp would decrease his risks. Since he had no teacher, he had to teach himself through trial and error or through other crude instruments, like guessing.

Regardless of the urgency of his need to know, he still had to start from ground zero! He had to build a reliable body of knowledge slowly on his own, one small piece at a time! He must depend on his natural curiosity. He must remain alert and receptive to what nature was teaching him. All his senses and his mind must be receptive to whatever nature was teaching him.

Unfortunately, nature was a non-verbal and a very slow teacher. Perhaps, the real fault was in the learner. He wasn't smart enough to understand what nature was teaching him. Still, he was learning enough to actually survive his impossible tenure of living in the swamp for three years!

Chapter Seventeen
The Tides and Fishing

Using his newly discovered wooden tub, he proceeded to explore the swamp seriously. At certain times, he enjoyed just floating around without any plan or destination. Some days, he loaded a fishing pole and some bait and paddled towards the East River. He was looking for beautiful vistas for his own enjoyment. He was craving for a good dose of natural beauty!

He had not yet discovered beauty in his immediate surroundings. Looking out into the open spaces made him feel less closed in. He discovered quite a bit of beautiful scenery. That was a real break from the gloomy atmosphere of the swamp.

However, he quickly learned the limitations of the tub. The basin wasn't river-worthy and he had to limit his explorations to the streams in his immediate environment. Still it was a vast area in itself. There were hundreds of smaller streams and creeks to explore, especially during high tides.

A Filipino dugout canoe

In order to explore properly the different sections of the swamp territories, he needed a regular Filipino dugout canoe to go out into the swift treacherous Rivers. From the Rio Este or Rio Oeste, he could choose and enter other larger streams that led to smaller streams. He had discovered that a primary stream dominated every section of the swamp.

Every dominant stream branched out into hundreds of smaller ones which, in turn, branched out into smaller and smaller creeks.

The Child Daredevil Hero

The swamps contained thousands of major sections that flowed, intersected and crisscrossed with each other. The swamp environment was an extensive maze of branching waterways. He had to devise arbitrary markers to find his way around the swamps.

After weeks of studying the configuration of the streams and the lowlands flooded by the tides, he concluded that the swamp areas were no different from the normal layout of most dry lands. Even before the ocean had flooded the swamps during high tides, the lands had already contained *small hills, plains and valleys.*

When the high tides first sent in salt water from the great Pacific Ocean to flood the inland, it naturally flowed first to the valleys, then to the plains and then to the higher grounds. However, the tidal water left out the higher levels of land dry. The dry lands were called *hammocks*, which became the natural destination of the tidal waters.

Conversely, the dry lands stopped the flow of the tides. The *hammocks* restrained the intrusion of the tides and allowed them to remain still and calm when they reached their peaks.

For at least twenty minutes, the peaceful waters became stagnant, flat and crystal like. The stagnant waters appeared like kilometers of solid glass.

Then, slowly and softly, the water flowed back to the ocean. Gradually, the flow accelerated and then cascaded precipitously! The low tide rushed out to the ocean to empty the land, until the swamps became almost empty again!

This tidal cycle happened twice a day. However, for about five or six days a month during the full moon, the high tide was reduced to only one. Because the high tide was higher than normal and the low tide was lower than normal, it took almost a day to complete one tidal cycle.

Junior wondered what caused the tidal cycles? Who or what was responsible and capable of making the giant ocean rise by several feet and make it flow inland into the smallest recesses of the swamps. Who or what sucked out the water that had invaded the swamps and spat it back into the ocean?

In order to answer these questions, he studied the tides and their relationships to the cycles of the moon and the other celestial bodies. After a long observation, he guessed that the moon and the other heavenly bodies affected the tides. By *marking the tidal levels on the bark of the mangrove trees*, he plotted out the gradual rise of the water in relation to the phases of the moon. He discovered that the highest tides coincided with the full moon.

Then, the tides started to wane as the moon's size decreased in volume. The connection between the moon and the tides became very obvious.

It was also quite clear to him that the other heavenly bodies must also affect the tides. However, he couldn't plot their relationships. There were simply too many planets and stars to contend with.

The different factors affecting the tides were too numerous and complicated for him to compute them. Fortunately these technical types of information were not necessary for his survival.

Junior discovered that the average cyclic rhythm of the tides was high-low and high-low every eight hours. This meant that every day, there were two high tides and two low tides. There were different heights to which the tides may rise or fall. The higher the height, the longer it took to reach it. And, the velocity of the outgoing current was relative to the height of the tide. In the same way, the lower the elevation of the tide was, the longer it took to reach it.

In the eternal rhythm of the tides, the first high tide may be higher than the second. The next day, however, the first high tide maybe equal in height to the second. However, the next day, the second tide maybe higher than the first.

As the first high tide kept going lower, the second high tide went higher. At some point, the two tides were the same level again. But, the next day, the first tide became higher again. It kept going higher every day until the tidal flow reversed itself.

When the moon became full, however, its gravitational pull pushed the tide to unusual heights. The gravitational effect pulled the water away from shallow areas of the ocean and left them dry for at least eight hours. The areas that became dry were the mud and sand flats near seashores. At least two kilometers of land that were usually covered by water were completely dry.

This was also the time of the month when there was only one high and low tide. Because of the unusual height of the tide, it took at least fifteen to twenty hours to complete the cycle from low to high tide. Hence, there was only one tidal cycle in one day. After five or six days, however, there was a short first cycle that lasted for only two hours. After the short cycle, the high tide resumed again for another fifteen or sixteen hours.

The next day, the first cycle lasted for four hours and the next day for six hours. As the first cycle lengthened, the second cycle shortened. Then, the double cycles came back to normal until the next full moon.

His primary interest in studying the tides was to determine *the best times for fishing*. Based on his observations, he concluded that there were *two best times*.

The *first best time*, especially for bait fishermen, was after the high tides had crested. For a few minutes, the water stayed very still, like a vast piece of glass.

The high tide had brought in a myriad of hungry fish eager to bite. They had traveled a long distance and were waiting for some kind of a reward. During this brief window of opportunity, he could hook at least twenty decent sizes of fish in a few minutes. He observed the whole process of fishing because the water was so clear. He could see the fish approach his bait. He snapped his pole right after the fish had swallowed the bait. His success rate of catching fish was very high!

Since he kept only what he could eat, he released most of what he caught.

The *next best time*, which was his favorite, was when the tide was at its lowest. The water in the streams was very low. The larger fish had already returned to the ocean with the receding tide. Still, many marine creatures had learned to remain in their territories.

He figured out why they remained in the swamp when the ebbing waters returned to the ocean. The small fish, for example, were too small to survive the trip to the ocean. There were too many predators out there that would gobble them up for a snack or a meal. They could never return to the sanctuary of the swamp again!

The newly hatched fish sought shelter in shallow waters, where the larger ones would be stranded. They learned early to form schools to give the impression of being larger. The small fish learned to hide behind objects like stones, logs, trees, roots, leaves and even in the shade.

Some marine creatures *buried themselves* in the muddy sand. This was the strategy of clams, shellfish and crabs. *Some attached themselves* to the side of the rocks, boulders, pilings and barks of mangroves, which was the *modus operandi* of the oysters and barnacles. Some *bore holes* into pilings and tree trunks, which was the style of mollusks and all types of worms.

Using a *suction system*, some residents adhered to the underneath surfaces of the stones and logs, which was the technique of some seashells and many other small organisms. And others *hid behind or under* solid objects like rocks, logs and tree trunks, which was the *modus operandi* of eels, snakes and other marine creatures.

All those territorial organisms were waiting for the return of the next high tide, which brought in all types of food.

At low tides, however, they were vulnerable to human predators. Harvesting shellfish, seashells, snails, stranded crabs, fish and eel was like picking fruits from the Garden of Eden. Junior picked and chose only the best specimens and only what he could eat for the day.

During this low tide fishing, he poked around and discovered oyster beds, clam beds and the gigantic snails with bow-like shell called abalone. Abalone shell was naturally shiny like the mother of pearl.

He caught brown mud crabs that were very large, thick and round. He also caught sand crabs that came in with the tides. They were smaller than the mud crabs. Sand crabs had wide light brown backs with sharply pointed projections on each side for defense.

He walked and fished along shallow streams using his bare hands. When he got tired of fishing, he just looked around and observed the behaviors of the marine animals. He studied the different mangrove trees, especially the red mangroves.

He also used the period of low tides to exercise his body. He felt he needed to release some pent-up energy. The activity became both practical and recreational. Some days, he walked more than he fished. The stream beds were excellent for walking because they were more or less level and the surface, though somewhat muddy, was relatively hard.

Whenever he felt inclined to go fishing, he waded through the streams and put his hands under rocks, logs or any solid object. Using this method, he frequently caught fish, eel, shells, snails, crabs and other marine animals.

Most of the areas of the swamp where he went fishing was heavily shaded. Hence, he couldn't see what he was touching under water. However, he learned to distinguish one creature from another by their texture, shape and behavior. If it felt like a snake, moray eel or a crab, he quickly let them go because they could give him a nasty bite. The snake maybe poisonous! If it was a crab, he used a stick to remove it from its hiding place. Then, he used the same stick to press its back and picked it up by its hind flippers.

Low tides gave Junior his first insights into the joys of living as a swamp hermit! The streams gave him new areas to explore and exercise his body. The discovery of various edible creatures provided him more than enough sources of food.

As he learned more about the swamps and its resources, life for him became more normal and enjoyable!

Chapter Eighteen
A Hermit's Social Life

Because his dream had shown him that everything in the swamp was alive and welcoming, he began to think of mangrove trees as persons with individual personalities. He gave them names and talked to them as he passed by. He began slowly to create a *swamp society* as suggested by his dream.

Before he cut down the roots of a red mangrove tree, which he had named Juan, he asked his permission first.

"Juan, *uh* ... please allow me to cut down two of your roots," he asked him respectfully. "As you see, *uh* ... my tub can't float through this portion of the stream. I understand your pain and discomfort for being mutilated. I'm sorry *uh* ... I have to cut these two roots so I can pass through here *uh* ... whenever I want to navigate this way. I know *uh* ... you can easily replace them whenever you want to. Is it all right, Juan?"

He waited for his answer. Somehow, he expected some kind of a sound. When he heard nothing, he assumed the tree had given him a silent permission. So he proceeded to use his machete to cut the roots.

After cutting them, he discovered something he didn't expect at all. He found a barnacle-like shell six inches below the high water mark. He had accidentally detached a shell, which he assumed was a barnacle.

Upon closer examination, however, the shell turned out to be the mouth of a much-coveted mollusk called *tamilok*. The mouth was attached to a round shell, which was the head. The body was a whitish cylinder that measured about half an inch in diameter and eight to twelve inches long. It was as delicious as abalone!

He was taking a serious risk by assumint that the mollusk he had discovered was *tamilok*. He had never seen or eaten a fresh *tamilok* before.

What he had eaten before the war was salted, which was the only way they were available commercially. He took the chance that the mollusk was *tamilok* because he was both thirsty and hungry. But, as he examined the shellfish inside the root, he became convinced that it had to be *tamilok*.

He thanked Juan for the discovery of *tamilok* especially because it became an added source of food for him.

Tamilok was a delicacy among aficionados because they were rarely sold commercially. Because of their short shelf life, they were usually sold in sealed jars. The salted *tamilok* had only a slight resemblance in taste to the fresh ones.

The shellfish that he had just harvested from its hidden cradle tasted sweet and just melted in his mouth like a spoonful of ice cream on a hot summer day! It was the most delicious shellfish he had ever eaten!

With this new discovery, he paddled around the streams looking for roots that blocked his passage. He hoped to find more *tamilok* and he often found several of them. He always asked for permission before cutting them down. He continued to harvest them whenever he had the craving.

He gave the trees both male and female names. He bestowed male names to most red and black mangroves because they were big, tall and strong. He made sure he gave enough female names to the smaller red and black mangroves so that he could match them up in marriage.

He performed short marriage ceremonies. He anointed himself as an ordained minister, with the authority to join swamp creatures in marriage.

He handed down mostly female names to the white mangroves because they were smaller and shorter trees. But he baptized enough males so he could match them up for marriage.

He apologized whenever he forgot their names and promised to remember them next time. After he had christened over one hundred of them, it became difficult to remember their names.

He devised a way of saving face. Every time he forgot a masculine name, he addressed him as Jose, instead. And, he called every female tree, whose names he had forgotten, Maria. When he was not sure of the gender, he called it, *Kaibigan,* which meant friend in *Tagalog.*

Like a typical lying politician, he called their wrong names with conviction, a smile and a nervous laughter! But, it worked all the time.

He knew he was a laughable caricature of the real politicians who told lies every day. Still, he was learning how to cover his forgetfulness because he had to. He could not possibly remember all their right names.

He tended to visit certain areas more often than others. Those living along his pathways became his close friends. He socialized more often with them. Those who resided outside his beaten path became simply Jose, Maria or *Kaibigan.*

He gave the primary stream leading to his hut an honorific name, Don Pedro, after St. Peter the Apostle, because he was swift and strong. He conferred on Rio Este the name, Don Pablo, after St. Paul the Apostle. He bestowed upon Rio Oeste the name of Don Juan, for St. John the Baptist.

When the tides came in, the water rushed in swiftly and aggressively. So, he conferred on the incoming tides masculine names. However, he bestowed upon the outgoing tides feminine names because they moved

The Child Daredevil Hero

slowly, gently and majestically in the swamp. He knew that those gentle waters would soon gather momentum and rush aggressively back to the ocean. He reasoned that women too had an aggressive side to them.

He handed out feminine names to the smaller streams because they flowed gently and amiably. They tenderly caressed the banks and the mangrove leaves that touched the water. They solemnly carried away the fallen leaves to bury them in the inner recesses of the streams or to far and distant places.

He created a social hierarchy among the trees. Some who were old and venerable, he honored them with the titles of 'Don' or 'Dona.' Some imposing and stately trees deserved the title 'Majestic.' He called the beautiful, symmetrical trees 'Handsome' or 'Beautiful' especially when dressed in their green summer finery.

He even introduced the trees to each other or talked about them to the other Majestic, Handsome and Venerable Trees. He was proud to have their acquaintance or friendship.

When he first met the old red mangrove, whom he called Don Pedro, he stared at his massive trunks. He admired his arching prop roots that started forty-five feet above the ground.

"Don Pedro, how large and awesome are *uh* ... your trunks and branches," he exclaimed to the tree. "I'm amazed as I gaze skyward at your broad canopy. How magnificent and elegant are your *uh* ... long branches!

"You must have lived a long time. You look like *uh* ... you're at least 100 years old. You must have seen *uh* ... so many interesting things in your life. I wish I'll live half as long as you have. I respect your age and wisdom, sir. Thank you for *uh* ... allowing me to visit with you."

Don Pedro seemed delighted with his visit. Junior stood there a while as he listened to what the tree had to say to him. He imagined that the tree was telling him stories about his exploits as a young tree, his many lovers and the females who flirted with him because he was so handsome.

During his first meeting with another red mangrove tree he named, Don Paulino, he held his breath while he admired his elegance. He was at the peak of his prime! He stood there majestically and serenely as his branches and leaves swayed gently in the breeze. He seemed to be saying, "Welcome, little boy. Explore the riches of the swamp and use its resources wisely. Take only what you can use and leave some for others to enjoy."

Junior kept nodding his head in agreement and said, "Yes, sir. I will."

He looked up to inspect his majestic canopy. After admiring its symmetrical shape, he said to the tree, "I admire your natural beauty, Don Paulino. You're simply awesome! I wish I have *uh* ... more room to stand on, without falling in the water. I want to have a *uh* ... fuller view of your gigantic spread. I guess *uh* ... I have to be happy with whatever space I have.

"I'll use my basin later on to find a spot *uh* ... from which I can have a better view of you. The trouble with the swamp, as you know, is that *uh* ... the mangroves are crowding against each other. It is very rare to see a majestic tree standing by itself. It's a shame *uh* ... some of your neighbors have encroached into your personal spaces. I guess that is life in the swamp. Encroach and be encroached! You must admit, it's a tough way to live."

It was difficult to carry on a conversation with those trees because of their height and wide spread. He kept straining his neck to have a good look at their canopies, branches and width. He couldn't hear their answers. However, he imagined them saying nice things about themselves and their families.

He also imagined them having the same problems with their children, as human beings have. He wondered whether anyone had the misfortune of having a 'Mabini' for a son. Some children can be rotten to the core!

He also imagined them being crazy about their grandchildren. As a happy human grandfather once remarked, "If I knew grandchildren are so much fun, I would have started with grandchildren first."

Like humans, those elderly trees deserved some joy in their golden years!

He met so many interesting personalities in the swamp in the few months that he navigated around. He was steering his basin around to organize them into his swamp community. He had a great time analyzing and examining different trees. He gave them names of his brothers, sisters, relatives, neighbors and friends.

However, there was a glaring exception. He didn't name any tree after his brother, Mabini. He didn't want to start hating any tree. If he named one after him, Junior was afraid he might also avoid that tree. And, he didn't want any tree nearby whose name he disliked.

As he explored the swamp in search of extraordinary personalities, he met many wonderful trees. They were truly the pillars of the community. He enjoyed their company and he christened everyone.

Soon, he ran out of names and he had to repeat the same names over and over again. That technique made remembering all of them impossible!

He laughed whenever he became mixed up with their names. He knew he could always use what he fondly called his 'political ploy.' He simply called them Jose, Maria or *Kaibigan*. Fortunately, they really didn't mind.

One day, he maneuvered his basin, which he called Pablito, to a mud flat section of the swamp. The mud flats had shallow water. He saw some white mangroves and some young red mangroves. It was a new discovery for him. He felt happy because the sun was shining brightly. Everything was colorful and full of life. It was like a different world!

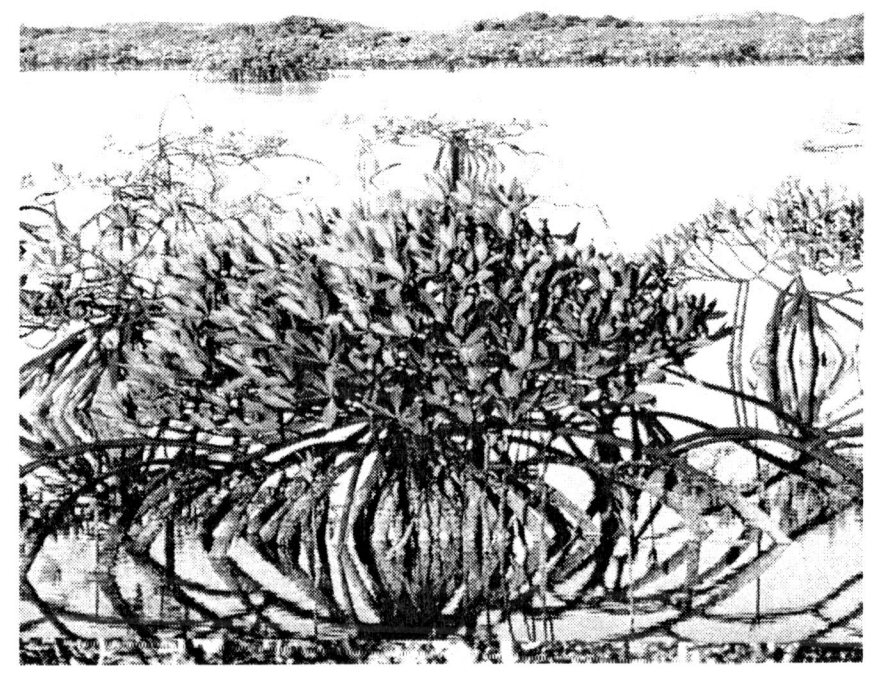

Young red mangrove Junior named Maganda

There, he saw thousands of baby red mangrove trees. There were several children of varying ages. And, there were nubile teenagers who were, like flowers, at the peak of their bloom. Their youth was so refreshing and seductive.

That was the time he met the beautiful young red mangrove he named *Maganda*. She was standing alone at the center of the mud flat. Her figure was symmetrical, balanced and feminine. Her new leaves were tender and reddish. They looked so fresh and edible, he had to restrain his hands from molesting her succulent beauty. Still, he allowed his eyes to feast on her youth and dazzling looks.

Sal Kapunan

"*Magandang dalaga,*" he said to her, smiling. "Do you know the meaning of the name I've just given you? It means 'beautiful girl' in *Tagalog*. It was a good choice because you're indeed very pretty.

"Oh! I can't believe you're blushing! Or, perhaps, it just so happens that your young leaves are reddish so that you look like you're blushing!

"I'm sure you know you're very attractive. Please forgive me for being forward. Looking at your youthful beauty *uh* ... has made me talk loosely like a drunken sailor.

"I don't have a camera to take a picture of you. What I'll do is *uh* ... to stamp your image in my imagination so I can remember you always. I'll come back again soon *uh* ... because I want to visit you and have more of this healthful sun. It has done wonders to your green complexion. I feel so alive myself and *uh* ... happy being in the open air. Goodbye, my lovely."

He also gave names to birds and fishes. He conferred only masculine names on kingfishers because he couldn't distinguish their gender. When he could distinguish the gender of the other birds, he bestowed on them both male and female names.

He christened all mullets only masculine names because they swam fast and leaped aggressively. However, he had problems recognizing birds and fishes so he pretended he recognized them anyway. Indeed, members of the same species really looked identical. They differed only in their sizes. Very often, he just called them *Kaibigan*.

Naming the different things in his environment made him feel powerful! He pretended to have the authority to give names to everyone.

It also made him feel he belonged to their *swamp society*. He was living in a society and he could socialize whenever he wanted to. By talking to the trees and other creatures, he was using his voice and relating to other beings. He was concerned that if he didn't use his voice, he might lose it.

He also christened his shack, Maria, because she was as comforting and nurturing as a mother's womb. To him, houses were females. They gave shelter and care to those living in them.

In the beginning, he got very excited every time he discovered new oyster or clam beds. He got excited every time he found the biggest clam or the biggest oyster. He wished he had a *compadre* or *comadre* to share his joy with. After forming his swamp community, it became easier to share his discoveries and happiness with any tree, crab, fish or bird.

When he found his first abalone, he said to the passing mullet leader, "Jose, look what I found. This is my first abalone and it is so delicious!

As they say, 'This is out of this world!' Yes, Jose, eating a fresh abalone is nothing like any abalone I had ever eaten before. It is just heavenly!"

Jose never heard a word he said because he was more interested in chasing Marieta or Josephina. Junior didn't mind because he didn't really expect the mullet to hear him. It was still a good feeling to share something so divine with someone, even though he happened to be a mullet.

After he had recruited enough members for his large swamp community, he decided to install himself as the *President*. Being a president appealed to him better than being a king. At least he knew something about presidents. He had been hearing a lot about the President of the Philippine Commonwealth, Manuel Quezon. His father admired Quezon as the leader of the Philippines.

In his small way, Junior would become president of his own community. Being a king sounded so European and alien to him.

He announced to the community that he would install himself as president the following Sunday. In fact, he was not just the president but everything else. He was going to be a benevolent little ruler, the very first of his kind.

In preparation for the event, he appointed few members of his cabinet. He didn't think anyone would object to nepotism since the cabinet members had only advisory capacities.

He appointed Don Mones Lopez and Dona Leona Lozada as his top advisers. They were his paternal grandparents and he was honored to have them stand next to him. He named two trees next to his cabin after them.

The two other advisers were Don Salvador, senior, and Dona Catalina Castaneda who were his parents. He named the next two trees near the cabin after them.

After his self-installation as president, he delivered a short speech from his cabin.

"Don Mones, Dona Leona, Don Salvador, Dona Catalina, ladies and gentlemen who are the residents of the swamp. As the President of this unique community, I hereby proclaim that it will be called from now on KALIGAYAHAN, which means happiness in *Tagalog*. I make my first decree today by banishing unhappiness, sorrow, sadness and gloom from our society. Anyone promoting unhappiness in the community will be banished forever!

"I want to encourage everyone to promote peace, friendship and of course happiness. As your President, I promise to be fair, understanding and friendly to everyone. I'm happy to be your President. However, don't call me Mr. President. Just call me Junior because that is what my family calls me. As of this moment, you are also members of my family. Let us all strive to foster Kaligayahan!"

With his society in place, he felt more stable, happy and at ease! It also felt good to be on top of his world in the swamp!

Chapter Nineteen
Digging a Well

His immediate priority as the new president was to solve the acute shortage of drinkable water. Potable water was always in short supply in areas near the sea and the swamps. Salt intrusion of the underground aquifers was a serious problem.

People built large cisterns to catch rainwater from their roofs. Still, there were times and seasons of the year when the rain was scarce. Some people dug wells and drank water with high salt contents. More often, however, they used well water only to wash their clothes and dishes.

Drinkable water in the swamp was even more difficult to obtain. The mangrove canopy diverted rainwater to flow down areas that were difficult to fetch. Even though he tried to save whatever rainwater he could, it was never sufficient. He needed to dig a well for potable water or he'll die of thirst!

Luckily, he had already discovered the existence of dry lands in the swamp. He went searching for new areas where there might be higher elevation of the dry grounds.

Unfortunately, the only dry land he found was a salt flat. The term *salt flat* was appropriate because it was flooded with salt water during storms and typhoons. The land was also flat. The vegetation was mostly grass, sedges, rushes, vines and bushes. The upper levels of the grounds contained high concentration of salt.

The highest elevation of the land that he found was only about three feet above sea level. Of course, he would have preferred a higher elevation.

He started to dig using only his bare hands since he had no digging tools. After two hours of work, his hands started to blister and stopped digging.

The next day he returned armed with a machete and a small bucket. He loosened the soil with the machete and used the bucket to scoop the dirt out.

After two weeks of digging, he had carved out a small well. It was six feet deep and three feet wide. He waited for the water to filter in. Then, he waited even longer for the water to clear up. The muddy particles slowly sank to the bottom and the water looked very clear and drinkable.

When he tasted it, however, it was very salty and spat it out! He felt really disappointed and discouraged. However, after working for long hours and feeling very thirsty, he forced himself to drink it. The taste was awful but he needed to quench his thirst.

When he didn't vomit or get sick from the water, he kept drinking a little bit every day. He kept increasing his intake until he got somewhat used to the taste. To his surprise, he reached a point when the water tasted tolerable!

He admired how nature adjusted to the awful taste. By making the natural adjustment, his system maximized its tolerance and minimized the pain. Whatever little he knew about human nature really amazed him!

Years later when he was old enough to drink liquor, he remembered this particular incident. He drank something that was even worse tasting because it was very bitter. The bitter drink that he found repulsive was beer, which he instinctively spat out. He guessed that beer must have toxic component, which was alcohol.

His friends laughed because they had the same initial experience. They assured him that he would get used to the taste. He said to himself, "If I could tolerate drinking salty water when I was just a child, I should be able to tolerate the taste of beer as an adult."

So, he persisted and drank beer with his friends. They were right. He not only tolerated it, he learned to like it!

He marveled anew at how human nature adapted to a noxious taste. He was also amazed at how human nature allowed even toxic substances such as alcohol and drugs in its system.

Of course, there were limits to nature's tolerance because such substances could harm and kill the abuser. Alcohol poisoning kills at lot of abusers every year!

Besides, some people have addictive personalities and become hopelessly addicted to harmful drugs.

His discovery of potable water in the swamp was absolutely essential to his survival. The heat in the tropics quickly drained fluid from his body. He needed to drink constantly to maintain the body's natural balance.

After six months of drinking salty water, he forgot the awful memory of the first experience. Every day, he fetched water from his well and drank it as if it were regular water. He also used the same briny water to cook his rice. To him, brackish water was regular water.

He was lucky to discover potable water in the swamp. That same year, the area where his family lived experienced severe drought. Even though he didn't tell his family about the well he had dug, the amount of rain water he received every week was never enough. If he didn't have his own salty well, he might have died from thirst! At least, he would have suffered from frequent bouts of extreme thirst!

After he had discovered well water, he became less anxious about his survival in the swamp wilderness. After a year of living in the wet forest, he realized that living alone was an excellent way to live. He loved living as a hermit and could live that way indefinitely! He couldn't make that claim before he had dug a well. Hence, the brackish well water was among his most important discoveries!

However, when his younger brothers, Trinidad and Ruperto, arrived to replace him so he could make his weekly trip to obtain food, he offered them his briny water. They tasted it but spat it out in disgust! They thought that he had served them water directly from the sea.

It was possible that the salinity of his well water was very high. Still, it prevented him from dying of thirst!

Chapter Twenty
New Ways of Fishing

After he took care of the water scarcity, he thought of new fishing techniques to add some variety and excitement to his fishing experience.

He had learned, back in his old town, how to use leaves of certain trees and bushes to poison fish. The mild poison forced the fish to float belly up. He found the same plants growing around the borders of the swamp.

He pounded the leaves with a pestle and carried the concoction in his coconut shell bowl. When he found a small pool of water during low tides, he scattered it around the pond and waited for the fish to go up to the surface.

The poisonous material quickly sank to the bottom where the fish were feeding. In minutes, the poison attacked their gills and forced them to go to the surface to inhale more oxygen. However, the toxin prevented them from getting the oxygen needed and they remained belly up. All he did was to pick up the dying fish from the water with two fingers.

The poison was not strong enough to affect humans, so the fish could be eaten safely. Just for greater safety, he removed the gills, which were the poisoned parts. He used this technique only a few times because it was too much trouble harvesting the plants and preparing the poison.

Moreover, he felt a certain psychological discomfort about eating poisoned fish. It reminded him of eating 'blow fish.' The fish had an interesting survival technique of inhaling air and blowing itself into a round balloon when threatened by predators. The fish increased its size by about six times.

The fish was also known to carry an extremely strong poison in its intestine. The poison was its most effective defense mechanism. It killed its predators within minutes!

Some specialty cooks in Japan knew how to remove the poison sack. The cooks made *sushi* from the fish, which they called *pogo* fish. Customers ordered the deadly fish because they were tempting fate! Some customers ordered the *pogo sushi* to prove their bravery to others.

Junior imagined himself eating a blowfish that could actually kill him every time he ate his poisoned fish. It always gave him a queasy sensation!

Catching crabs, fish and gathering shellfish and other marine fare with his bare hands was always exciting! The excitement was due to the danger involved and the degree of competence necessary to execute the process.

Sometimes, he felt like a professional when he quickly bent over to pick up clams, shellfish and crabs with his bare hands.

He found it fascinating to watch skillful fishermen harvest all kinds of mean-spirited sea creatures, without any fear of being bitten, pinched or punctured. Long experience had made them look so competent.

In waist deep water, he used his bare feet to scour through the mud and sand for clams, abalone and shellfish. Marking their location with a stick, he dove underwater to pick them up with his hands. Using this method, he harvested several types of shellfish.

In clear shallow water, he learned to press his big toe on the back of crabs and bent down to grasp the back fins of the crustaceans. He removed their claws and placed them in his basket. Sometimes, he used the index finger of his left hand to press on the back of a crab, and then used his right hand to grab its back flippers.

Catching crabs was easy because they partially buried themselves in the mud or sand to hide from predators. Nevertheless, they betrayed their presence by their protruding eyes and antennae. Their camouflage might be good enough protection against most natural predators but not enough from skillful fishermen. Still, the human eyes had to be trained to see the partially hidden crabs. The novice crab hunter simply wouldn't see them.

His feet and hands worked together as paired instruments that kept him busy and prevented him from going hungry. He could live as a swamp hermit for many years. Every day he was learning new tricks and skills.

He was also learning about crab psychology and behavior. For instance, when he saw a crab crawling on the sandy bottom, he knew what it would do if he threatened it in any way. It would quickly bury its body in the sand or mud. Once the crab had buried itself, he no longer had to chase it. He could harvest it by using only one hand.

Since he harvested only what he could eat for the day, he spent less and less time in harvesting food as he became more proficient. He was able to devote more time to his *new hobby*, which was *thinking*.

He found it ironic that, in the beginning, he found thinking as the curse of his existence! Gradually, he discovered it as his dear friend and companion!

As discussed in chapter seventeen, 'The Tides and Fishing,' there were days every months when the low tide was very low and the high tide was very high. Because it took at least fifteen hours to climb from low tide to the higher peaks of high tides, there was only one low tide and one high tide in one day. Normally, there were two high tides and two low tides. This apparent aberration was caused by the *full moon*. The moon was closer to the planet earth and its gravitational pull sucked up the ocean. Inevitably, the gravitational pull left vast areas of sand or mud flats dry.

The drying of the flats may last for at least eight hours. And, the moon stayed full for five to six days.

As the water receded quickly, various types of marine organisms got stranded in little pools of water. The stranded fish became easy catch for Junior.

But, the biggest group of stranded marine animals were the mollusks, especially the gastropods (snails) and the bivalve shellfish. Large gastropods like whelks, cockles and conchs were stranded on sand or mud. The only bivalves that escaped with the fast receding waters were the **scallops**. They used jet propulsion.

Junior went down to the dry flats to study everything about the life cycles of the mollusks. He observed how they tried to survive under those unnatural and perilous conditions. Their lives were not only exposed to predatory humans, they were also exposed to small mammals, reptiles and all kinds of birds. He saw all kinds of wading birds cracking bivalves.

He watched the gastropods walk on sand and devour smaller shells. One day, he watched two small fighting conchs gang up on a large whelk.

He studied the egg casings that the shells buried in the sand that contained several egg shells in disks. Each egg casing contained at least seventy circular disks. In a month or so, fully functioning shells escaped from the disks and walked, ate small preys and grew.

He studied the anatomy of each type of gastropod. He discovered feet, eyes, proboscis, mouth and sexual organs. He performed an autopsy on recently deceased mollusks to study their anatomy and their interior organs. He also examined the shell remains of long dead mollusks.

Based on some shell remains, he discovered that some of them were carnivorous. Many of the dead shells had small holes on one side carved out by the predator mollusks. Then it sent in its long proboscis and devoured the meat.

He found out that mollusks had very active lives. They had highly developed physical properties for walking, seeing, eating, breathing, procreating and burrowing in the sand or mud for escape and protection. Some of them, like the 'fighting conchs,' were feisty! When he picked up a fighting conch, the gastropod sent out its long foot to attack his wrist. It pushed hard against his wrist to try to escape.

In contrast, most of them were gentle and docile. When in danger, they quickly withdrew into their protective shells, which they covered with a shell-like trapdoor. The trapdoor was naturally attached to the bottom of their foot. After they had pulled in their trapdoors, the opening became hermetically sealed. Sealing themselves inside was their last defense.

Their first defense was to avoid predators with the use of a natural camouflage created by the natural coloring of their shells. Their second defense was by hiding in the sand. The third was by moving away; and, the fourth was by fighting!

Of course, Junior also ate some tasty cockles by forcibly opening their valves with a machete. He ate them directly from the shells. Moreover, he selected some large conchs to broil them on embers in his cabin.

With so much marine life in the swamps, Junior knew he would never go hungry! Having found their exact locations in the streams when the flats were dry, he could easily locate them in the water when normal tides came back. Knowing their locations and their abundance in the swamp made Junior feel more confident that his hermitic life could continue indefinitely!

Chapter Twenty One
Important Insights about Nature

As discussed in chapter fifteen, the author explained how Junior formulated his personal philosophy of life, which guided his daily life. He became a child of nature and was effortlessly absorbed into the existing processes and rhythms of the natural world. He became part of nature and the swamp was no longer alien to him.

If he had thought that nature was an enemy, which he had to subdue and tame to follow his will, nature would have crushed and destroyed him! The forces of nature that he faced, such as the awesome tides, the brooding and suffocating gloom of the woods and the pervasive foul smell of the rotting vegetation, would have killed his spirit and led him to despair and suicide!

After he discovered the resources of the swamp and understood its nature and rhythms, he fell in love with a *lifestyle* that followed the laws of nature! Living alone was a special privilege because it gave him complete freedom. He was free from any stress because nobody pressured him to follow arbitrary rules. He was also free from daily family obligations.

By blending seamlessly with nature, he got used to the foul odor of the decaying leaves. He finally became convinced that the many *predators* he had imagined *didn't really exist*!

By studying the marine life in the swamp, especially during low tides, he concluded that the swamp, where he lived, was the *nursery* of marine animals. Virtually all the fish that remained in the swamp during low tides were babies and young organisms.

He concluded that the big predators would not be living in a habitat where the preys were small. He became convinced that the carnivorous predators would not live there since the fare was only small marine animals. All the predators that he had imagined did not live in his swamp! This realization relieved him of severe anxiety and fear of death!

He saw some small snakes and he assumed that some might be poisonous. Still, they were more afraid of him than he was of them. He also saw small lizards but they were no bigger than a gecko.

It is interesting to note, parenthetically, that the coastal swamps in Southwest Florida, USA, where Junior lives seven months a year, have large alligators and crocodiles that feed on larger fish. He was just lucky that he lived in a swamp, in the Philippines, which served as a nursery for marine life.

The Child Daredevil Hero

Hence, it would be erroneous to generalize about swamps from a single or few samplings. What marine life may thrive in one swamp may not be the same in another. Each swamp is an ecological system, which sustains only the lives that are suited to that particular environment.

He also found out that the swamp where he lived in Makato was a *unified ecological system.* This was a major natural revelation to him!

The heart of the ecological system was the ocean and its vascular system were the Rivers, the estuaries, the streams and their branches and little creeks. However, its life forces were generated and controlled by the moon, the earth, the sun and the other celestial bodies.

The swamps, therefore, were part of a big continuum that included the wide Rivers and the vast Ocean. By living in the swamp, he was in a privileged position to observe the nurseries, the cycles of marine lives and the rhythyms of nature. He could directly observe the processes of nature. From what he learned and understood, he knew what to do to adjust his thoughts, attitudes, feelings and behavior so that they conformed to natural laws.

By following the naturalistic philosophy that he had developed, his life was in synchrony with nature! He reached the point when he felt that he truly understood the natural processes and felt more at home with his environment.

He understood that the *mangrove vegetation and the swamps provided the natural link between the dry land and the wet sea.* Hence, the land and sea also formed a continuum. The organisms living in the swamps lived in a *hybrid environment* and could survive the dry conditions of the land and the salty waters of the sea.

The *mangrove trees* were especially *drought-tolerant* because they could extract fresh water from sea water.

Some mangroves were *salt-tolerant* because they developed glands that excreted salt. Some of the vegetation survived the salty conditions by blocking salt in their root system. The salt-tolerant plants were among the most marvelous living organisms in the world!

The mangrove trees were the living proofs of the natural continuity between the land and the sea. They served as the natural bridges between the two worlds.

Junior realized that he lived at the very center of the *fulcrum of nature* and was privy to many of its secrets!

Chapter Twenty Two
The Good Happy Life

After his life had conformed to the rhythms and cycles of nature, it ceased to be boring or depressing. Every day he was busy doing whatever he liked to do. He was happy to be alone, to be his own boss and to follow the simple natural rhythms of life.

He discovered that being alone didn't mean being lonely. He was proud of his knowledge of the mangroves, the swamp and the natural world around him.

Most of all, he learned a great deal about himself! He was naturally curious and inquisitive. As he needed them, he learned manual skills on his own. Like his father, he was resourceful, versatile and quite clever. He could do whatever he wanted to do. This was a special trait that went back, at least, to his paternal grandfather, Don Mones.

In the beginning, he was afraid of nature and of the dark. Some nights were so dark he couldn't see anything because the thick forest canopy blocked the light of the moon.

However, when his eyes got used to the darkness, many things became dimly visible. Consequently, he no longer feared the darkness. He started to think of darkness as a protection from being seen by Japanese flyers. What had been strange and frightening became his friend and ally.

He got used to the different sounds made by the jumping mullets, insects and many other strange sounds he didn't recognize. When he became familiar with them and realized they were harmless, they became comforting and entertaining.

As he learned more about the different rhythms, such as the rising and setting of the sun, the changing phases of the moon, the ebb and flow of the tides, the changing patterns of the weather and the circadian rhythm of his own biological system, he became more comfortable and happy with the world around him. He realized that nature was also in him. And, the rhythms that occurred in him were also connected to the rhythms of nature as a whole.

He developed a routine in his life, which was a form of a rhythm. He naturally awoke at daybreak and went to sleep when he felt sleepy, around eight.

Most of the time, he didn't make any plans for his activities during the day. He didn't intend to do anything productive or practical. For a change, he found it wholesome to follow his natural inclinations. This was one luxury he really enjoyed!

He was glad that nobody was there to order him around and disturb his peace of mind.

Making plans demanded a lot of thinking and comparing the relative merits of the activities. Making meticulous plans for the day could mentally tire anyone.

When he didn't make any plans and just decided spontaneously, he felt that it was *more natural* that way. He became more relaxed and enjoyed himself more. *Spontaneous living* really appealed to him! It simply meant doing what came naturally!

Very often, he just watched the fish frolic in the water. The mullets were playful jumpers. When they leaped above the water, they seemed to be looking right at him. He was sure they were trying to show off and wanted to socialize with him. They leaped above the water to find out what he was doing.

They leaped over wide expanse of water when they were escaping from predators, when nervous or just playing around. There were times when ten or twelve mullets would jump at the same time because they swam in a school. Jose was their strong confident leader. Junior thought that Jose winked at him the last time he was up in the air. Their presence always created some excitement in him!

He liked to watch the kingfishers dive for their prey. They were graceful and efficient predators. Sometimes, he pitied the poor fish especially when he recognized them. It was a one-sided affair, with the bird always winning the waiting game.

He felt that way, until he happened to observe the clever behavior of some of the fish.

One day, he thought he was watching a happy coincidence. He was watching a leaf move with the current. It so happened that a fish, he had named Pepito, was also moving in the same direction with the current, underneath the leaf. He said to himself that Pepito was very lucky to be under a leaf because there was a kingfisher perched right above on a tree branch. He assumed that being under a leaf was just a coincidence and luck.

However, he noticed the same incident several times involving other fishes that he didn't recognize. He suspected that the fish knew exactly what it was doing. Unbelievably, some of the preys outsmarted their predators!

Several times, he observed the same technique of using a cover to live another day. The fish had figured out to hide under floating leaves until out of danger.

Even fish have intelligence and could learn to defend itself from predators.

After he realized how smart some fish could be, then he felt sorry for his friend, Diosdado, the kingfisher because he was just sitting up there hungry and frustrated.

For hours, Junior observed the tides and watched the behavior of the fish, the birds and everything around him. He watched the mangrove leaves and branches playing with the rising water.

The current purposely caught and dragged down some of the mangrove branches for a few minutes. Then, suddenly, the branches leaped to the air to escape the grasp of the rushing waters.

However, before long, the rising water would grab the branches again and the tree would pull its arms away again and again! The fierce struggle went on for minutes until the waters completely overpowered the branches and sent them down under to drown.

When the tide receded later on, however, he observed the same leaves and branches still playing the same game with the outgoing current. The branches and the leaves didn't drown. The waters merely pushed them down under but they still managed to survive.

They learned to have fun while surviving the daily cycle of the tides. The next day, the tides and the branches played again and again until they grew bigger and higher; or until the waters broke them off for good!

He was fascinated to watch the wooden pilings that fishermen had installed as fishing devices along the streams and rivers. The pilings would violently shake back and forth and sideways as if some angry squids were shaking them underwater. Sometimes, he watched an entire row of pilings shaking together as if protesting vigorously the water intrusion or making some terrorist threats! He found their collective behavior amusing!

Some mangrove leaves, in contrast, gently shook as the rising waters caressed them. There was something quietly dramatic about the behavior of the incoming waters as they moved up to kiss the parched lips of the streams and rivers. The moisture of the kiss made their lips expand and they enjoyed the token of affection from the tidal waters.

He was excited to observe the stiff militaristic behavior of the rising waters as they executed the cyclical command to invade and occupy the swamp territory. Large volumes of water parted unerringly as they hit solid objects. They appeared preordained by some inherent command to

The Child Daredevil Hero

separate to the right or the left and to converge again after passing the obstacles.

The tidal march was always purposeful, intentionally seeking the valleys first. Then they colonized the plains and the higher regions until the whole area had been occupied. Molecules of water marched one after another as precisely as trained soldiers.

He found it amusing and enlightening to observe the behaviors of every creature around him. Like him, they also followed the natural laws within and around themselves. Their behaviors of eating, drinking, defecating, fighting, mating, fleeing or sleeping were also naturally instigated. Like humans, they felt certain natural urges and followed the natural cycles and rhythms.

By the age of twelve, he concluded that a *good life* was one that followed the laws of nature as he observed it around him and in him. He knew even then that nature followed certain laws and that events occurred regardless of whether or not he intervened.

He realized that his favorite and most satisfying activity was *thinking*. This was the activity that terrorized him in the beginning, when he was just ten-years-old. He thought of thinking as a natural curse! Yet two years later, it became his constant companion and comforting friend!

Sometimes, his thinking processes were connected to the five sensory organs: eyes, ears, tongue, nostrils and skin surfaces. He thought about what he was observing, hearing, smelling, tasting or touching. Nevertheless, his most satisfying thoughts had nothing to do with the senses.

He became absorbed in reasoning, speculation, understanding the relationships of things, causes and effects, trying to understand the natural laws that governed the universe and many other subjects.

He became engrossed in his own thoughts for hours! His life as a hermit made it convenient to think endlessly about anything. He believed that he was destined to become a philosopher even before he knew what philosophy meant. He was already doing philosophy without knowing it.

Having ample opportunities to think freely, he learned to take advantage of his leisure times. He used every opportunity to think and loved the simple indulgence of this most noble of all human activities! He also regarded it as a great blessing!

He concluded that the *good happy life* was the life of the mind! After sixty years, he still maintains the same belief. The joy of insight, inspiration and understanding far exceeded the pleasures of the senses, which were fleeting and ephemeral. It was not as good as orgasm but it lasted longer!

Chapter Twenty Three
Famine!

The evacuees from Ibizan left for Makato in order to live in the swamps. However, after they arrived in Punta Oeste, it became obvious that it was better for their families to live in the fishing village rather than in the swamps. The prop roots of the red mangrove trees made every movement in the swamp almost impossible.

The *aerator roots* of the black and white mangroves carpeted the surfaces with four to six-inch daggers sticking up from the grounds. The menacing protrusions covered the grounds so thickly that they naturally discouraged anyone from walking on them.

To make the living conditions in the swamps even worse, high tides flooded the whole area twice a day. Except during the times when the tides were at their lowest, walking around was almost impossible. Everything was wet and the water in the streams, even at low tides, was at least ankle deep.

The children, with their boundless energy, would feel terribly restricted in their movements. They would feel miserable and uncontrollable.

Living at the seashore, in contrast, would allow them much more activities on the beaches, under the coconut groves, in the village itself and in the wide open ocean. Life in the Punta Oeste village would be ideal especially for the children!

Instead, Badong and Paing built a hideout in the swamp where the refugees could escape to in case the marauding Japanese soldiers raided the seashore village. They could survive in the wet woods during brief invasions.

They estimated that the raiding soldiers would be gone in one or two days, at most. In fact, the invaders might stay only for a couple of hours, while they slaughtered some small animals. They might also load rice, corn and other edible things they happen to find.

The hideout in the swamp was ideal because it was completely inaccessible to the enemy. Besides, Junior lived there to guard it, to keep it clean and to maintain it. Therefore, the hut was always ready for use whenever it was needed.

Even though the children in the village had limitless leisure and activities, the village life was far from ideal. Badong complained to Juan, his new neighbor and village leader.

The Child Daredevil Hero

"Juan, my family is starving at this moment! We have no food and I don't know where to obtain them."

"Badong, for centuries, da village couldn't grow staple foods. Da salty ocean had invaded about twenty-five kilometers inland and one hundred kilometers along da coastline. Da sea had turned da land into tidal swamps."

"In that case, where do you obtain your staple food?"

"We obtain rice, corn, fruits and vegetables from da farmers inland. Des types of food were always in short supply here and were very difficult to obtain.

"Ya have to navigate a canoe through a Japanese occupied region. Da nearest farm is at least thirty kilometers away."

"Can you get to the farms by walking?"

"In teory, yes. But, it will be more difficult and dangerous! Da hikers are more visible to da Japanese sentries.

"On da oder hand, canoeing on one of da two swift Rivers will give ya some natural protection because da Rivers are located in a canyon. Still, da dangerous trip goes through heavily guarded Japanese-occupied areas. Such missions could easily cost da lives of dose involved."

"Why is it so dangerous, Juan?"

"Because da occupying soldiers consider every Filipino civilian hiding in da forests, swamps, caves and in remote hiding places as disloyal subjects. Dere is a standing military order to arrest or kill civilians who did not surrender to da Japanese authority!"

"Have the soldiers tried to capture or arrest the civilians?"

"Only when da civilians try to go through da occupied areas. Dey target especially dose who navigate deir canoes to obtain food from da farmers. Da Japons know dat da beach residents have to obtain food from da farms. So, dey wait for da canoes to pass under da bridges and kill dem! Ah believe dey assign soldiers to guard da bridges.

"It is commonly known dat Japanese soldiers routinely kill civilians in canoes wherever and whenever dey see dem!"

"Juan, I didn't expect immediate hardship waiting for us upon our arrival here in Punta Oeste. We had escaped from physical danger in Ibizan but *um* ... only to land here where starvation is already stalking us! This is a bad exchange of one misery for another!"

"Ah'm sorry for yar problems, Badong. But, for hundreds of years, *um* ... my people have always lived in constant shortage of food in dis village. Der was never *um* ... a time when we could grow staple food here.

"It is true dat after da Japanese occupation, *um* ... our situation became more critical! We eat only after *um* ... one or two of our men succeeded in eluding da Japanese guards and obtaining food from da farmers."

"You're a native here, Juan. You must have many relatives around to help you out."

"Yes. But, ma relatives are *um* ... like me. Dey're also fishermen."

"So, what do you do to solve your problem with the food?"

"Since da war began, *um* ... it has been a constant 'hide and seek' game. It can be a deadly sport! Ah had two cousins, from *um* ... Punta Este, who were shot and killed by da *Japons*. Dey were on deir way to a farm. It was late afternoon. Da soldiers took ... perverse pleasure in killing dem."

"Why do you say, perverse? Did they torture them?"

"No. Der were two oder *um* ... relatives in anoder *banca*. Dey were hiding in da bushes. Dey had tried to persuade *um* ... cousins Pablo and Pedro not to pass under da bridge during the day. My broder Guillermo and *um* ... cousin Ismael told dem to wait until dark. But dey tought *um* ... noting bad could happen to dem."

"So, what happened?"

"Some soldiers saw dem pass under da bridge. Dey started shooting dem with *um* ... machine guns. Da whole truck load of soldiers were *um* ... laughing! Dey tought it was funny and fun! Dat is why ah call deir behavior sick!"

"I'm sorry to hear about the death of your cousins!"

"Tank ya, Badong. As ya see, going to da farms *um* ... to get food can be a deadly business!"

"I see. I had no idea that it can be that serious!"

"Yes, Badong. Ah won't tell ya now about oder relatives who were *um* ... only wounded. Ah'll tell ya da stories some oder time."

"Juan, I'm deeply disturbed to watch my younger children starve! If I knew that a life or death situation was waiting for us here, I don't think we would have left Ibizan at all!"

"Ah understand yar disappointment, Badong. But ya have to tink of da *um* ... great abundance of seafood available for ya here. Even if all ya eat is *um* ... fish, shrimp and crabs, dey are still food dat will sustain life. Ya might have an unbalanced diet; but *um* ... no one will really starve to death here! Dat is important for ya to understand!"

"You're right, Juan. Perhaps, my expectations were too high. Hence, I'm disappointed!"

"Badong, ya have to learn *um* ... how to survive here like my people have done for *um* ... hundreds of years. Ya must find a way of *um* ...

converting seafood to oder types of food. Dat way, *um* ... yar family can eat balanced meals.

"Coastal villagers have always bartered deir fish, shrimp, crabs, fish sauces and salt for *um* ... da farmer's rice, corn, vegetables and fruits.

"Because da *Japons* now control da roads, we *um* ... have to sneak into da farms and *um* ... barter or buy food trough da Rivers. And, we can only do dis while *um* ... da Rivers are still open. It is possible dat *um* ... da *Japons* might want to starve us by blocking every boat passage to da farms."

"Why would they do that?"

"Badong, ah can think of several possible reasons. But da most important reason depends on da *um* ...tactics used by da Filipino guerrillas. If dey use da Rivers to deploy deir forces and *um* ... attack da Japanese garrisons, den *um* ... da *Japons* might guard da Rivers to prevent dem an easy access."

"I see that possibility. But can you think of some other probable reasons?"

"Da oder reason ah can thank of is *um* ... if some civilians do da stupid ting of attacking da *Japons* from da Rivers."

"Why would they do that?"

"Just out of anger of da *Japons* or *um* ... for any irrational motives."

"If the occupiers seal off the passages, what can we do then?"

"We will have to do more heroic acts, like *um* ... attacking da guards while some civilians sneak trough da guarded areas. We will probably lose many lives. But, *um* ... we will do whatever we need to do to survive!"

"I suppose so. I hope we don't have to do that."

"While we know dat da farms are still *um* ... accessible, at least **at night**, ya have to survive by *um* ... doing exactly what we do."

"All right! Tell me what should I do?"

"Ah suggest dat ya send *um* ... a couple of yar men to risk being killed by navigating a canoe trough the occupied territories. Dat is a very serious decision to make!

"Fill a canoe with marine goods dat *um* ... dey can barter with da farmers. Let dem paddle against da swift current, *um* ... elude da guards and do business with da farmers. Der is no oder alternative!"

"Juan, I know now that I might have to do that. But before I follow your suggestion, let me pursue a possible alternative.

"I see a big island across the ocean, north of us. I believe the island is called *Romblon*. I still have the outrigger sailboat that we had used to sail from Ibizan. I'm tempted to sail across and investigate that island. Do you think it is worth my effort to do that?"

"Ah have never sailed to dat island; but *um* ... some fishermen from dis village had sailed der before. Based on deir stories, *um* ... it is not wort da trouble. Da island is famous for *um* ... beautiful marbles but not for food. It is completely rocky and *um* ... not habitable by humans."

"I'm disappointed to hear that. Still, I'm glad to have inquired about it. In that case, I'll figure out how to make the canoe trips to the farms."

"Listen to me, Badong. I've been sending *um* ... a younger broder to obtain food for my family. Da best time to do dat is only at night because *um* ... da soldiers don't seem to patrol the bridges during dose times.

"Let dem start from here no later dan eight in the morning. By da time dey reach da first bridge, *um* ... it will be almost dark. Tell dem to wait until it is completely dark.

"Den, let dem navigate silently along da banks until *um* ... dey are past da Japanese garrisons. Den, let dem find some of da farmers and *um* ...talk to dem about bartering goods. Badong, dat is da only way for now."

"Juan, do you have relatives among the farmers whom we can try to find and barter food with?"

"Yes, ah do. Dey are distant relatives. But, dey are already *um* ... committed to help us for da duration of da war. Dey own only small farms and *um* ... deir harvests are unpredictable. Ah would suggest dat ya make yar own contacts. Dere are many oder *um* ... farmers who would be happy to barter with ya."

"My family is already going through what I call, 'starvation diet.' I have already reduced meals to two a day. The first meal is only a small bowl of porridge. The amount of rice eaten for supper is also getting less and less. Every day, the food situation is becoming more desperate. Starting tomorrow, I will limit food to only one meal a day!"

"Badong, ah have done da same ting for my family *um* ...when food supplies were too low. In da past year, dere were monts and *um* ... weeks when food was very scarce. Da monts of June, July and August are notorious for food shortages. Dere were days when *um* ... we ate only once a day. And, dere were oder days when *um* ... we didn't eat anyting at all!"

"So, you have already experienced some really bad times before, Juan."

"Ah don't want to tell you dis; but believe me, *um* ... we will have many more bad times coming to us before dis war is over! As da war progresses, *um* ... dere will be days and weeks when food will be insufficient! Famine has been threatening dis village *um* ... every day since da war broke out!"

The Child Daredevil Hero

"From my point of view, Juan, we are now experiencing a famine. If we don't obtain new supplies of food soon, the young children and the sickly might starve to death!"

"Badong, ah have a *um* ... sack of rice ah can lend ya until ya get yar own supplies. Ah know ya'll pay me back later on."

"Thank you for your generosity, Juan. I'll definitely pay you back. But, tell me how my boys can find the farmers?"

"Just send dem inland, past da occupied territories. Dey will see *um* ... small farms on bot sides of da Rivers. Dere is, however, one problem. Ah told ya earlier dat da riverbanks are *um* ... very high because da Rivers are situated in a canyon. So, dey have to *um* ...climb a precipice and get to da top. Da farms are situated beyond da River rim."

The high precipice of a canyon

"How high are the cliffs?"

"It varies. In a worse case, *um* ... it might be one hundred-fifty feet. Am not sure of ma estimate because *um* ... ah never counted da number of steps."

"Are there ladders or steps purposely carved out of the muddy cliffs?"

"In some cases, yes. Some farmers made ladders out of bamboo logs. But, da frequent floods just *um* ... washed dem away or destroyed dem. So, most farmers just *um* ... make mud steps like narrow terraces. But again, da rains and *um* ... da floods just eroded and destroyed dem."

The Child Daredevil Hero

"I suppose that in some situations, the vertical cliffs are impossible to climb."

"Yes. But, da farmers somehow *um* ... find a way to climb dem."

"I'm sure, they do. But, how will my boys find their secret ladders in the dark?"

"Badong, ah have to admit dat *um* ..., in some cases, it can be a real problem. Perhaps, yar boys should wait until *um* ... day time before climbing da river bank."

"Where are they going to spend the night? In the canoe?"

"Badong, ah realize now dat *um* ... dese trips might be more tricky for people like ya. Ya're not familiar with da Rivers and da farms.

"In our case, *um* ... ah have been making trips to da farms of my relatives since ah was a kid. Ah have taken everyting for granted. Ah admit, it is much more complicated *um* ... for dose who didn't grow up in dis part of da province.

"Ah wouldn't advise dat dey sleep in deir canoe. Dere are crocodiles *um* ... especially in da upper levels of dese Rivers."

"So, where can they sleep while waiting for the sun to rise?"

"In some places, *um* ... dere are *secondary banks*, which are da lower levels of land, *um* ... next to da water. Dey are like mud and gravel beaches dat are deposited by da water current. Dere are many of dem along da River banks."

"I understand what you're saying. But, it would be impossible for my boys to find them in the dark."

"Ah agree, Badong. Am convinced now dat dese trips will be difficult for dem. Hence, ya should send boys *um* ... who are mature enough to figure tings out. Dey should be able to solve problems as dey come."

"That is a big problem for me, Juan. I can't go myself because I'm the head of my refugee group. I can't send Paing, my brother-in-law, because he is the leader of his family also. We have to be around to lead our families through all kinds of emergencies!

"I'll sleep on this problem and hope to find a good solution tomorrow."

"Badong, am sure ya'll figure it out."

"Juan, I see now how fortunate you are because you have relatives among the farmers. That is one big advantage of being a native of Makato.

"Still, I feel fortunate to have found a refuge in your village. For this reason, I appologize for making some negative remarks about your village yesterday."

"Ah accept da appology, Badong. Ah assure ya dat *um* ... after ya solve dis problem with food supplies, ya'll find living here safe and almost normal.

"We do hear some of da fighting between *um* ... da guerrillas and da *Japons*. But da shootings sound quite far away. Ya'll see dat *um* ... living here is quite peaceful."

"Juan, let me inquire further about the specifics of making the trips inland. After the first meeting with the farmers, I assume that it becomes easier afterwards."

"Of course. Yar boys will be *um* ... more familiar with da way to da farms. Da farmers will give dem more specific landmarks so dey find da farm more easily. More importantly, ah predict dat *um* ... dey will become good friends. After da first meeting, da boys can make deir trips as often as dey need to.

"Yar primary problem is *um* ... choosing yar food hunters. In my opinion, dat is a big decision because ya're asking dem to risk deir lives for da sake of yar family! Yar next problem is how to elude da Japanese guards and stay alive."

"I really appreciate all these suggestions, Juan. But, suppose the farmer's food supplies are low, what should they do then?"

"What yar men should do is *um* ... to go to da next farms and barter with da oder farmers. Da chances are good dat *um* ... da oder farmers will be happy to do business with dem."

"Juan, let me be the devil's advocate. What if the farmers they approach don't want to do business with them? What should they do next?"

"If da farmers dey meet can't do it, *um* ... ask dem for recommendations to oder farmers. Dere are *um* ... literally hundreds of little farms inland. Unfortunately, *um* ... most of dem maybe far from da River. Still, dere are enough farmers *um* ... whose farms are along da riverbanks."

"Have you tried bartering with the other farmers other than your relatives?"

"Not yet. But, am prepared to do dat. If my relatives are no longer able to provide us da food, den ah'll approach deir neighbors. Ah won't have problems since ah already know deir neighbors."

"Juan, you know all the problems involved in making the trips to the farms. What is the most difficult part of the mission?"

"Honestly, dere are many problems! Ah really never figured out which ones are worse. Definitely, da possibility of getting killed by da *Japons* comes first. But, ah think traveling in da dark is among da worst! Tink, for example, of how dangerous it is to navigate a banca in da dark since da current is very fast. If and when dey reach deir destination, how are dey going to climb a precipice in da dark?"

"I see what you mean. Climbing the steps in the dark would be impossible!

"Juan, you must give me more information and suggestions at some other time. You must help me make this food mission possible for my boys."

"Ah'll help ya Badong. Ah tink, yar most difficult decision is choosing da right people to do da job! Let me know when ya have chosen dem."

Chapter Twenty Four
The Treacherous Rivers

"Juan, tell me about the boat trip itself. Is it difficult to navigate the Rivers? What should my boys watch for with respect to dangers and difficulties?"

"Badong, *um* ... da possible dangers within dose two Rivers are many and difficult to predict. Da biggest problems are da heavy rains and flush flooding. Rains are easier to predict *um* ... because of cloud formations and weader conditions. When dey see da rain clouds forming overhead, *um* ... dey know da rain will pour in a matter of minutes.

"However, floods are *um* ... more difficult to predict or foresee. Da headwaters of da Rivers are many *um* ... kilometers away in da mountains. If a heavy rain is falling where da headwaters are, *um* ... even if da weader is perfect down here, floods *um* ... may occur suddenly. Yar men have to be *um* ... on constant lookout for deir safety."

"What should they do if they notice a sudden flood is approaching?"

"Dey should immediately look for *um* ... an inlet where da current is slower. Dey should tie up deir *banca* to a tree or a bush. Make sure dat dey leave a lot of slack to allow da boat to float with da rising waters.

"As da water rises, *um* ... dey should keep adjusting da rope. Dey might even tie up da boat higher in a tree, if necessary.

"Den, dey have to wait patiently *um* ... until da flood reaches its highest level. Dey'll have to constantly adjust to da ebbing flood *um* ... and allow da canoe to go down gradually with da water. If dey don't watch it, *um* ... deir boat might get stuck in a high dry ground. Den, dey'll have serious problems bringing it down."

"What if they can't find an inlet? What must they do?"

"Den, dey should turn around and paddle down stream until *um* ... dey find da best place to tie up. Dis maneuver might give dem *um* ... extra time to figure out what to do.

"Honestly, Badong, *um* ... dey have to estimate very quickly how much time dey have *um* ... before da flood arrives. Den, dey must do da best dey can! Dere is no way to predict what can happen. Let me be frank in telling ya *um* ... dat serious disasters do happen! Every month, people drown in da Rivers!"

"I assume that disasters may happen. How long will a flood last around here?"

"It depends on da amount of rain. Most rains last only for a few hours. Some rains, however, *um* ... last for a few days. And dere are rains dat last for weeks."

"I assume, then, that a trip may be delayed for days. Is that so?"

"Of course. Trips on da Rivers are unpredictable. Da travelers don't know what difficulties dey might encounter."

"Yes, Juan, I happen to know that. I had made several trips on the Mambusao River that took me weeks to complete. As you said, it depends on many circumstances."

"Exactly! After da flood subsides, *um* ... dere are still logs and all kinds of debris floating in da River. Some big and heavy logs *um* ... might be floating under the water surface. If a log hits yar canoe, it will capsize and break apart! Ah have seen and experienced such accidents!"

"Apart from logs, what else can they expect to find in the River?"

"Every flood causes all kinds of damage and casualties! Derefore, dey might find trees *um* ... and corpses of people who have drowned. Ah have seen houses, horses, pigs, *carabaos* (water buffaloes) *um* ... rafts, *bancas* and all kinds of things ya might not even imagine."

"Yes. I have seen some bad floods before! But, the Mambusao River is like a creek compared to your Rivers here."

"Indeed, dese Rivers are vicious! Dis is why dey should not resume deir trip while da River is still flooded. It would be wise *um* ... to wait until da water level is almost completely back to normal before *um* ... trying to navigate it safely again."

"I agree, Juan, that it would be wise and prudent to wait. But, what happens when our food supplies are very low?"

"Dat is an excellent point to consider. During da rainy seasons, *um* ...da Rivers might be flooded almost all da time. Da River trips would be impossible to make. For dis reason, yar men must *um* ... load as much food as possible to save for da rainy days."

"I realized, as you were speaking, that we must always save food for those times when food is impossible to obtain."

"Sorry to tell ya, Badong. It happens more often dan ah care to count. Food shortage is *um* ... a constant worry!"

"Let me bring up two oder factors, which are connected with da rain. Dey are tunder and lightning! Several people are hit by lightning every year. Most of dose dat are hit die instantly."

"We had the same problems in Mambusao. But, what would you suggest that they do to be more safe from electrical storms?"

"Ah don't tink anyone knows what to do to be safe from lightning. What ah have noticed is dat lightnings hit tall trees. Derfore, ah stay away from trees when der is lightning going on."

"Are there big trees on the bank of the Rivers, Juan?"

"No. Da tall trees are above da rim of da precipices. Dey are quite far from da water. However, dere are small trees on da secondary banks. Still, ah would suggest dat dey tie up da canoe during da electrical storm. Dey should lie down on da ground so dat dey are low targets of da lightning. It is less scary dat way!"

"How about the River bends that produce *whirlpools*? Are there very strong whirlpools that can capsize canoes?"

"Badong, dese Rivers have very strong currents because *um* …dey flow precipitously down from da mountains. Any abrupt bend in a River would produce whirlpools. And dey are not just one but several of dem. Ah have seen *um* … several whirlpools spinning in a row! Dey're very dangerous to navigate!"

"How many bends are there that you consider dangerous, Juan?"

"Every River *um* … naturally meanders down like a very big and long snake. Hence, dere are *um* … hundreds of bends in dese Rivers. Fortunately, most of dem are just gentle ones."

"Are there *notorious bends*, where the whirlpools are extremely dangerous?"

"Yes! Dere are at least *um* … tree or four infamous ones where da Rivers flow over rocky areas. Da solid rock formations on da banks have *um* … prevented da Rivers from forming more gentle curves. Ah have found some bends *um* … dat are very abrupt and sharp!

"To complicate da danger, *um* … dere are island rocks nearby dat are difficult to avoid. Dose islands are monstrous boulders dat, at one time, *um* … were parts of da riverbank. Da water current had cracked and broken dem off and *um* … pushed dem out, right where dey can do tremendous damage! Hitting dose rocks could capsize *um* … and sink any boat and leave da passengers stranded or worse!"

"What do you do to handle the whirlpools and avoid the treacherous islands?"

"Dere are so many teories on how to survive dose bends. It has been da *um* … favorite discussion topic among men for many … many years. Everyone has formed a routine of what to do. Derefore, *um* … ah can only tell ya what ah normally do."

"That is fine, Juan. Give me your theory and the routine that you follow."

"First of all, dere are what are called *secondary whirlpools*. Dey are da spin-off water *um* ... dat are thrown off from da main current. Instead of flowing down da River, *um* ... da small whirling waters flow upstream, below da main current. Dey form a kind of a backlash called *eddies*.

"What ah normally do is to ride da eddy to where ah plan to cross da smaller whirlpools. Ah *um* ... position my *banca* just outside da main current. Ah choose a spot, between da bank and da rock island. Den, ah *um* ... wait patiently for a series of weaker whirlpools. When ah spot da opportunity, ah den paddle across to safer waters!"

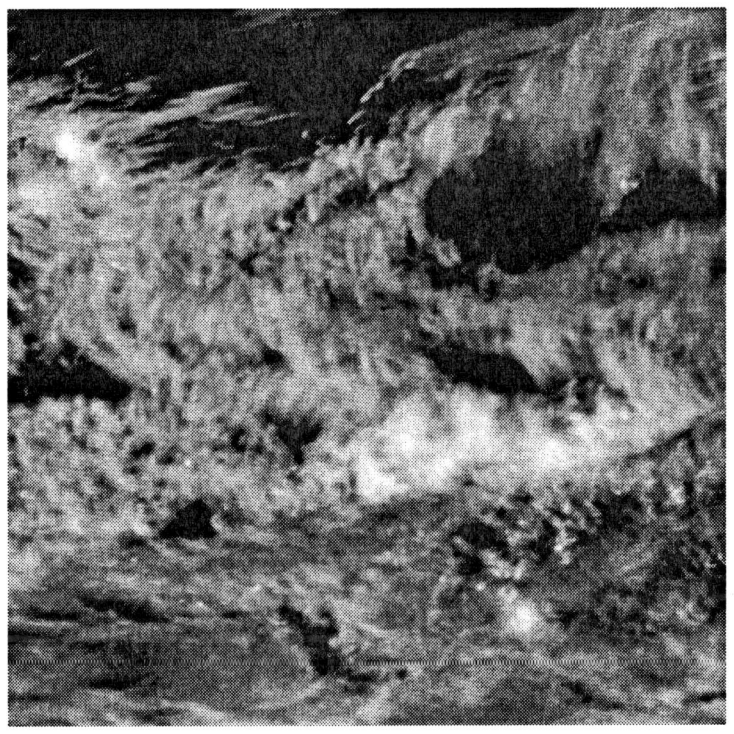

Turbulent river current but not as disastrous as whirlpools!

"What will happen, Juan, if you choose wrongly and paddle across a strong whirlpool?"

"*Caramba*! Dat would be a disaster! Da vortex of da whirlpool can *um* ... really pull a canoe down to da bottom of da River! Few people can survive such a catastrophe!"

"Juan, you're talking about an extreme condition where people can drown and die!"

"Yes! Of course! People drown every day, if dey are not careful!

"What is very important for people, who are not familiar with whirlpools, is *um* ... to study everyting about dem. Da more dey know about whirlpools, da less dangerous dey become. Dey should be patient and *um* ... wait for da smaller ones. If dey are lucky, *um* ...dey may have a series of small 'spinning holes,' as ah call dem. When dey spot da opportunity, den *um* ... dey paddle across like maniacs!"

"Wow! Juan, those Rivers are more vicious than I had expected! But, my men will try to meet the challenges as they come!"

"Let me also point out dat dose whirlpools are bigger and more dangerous when da Rivers are flooded."

"I hope they don't navigate the Rivers when they are flooded. That would be stupid and suicidal!"

"Ah hope so too, Badong."

"Since there are two Rivers, which of them should they choose to get to the farms?"

"Bot Rivers pass trough da *um* ... population center of Makato, where da Japanese have deir headquarters. Ah prefer to take *Rio Este* because *um* ... it seems more straight, but no less treacherous. Besides, *um* ... it leads me directly to da farms of my relatives. For dis reason, it is more familiar to me.

"Ah suggest dat *um* ... dey take eider one and let dem judge, which of da two is better. Ah know some people who prefer *Rio Oeste*."

"I guess that they'll take *Rio Este* for the first trip and then take the other, the next time, and compare them."

"Badong, *um* ... ah have a better suggestion based on my experience. Let dem take *Rio Este* and let dem contact a farmer dere. After deir first successful barter, *um* ... my guess is dat dey'll continue to take da same route because *um* ... dey want to go back to da same farm."

"That makes sense to me, Juan."

"What other factors should my boys watch for?"

"Well, dere are da bridges, which are quite low. Da Japanese soldiers use dem *um* ... constantly during da day and in early evening.

"Navigating under da bridges *um* ... during daytime would be courting disaster! Da passing vehicles can easily see people underneat trough *um* ... da spaces between da wooden boards. Dere is always a chance *um* ... dat da *Japons* might look down and see dem. Moreover, ah said before dat ah suspect dat some soldiers might be assigned during da day to arrest or kill da civilians who go to da farms."

"So, what is your advice?"

"Ah tink dey should *um ... completely avoid traveling trough da occupied areas during da day*. So, dey should always wait until it is *completely dark*, before going under da bridges."

"Juan, that is a prudent advice."

"Tank ya, Badong."

"What about predatory animals, like crocodiles? Are there many of them in certain parts of the River?"

"Yes. Dere are many crocodiles in da Rivers, *um* ... especially in da upper levels where da current is more gentle. Da *buayas,* as we call dem, *um* ... don't like swift waters. Some areas have more crocodiles dan oders.

"Tell dose who pilot da canoe trough da Rivers *um* ... not to trow scraps of food into da water. Dey act like ground baits dat *um* ... may attract da animals to people. Da crocodiles have a very strong sense of smell."

"Are there many known crocodile attacks on people?"

"Of course! But, dey prefer small preys *um* ... like dogs, goats and fish. However, if dey are hungry, *um* ... dey'll attack any animal dat strays into da water. Dat includes human beings."

"What should my boys do to protect themselves from crocodiles, apart from not throwing chums in the water?"

"When dey sleep on da riverbank, *um* ... dey should stay far away from da water's edge and as far away as possible. Tell dem not to sleep in da canoe where *um* ... da *buayas* can easily attack dem."

"What about the fish cargo in the *bancas*? Will the *buayas* attack the canoe to eat the dried and salted fish?"

"Not likely. Da processed fish has *um* ... a different smell and taste from da fresh fish dat dey eat. Fortunately, yar cargo is virtually safe."

"Thank you, Juan, for all these suggestions and information. We will select a couple of people to make the dangerous journeys. Hopefully, they'll save us from this persistent starvation!"

"It was no trouble, Badong. Just let me know if *um* ... ah can be of greater help."

Chapter Twenty Five
Selecting the Food Hunters

In order to determine who would undertake the dangerous missions, Badong decided to call a meeting, with both the Lopez and Castaneda families in attendance. He required even the children to attend. The group decision would, in theory, make everyone partly responsible in case the persons assigned died or killed.

The choices were very important because the survival of the twenty-five refugees depended on the success of the missions. The group meeting gave the semblance of a democratic selection.

In fact, it wasn't democratic at all. Badong had already selected the hunters based on the assumption that a woman and a little boy, if caught, would not be killed. He based his decision on a mere *wish* and a *hope* that, if the Japanese caught them, they might let them go. Of course, nothing was assured!

Hence, the selection process was already prejudiced. The group reached a decision without too much trouble. They chose Junior, a puny ten-year old, and his ninety-pound mother, who was the mother of nine children.

It was a lightweight team against formidable obstacles! They had to contend with the treacherous Rivers, the flooding, thunder and lightning, the mysterious whirlpools, the slippery rapids, the hungry crocodiles and the trigger-happy Japanese soldiers! The choices didn't look right. They didn't look equal to the task!

Because of the gravity of the responsibility, Badong went to the swamp cabin to explain the family's decision to his son, Junior.

"Son, I have an important news to tell you," he began. "We had a family meeting the other night that included Paing's family. Everyone agreed that you and your mother are the best choices to go to the farms and barter our seafood for some rice, corn and other goods.

"I don't expect you to be pleased with this news. The fact is that there is no more food around and somebody has to take the risk and do the job! Unless you and your mother make these trips for the family, we'll all die of starvation!"

The news sounded like a death sentence to the ten-year old! The assignment shocked him! He became angry to be singled out again and sacrificed to die for the sake of the family. He was absolutely certain he was going to die and felt extremely scared!

A sharp pain stabbed his heart and felt very sad with the thought of dying so young! He cried unashamedly as if he was already mourning at his own funeral! He cried until his tear ducts became dry!

He thought that a large part of him, particularly his heart, had already started to die! He quickly became emotionally drained and felt tired! So, he went to sleep without intending to.

When he woke up, he had no idea how long he had slept. He found himself slumped in his seat. His father was still sitting across from him. After he had regained his composure, he asked him some questions.

"Why did you choose me?" he asked, sounding very angry. "I think *uh* ... Mabini and Paterno should go. They're *uh* ... bigger and stronger. They can *uh* ... overcome the strong River current. And, they can *uh* ... better endure the long journey."

"I agree, it would be better," he responded, looking conflicted. "Mabini is now sixteen and Paterno is fourteen. But, the *Japons* will surely kill them if they get caught. They look like grown men already at their young age."

"On the other hand, *uh* ... mother and I can also get killed," he objected, as he raised his childish voice. "When the *Japons uh* ... burned down our town of Mambusao last year, they killed everyone they found. They also killed women and children. I don't think they made any *uh* ... exception for women and children!"

"That's true. However, it's a question of what is more or less probable. If you and your mother get caught, it's more probable that the *Japons* might confiscate the food, but let both of you go. However, if your uncle Paing and I were to get caught, I'm certain they'll kill us and also take the food."

"I see your point," Junior said, sounding conciliatory. "However, *uh* ... you're forgetting that I just turned ten a week ago and *uh* ... I think, I'm small for my age.

"I'm just a small child, *tatay*. I don't have *uh* ... enough strength to overcome the River current. And, *uh* ... mother may not even know how to paddle. And, *uh* she's so little. She doesn't have much strength!"

"Son, I didn't come here to argue with you. If I thought you couldn't do this assignment, I wouldn't have asked you," Badong said, sounding more authoritative! "I've watched you navigate a *banca* in the Mambusao River. I've admired your skills for someone so young. I admit your mother might not be of much help. But, I know you're capable of making this trip!"

"Thank you for your *uh*... confidence in me. But, why should mother be going? She has *uh* ... nine children and two are still in their infancy. Don't you think *uh* ... she's risking too much by making this trip?"

"I'm aware of the risks and your mother knows the dangers. Still, she volunteered to go. I tried to persuade her not to risk her life, but she insisted!"

Junior suspected that his father might have twisted his mother's arm, so to speak.

"I don't understand why *uh* ... mother would do something so dangerous. Juliet and Diadema need her care.

"If you don't mind, *tatay*, *uh* ... I'd like to talk to her by myself. I want to understand why *uh* ... she thinks she should take this risk."

"That's fine with me," Badong replied, sounding more relieved and triumphant. "Get ready and come with me to the village. You can talk to your mother as much as you want."

Taling was cooking lunch when they arrived. She was surprised to see Junior. As their custom dictated, the son approached his mother and kissed her forehead. Then, he proceeded immediately to ask her questions.

"Is it true, *nanay*, that *uh* ... you volunteered to make this dangerous trip with me? If the *Japons* should kill us, you'll be *uh* ... leaving eight orphaned children, among whom are two very young children!"

"Listen, son," she said gravely, looking right into his dark eyes. "I'm perfectly aware of the risks I'm taking! There's not enough food to last for two days. If we don't get more food right away, the whole family will starve!

"To a certain extent, we've been starving already. Two small meals a day are not enough to survive on in the long run. Breakfast is hardly a meal.

"Do you realize that everyone has been losing weight? I've been losing weight myself and I'm constantly hungry!"

Junior stared at her sunken face and felt horrified! "How much weight have you lost, *nanay*?"

"I don't have a scale, so I don't know for sure. I go more by the holes in my belt. I've been tightening it to the point where there are no longer any holes left. Look at how loose this belt is!"

Junior became alarmed by her emaciated figure. He had been feasting on so much abalone, oysters, shrimp, crabs and *tamilok* in the swamp that he had forgotten his starving family. He knew he didn't lose any weight and he didn't feel hungry.

However, the most telling statement that stopped all his objections was when she said, "I'm risking my own life because I'd rather die than

The Child Daredevil Hero

watch any of my children starve to death! I refuse to wait for death to come to me! I'm willing to die to save especially the little children!"

"All right, *nanay*, I'll go if *uh* ... this is what you want to do! I'll load the boat right now and we'll leave *uh* ... early tomorrow. I'm sorry, *nanay*, *uh* ... you've suffered from hunger! I love you so much, I'll do anything for you!"

Jose and others helped load the canoe with dried and salted fish, cooked shrimp and crabs, cans of salt and bars of soap that Badong had made. Although the boat was filled to the hilt, Junior made sure there was enough room for his mother and himself to move freely. He needed all the freedom to maneuver the canoe efficiently.

Early the next morning, Badong conferred with Taling about the dangerous journey. He told her everything that Juan had told him about the treacherous bends in the Rivers, the problems she might experience and the crocodiles.

"Taling, dear! Are you up to this journey with Junior?"

"I'm as ready as I can possibly be. What time do you think we should leave?"

"Juan said that you should leave no later than eight in the morning. That way, you arrive at the Japanese-occupied area late in the afternoon. You might want to leave sooner and analyze the different problems as you encounter them.

"For example, you're supposed to see violent whirlpools at some bends of the River. You should be able to deal with them better if you see how they form, their sizes and their directions. Juan warned especially against the 'giant spinning water holes' as he called them."

"Yes, Badong. We'll do whatever we need to do. I'm too nervous just to wait around! I'd prefer to leave as soon as we can. Then, we can kill some time while we study the whirlpools and other obstacles. If we arrive too early, we'll cool ourselves in the shade and rest our muscles."

"Where do you think you'll spend the night? Where will you sleep?"

"I have no idea! If we arrive at the farm region tonight, we will not meet the farmers until the morning. We can't climb the precipice in the dark. We have no torch or any light to guide us. I hope that the moon will shine over us so we'll have some idea about our location."

"Your arrival at the farms will be the most difficult part of your journey. Indeed, you can't do anything until the morning. So, after you pass the Japanese occupied areas, you should tie your *banca* to a tree or a bush and sleep until morning. But, finding a tree to tie up the canoe in the dark can be very difficult. Everything will be unfamiliar to you!"

"The terrible thing, Badong, is that I don't know what to expect! We have no past experience to guide us. So, we will decide as we go along."

"I wish I can be of greater help, Taling. I wish I had asked Juan for more specific information about what you can do upon arriving at the farm area. I should have asked him where you can tie the banca and where you can sleep."

"Don't worry about it, Badong. Even if he told you where to go, finding places in the dark is very difficult if not impossible! Junior and I will figure out what to do when we get there."

"After you establish contact with a farmer tomorrow, it will be much better after that. So, your next trip will be much easier."

"Yes. That is what I expect."

"I have no clear idea how they barter the food. I don't know if they have cleaned rice and corn to barter with you. If they don't have harvested rice already, then they might invite you to harvest rice and corn with them. By tomorrow evening, you can return home with the needed food!"

"That would be nice! I hope and pray that we succeed!"

"Taling, do you plan to navigate the *banca* or do you want Junior to do that?"

"I'll ask him to do that. He knows more about it than I do."

"That is a wise decision. I trust that the boy will handle the canoe very well."

"We should be going, then."

"*Adios*, Taling. Be very careful! I and the children will be thinking of you!"

"*Adios*, Badong. I'll say goodbye to all the children and leave."

Chapter Twenty Six
The First Food Hunting

Their first departure to find food was like a funeral! Everyone was crying uncontrollably! Everyone knew that the two food hunters might never come home! The younger kids were pulling their mother's skirt and didn't want her to leave! The scene was heartbreaking!

Junior and his mother starting their dangerous journey to procure food for twenty-five refugees

Badong pushed the stern of the canoe to get them started. Junior and Taling furiously paddled to overcome the tidal current! At first, they actually lost a couple of meters to the swift current. Junior corrected the situation by making bigger and deeper paddle strokes. He knew before hand that overcoming the current would be a big struggle!

He could see that if he had to exert that much effort throughout the journey, they would never reach their destination. Because of nervousness and lack of sleep, he feared that he didn't have much more stamina left. He was very pessimistic about the outcome of the trip!

Perhaps, he was having a hard time because he really dreaded the assignment! He felt very tired before he even started. He had slept only two or three hours the night before because he was crying for fear of dying! When he finally went to sleep, he had nightmares about being shot by the Japanese soldiers!

He was still angry with his father and resentful of the teenagers for shirking their obligation of relieving their mother! He couldn't believe that he was the one paddling the canoe instead of his bigger brothers or one of the adults. He wondered whether he could overcome his intense resentment against his father and brothers.

He assumed he was the navigator when his father told him to sit at the stern. Still, he expected his mother to make the decisions. He felt he didn't know that much about steering a canoe. He had paddled canoes before but only for fun. He had never paddled to travel a long journey.

He watched his mother paddle as hard as she could. He didn't even know she could use the paddle properly. She was a very good canoer and was working harder than he did. Watching her work so hard made him feel guilty. For her sake, he made the resolve to put in the necessary effort, even if it killed him.

So, he increased the rate, depth and length of his strokes. They were finally winning against the current but at such a large cost of physical energy!

Because he continued to struggle with the current, he decided to explore other ways of overcoming it. He kept saying to himself that his legs were stronger than his arms. If he could only use his legs to help his arms, he could win the tug-of-war with the current.

Suddenly, he felt the urge to walk along the bank of the river with the boat. He felt sure that if he pulled the boat with a rope, he could definitely overcome the current.

He said to his mother, "I'll try something different, *nanay*. I'll tie up the canoe on the left bank of the River, just for a little while. I plan to pull the *banca* with a rope and I want you to control the movements of the bow uh ... so it doesn't hit the riverbank. I'll show you what I have in mind."

"That's fine, son. Try anything that might help our trip."

After he had tied a long rope to the bow of the canoe, he said to her, "*Nanay*, I want you to use your paddle as a rudder. You hold it vertically with your uh ... right hand, against the right side of the *banca*, like this. Then, uh ... put your left hand on top of the paddle handle, like this. With that position, uh ... you can make the bow move to the right or left. You can even make the canoe turn around completely, ... if you want to.

"If you want the bow to move to the right, uh ... you turn the rudder to the left, like this. If you want the bow to move to the left, uh ... you do the opposite, like this. Think of opposites, nanay: uh ... bow going right, rudder pointing left and vice-versa. Did you understand my explanation, nanay?"

"Let me repeat what you said. Bow turning right, rudder pointing left and vice-versa."

"That is right. In order to make small adjustments with the boat direction, *uh* ... turn the rudder slightly more to the right or to the left, like this.

"You need to understand, *nanay*, that *uh* ... the bow will naturally move towards the bank as I pull the rope. What you need to do is *uh* ... to prevent that left movement by *uh* increasing the angle of the rudder to the left, like this."

"Son, why should the bow move to the left when you pull the rope?"

"Because I'm pulling the boat from the riverbank and not from the front of the bow."

"I see what you mean, son."

"Let's practice until *uh* ... you get the feel of the movement of the boat. Keep making the adjustments *uh* ... very slightly until the boat is cruising smoothly, parallel to the bank."

"How can I make the movement of the boat parallel to the bank? That seems difficult to do, son."

"It's not difficult, mother. It is just a *uh* ... question of practice and *getting the feel of the movement*. What I mean is *uh* ... that you should feel the effect of what you do with the rudder. I think that *uh* ... you should also *feel your power and control* of the boat!"

"Wow! You said power and control of the canoe? I like that idea! I do want to acquire the skills so that I can control the movements of the banca!"

"In that case, let us start. N*anay, uh* ... position your rudder vertically and I'll start pulling the canoe. ... Now, adjust the rudder *uh* ... a little more to the left. That's the correct angle! Keep it steady! ... Turn the rudder more to the left. That is it, *nanay*!"

"I feel so awkward, son. I'm afraid I might lose the paddle."

"Don't be afraid of losing it. It's made of wood and *uh* ... it will stay afloat. I can easily get it back to you. Let's try it again."

"All right, son. I'll try it again. ... I think ... I'm getting the right idea! ... Now, ... I know what you mean by my power and control of the boat. Oh! ... I like doing this better than paddling! It's very restful! ... Wow! ... I'm enjoying it!"

"I knew you'd like it. You'll be using *uh* ... much less energy this way."

Pulling the boat definitely allowed Junior to overcome the current! He felt fortunate to have thought of the idea. He thought of the saying, "Necessity is the mother of invention," which his dad often quoted when he was solving some problems. He wondered whether his dad really expected him to invent new techniques in the process of carrying out the mission. He was only a ten-year-old child, not an adult!

Unfortunately, he had to give up his clever technique after walking about ten kilometers. The riverbank suddenly became a high precipice. The rope was not long enough to continue pulling the canoe. He had to paddle again the hard way.

Navigating upstream had been really hard because they had never paddled that much in their lives. Their muscles were starting to ache but they couldn't afford to take it easy or the current would pull them back. They could not afford to stop and rest because they had no idea how far they had to go.

The heat and humidity were stifling! They thought they would never make it! Yet somehow, they kept going on because there was no alternative other than death, and they didn't want to die! Not yet!

After steering the canoe for less than three kilometers, they approached the first treacherous bend that Juan had warned Badong about. As they came closer, Junior noticed an upstream moving current on the side of the main current. It was called an eddy.

"Nanay, I'll move the canoe outside the main current and ride the upsteam current. This way we have a free ride and get some rest!"

"Do it son. This is unexpected bonus!"

Junior noticed *several currents* of water. He watched how one current bounced off a rock island at the middle of the River. It entered what looked like a rocky cave on the left side of the precipice.

What came out of the cave were whirling formations of water. The whirling motion accelerated and tightened the water spring and, thus, formed gigantic whirlpools! The spinning bodies of water formed different sizes of gyrating eyes! They looked like spinning water tops parading diagonally towards the opposite side of the River.

As the series of whirlpools approached the center of the two-hundred-foot-wide River, the rotating eyes became high- velocity spinning holes that quickly disappeared into the bottom of the River!

The vortexes seemed to explode at the bottom and dissipated their aquatic force! The surface water above the explosion, however, looked like a giant cauldron of boiling liquid. But, twenty to thirty feet away near the right precipice, new but smaller whirlpools were forming. He guessed that they were the residues of the spent out whirlpools.

The power of the whirlpools awed and scared them! They didn't know what to think or what to do. They kept staring at the whirling phenomena! They were trying to understand them and figuring out what to do!

Junior also noticed that at the right side of the river was a straight current, with stronger and faster velocity than the whirling waters. The current flowed like wavy rapids except that the water didn't make any noise. He guessed that the River was very deep.

The straight current collided with the remnants of the exploding vortexes. The colliding currents caused the formation of new but smaller whirlpools.

Junior assumed that the whirlpools continued to form down the River as the currents meandered. There were different currents interacting against each other in some mysterious aquatic ways.

Junior sensed a very serious danger at hand! He had never seen various sizes of whirlpools parading diagonally across a river before. He had seen whirlpools in the Mambusao River but only when it was flooded. But, they were babies in comparison to the giant monsters he was staring at!

He wanted to determine their relative danger to the canoe and to themselves.

"Nanay, *uh* ... I picked up some floating sticks. Let us see how dangerous these whirlpools are. I'll throw a stick into the eye of a giant whirlpool and *uh* ... see what happens to it. There! I threw a stick into the big one. Let us watch what happens to it. ...

"Wow! Did you see what happened to the stick? The whirlpool pulled it down and sucked it into its stomach, as it were! Let us watch where the stick will surface. ... Look at where the stick came up! That is more than fifteen meters away!"

"All right, son. Throw another stick into the eye of a medium sized pool and see what happens to it."

"Yes, *nanay*. ... There! I just threw a stick into a smaller eye. See that? The eye also swallowed it but let it go only about eight to ten meters away."

"Now, son, let us select the smallest whirlpool. There is one coming. Throw a stick into its eye. ... Look! The stick came up only about three meters away."

"That was an interesting experiment we just made, son. We have just learned how dangerous those large whirlpools are! We also learned that we must avoid them at all cost! For safety, Juan had suggested to your father that we should wait for small whirlpools and quickly paddle across them."

"Yes, nanay. That strategy might work. But, I think I have a better idea. Instead of navigating to the left of the rock island, where the water is very rough because of the whirlpools, *uh* ... we should paddle to the right of the rock island and close to the right bank."

"Why do you think that the right side is better?"

"For several reasons. If you look to the right side of the River, *uh* ... the water current comes straight down. And, no whirlpools are forming. Hence, the water current is smoother and less dangerous."

"But son, the current there is much faster than on the left side of the river."

"Yes, mother. But, *uh* ... we can overcome that by making our paddling motions larger, deeper and faster!

"There is another important reason. Look at the pattern of movements by each whirlpool. Watch the whirlpool that just came off the wall ... and follow its behavior."

"All right. I'm looking. Let us count the number of turns it makes. One, two ... I counted about eleven."

"Yes, mother. I counted about ... twelve. Did you observe that the rotation of the water in the eye became faster and tighter? Then, did you notice that the eye suddenly sunk and disappeared at *uh* ... about the middle of the River?"

"I didn't notice it. But, I'll watch more carefully and observe what you just described to me."

"*Nanay*, watch especially the big ones, *uh* ... the center of the eye will disappear as it approaches the center of the River. Watch and follow again a single whirlpool. There! Did you see the eye sink and disappear into the bottom?"

"I saw that, son. Does it mean that the whirlpool is completely gone?"

"To a certain extent, yes. After the water spring explodes at the bottom, it loses most of its power. The water is still spinning but it is no longer a dangerous whirlpool. Therefore, it would be less dangerous to cross it after its energy had been used up."

"Explain it to me in another way, son. I didn't completely understand your explanation."

"As I understand it, *nanay, uh* ... a whirlpool is a water spring. It is like a wire spring ... of a clock that you wind.

"The water spring starts to be wound up as *uh* ... water enters a cave-like chamber at the left wall of the cliff. The chamber rotates the water. After the whirling water is released, *uh* ... the winding process continues and an eye is formed. After it spins around for at least ten times, *uh* ... it becomes the time when the eye sinks into the bottom!

The Child Daredevil Hero

Different currents and underwater obstacles in a river

"As it hits the bottom, the energy *uh* ... explodes and the power of the whirlpool is almost completely used up.

"When the remnants of the whirlpool surfaces, ... it is no longer the same bundle of energy. It continues to spin but with much less force. It is like a wobbly top that is about to stop."

"Where does the spent up whirlpool surface again, son?"

"It depends on the original size of the pool. The bigger they are, the further away they'll resurface. Remember when I threw a stick into the eye of a giant whirlpool?"

"Yes. I remember it well."

"When the stick came up, it was several meters away. I believe *uh* ... that the used up whirlpool resurfaced where the stick came up."

"So, are you saying that while the whirlpool is exploding at the bottom, it is safe to navigate the water on the surface level?"

"I think that is what I'm trying to say. What I observed was that the water *uh* ... on the surface was still agitated as if it were boiling."

"That is what I want to clarify, son. Is it safe to steer the canoe through the rough agitated waters?"

"Yes, *nanay*. I think it is safe."

"I think what you're saying is that there is still a lot of water energy on the surface, but the energy is diffused or disorganized."

"That is right, *nanay*! That is why we don't have to wait for *uh* ... smaller whirlpools to arrive in order to cross the River. We can just paddle through the rough waters that do not have whirlpools!"

"Are you sure that your analysis is correct? If it is not, we might drown right here!"

"I'm not absolutely sure, *nanay*. But, I think *uh* ... it will work."

"In that case, let us move the boat towards the right side of the River. Let us continue to use the eddy and position the canoe to go across. This is the life and death test of your theory, son! If you're wrong, we die! But, if you're right, we live!"

"That is right, *nanay*. We have to take the risk or *uh* ... we will be stock here all day."

"You are right, son. I think your analysis of a whirlpool makes sense. Now, let us go ahead and paddle through this rough water, son!"

"Yes, *nanay*. But we have to paddle harder and faster as soon as we get to the right side of the River. The current ahead of us is *uh* ... definitely stronger! Let us go ahead and paddle. One, two, three! Go! ..."

"*Dios mio*! We made it! That was really a dangerous river bend! I think, we were lucky to get out of there safely!"

"Yes, *nanay*. But, just remember, *uh* ... we have to cross several more whirlpools later on."

"I understand, son. Your father told me all about them. From his explanation, however, I had no idea that they were as treacherous and deadly as they really are!

"I'm glad that you figured out how those whirlpools worked and especially how to avoid them."

"Yes, *nanay*. I'm glad to find out that *uh* ... my analysis was correct! Those whirlpools could have killed us!"

Having survived the first treacherous river bend, they felt more experienced and comfortable dealing with the second and third bends.

The Child Daredevil Hero

They had a better understanding of how whirlpools were formed. More importantly, knowing where they naturally exploded their energy gave them the clue to where the safer water pathways could be found!

By the time they were about to cross the fourth river bend, they thought they had learned everything about the fast spinning whirlpools.

However, they were somewhat surprised to come across several rock islands scattered around the middle of the River. Obviously, they had been gouged out from the banks of the River.

As they paddled further up, they saw a very large rock island that forced a large portion of the current to bounce off the wall at the right side of the River. Constant water pressure on the wall had eroded and dislodged large chunks of rocks. There was a cave-like indentation in the wall that forced the water to churn, bubble and create a fine mist.

The cave formation was like a whirlpool factory. The water that entered the cave turned into giant whirlpools, bigger than what they had seen earlier. The whirlpools that came out of the 'factory' were fully formed and programmed for immediate destruction!

Fortunately, the navigators had already learned from earlier whirlpools that the 'water springs' would expend their energies around the middle of the River.

Even though the menacing 'spinning corkscrews' were large and deep, they just waited at a comfortable distance beyond what Junior called, 'the whirlpool grave yard.' After expending their wound up powers, they suddenly became harmless little vortexes.

After they thought they were out of harm's way, however, they faced a completely new set of obstacles. Juan Capistrano forgot to inform Badong that there were *swift rapids* and *shallow waters* at the higher elevations of the River.

In the rapids, there was a drastic narrowing of the water passage. Due to constant erosion and sediment build up on various sections of the waterway, the water passage was restricted in some sections of the River. As a result, partial dams were created, which held back the water. Then the water level rose above the obstacle until the River flowed downwards on a slide!

As the water rushed down, the speed of the current seemed to quadruple. The current was so strong that the paddles alone couldn't overcome the natural force of the water.

In a panic, they used their paddles as poles to push the canoe against the swift current. They planted their paddles into the gravel bottom to prevent the boat from floating away.

However, every time they lifted their paddles to steer the canoe forward, they immediately lost grounds to the rapids.

Junior tied two ropes to the bow of the boat and both of them pulled the *banca* from the opposite sides of the sedimentary embankments. They pulled hard to overcome the speedy current. After about an hour of hard work, they overcame the first rapids!

The white waters of the rapids. Obstacles in the flow of the liquid forced the water to rise and create waves. The rapid flow of water is caused by the steep descent of the liquid just past the obstacle

They encountered several other rapids with varying degrees of difficulty. Fortunately, they had already learned what to do.

Suddenly, there was an abrupt change of elevation of the riverbed. The water was suddenly too shallow to float the canoe on its own. The water was only ankle deep in some places. Both Taling and Junior waded through the shallow waters, while partly lifting the *banca* from the rocky bottom. They pulled the craft through the shallow riverbeds for at least two kilometers.

Junior realized that the riverbeds were on a much higher elevation than at the seashore. He estimated that the difference of elevation was at least a kilometer.

He understood, for the first time, why the river current was very swift especially close to the mouth of the Rivers. He imagined that navigating down the River would be like riding a water slide!

Shallow waters also formed rapids. The riverbed acted as a dam that slowed down the water and caused it to rise.

Rio Este also became narrower and the current became slower. The River looked and felt more like an elongated lake.

Suddenly, Junior became afraid of crocodiles! The placid waters seemed ideal for crocodiles to thrive in. He remembered seeing crocodiles in similar environments in Mambusao.

Soon, Junior realized that they were approaching the town of Makato when he saw a couple of bridges at a distance. He saw the impressions of trucks, some motorcycles and jeeps crossing the bridges. Unexpectedly, he felt scared and nervous! This was the first time that they saw the dreaded enemies!

Taling also became aware of the same change of surroundings and whispered, "Listen, Junior, we're approaching the town proper. We'll have to speak in a whisper so no one will hear us!"

"Yes, *nanay*," Junior whispered back. "We must also stop using the paddles *uh* ... because they hit the side of the boat and make some noise. Let's stop using them as soon as *uh* ... we come close to the first bridge."

"How are we going to move the canoe then?"

"We'll move it forward by pulling on *uh* ... the vegetation."

"That's a good idea. But, Junior, we must wait right here until it is dark. Juan told your father not to travel under the bridges during the day."

"That is right, *nanay*. We must wait here until it is completely dark. For now, I'll tie the *banca* to a bush. We don't have too long to wait. It is already uh ... getting darker by the minute."

They were killing time while moored less than half a kilometer from the first bridge. After a little while, they heard soldiers marching in columns. Both crouched very low and watched the dreaded enemies cross the first bridge. The soldiers were marching westward. Then, they noticed trucks loaded with soldiers were moving in the same direction on the other bridge, which was not too far from the first.

The soldiers and the trucks were crossing the bridges for what seemed like an hour. They had no idea how long the mobilization would take.

When it was sufficiently dark, however, they pulled on the vegetation to move forward. By the time they passed under the first bridge, the Japanese mobilization was over.

They kept using the same method until they had passed the town by at least a kilometer. Then, they paddled for another seven or eight kilometers in almost complete darkness.

Junior finally complained, "*Nanay*, I can no longer see anything! We have to stop and *uh* ... look for a place to tie up the canoe."

"I can't see anything either. But, we can't just suddenly stop. Perhaps, you should turn the boat around and let it drift slowly. Let us grope, by using our paddles, to find a place to tie up. Without any light, this is an impossible thing to do!"

"Yes, mother. I had no idea it would be this dark! I'm only glad that *uh* ... we're outside the occupied territory. Or, *uh* ... we might drift into the Japanese hands.

"I'll poke the river bank with my paddle to find a place to tie up."

"I'll try to do the same, son."

"Mother, I'm afraid *uh* ... of crocodiles and other predatory animals!"

"Control your imagination, son. You're making me nervous!"

"I'm sorry, mother."

"Keep drifting slowly and feel for any low land."

"All right. I'll keep feeling my way but *uh* ... I'll use only the paddle. I'm afraid to use my hands *uh* ... because a crocodile might be waiting to bite them."

"Stop this talk about crocodiles, Junior! First of all, you don't know that there are crocodiles around here. You're making me feel scared!"

"I'm sorry again, mother. It is true I don't know for sure. But, uncle Juan said that they are all over this River. Somehow, I just feel that they are around here!"

"Even if they are, I order you to stop talking about them! I'm becoming terrified!"

"Yes, mother. I'll stop as you ordered me."

"What are you feeling with your paddle, Junior?"

"I'm touching a muddy cliff, *nanay*."

"I wonder whether we should cross over to the other bank."

"I don't think so. I'm afraid to paddle across because I can't see anything! We could hit a rock island and capsize!"

"All right. Let us remain on this side of the River. Keep poking with your paddle until we find something suitable."

"I feel like a blind boy. I can't see anything."

"We're both blind, Junior. Remember that blind people are able to do a lot of things. After a while, we'll be used to our blindness."

"Wait a minute! We are coming to a more open body of water. Suddenly, I feel the wind. ... Oh! ... I think I've found something! It feels like a flat muddy ground."

"I'm so glad you have found something!"

"I'll disembark, *nanay*. ... Now, I'll *uh* ... grope for a shrub or tall grasses to tie up the canoe."

"Be careful not to fall into the water!"

"Yes, *nanay*. I'm being careful. ... I found some tall grasses. I'll tie up the canoe to a clump of grasses."

"How far is the precipice from where you're standing?"

"I'll walk to it and *uh* ... I'll tell you in a couple of minutes. ... It is about twenty feet, *nanay*."

"That is a good distance from the water's edge. Now, help me get off this *banca*. I need to stretch my legs!" ...

"Do you want to search for the steps going up the cliff, mother?"

"No, son. That is a futile search in the dark. Besides, I don't want to climb a precipice in total darkness. We could fall and get seriously hurt."

"You're right, *nanay*. We should wait until *uh* ... tomorrow morning when we can see."

"Junior, your talk about crocodiles has made me anxious! Perhaps, there are crocodiles around here."

"I'm glad you're talking about them. I still feel that this River has crocodiles."

"All right. Just for precaution, let us move as close to the precipice as possible. We shouldn't sleep so we can hear any animal that might try to attack us. Hold the paddle in your hands and use it as a weapon, if necessary!"

"That is a good suggestion, mother. I'm now moving towards the cliff."

"I'm doing the same, son." ...

"Should we spend the whole night watching for crocodiles, mother?"

"Only until early dawn when some light will allow us to see our way around. Then, we'll climb to the top of the cliff."

"Mother, I'm sorry! I'm suddenly feeling really tired. Do you mind if I sleep for a few minutes? After an hour, wake me up and I'll do the guarding, while you also sleep."

"Do that, son. Go to sleep. I'll wake you up in an hour or so."

Taling never awakened Junior until about six in the morning. She thought the boy needed his sleep more than she did.

Junior looked down to check their canoe, which was still tied up to its moorings. He looked around and checked their surroundings. Then, he saw the muddy, crude steps that the farmers used to climb the precipice.

"Mother, let us walk up those steps and *uh* ... find out where we are."

"Sure, son. Let us do that. Those steps look very primitive but interesting."

"They also look very slippery! Can you imagine us climbing these steps in the dark?"

"It is difficult to imagine."

"That is not only difficult, it is impossible to do. By the way, *uh* ... why didn't you wake me up during the night?"

"That is all right, son. I wanted you to rest; you did a lot of work yesterday."

"But, you worked as hard as I did. You should have *uh* ... awakened me, so you could also rest."

"Son, I'll make up for the lost sleep in the next few days. Don't be worried about me."

"Mother, we are now reaching the top of the precipice. Just two or three more steps. ...

"Wow! It is so beautiful up here! Look at that scenery! Look at that uh ... deep canyon, which cradles the River! ..."

"You're right, Jun. It is very beautiful and refreshing up here. Let us see what we find. ... There is a house over there, son. That has to be the farmhouse."

"Yes, mother. But, I don't see anyone moving or doing anything."

"Just the same, let us check the house and see what we find. But, before we do that, go down to the canoe and pick up a basket of cooked crabs. Let us offer it as a gift."

"Yes, mother. I'll do that."

They knocked at the door but nobody answered. Still, it was obvious that people lived there. There were chickens running around and some pigs were roaming under the house.

They walked on the rice paddies and saw rice stalks bending and nodding in the wind. The rice crops were ripe for harvesting.

Suddenly, they heard a man's voice calling, "Pedring! Bring one *carabao* over here. I'll start plowing da field right now. Pedring! Do ya hear me?"

"Yes, *tatay*! I'll bring da *carabao* immediately."

A Filipino farmer uses a water buffalo for plowing

As was customary among the Filipino farmers, the family had awakened at dawn or earlier. They worked in the fields before the sun became unbearably hot. It was only few minutes after seven o'clock but they had already worked for an hour weeding the fields and harvesting some rice.

Taling and Junior walked towards the source of the voices to introduce themselves to the farmers.

"Senior, my name is Catalina Lopez and my son is Junior. Just call me Taling and call my son, Jun.

"We came from Punta Oeste at the seashore. We're here to barter some of our sea foods for rice and corn."

"Taling and Jun, welcome to our humble barrio. Ma name is Jose Custodio. Ma son is Pedro. Just call me Pepe."

"Call me Pedring," the boy said.

"Let me ask ya a question, Taling. How did ya arrive here so early?" Jose asked.

"We actually arrived last night but we didn't know where we were. We spent the night near our boat on a low embankment on the bank of the River. We waited until morning to climb the precipice. Then, we went to your farmhouse but found no one there."

"Did ya sleep at all last night, Taling?" Jose asked. "Da reason why ah asked is because ya look sleepy and tired."

"Jun had a good sleep; but I didn't sleep at all."

"Dat was a shame when our comfortable house was so close by. But, ah understand. Besides, ya can't really climb da cliff in da dark."

"That is true. It is impossible to climb it at night."

"Why couldn't ya sleep, Taling? Was something bothering ya? Were ya afraid of da crocodiles?"

"Yes! I was definitely afraid of crocodiles! Are there crocodiles in this River, Pepe?"

"Sorry to tell ya, yes! We have some. It is hard to say how many of dem live around here. Ah guess dat dere are at least four or five. Dey move around where the food is more plentiful. Dey migrate depending on da seasons."

"Jun was right. He thought there were predatory animals in this River. Have they attacked your work animals, Pepe?"

"Unfortunately, yes. Sometimes, our *carabaos* break deir rope dat we use as leashes. Den, dey go down to da River to cool off. We have lost some of our work animals dis way."

"Now that I know that there are definitely crocodiles here, I'll be more scared of them," Taling remarked.

"You have a good reason to be afraid, Taling. Dose reptiles have attacked and killed people. So, continue to be very careful!"

"Pedring, go and ask yar moder *um* ... to come home and cook breakfast for all of us. Tell her dat we have visitors from Punta Oeste."

"Yes, father. I'll walk over to get her and Mila."

After Pedro had left, Jose explained, "My wife, Magdalena, and my daughter, Milagros, are *um* ... planting bean seeds. Dey started da new vegetable patch only last week. Dey are also weeding it. Dey will be home in a few minutes.

"Taling and Jun, *um* ... walk with me to our home. Ma wife and daughter will be home in a little bit. We don't eat breakfast until about *um* ... eight or nine o'clock. Dis is our first break from work."

"When do you start working?" Junior asked.

"Pedring takes out our *carabaos* to graze at *um* ... around four o'clock. By daybreak, we use da *carabaos* to plow the fields or *um* ... whatever we need to do for da season."

"Does Pedring do that everyday?" Taling asked.

"Yes. Unless, ... he's not feeling well. Den, Mila or ah *um* ... take out da *carabaos* to pasture."

"Pardon my ignorance, Pepe. I don't know too much about farming," Taling interrupted. "Why do you work so early? Couldn't you wait later in the morning to take the *carabaos* to graze on grass?"

"No, Taling. If we waited until later *um* ... to make da animals graze, den *um* ... we put dem to work when da sun is already hot. Da animals will be thirsty in less dan thirty minutes. Dey will be *um* ... frothing in deir mouths like mad dogs.

"We have to stop working and *um* ... give dem water to drink. If we don't do dat, dey start to pant and simply refuse to work.

"However, if we take dem to pasture early, we also start to work early. Den, *um* ... dey can work for two hours straight, without resting."

"That is interesting to know," Junior observed. "I didn't know *uh* ... you work that early."

"Pardon my curiosity also, Taling. Ah noticed dat *um* ... ya don't speak our Aklanon dialect. However, ya speak Ilongo with a *um* ... Capiz accent. Where are ya from before da war broke out?"

"We're from Mambusao, which is south of Capiz City."

"Ah know where Mambusao is, Taling. Ah have some nephews and nieces who *um* ... went to work in Mambusao during harvest seasons. Yar town is known here as a rich community."

"Maybe it was, Pepe. Now, most of the land is not being cultivated because of fear of the *Japons*. They burnt down our town and we have been hiding from them since then."

"Taling, ya have come a long way. How did ya find *um* ...yar way to Punta Oeste from Mambusao?"

"Pepe, that is a long story. Let me just say that we evacuated to Ibizan, which is south of Capiz City, until the *Japons* raided the village. Then, we sailed from Ibizan to Punta Oeste because my sister-in-law was born there."

"Now, ah understand why ya and Jun *um* ... don't know too much about farming. Ah suspected dat *um* ... ya folks must be landowners from some town in Capiz."

"You're right, Pepe. We're landowners but we're only small landlords."

"Dat is where we differ as landowners, Taling. Ah also own and *um* ... work da land maself with my small family. Whereas, ya only owned da land but *um* ... ya had tenants who worked for ya."

"That is a correct description, Pepe. We did have tenants who now virtually own our lands since they keep all the proceeds of their farming."

"Ah suppose so; at least for da duration of da war."

After his wife and daughter arrived, Jose introduced them saying, "Taling, may ah introduce to ya ma wife, Magdalena, and daughter, Milagros."

"I have already heard about both of you from Pepe. Just call me Taling and my son is Jun."

"Just call me Magda and call my daughter, Mila."

Taling felt that it was time to explain again the purpose of her unexpected visit to the farm.

"Pepe and Magda, for the sake of my family and relatives, I want to barter our seafood for your rice, corn, fruits and vegetables. I have never done this before. So, I really don't know what is a fair exchange."

"Taling, we had done dis many times before," Jose said. "But *um* ... we did it only with our relatives from da shore. We want ya to *um* ... keep coming back here to barter with us. We also need yar kind of food. So, *um* ... we'll be as fair to ya as we can."

"More dan dat," interrupted Magda. "Because ya had miraculously found us, we now regard ya as members of our family. Ya came with a *banca* full of seafood. So, we will send ya home with a *banca* full of rice, corn and whatever ya can load."

"That is so generous of both of you, Pepe and Magda. We are so thankful for your hospitality and generosity."

"We are also inviting ya *um* ... to harvest rice, corn and whatever fruits and vegetables dat ya like," added Jose. "Whatever ya harvest is yars. So, spend da rest of da day *um* ... harvesting whatever ya like. Den, after supper tonight, *um* ... ya can return to da shore with yar food."

"I would like to harvest some mangoes, *nanka*, guavas, *ates* and *cacao*," Junior requested.

The Child Daredevil Hero

"Yes, Jun, ya can have whatever ya can harvest," Jose offered. "Everything ya bring down from any tree ya climb is yars!"

"Thank you so much, Tia Magda and Tio Pepe," Junior said.

After supper, Taling and Junior were ready to leave for the shore.

Jose said effusively, "Remember Taling, *um* ... ya can come back any day ya need more food supplies. Make sure ya remember *um* ... da *balite* tree as yar landmark to find our farm."

"Thank you again for your hospitality and generosity. Jun and I will return next week and for many other weeks during the war."

"Please, feel free to come back as often as ya want," Magda said. "Remember da big *balite* tree as yar marker."

"Yes, next week we'll come back," Taling explained. "We will continue to sleep at the river embankment even though we are open to crocodile attacks. We'll see you after waking up the next morning. Then, we will harvest whatever we can. And, like tonight, we will return to the shore after supper."

"Taling, it's too bad dat ya can't come up and sleep with us," Jose said. "But ah understand dat ya must sleep at da lower bank of da River. Da cliff is impossible to climb at night."

"I won't forget the *uh* ... *balite* tree as my guide," added Junior. "For me, I can never thank you enough!"

With joyful hearts, Taling and Junior paddled their canoe with the help of the strong down stream current. High spirited and jubilant, they paddled with confidence.

Soon, they were approaching the town of Makato. They didn't use their paddles as they approached the town. After they had passed the center of Makato, they felt relieved that they had made it safely thus far.

They were very eager to reach home and paddled even faster. Even though they were traveling in the dark, they seemed to travel three or four times faster than when they were paddling against the current. Somehow, the River was familiar and they were navigating instinctively.

They made sure they avoided the whirlpools by staying away from the river walls that manufactured them. Junior developed a safety policy of navigating only where the current was straight. This policy made them avoid the whirlpools!

The rapids, however, presented a very serious problem! To have a good control of the boat, Junior thought of tying two ropes from the stern of the canoe. He and his mother could walk on the opposite banks of the River and control the speed of the craft by pulling the ropes.

However, the rapids tempted him to ride them and experience a cruising speed he had never known before. Because of the great risk involved in navigating through the rapids, he conferred with his mother.

"Mother, we are about to hit the first rapids. In order to arrive home sooner, *uh* ... I'm tempted to just ride the current, however fast it might be. I feel *uh* ... I can control the canoe even at a very high speed. What do you think?"

"That sounds very scary to me! In a way, it will be the simplest solution to the problem of dealing with the rapids. However, if the canoe capsizes, we will lose all the food that we worked so hard to obtain. Our family really needs everything we are carrying.

"Son, we have no experience in steering a canoe through the rapids. Maybe we can ride the rapids later on, after we have some experience dealing with it."

"So, what is your suggestion?"

"I suggest that you tie a rope to the stern and you control the speed from the embankment of the River. I'll stay in the boat and paddle upstream by facing the stern. Both of our actions should slow down the speed of the boat. What do you think of my suggestion?"

"Mother, I agree with it wholeheartedly. You're right. We can't afford to *uh* ... lose our valuable cargo. Let us do exactly as you suggested."

The maneuver through the first rapids was barely successful. There were times when Junior had to use every ounce of his energy to slow down the canoe. Several times, he felt tempted to let the boat go. If he held his ground, the canoe might drag him through the embankment and get seriously hurt!

However, he decided that letting go of the canoe was not an option. He couldn't leave his mother alone in the boat. And, there was no way he could catch up with a runaway boat in the rapids! There was danger that they might be separated!

He thought of a second option in case he lost control of the canoe. He intended to jump into the water with the rope and try to board the canoe. This move would keep both of them together. And, hopefully both of them might control the boat by using their paddles.

Fortunately, the first option succeeded! They were able to slow down the canoe as his mother had suggested.

He could only guess what might have happened if he had jumped into the water and swam to board the canoe. His guess was that the canoe might move faster than he could swim and drag him down the treacherous rapids. It was also possible that he might not be able to hold on to the rope. If that had happened, mother and son might have been separated.

With such adverse possibilities, he was so grateful to survive that obstacle!

When they hit the next rapids, Junior insisted that he tie two ropes to the stern and both controlled the canoe from the land. He figured out that they could use shrubs, bushes and rocks to slow down the boat. This technique was more successful!

Inexplicably, there was a little bit of moonlight when they passed the dreaded whirlpools. They were able to choose the safer pathways and escaped disaster! Junior wondered what it would be like to travel in complete darkness. He shuddered at the thought!

They arrived home about an hour after midnight. Badong and the older children were still awake, waiting for them. They were surprised but happy to see them return.

Badong was beside himself with joy! He bragged, "I knew you could do it! I'm very proud of both of you! Welcome home! You returned sooner than I thought."

He hugged both of them and wouldn't let go for what seemed like at least two minutes. He started to cry with joy! Then, he grinned from ear to ear like a little boy!

As dictated by their custom, everyone approached Taling and kissed her forehead and hugged her. Junior, however, got only a hug from each one. It was enough. Everyone in the family gazed at them admiringly like they were returning heroes!

Everybody was very happy because they had food to eat finally and because the adventurous food hunters came home safely.

Badong waited patiently until everyone had expressed his or her greetings. He had something important to say to the family.

"Listen, everyone! This event is extremely important; it marks the turning point of our *starvation crisis*! For weeks now, I've endured hunger and feared that it might be with us for a long time. I was even afraid that the famine might claim the lives of some of us!

"Well, your mother and brother have saved us from starvation! They are our real heroes; they saved us from famine! Tonight, I'm saying goodbye to famine and hunger! We have enough food to eat. Let's have a feast right now!"

"Bravo!" yelled Mabini and Paterno.

"Jose, go to Paing's house," Badong instructed his male servant. "Go and invite everyone to the party. I know it's late and he'll think I'm crazy. Tonight is special and very important. Let's celebrate! I'll explain everything to our neighbors tomorrow."

Everyone ate whatever appealed to him or her. They had not eaten this way for quite a while. Everyone was relieved and happy to eat contentedly!

Eight-year-old Leona said, "I was afraid! I cried *uh* every time I think you might not *uh* come home!"

She cried with joy and ran to hug her mother.

"We're so happy to see you home safely!" Badong said, still grinning from ear to ear. "And we're happy to be a whole family again!"

Taling picked up the little ones, Juliet and Diadema, who felt more secure in her arms!

Chapter Twenty Seven
The Vicissitudes of Food Hunting

The success of the first mission encouraged Junior to repeat the dangerous ordeal with much less hesitation. Still, he knew that each trip would be a life or death situation! Night travel would continue to be nightmarish!

The whirlpools could swallow their tiny canoe and dash them to the bottom of the river. The rapids could smash their canoe against the ubiquitous rock islands. The crocodiles could attack and turn them into a meal. The Japanese soldiers could arrest and use them for target practice, as they had done to some other civilians!

He and his mother had devised a successful way of eluding their potential captors. He felt a bit more familiar with the layout of the land. He had figured out how to neutralize the awesome powers of the whirlpools and the rapids! They had already established a bartering account with the Custodio family. And, they had established landmarks to find their way to the farm even at night.

However, he was still angry with his father for not getting a relief for his mother. He was still resentful of the teenagers for not volunteering to relieve her. He couldn't understand why they would allow their own mother to risk her life. She was essential for the survival especially of the younger children!

They followed a simple routine. Taling decided when to go back to the Custodio farm. Her decision depended on the amount of food supplies left in the house. It also depended on some special occasions like holidays and birthdays.

On average, they made the trip about once a week. However, there were times when they went to barter food about three or four times in two weeks.

Taling sent her younger sons, Trinidad and Ruperto, to the swamp cabin to replace Junior. Then, the older boy rode the canoe back to the village where he spent the night. The next day, around eight, they left for their dangerous journey!

After a while, the dangerous trips became just weekly routines. The inherent risks, however, didn't change. They could possibly encounter the soldiers if they were at the River bathing, fishing, guarding or for whatever reason. They could possibly get caught in a crossfire between the Japanese and the guerrillas. The possibilities of getting caught by the Japanese or the Constabulary were difficult to estimate.

They didn't know enough regarding the whereabouts of the Japanese soldiers and the pattern of their movements. They merely assumed that the Japanese didn't patrol during the night. But, a sudden change of Japanese policies could change their routines and their fate! They could station guards along the River and arrest them when they went out to obtain food supplies!

The Japanese could even close off the Rivers and prevent every access to the farms! Japanese sentries could shoot and kill them any time! The family wouldn't even know what had happened to them.

They were working on uneducated guess work and blind luck. Working with unknown parameters only aggravated their fears!

To Junior, however, the Japanese soldiers were not his primary concern. His greatest fear was traveling at night, especially on their return to the shore! There were nights when they were navigating in almost total darkness! Junior didn't have any light to help his navigation. He didn't even know that flashlights existed. What his parents used for lighting at home were torches fueled by coconut oil. Carrying a torch in the canoe would have called the attention of the Japanese guards!

They had to return home at night in order to elude the Japanese soldiers. And, traveling in the dark was always a nightmare! Several times, they had to tie their canoe to a bush while waiting for early dawn to light their way. Every delay in their arrival always caused concern and worry on the part of Badong and his children! There was always a possibility that they were late because the Japanese had killed them!

The greatest nightmare they had ever experienced was trying to climb the slippery steps of the precipice upon arriving at the Custodio farm. Because of their fear of crocodile attack, they tried to climb the precipice on their third visit to the farm. After they had climbed about twenty steps, Taling said, "Jun, we must give up this attempt to climb in the dark! We can fall and get seriously injured or worse!"

Jose Custodio had left a lighted torch at the rim of the precipice. The torch, however, was too far to light the lower steps. So, they decided, as matter of policy, to spend the night at the low embankment on the riverbank. This decision, however, made them vulnerable to hungry crocodiles!

Their weekly departures continued to be highly emotional! They might not be lucky this time around. Still, the departures were less intense than the first time. To the little children, however, every departure was final! They cried as if they would never see their mother again!

Junior's fear became somewhat repressed too, except during the days when they were actually carrying out their dangerous task. He could feel himself getting tense even before they left the shore. And, the fear increased as they approached the occupied territories! The fear level remained high until after they had passed the occupied areas, on their way home.

He didn't relax completely until he was back safely in his swamp society.

Every trip was, in fact, unique because of the various circumstances and obstacles they had to overcome. The worst obstacles were the *rains* and the *floods*. The inundation directly affected the size and ferocity of the whirlpools and the velocity of the rapids!

Every time it rained, they faced sudden changes in the water level. Mentally, Junior measured the amount and duration of every rain. If it rained for more than two hours, he became apprehensive about the possibility of a sudden flood coming down from the mountains!

When the rains came while they were still at the shore area, they could easily tell the effects of the rain by checking the Rivers. If the water elevation was much higher than normal and the velocity of the water current was impossible to handle, they had to stay at home until the water level had returned to *normal.*

Junior quickly learned, however, that "normal" had a relative meaning. When the food shortage was acute, the meaning of normal could include minor flooding. There were times when they ventured in search of food even though the Rivers were still dangerously flooded. As long as they could gain a headway against the current, it was business as usual!

Every time the rain caught them while in transit, there was always some degree of flooding. Sometimes, the tropical rains poured down vast amounts of liquid like one would see in waterfalls! There were times when they watched in horror as the River rose and swelled before their eyes!

When the color of the water became suddenly muddy, they stopped and searched for a haven to tie up in safety! They knew that severe flooding would occur within minutes!

The first time they encountered a real flood while in transit, they almost lost their lives! They kept paddling in the rain, completely unaware that a two-foot-wall of water was rolling down from the mountains! When they saw the wall coming down, there was no time to get out of its way!

The liquid wall submerged the boat and knocked them off their seats! The canoe completely disappeared and was never seen again! The flood and the ferocious whirlpools must have broken it into pieces. They swam to the nearest bank for safety!

A hospitable family provided them food and lodging for three days. When the river became navigable, the family lent them a canoe so they could return home to the shore.

After buying enough seafood for the next trip, they towed the borrowed boat and returned it to their Samaritan owners. It was filled with seafood. They felt lucky to have survived the *tsunami*!

Every time they were stranded, they sought shelter and lodging wherever they could find them. Very often, they found some families willing to provide them with food and lodging. After the flood subsided, they negotiated a limited food exchange with their hosts and returned to the shore to replenish their cargo.

Unfortunately, there were times when they found themselves in a "no man's land." Those were the cases when they were stranded in Japanese-occupied territories or very close to them.

When they were stranded near the occupied territories, they were vulnerable to the Japanese soldiers! They made sure that they hid their canoe in the vegetation. Then, they crawled on the ground to prevent detection!

However, what they dreaded the most was being stranded in areas actually occupied by the Japanese soldiers. Taling said to her son, "Jun, let us make the policy of moving on through the Japanese-occupied areas. We have to keep moving even though a flood might be raging!"

"But, mother, that could *uh* ... lead us to disaster!"

"Perhaps. But, I'd rather die in the flood than *uh* ... in the hands of the *Japons*!"

"What should we do to *uh* ... make sure we will not be stranded in the Japanese occupied territories?"

"Either we turn around and go home or stop where some Filipinos can give us shelter."

"Yes, mother. I think we should do that."

In spite of this policy and strong determination to keep a safe distance from the Japanese, there were times, when a destructive flood caught them in a "no man's land," while in transit. The flood level was too dangerous to keep going on! They had to tie up the boat anywhere they could find a tree or a bush near the River!

To make the situation even worse, they had to wait for the flood to crest and waited even longer for the flood to subside. The waiting could take several days. One time, they waited patiently for ten days!

They spent their days on their stomachs or their backs to maintain a low profile. They were frozen in fear of being seen by the enemy!

They ate the uncooked food they carried with them. By the time the flood had returned to normal, they had no more food to barter. They returned home to reload their canoe for bartering.

At another time, they had waited for seven days and ran out of food and water. Taling insisted not to eat the food in the canoe but to scavenge for whatever seemed edible. In their hunger, they ran the risk of eating something poisonous.

Mushrooms were especially tempting because they were delicious and were all over the grounds. Unfortunately, they had never learned how to identify the edible ones properly. For safety, they resisted the temptation even when they were very hungry!

Junior narrated an incident when the flood had lasted for five days.

"We were hiding from the *Japons* because *uh* ... the occupied area was only a kilometer away. We hunched our backs and hiked by bending low for over a kilometer *uh* ... before we found an abandoned house.

"The house was manually locked, using wooden crossbars. I managed to unlock the door and crossed the threshold. Right after I had stepped in, a large stone that weighed thousands of kilos fell just behind me! I was sure the crude device was positioned to kill or maim any intruder! I couldn't figure out why the stone missed me.

"We slept on the bare floor made out of strips of bamboos. The flooring strips had been nailed down about half an inch apart for floor ventilation and cooling. The wind blew in through the floor and the rickety walls. It was cold during the night and we had nothing to keep us warm.

"There was no food to eat or water to drink. We had food in the canoe but *uh* ... we didn't eat it because it was set aside for bartering with the farmers.

"Using a small machete, I cut down some banana trees and *uh* ... opened their trunk to get to the pith of the plant. The moisture in the banana stalk *uh* ... quenched our thirst but we felt hungry all the time. There was *uh* ... little or no nutrition in what we were eating.

"We ate *uh* ... very young green bananas, which had no taste. We also ate the heart of the banana stalk, which contained the immature banana flowers and seeds that didn't turn into fruits. The reddish heart-shaped appendage was edible if cooked; but we had no cooking facilities. We ate it just the same. It tasted bitter and *uh* ... difficult to digest. I had diarrhea for days.

"We kept checking the River for the flood level and drank the *uh* ... polluted River water. The dirty water just aggravated my upset stomach.

Sal Kapunan

"After four days, when the water level was almost normal, we *uh* ... decided to float back to the shore. We aborted our journey because *uh* ... we were too sick to resume our trip to the farm!"

The rainy season, which lasted for about six months, presented many difficult situations. The Rivers flooded almost every week. Still, they navigated the *Rio Este* even though the water level was slightly elevated. Crossing and surviving the whirlpools became major achievements! During a flood, there were no small or baby whirlpools!

In some cases, Taling ordered Junior to wait for a few hours or even a whole day before they attempted to paddle through the spinning and whirling waters!

In a couple of cases, while returning to the shore in the dark, a whirlpool caused the canoe to capsize! They lost the canoe and their cargo. They were lucky to survive what could have been a fatal catastrophe! A nice family gave them shelter and food. Their hosts also lent them an old canoe so they could return home to the shore.

After such mishaps, they returned to procure food after only one or two days to minimize starvation. There was never enough food to eat during the rainy season!

The rapids too became serious problems during the rainy days. Any added rainwater in the River increased the velocity of the rapids.

One time, they under estimated the force of the rapids. The current velocity was so extreme that they had to let their boat go; or else it would drag them down the River!

Instinctively, they yelled for help and two strong young men came down to intercept the runaway boat. The men kept running along the bank of the River until they reached the area where the river current was slower. After they were ahead of the boat, they ran down the precipice and swam and caught up with the canoe. They brought it back to the hysterical mother and son team! The men also helped them pull the *banca* through the rapids!

But, their most dreaded nemeses were the crocodiles! During the day, Junior watched the crocodiles from a distance, while the giant reptiles were sunning on the lower embankment of the River. They were cold-blooded animals and needed the sun to raise their body temperatures. While sunning, they kept their mouths open to attract the flies. Every now and then, they'd suddenly close their mouths to trap the insects. They made loud scary noise because of the echo generated by the cliffs! The clamping sound and the mere sight of them sent shivers down his spine!

As the canoe moved closer to the animals, they always jumped into the water. Junior thought that they were positioning themselves to intercept and attack the small vessel! The crocodiles were larger and longer than the canoe they were navigating. It was always a scary experience while expecting the attack! For the next ten or fifteen minutes, Junior was always in a state of terror!

One night, while they were looking for the *balite* tree as their landmark to the Custodio farm, they became completely disoriented in the heavy rain! After going back and forth for three or four times and still not finding their guidepost, they decided to tie up at the nearest embankment.

Taling said, "Let us settle here and wait until daybreak to find our destination. This rain is just pouring and I hope that the flood doesn't come up to where we stand. Let us monitor the rising water for our safety. If the flood rises to where we are, we have to tie up the canoe to a shrub at a higher level."

"Yes, mother. That is a good idea."

"After you have tied up the boat, you might consider going to sleep even in the rain."

"How about you? Will you try to go to sleep also?"

"I don't think so. I can't sleep under these conditions. Besides, I'm scared of the crocodiles! I'll stay awake and guard our safety."

"Please, wake me up after *uh* ... two or three hours and I'll relieve you."

"Go ahead, son. Sleep! I'll wake you up later."

"Goodnight, mother."

Sometime during the night, Taling yelled for help and awakened Junior.

"Help me, son! A crocodile has bitten my right thigh! It is dragging me to the water! Hurry! Help me! *Aroy! Aroy!*"

"I will, mother! Fight it off! Hit it with your paddle!"

"I can't! I don't know where it is!"

In the dark, Junior groped for the head of the monster. He hit it hard with both fists but the beast wouldn't let go of her limb. He tried to pry the mouth open. But, he wasn't strong enough to make any difference.

Then, he thought of hitting its eyes. Pounding them made the animal grunt and raise its head, causing Taling to yell in extreme pain, "*Aroy! Aroy!*"

Junior realized that the animal was not comfortable with what he was doing to its eyes. So, he stuck his five fingers into an eye and tried to gouge it out. The animal reacted even more violently and tightened its jaws! It forced Taling to yell in greater pain!

So, Junior used all the fingers of both hands to poke into the crocodile's eyes. He kept pushing his fingers deeper into the sockets and tried to gouge them out!

Suddenly, the animal tossed the boy into the air with its snout, as it let go of Taling's limb! He finally saved his mother from a certain death!

In the dark, Taling used her skirt as a bandage to stop the bleeding. After the fabric became saturated with blood, Junior used his under shirt as a bandage. He washed the skirt in the River and spread it on the grass to dry. He kept alternating the bandages until the blood stopped flowing.

Early in the morning, Junior examined his mother's wounds. She had about twenty five punctured wounds on the top and bottom of her right thigh. Four of the wounds were very deep and wide; they were punctured by the incisor front teeth. He loaded her in the *banca* and looked for the Custodio farm. They were only less than two kilometers away.

He ran up the steps of the cliff and informed the Custodios of the attack. Magda brought some homemade ointments and clean bandages. She washed, treated and bandaged the wounds.

She said, "Taling, you're very lucky to have survived da attack. Da wounds are deep because dey are da marks of da crocodile's front teeth. But, dey will heal quite quickly. Try not to use yar legs until da wounds have healed."

Jose Custodio said, "Taling, I'm very sorry for da crocodile attack. Pedring and ah will *um* ... carry ya to our house. Rest for a few days or *um* ... until ya're healed."

"Pepe, I can't stay here for more than a day," she protested. "My husband and family will be very worried!"

"Yes, of course!" Jose said. "Da fact is *um* ... dat ya had been attacked by a large crocodile. Ya need to recover from yar wounds. When dey find out dat *um* ... ya're well, dey'll be happy for ya."

"Dat is right, Taling," Magda agreed. "Ya need to rest and recover! It's too bad dat we have no way to communicate with yar family right now. But, I agree, dey'll be happy when dey find out dat ya're alive and well."

"How long do you think should I stay here?" Taling asked.

"Give yarself at least a week," Jose said. "We want to clean da wounds *um* ... every day and make sure no infection develops. If dere is no infection, *um* ... ya'll start healing almost immediately."

"What will I do for a whole week?" Junior asked.

"Ya harvest rice and all yar favorite fruits," Mila answered. "Ah'll even help ya."

"Thank you Mila. But, if it is all right with you, *nanay*, uh ... I'll return to the shore so our family will have the food. Also, that way, *uh* ...they'll know that you're all right."

"I like your suggestion, Junior. Go ahead and return to the shore. Tell everyone I'm doing well and I'll be home soon."

"When should I come back to pick you up, *nanay*?"

"Why don't ya come back in a week and bring us more of da delicious crabs and shrimps," Magda suggested. "I'll take good care of yar *nanay*. By dat time, she might be ready to ride home with ya."

"Magda is right, Jun. Come back in a week."

After two weeks, Taling was still hurting but her wounds had started to heal. The Custodios helped load the *banca*. With the help of Jose and Pedro, Taling managed to walk slowly to the bank of the river. But, Juan and Pedro carried her down the steps of the cliff and loaded her in the *banca*.

Junior paddled carefully and made sure his mother was comfortable. She didn't do any paddling but her spirits were high! She was on her way home!

When they arrived, the family was delirious in their welcome! They had been terribly worried about her safety and health!

"I'm so sorry for what you went through, Taling," Badong said. "But knowing that you had survived what could have been a fatal attack is beyond words! Once again, I'm thankful to Jun for saving his mother's life! What he did was heroic and extraordinary! He looked for the vulnerable part of the crocodile, which were the eyes. How he figured that out was unbelievable! If he didn't do what he did, Taling might not be with us today!"

"Jun, let me take this opportunity to thank you for saving my life! You're truly my hero!"

Everyone cried as an open expression of their feelings of gratitude and happiness!

They endured these terrifying ordeals for almost three years. Junior suspected that each trip extracted a certain amount of physical and psychological toll on them. He suspected that the pains and sufferings they had incurred might shorten their lives! But, he was glad that they were still alive!

His simple hope, for the moment, was to survive the perilous journeys and to recover completely from the traumas after the war was over!

Chapter Twenty Eight
The Liberation of Manila

In February 1942, General Douglas MacArthur and his beleaguered troupes were taking their last stand against the Japanese in the Bataan peninsula and the tiny island of Corregidor in Manila Bay.

Insufficient food and malaria weakened the Bataan and Corregidor defenders. Every allied soldier was sick of malaria and other illnesses. The Japanese attack was relentless and the defense appeared doom to fall! It was just a matter of time!

The Washington administration ordered MacArthur to abandon his command in the Philippines and escape to Australia. Before leaving the Philippines, the press had quoted him for saying, "I shall return!" The general's parting words became the guerrilla mantra of resistance and patriotism!

In 1944, MacArthur was finally poised to fulfill his promise to return. However, the US Navy didn't share his enthusiasm to liberate the Philippines. To Admiral Chester Nimitz, the Philippines was strategically irrelevant! Nimitz's plan of action from the South Pacific was to leapfrog over the Philippines into Taiwan, which would place the allies only three hundred miles from their bull's eye: Tokyo!

When MacArthur learned of the Navy strategy, he was appalled and warned President Roosevelt that ignoring the archipelago would incur the open hostility of the Filipinos and damage the American image in Asia.

To pacify MacArthur, Roosevelt called a meeting between Nimitz, MacArthur and the President in Hawaii in July 1944. MacArthur put tremendous importance to the meeting. Roosevelt, on the other hand, used the occasion for political propaganda. He had just been nominated for the unprecedented fourth term by the Democratic Party. The General realized that he was just part of a political picture-taking junket.

In a private meeting with the President, MacArthur won a minor concession of a limited action in the Philippines by landing in Leyte and conquering the Capital. In exchange, MacArthur promised quick and dramatic results in his Philippine campaign!

On October 20, 1944 General MacArthur landed in Leyte and fulfilled his promise. The press photographed the General wading through the surf in Leyte. The photograph alone proved that he had fulfilled his promise.

General MacArthur landed in Leyte on October 20, 1944 with the new Philippine President Sergio Osmena. President Quezon died in New York in August 1944.

The allied forces immediately supplied the guerrillas with state of the art weapons and ammunitions. Many able bodied Filipinos who saw the imminent end of the war took the opportunity to become liberators of the Philippine Commonwealth and become war heroes. They joined the guerrilla groups in their own provinces.

Instead of occupying and defeating the Japanese forces in every island in the Philippines, General MacArthur used the 'leap-frogging technique,' which he and the US Navy had used in the South Pacific. The allied forces purposely bypassed thousands of islands in the Solomon and the Caroline Islands. In some cases, they bypassed some islands because the enemies were too well fortified. In other cases, they bypassed islands because there were only few Japanese soldiers to bother with. They selected only strategic islands.

MacArthur used the same leap-frogging technique in the Philippines. For example, he bypassed the big island of Mindanao and thousands of islands in the Visayan region because there were few Japanese soldiers in them.

He concentrated his forces primarily on the small island of Leyte, in order to land his forces in the Philippines. He could then formally claim that he had returned!

Then, he took a small swath of land through the big island of Luzon, on his way to liberate the Capital City of Manila.

In *Leyte*, the allies overwhelmed the 20,000 defenders with 200,000 troops and 700 crafts, warships and transports.

After only two months of fighting, he declared Leyte liberated on December 26, 1944. In fact, there were still many Japanese soldiers hiding in the hills. The General left the job of 'cleaning-up' to the Leyte guerrillas. Then, the allies quickly liberated small portions of the island of *Mindoro*. The primary purpose was to build airfields there for the liberation of Manila.

The Mindoro airfields would provide air cover for the allied forces as they marched from the Lingayen Gulf, in Pangasinan province, to Manila.

MacArthur expected General Tomoyuki Yamashita, the commander of Japanese forces in the Philippines, to put up a heavy defense at the Lingayen Gulf. To soften and prepare the landing of the allied forces, he sent a U.S. flotilla to pound the coastline before the forces landed.

As the US ships entered the Lingayen Gulf, swarms of *kamikaze* fighters attacked them from every direction. After a week of suicide bombings, the Japanese airforce ran out of planes and pilots. By then, however, the suicide bombers had destroyed twenty-four ships and damaged seventy.

When the allies landed in Lingayen Gulf on January 9, 1945, the Japanese resistance was no longer a factor. He landed with 300,000 troops and marched south to liberate Manila.

There was little opposition to the 'conquering horde' except in the hills near Clark Air Base, in Angeles, Pampanga. General Walter Krueger headed a ground force that engaged the defenders. After a week of fierce fighting, the allies routed the defenders.

Then, they marched south to Manila. There, Rear Admiral Sanji Iwabuchi, Japanese commander of the naval defense force, deployed about two-hundred thousand navy men on every street, in private homes, in historical landmarks like the Manila Hotel, the Philippine General Hospital and the walled city called Intramuros.

Iwabuchi issued a 'scorch earth policy' by burning everything, including docks, warehouses and port installations. Then, they embarked on an orgy of attrocities! They impaled babies on their bayonets, raped women, beheaded and mutilated corpses! They raided hospitals and strapped patients to their beds and set the buildings on fire!

The soldiers shielded themselves with thousands of captive Filipino civilians. The tactic was intended to slow down the advance of the allies to Japan.

The Child Daredevil Hero

In February 1945, MacArthur ordered his soldiers to search for the defenders from block to block, house to house, room to room, basement to basement and attic to attic. They had to physically hunt and kill the Japanese soldiers, who were hiding in basements and attics. The allies used flamethrowers and explosives. The flamethrowers literally glued the Japanese soldiers to the walls so that their charred corpses became part of the wallpaper!

Nevertheless, by March 1945, the allies had liberated the City of Manila. Unfortunately, they left the city in rubbles with a pervading stench of unburied corpses. The intense search for the Japanese defenders forced the conquering forces to destroy every building where the enemies were hiding. They left the City of Manila in total ruins with a dubious distinction of being "the most totally destroyed city, next only to Warsaw!"

The Manila campaign cost the Japanese two hundred thousand soldiers. At least one hundred thousand Filipino civilians lost their lives. Only eight thousand American soldiers died.

Some allied soldiers made some meaningless assaults of General Tomoyuki Yamashita's forces in northern Luzon. But, most of the allied forces went on to take Taiwan, Okinawa and Iwo Jima on their way north to invade the Japanese mainland.

General MacArthur left the *guerrillas* in charge of liberating the rest of the Philippine Islands. From his point of view, however, he had already liberated the Philippine Commonwealth.

By capturing Manila, the Capital, he had already decapitated the enemy; and, therefore, was already virtually dead! He believed that after the head had been severed, the body would necessarily follow. He knew that the term 'capital' came from the Latin *caput,* which literally meant *head.*

In fact, however, there were still at least 7000 islands to liberate from the Japanese. The General left to the guerrillas the tedious job of actually liberating every island.

In Panay Island, the guerrillas went to work as soon as they received weapons and ammunitions from the allies.

In the Makato region, where Junior lived, the guerrillas attacked the garrisons and ambushed the Japanese reinforcements, coming from Capiz City.

Large areas of the Rivers that the civilians used for navigating a canoe to obtain food became *battle zones.* The most active areas were those occupied and controlled by the Japanese. The guerrillas targeted their headquarters!

The last nine months of the war became hellish for Junior and his mother. They had to dodge the bullets every time they made their usual trip to procure food for their family.

Every week, they heard or actually witnessed the fighting. Unfortunately, their boat travels had to cross the battle zones.

Junior predicted that before long, they would find themselves in the line of fire and probably die! He and his mother had committed themselves to a weekly procurement of food to feed twenty-five refugees. They felt obligated to fulfill their missions, regardless of the escalation of hostilities especially from the Filipino and American guerrillas!

Chapter Twenty Nine
The Guerrilla Fighters

The guerrilla soldiers, in the Philippines, were the underground resistance fighters against the Japanese occupiers. Because they were in small groups of poorly armed fighters, they fought sporadically and only when they had the advantage. Their primary tactic was "ambush and run!" Their old guns and rifles had little or no ammunitions.

Throughout the war, they continually disrupted and weakened the Japanese forces. They ambushed, killed and maimed the enemy at every opportunity.

They developed a *special information arm* that collected war news from underground radio stations. They collated, printed and distributed the information to the other guerrillas and to some literate civilians.

Some guerrilla fighters were Filipino soldiers who refused to surrender and give up their arms. They fled to the hills and mountains and hid in the caves.

Some were American soldiers who had also chosen to fight rather than surrender. Some were escapees from the infamous Bataan death march.

Others were civilians who hated the invaders: ex-teachers, tradesmen, day laborers, communists and other heroic characters. The communists were numerous especially in the large island of Luzon. The group would serve as the core of the communist organization that would try to overthrow the Philippine government after the war.

In order to be more effective, Filipino ex-military officers organized the guerrillas into trained units. In areas where the Japanese were at a safe distance away, they drilled, held target practices and combat exercises.

Wherever possible, they wore simple uniforms. These trappings of the military legitimized their status as soldiers. They maintained a connection with the armed forces, to which they loosely belonged. It was important to them that the military headquarters of General MacArthur in Australia knew they existed as fighting units. Indeed, they were part of the allied forces. They received military benefits after the war.

Some guerrilla units were well organized. They succeeded in installing radio stations. They contacted the Southwest Pacific Headquarters of General MacArthur in Australia. MacArthur was able to send them military supplies through submarines that surfaced at night, at predetermined ports in Mindanao and the Visayan Islands. The submarines were also able to load and take away the wounded and the sick.

One of the best-organized groups was situated in the southern section of the island of Leyte. Col. Ruperto Kangleon, who had been a Philippine army officer, headed it. The unit included both Filipino and American guerrillas and had over 7000 members.

One of the American guerrilla heroes was David Richardson who became Kangleon's chief of staff. He became an expert in radio communication and kept MacArthur informed in Australia. In 1945, war correspondent Ira Wolfert wrote, 'American Guerrilla in the Philippines,' which portrayed Richardon as an extraordinary romantic adventurer and war hero. Hollywood made the book into a movie.

They cooperated with the civilian population. They installed a civil government that printed its own money. Each guerrilla soldier received a weekly salary.

Several times, a US submarine surfaced at night in the Gulf of Leyte. They unloaded various military supplies, weapons and ammunitions. As a result, the Leyte unit was the best armed of all the guerrilla forces.

The Leyte unit also had the best-trained people in radio communications. As mentioned earlier, Richardson provided MacArthur the pertinent information about the Japanese forces in Leyte. He described the types, sizes and numbers of destroyers, carriers, cruisers and planes. And, he informed the MacArthur headquarters where the Japanese armaments were stored.

Richardson also informed the General that there were only about 20,000 Japanese soldiers in the island. The American guerrilla found out that the enemy forces were deployed at around twenty kilometers from the coastal region. This was the newly modified Japanese strategy developed by General Yamashita to minimize losses along the coastal regions. This information was important! It made landing safer and easier for the allies.

The pertinent information provided by the guerrillas prepared the allied landing in Leyte. In truth, the guerrilla assistance was the reason why MacArthur chose to land in Leyte. The Philippine archipelago is composed of over 7000 islands. Theoretically, some other island could have been chosen for the landing.

MacArthur was simply looking for a seashore in the Philippines, where the photographers could take his pictures. He intended to wade through the surf. The photographs could then prove to his Filipino friends that, indeed, he returned as he had promised.

In fact, the original plan of MacArthur was to land in southern Mindanao. He was moving his forces from New Guinea, in the South

Pacific, to the Philippines. His forces would have to pass Mindanao before reaching Leyte.

He bypassed Mindanao, however, after the guerrilla soldiers there had informed him that there were only few Japanese soldiers stationed in that large island.

After the allied landing in Leyte, the number of guerrilla fighters throughout the islands swelled to over 500,000. The allies were only happy to provide them with modern firearms and ammunitions.

As the fighting in Makato will show, the reinforced guerrillas used their new armaments to attack the enemies. They tormented and systematically weakened the defenses of the Japanese forces. The guerrillas would, in fact, become the actual liberators of the Philippine Archipelago!

Understandably, the history books will continue to give the honor of liberator of the Philippines to General MacArthur and the allied forces. Strategically, they had set the course of liberation. They also provided the necessary arms and ammunitions.

General MacArthur would have been happy to finish his work of liberation if his bosses had allowed him. However, President Roosevelt deferred to to his joint chiefs to deploy the allied forces right at Japan's front steps.

In truth, MacArthur's retaking of Leyte and Manila was merely symbolic! It was a concession due to his personal ties to the Philippines.

In retrospect, Admiral Nimitz and the Navy were right! The liberation of the Philippines was not necessary to win the war. Still, even to the Filipinos who were not yet liberated, there was a 'psychological liberation' in knowing that small parts of the Archipelago had already been liberated! It was akin to seeing the light at the end of the tunnel. The people were telling themselves that being free from the Japanese occupation was just a matter of time.

Nevertheless, the work of the guerrilla forces to eradicate the Japanese from the islands was no less heroic! The guerrilla forces were the fighters who actually finished the work that the General had begun. The guerrilla soldiers were true heroes!

Chapter Thirty
Daredevils and Heroes

Once the guerrilla soldiers saw the probable defeat of the enemies, they became determined and aggressive! They were motivated to annihilate the invaders. They attacked them wherever and whenever they could.

This heightened guerrilla activities made Junior's and Taling's trips to the farm much more risky! Every time they left their cocoon at the shore, they could hear fighting on either side of the *Rio Este*. They heard the hostilities soon after they passed the swamp areas.

Fortunately, they had a natural margin of protection provided by the high rims of the canyon. Their canoe was, on average, about fifteen feet below the rim. As mentioned earlier, the riverbed was in a relatively deep canyon. The walls of the riverbanks were high precipices.

Because of this margin of protection, they carried out their regular weekly mission without too much concern. However, due to the escalation of the guerrilla fighting, they felt more vulnerable. Moreover, the riverbanks were not uniform in height. They were, in fact, more vulnerable in some areas, where the height of the river rim was much lower.

When they were navigating close to the town of Makato, there was a greater probability of getting in the line of battle. In the Japanese occupied area, the margin of protection by the rim was no more than eight feet.

When you subtract the height of the boat and the height of a seated canoer, the margin of protection went down to less than five feet. That margin was too scary even if one wore a helmet. Of course, the food hunters had no such protection and carried no weapons.

Every week that they cruised the *Rio Este*, their emotional state was getting worse! Junior's nerves were getting frayed and he suddenly contracted tension headaches!

Just listening to the shelling or seeing bullets whisk over their heads was nerve-racking! He knew that sooner or later, they would get caught in a real line of fire that would endanger their lives!

Strictly speaking, they had already been in crossfires! Fortunately, the canyon configuration of the River prevented any physical harm done to them. The psychological harm, however, was considerable!

Junior also knew that it was possible that fighting could take place while they were cruising through certain regions, where their heads could become shooting targets! The first ten kilometers after passing the swamp territory, the River rim was less than five feet high.

The first time Junior heard guerrilla activities in the town of Makato was around November 1944. The fighting was at a safe distance from them. It was somewhere at the right side of the River. The shots sounded far, at least fifteen kilometers away. Because of the distance of the hostilities, he hardly paid any attention to them. It was wartime and hostilities could be expected. At the time, he didn't even know that there were organized guerrilla forces.

In the month of December, however, the armed encounters seemed to escalate. And, the fighting seemed to be coming closer to *Rio Este*.

Junior wondered why the fighting occurred every week at about the same time. They arrived at the occupied area, close to the bridges, between four and five in the afternoon. They hid in a river alcove, while waiting for the cover of darkness. They resumed their travel in almost total darkness.

Since early January 1945, they could hear hostilities every time they arrived late in the afternoon. The hostilities, however, were still quite far from the River. He wondered whether the fighting occurred all day long every day. He also wondered whether the fighting actually started late in the afternoon.

He found it odd that hostilities would even go on late in the afternoon. After all, the fighting would have to stop when it was too dark to see the enemy.

Yet, he strongly suspected that there were hostilities that started late in the afternoon. Again, he wondered what the explanation might be.

On the other hand, he also suspected that the fighting late in the afternoon might be the tail end of the day's hostilities. This pattern didn't make sense to him bcause the guerrillas were too few and unequipt to engage the enemy for a full day. They were known to engage the enemy for only few minutes. Their favorite mode of operation was *ambush and run*!

In late January, the fighting had escalated even further. The hostilities had also moved closer to the town proper. Again, the skirmishes regularly occurred late in the afternoon. At least, they happened while Taling and Junior were approaching the occupied areas of Makato. Still, the fighting was limited to the outskirts of the town.

In mid-February, however, the skirmishes occurred within a kilometer on the right side of the River. Again, the fighting happened in the late afternoon. Suddenly, Junior saw a vague pattern in the hostilities that begged for some rational explanation!

He guessed that the guerrillas had developed a strange pattern of attack. Since they arrived at the war zone on foot, they got there by using the road system. Walking from their hiding places in the mountains and caves, they converged at the outskirts of the town. The meeting place happened to be at the right side of the River.

He guessed that as soon as there were enough fighters assembled for an attack, they moved covertly on foot towards the town. Their objective was to attack the Japanese barracks and garrisons, kill the defenders and destroy their armaments!

He guessed that the fighting at the outskirts of the town might be ambushes by the guerrillas. Or, the Japanese soldiers might be attacking the guerrillas at the outskirts of the town as they were arriving, as a defensive tactic. By attacking the guerrillas away from the barracks, they also prevented them from attacking the barracks and their military compound.

The guerrillas might have suffered severe casualties, in the beginning. But, they were increasing in numbers especially after the allies had liberated Leyte and Manila. They were getting state of the art weapons and ammunitions from the allied forces.

Week after week, the guerrilla activities hurt the Japanese. The native fighters and the American guerrillas continually pushed the Japanese soldiers back to their headquarters. The attackers were gradually forcing the occupiers to be defensive!

Junior formulated a *theory* of why the guerrillas tended to attack late in the afternoon. Because they had no vehicles, it took them a long time to mobilize their troops and armaments.

What really slowed them down and prevented them from launching earlier attacks were the quantity and the combined weight of their weapons and ammunitions.

They were still using primitive technology to harness and deploy their resources. For example, they were still using the lumbering *carabaos* (water buffaloes) to move their armaments and amunitions into offensive position. The water buffaloes slowly pulled the rickety carts that contained all their hardwares. That was indeed a very primitive and slow process!

In spite of their outdated technology, the guerrillas were determined to cripple the enemy. Every week, they pressed their noble cause and pushed the enemy back to Japan, if possible.

Junior could see and hear the new reinforcements they were getting from the allies. Their new supplies enabled them to physically force the Japanese back to their barracks. He sensed that the guerrillas were getting stronger every week!

The Child Daredevil Hero

The first time Junior felt that they were in mortal danger was in late February 1945. They were approaching the town proper late in the afternoon. Somehow, Junior expected gun shots to start any time because the guerrillas were moving closer and closer to town every week! He was surprised that nothing was actually happening.

That particular afternoon, he had a premonition that a catastrophic battle was about to occur! It was a matter of logical deduction, based on how the fighting was escalating. The guerrillas were no longer limiting their fighting strategy to ambush and run. They were numerous enough and armed enough to hold their ground. They had already reached the point of dictating the hostilities!

Of course, he dreaded being caught in a battle zone! But, just the expectation of a major confrontation suddenly made him tense! His paddling motions became shorter. His jaws became locked and his teeth and gums were aching from clamping them so tightly. His tension headache was worse than usual!

Fear felt like invisible insects crawling all over his skin, especially over his face, spine and at the back of his neck. He could feel his body hairs standing at attention, like porcupine quills warding off potential harm!

He was uncontrollably shaking because he was terribly afraid! His throat and mouth became very dry and his breathing became short and labored!

They were less than one kilometer and a half from the town of Makato. Finally, he heard occasional shots from afar. They had stopped navigating by holding on to the vegetation on the riverbank. They were waiting for darkness before resuming their trip.

Suddenly, however, the guerrillas lobbed four inch canon balls over their heads from the right side of the River. The firing went on for about ten minutes without any response from the Japanese.

The guerrillas seemed to be moving towards the bank of the River. The sound of the canon shots was getting progressively louder. As soon as they reached the bank, Junior could hear several types of rifles, bazookas, carbines, machine guns and other weapons firing!

They were using everything they had as a show of force! Junior doubted whether most of their shots did any damage. It seemed like the guerrillas were just eager to make a very loud noise! This was the closest perimeter that they had reached in their attempt to destroy the enemy!

Then, suddenly, four or five inch canon projectiles started flying from the left side of the River, which he assumed came from the Japanese weapons.

All kinds of firearms were firing from both sides of the River. The noise level was deafening!

Even though the riverbanks protected them, being in the firing line was very scary! They could see some stray bullets hitting the waters close to them.

Junior instinctively knew that they had to get out of the area! He allowed the boat to drift with the current. Then, he started to paddle down the River.

He looked at his mother and saw her curled in a fetal position! She was crying hysterically!

Junior was too numbed to cry or say anything. They had to abort the mission, even though they were just seven or eight kilometers away from their farm destination. They went home empty-handed!

Whenever they were short of food supplies, they had to take greater risks. They were going to die anyway if they didn't eat. In order to minimize their starvation, they made another trip to the farm two days later. Surprisingly, there was no fighting at all that day. Perhaps, the guerrillas had used up all their ammunitions. They couldn't attack again until they received new supplies from the allies.

In March, they literally ran out of food and they felt very desperate! Every time they made the trip, however, they could tell that the battles were escalating even more! The new battles were already taking place at the left side of the River.

This meant that the guerrillas were moving closer to the Japanese barracks. It also meant that the Japanese were becoming more defensive. Instead of engaging the guerrillas as they converged outside of town, they were waiting for them to attack in the town. The battles were getting fiercer!

The escalation of hostilities put their trips in greater danger! By the end of March, both Taling and Junior were reluctant to make the trips! But, no one else dared to take their places. Predictably, famine again returned with a vengeance!

The starving children cried for help! When the food procurers agreed to resume the dangerous trips, it was on the condition that the intervals between the trips be made longer, at least ten days apart. As a result, Badong had to ration off the available food to two meals a day. Then, he reduced it to only one a day. It was a slow starvation diet!

Meanwhile, Taling was going through a personal and psychological transformation! Faced with a serious food shortage, her conscience bothered her! She felt guilty and ashamed of her cowardly behavior the month before. And, the partial starvation of eating only one or two small meals a day bothered her terribly!

The younger kids became hard to control because of the pangs of hunger! They were crying almost all day long from hunger pains! She also cried with them! She couldn't bear to watch her children suffer!

After leaving for another food mission, Taling talked frankly in a manner that actually shocked Junior!

With uncommon seriousness, she said, "Listen son, I'm sorry for how I acted last month. I simply fell apart! I didn't expect the fighting to be so close to us. I wrongly thought that the *Japons* would retaliate immediately. I was sure that the Japanese rockets would hit us because we were close to the guerrilla location! Somehow, I thought that it was the end for us! Being caught in the line of fire was what I had dreaded for a long time!"

"It was true, *nanay*. We were in the line of fire!"

"Still, I think we should have waited a kilometer or so away. We could have waited until nighttime. We should have resumed our trip! That way, we could have obtained the necessary food!"

"It was true, *nanay*, that we could have waited until dark and resumed our trip. But, what happened *uh* ... was too scary to continue! Both of us panicked!"

"Indeed. We panicked!"

"*Nanay*, the incident bothered me very much so that *uh* ... several nightmares interrupted my sleep! In one nightmare, I dreamt of *uh* ... getting shot in the back! When I woke up, *uh* ... I was happy to realize that it was just a bad dream!"

"Son, I also had nightmares in which the *Japons* were shooting at us. The bullets were literally hitting just inches away and I kept waking up!"

"*Nanay*, when you have a nightmare, like that, are you able to go back to sleep?"

"Sometimes, I return to sleep. But more often, I refuse to go back to sleep because I'm too scared of my dreams!"

"I do that, too, *nanay*."

"Just the same, we shouldn't have gone home without any food! I'd rather die than listen to my children cry in pain! It has been just too painful to watch the young children ask for food. I can no longer nurse them because my milk had dried up.

"My heart was breaking in knowing that I couldn't do anything about their hunger! I haven't been able to sleep properly. I'll probably die from fear and sorrow any way!"

"I understand why *uh* ... you feel that way, *nanay*. What do you propose *uh* ... that we do differently?"

"I have thought hard about that incident last month. I asked myself what we could have done otherwise.

"I feel that I have to be a braver person! If we try to play it safely, we'll never be able to procure enough food again. These trips have become more dangerous to accomplish! Now, that the guerrillas have become more active and daring, we can expect more fighting every time we come out here!"

"I know you're right, *nanay*. I was thinking *uh* ... that it is possible that the combatants might shoot at each other across the River. If we happen to be in the area when that happens, uh ... the *Japons* can see us and may shoot us at will!"

"Yes, Junior. That is a possible situation."

"So, what do you think *uh* ... we should do that is more daring but safe, *nanay*?"

"Junior, we are like soldiers with a specific mission, which puts our lives in danger. Like fighting soldiers, we have to decide how we'll live or die.

"Either we die by starving in safety in our hideaway or we die by trying to overcome the most extreme dangers. Son, I want your opinion on this matter!"

"*Nanay*, are you asking me *uh* ... to commit suicide with you? Why are you talking about *uh* ... dying?"

"Son, I'm asking you to do things with me that some people might interpret as committing suicide!"

"*Nanay*, I *uh* ... don't want to commit suicide; I don't want to die!"

"I don't want to die either. But, we have now reached a more dangerous situation! We might die at any moment!"

"*Nanay*, I'm shocked! Why are you talking this way?"

"Son, let me put it bluntly! In order to accomplish our missions, I want to increase our tolerance of danger to the *extreme degree*! Anything less will force us to fail and not bring any food home! This change in our tolerance of risk might mean we die instantly!"

"*Nanay*, *uh* ... please explain what you mean by 'extreme degree'? Does it mean that *uh* ... we never withdraw from any situation, even if we die in the process?"

"I'm not too clear about it myself. Let me explain it in another way. We need to increase our tolerance of risk to the point when we might get killed at any moment!"

"*Nanay*, I think you're *uh* ...*uh* ... asking too much," he answered and started to cry. After he had calmed down, he said, "I'm not sure *uh* ... *uh* ... I can go along with your plans. I think *uh* ... you're turning us into *uh* ... **daredevils!**"

"Son, we have to be daring enough so we can accomplish what we need to do. If you think that is being daredevils, then we are!"

"What if I *uh*... refuse to go along with your proposal?"

"Then, we have to stop making these trips and starve to death in hiding!"

"Will someone else *uh* ... make these trips for me if I stop going?"

"Honestly, I don't think so. I don't think I can tell your father about what I have just proposed to you. He'll be dumbfounded and think I'm crazy! He might even decide to do it himself. But, I don't want him to do this. His survival is essential for the survival of our family and the whole group."

"Perhaps, *nanay uh* ... I don't really understand *uh* ... how much more risk you want us to take. Still, I love you so much, I *uh* ... won't deny you my company!

"Will you please, *uh* ... give me a few minutes to think about your suggestion?"

"Yes, son, think about it; while I also try to clarify my thinking."

They kept cruising without saying a word for at least an hour. Junior kept thinking about his mother's daredevil proposal. He kept vacillating because the thought of dying was very scary to him!

Nevertheless, he was certain of one thing: he loved her more than he loved life! He was willing to die for her and with her! After he had sufficiently clarified his thoughts, he was eager to talk!

"*Nanay*, I have thought long enough about your proposal. All right! I'll *uh* ...risk my life with you, even if we die *uh* ...in the process!

"I agree with you that we have to increase *uh* ... our courage! We will do *uh* ... whatever we need to do!"

"Thank you, son, for your commitment! I love you very much, son. You've always been my favorite child! I want you to know that, now! I may not have the chance to tell you later on. I no longer know if there is even a tomorrow for us!

"I hope this is not too soon, son. I expect you to try our resolve today! I expect to go through very heavy fighting this afternoon. And, I'm determined to bring food home!

"Is it all right with you, son, to start our new resolve today?"

"Yes, *nanay*! You have my *uh* ... full cooperation! Based on the *uh* ...weekly increase in the fighting, I agree we might be *uh* ... going through hell today!"

Junior couldn't help crying. The thought of dying made him feel so sad! He wasn't ready to die! He was just a child; he had not yet lived as he had dreamed of living! Yet, that day might be his last day alive!

Silently, he said goodbye to the birds, fishes and trees in his swamp family. He said goodbye to his father and to everyone in the family. He even said goodbye to Mabini. He bid *adios* to his beloved town of Mambusao, to his province of Capiz and to everyone in his swamp community. He expected to die that same day!

To his surprise, he was at peace with himself! He was resigned to die!

When they were about five kilometers from the town, Junior could hear fighting going on at the left side of the River. He steered the canoe to the left bank for more protection from stray bullets. The farther they navigated towards the town, the closer the fighting sounded to him. He saw some stray bullets hitting the water at the right side of the River.

He kept thinking about his mother's resolve to push the risk factor to the extreme. He really didn't know what that meant. But, he trusted that she would tell him whether they were reaching the extreme or not! He was also determined not to turn back. He told himself to stay the course, unless his mother ordered him to do otherwise. He had already given her his word. He was willing to die with her, if necessary!

From his point of view, however, what they were experiencing already bordered on suicide! They could get killed at any moment! Bullets were hitting the water close to their boat. They were literally going into a direct line of fire!

If the decision were left to him, he would have escaped from the extreme danger minutes earlier!

The noise level was so loud that even if Taling had ordered him to turn back, he might not have heard her!

On his own, he decided to paddle furiously forward to get out of the battle zone! He noticed that his mother was doing the same thing. After a while, he became sure that they were relatively out of danger. They exhaled loudly for relief!

He felt lucky to get out of that scene alive! The stray bullets kept hitting the water just a few feet away!

He kept asking himself whether, from his mother's point of view, they had already reached extreme risk. Since he didn't hear anything from her, he assumed that, to her, there was still a margin of safety.

That was the first time when he seriously believed that *she had become a true daredevil*! Or, perhaps, she had become suicidal because she was so desperate to obtain food! In either case, he realized that they had definitely increased their tolerance of risk to the most extreme degree!

Even though they had survived the near-death episode, Junior felt more severely traumatized than ever before! His paranoia seemed more extreme!

He was sure, for example, that some Japanese soldiers were directly shooting at them! He looked back a few times to look for the Japanese soldiers but saw no one. He reasoned that it was possible the bullets were only straying from their intended targets.

However, he felt sure that some Japanese soldiers were shooting at them, as he had seen in his nightmares! He was getting confused between his nightmares and reality!

Towards the end of May, they made another trip, which Junior was very reluctant to make. His nervous condition had gotten considerably worse! His brain felt numbed. At the same time, his headaches were hard to bear, especially at the base of his head.

When they were about five kilometers from the town of Makato, they could hear a fierce battle going on above the left bank of the River.

Perhaps, because of his mother's daredevil new attitude, he ignored the fighting and just kept paddling briskly forward. He was vaguely surprised at his own behavior. He wasn't sure whether he had become braver or just resigned to die! He was paddling the boat casually, while bullets were hitting the waters around them!

Somehow, nothing seemed to matter anymore! By then, he was prepared to die! He thought that if they died, the family would have to form another daredevil team because they had to. The conditions surrounding their trips excluded cowards!

He wondered whether there were different degrees of extreme danger. He was curious how long he could go before the lethal bullet actually hit him. He was seriously puzzled whether getting wounded or dead was just a matter of luck!

He had expected to get wounded for sometime. Yet, he and his mother have been lucky so far. He asked himself whether some people were born lucky and others were just unlucky. It was clear to him that there was nothing special that they were doing except that they had increased their daring. This change would definitely increase the odds of getting killed!

Since his father had chosen him to live in the swamp, he had classified himself as among the unlucky ones. He was unlucky to be the runt of his family. He was unfortunate to have been chosen to make those death-defying missions through the battlefields. He felt certain that it was also his predestined bad luck to die at any moment soon!

He felt helpless and resigned to whatever might happen. They were in the line of fire! There was nothing he could do except to keep on going forward. He expected the right bullet to strike him down!

He reasoned that turning around and going back would not help. The fighting was extensive! The combatants just happened to be near them. He assumed his mother was thinking in the same way. They couldn't really communicate verbally. The noise level was so loud!

After surviving that harrowing experience, he felt emotionally calloused. He believed he had experienced the most extreme fear and survived! He suspected that nothing could scare him anymore!

He was curious whether he was becoming more daring or just emotionally paralyzed. He experienced a certain degree of liberation from fear. It felt good not to be so afraid!

He even thought that the daredevil experience might increase his courage. However, he also wondered whether he might become more reckless.

In fact, the cumulative effect of extreme fear was not what he had expected. What he experienced was *emotional paralysis*.

He had become an emotional zombie! This was nature's way of protecting the psyche. It was like having an amnesia, which protected consciousness from unbearably painful memories. He had made those dangerous trips for so long, he became emotionally flat. His emotion of fear had reached its limits. He could no longer become more afraid! It was an interesting experience and realization!

Every time they made another dangerous trip, they could hear fighting either at the left or the right side of the River. When the fighting was at the right side of the River, Junior guessed that the Japanese soldiers must have ambushed the guerrillas before they could cross the Rio Este Bridge. He thought that it was a good defensive strategy. It prevented the attackers from having an immediate proximity to their barracks.

There were also times when the combatants were attacking each other from each side of the River. Every week the battles were escalating! He wondered how long the Japanese could hold out. Every week the guerrillas were hitting and hurting them badly!

During the first week of July, the family was again short of food supplies. Taling was especially determined to complete the mission. However, as soon as they got out of the swamp area, they could hear fierce fighting on both sides of the River. The whole atmosphere was threatening and ominous!

The volume of firepower was like firecrackers on New Year's eve or like millions of popcorns popping out in rapid succession! The only difference was the loudness of the explosions. The noise level was so loud that Junior didn't hear his mother's voice when she yelled, "Let us turn back and get out of here!" She had to repeat her order three or four times before he got the message.

After they were out of danger, Taling said, "Let us try it again tomorrow. I hope the fighting won't be as bad!"

"*Nanay*, I was quite surprised by your decision," Junior remarked with a smirk on his face. "I had suspected that *uh* ... no amount of danger can scare you anymore!"

"Son, I have definite limits to my tolerance of risk," Taling responded with irritation that bordered on anger. "I'm willing to take extreme risk, but I don't want to commit suicide! That situation was just too risky!"

"I'm sorry, *nanay*. I was just teasing you."

"Junior, this is not a teasing matter! Don't ever make any more frivolous remarks in the future! Understand?"

"Yes, *nanay*. I'm very sorry!"

That was among the few times that she ordered him to turn around. They had traveled only about twelve kilometers from their house.

They didn't try again until two days later. That day, the fighting was farther away at the right side of the River. As they paddled upstream, past the battle zone, the fighting suddenly shifted towards the River. Junior suspected that the fighting might move towards their specific location!

He guessed that the Japanese might be retreating and the guerrillas might be chasing them. Or, it could be the other way around.

This was one situation he really wanted to avoid. If the Japanese crossed the River to escape, the guerrillas would be shooting at them. Junior was afraid that they might be in a crossfire!

He was in a quandary whether to turn back or continue. Taling said nothing. To him, it seemed easier to continue because they had already the momentum of moving forward. So, he increased the rate of his paddle strokes to get out of danger!

They were trying to read each other's mind. As long as Taling didn't object to what he was doing, Junior assumed she was in agreement.

He decided to stay close to the right bank of the River to avoid the stray bullets. They paddled in a frenzy because they could hear bullets and projectiles flying over them. They could also see some bullets hitting the water on the other side of the River!

They continued moving in a hurry even after they were out of danger. It was fear that forced them to keep on moving even when they were already safe.

They never knew whether the Japanese or the guerrillas, in fact, crossed the River. After they got out of the danger zone, the question became purely academic. They had moved out of danger faster than usual. Junior suspected that the past three years of using the paddle, they had become physically stronger. They had also become better canoe navigators!

Chapter Thirty One
The Last Days of the War

Jose Custodio informed Taling and Junior before they departed for the shore, "Ah just heard a good news over our underground radio! Germany has already surrendered to da allies! Hitler committed suicide!

"Japan is badly losing da war. She wouldn't be fighting too long without any ally."

"That is indeed good news, Pepe!" Taling responded. "Now, I know that the war is finally coming to an end!"

"Yes, Taling! Still, ah advise ya to be careful as usual. Avoid da Japanese soldiers *um* ... as much as possible. Dey are becoming more desperate. Dey are retaliating *um* ... on da civilians and are killing dem indiscriminately."

"Yes, Pepe. We'll be careful. I'm afraid they'll go down to the riverbanks and kill innocent people like us!"

"Am sorry, Taling. Am afraid ah scared ya! Ah don't think dey'll do dat. Dey have actually suffered tremendous loses. It is rumored dat dey are now reduced to defending deir garrisons. Hence, deir aggression has been more limited."

"But, you just said that they have killed civilians indiscriminately."

"Yes. Ah said dat. Yesterday, two Japanese soldiers went berserk and killed ten civilians in barrio Isidro. Dey were disperate and wanted to die. Da oder barrio people hacked dem to death! But, dat was an isolated incident."

"Does it mean that they are no longer using the bridges?" Taling asked.

"Yes. We have not seen deir vehicles cross da bridges dis past week. Ah have recently made it a hobby to observe deir movements.

"Am finding it interesting to watch how dis war is coming to da end. Ah know dat everything happening now is historic. Don't ya think, Taling, dat everything is becoming more interesting?"

"You're right, Pepe. For example, just about a month ago, we saw plane dogfights especially near the shore."

"Uncle Pepe, I *uh* ... enjoyed the dogfights every time they happened," Junior interrupted. "I would hear *uh* ... two or three Japanese airplanes flying in the sky. I think they were flying *uh* ... towards the south.

"Suddenly, *uh* ... two or three American 'double bodied planes' showed up. I didn't know where they came from. The Japanese planes dove down to *uh* ...get away from the Americans. The 'double bodied planes' also dove down and shot down the *Japon* planes."

"Did da Japon planes give da Americans any competition?" Jose asked.

"Yes. But, the competition was short. They were shooting at each other for about *uh* ... five minutes. Then, suddenly, *uh* ... the Japon pilots became scared. They made their planes dive down. But, they couldn't get away from the Americans.

"Every time I watched the dogfights, the 'double bodied planes' always won! The Japanese planes always ended *uh* ... at the bottom of the ocean."

"Jun, what ya call double bodied planes are really called P-39. Da capital letter P stands for *pursuit*. Dey are good for pursuing enemy planes because dey are fast."

"What makes them faster than the *uh* ... *Japon* planes, uncle?"

"Da P-39 has two propellers. Da Japon planes have only one." Jose answered.

"Now, I understand why *uh* ... the P-39 always wins."

"Ah have also seen some dogfights over my barrio. Just da oder day, ah saw a P-39 shot down a Japanese plane. Da burning plane dropped near da Japanese garrison.

"Ah wanted to run over dere to watch it burn. But, ah was afraid da Japanese soldiers might shoot and kill me."

"Over at the shore, the burning Japanese planes usually drop into the sea," Taling said. "But, last week, one Japanese plane dropped on land. My husband, Badong, and several kids ran towards the downed plane. They were curious and thought that it was only about two or three kilometers away.

"It was, in fact, over seven kilometers away. He told me that by the time he got to the downed plane, it had been completely stripped by the civilians of everything they could use. They removed even the aluminum skin of the plane. Still, he was able to remove about two feet of structural aluminum. He made several combs out of the material."

Jose asked, "What happened to da pilot? Did he survive?"

"He jumped out in his parachute. But, the civilians killed him as soon as he landed."

"Am not surprised," Jose remarked. "If ah were dere, ah'd kill da *Japon* myself!"

Taling interrupted, "Pepe, let us go back to the topic of the *Japons* in Makato. You said that they just stay in town to defend their garrisons.

Does it mean that we can now cross under the bridges even during day?"

"Ah hesitate to advise ya to go ahead. However, if ya're up to it … go ahead and try. But, be very careful! Don't use yar paddles when pass under da bridge. Move yar canoe slowly up da River."

"But, why should we be careful if the Japs are no longer using bridges?"

"Ya're right, Taling. Ah think ah'm still afraid!"

"I asked you that question because I intend to arrive here earlier week. I'm tired of arriving here in the dark and sleeping on a mu ground. We have made ourselves vulnerable to crocodile attacks! As known, I had been attacked by a crocodile a few months ago. So, my of the animals is warranted!

"I want to stay overnight with you and sleep in a warm bed. I wa visit with you and talk about subjects that interest me."

"Dat is a wonderful plan, Taling," Magda said. "Every week worry about ya being open to crocodile attacks. Ah feel dat we can ha good conversation about a lot of topics."

"Ah agree with Magda," Jose added. "We have a lot to talk a In da past, we really had no chance to talk because everyone was so harvesting. It would be nice for ya to sleep in a real bed and not op crocodile assault."

"So, expect us to arrive late in the afternoon next week. We wi supper with you and celebrate the allied victory over Germany!"

"Yes, Taling," Magda said. "We will expect you and Jun to a earlier. We will be eagerly waiting for your arrival!"

Around the first week of August, Taling and Junior left at ar seven-thirty in the morning for the trip to the Custodio farm.

Taling said, "Jun, let us try to maneuver our boat under the b today. That would be a real experience! For three years, we have waiting at the outskirts of the town until dark. We were afraid of seen by the *Japons*."

"Yes, *nanay*. Let us finally defy them! It might feel good *uh* … feel afraid of them any more!"

"I can't wait to arrive in the farm and climb the precipice upon a It would be nice to start harvesting rice and corn as soon as we arriv

"Yes, *nanay*. It would be a different experience to climb th during the day. For three years, *uh* … the cliff has prevented us seeing the Custodios until the next day. Today, we'll climb the cli see the Custodios right away."

ight, Jun. Beginning today, our trips to the farm will be easier
)yable!"
ay. Let us paddle faster so we arrive there earlier!"
ll be there before we realize it!"
ight they were lucky not to hear any fighting as they
e town. Junior suspected that the war might be over because
cted that it could be over any day soon.
relieved especially after reaching the town and still nothing
. Just for greater safety and by the force of habit, they were
the vegetation to move the boat forward.
however, several canon shots came from the right side of
d become the pattern of the guerrilla fighters to attack from
hots started from afar, about two kilometers away. Again,
hat the guerrillas were moving towards the riverbank.
e getting progressively louder. He thought he heard also
id bazookas firing.
rd and saw four-inch canon projectiles zooming across
on as the guerrillas got close to the bank, they unleashed
had! He could hear carbines, bazookas, machine guns,
and canons. The sound was deafening and numbing.
if the guerrillas were already celebrating their victory!
vere shooting into the air and yelling, "*Mabuhay ang
g live the Philippines.) This patriotic phrase was used
tic festivals.
hots of canons, including machine guns, were coming
Junior knew that those were the Japanese fighting back.
defend their position.
the volume and power of the guerrilla attacks, it became
hat the guerrillas had finally gained the upper hand!
y had obtained more arms and ammunitions from the
using all their weapons to let the Japanese defenders
e better armed than before. For a change, the guerrillas
idate and humiliate the occupiers!
d to Junior, by nodding her head, to keep moving
dled in a frenzy and moved faster than usual! They
me more skillful and vigorous navigators.
boat close to the left bank. He figured out that any
d other bullets, coming from the Japanese side, would
e of the River.
ved at the Custodio farm, they could still hear the
oting from both sides of the River. Mr. Custodio told

them, "Da *Japons* are getting hopeless and crazy! Dey are killing more civilians, including women and children in da barrios. Dey are retaliating on da defenseless people."

"Pepe, aren't you afraid that they might come here and massacre us also?" Taling asked.

"Of course, am afraid. Dat is why *um* ... am happy when da guerrillas are attacking and killing dem.

"However, da danger is getting much less everyday *um* ... as da Filipino guerrillas are killing dem and destroying deir ammunitions. Da guerrillas set fire to deir *bodegas* (wharehouses) dat contained deir ammunitions only last night. Obviously, dey have oder storage facilities because dey are still shooting, as ya can hear."

Junior took Jose aside and asked, "Uncle Pepe, didn't you tell us last week that *uh* ... the war may be over any day now?"

"Yes, Jun, ah said dat. But, from what ah have read in da underground newspaper, *um* ... dere are powerful Japanese Generals who want to fight to da last man. Dey are da *bushido code* fanatics. Nobody knows, at dis time, *um* ... when da end will come."

"Still, the end must be *uh* ... coming very soon; I hope so," Junior muttered in discouragement!

"Jun, why are ya suddenly impatient about da war? Is dere something wrong?"

"Yes, uncle. I feel like I am about to have a nervous breakdown!"

"Am sorry to hear dat. How do ya feel right now?"

"I'm feeling shaky and anxious! I'm afraid my health is falling apart!"

"Take my advice for what it is worth. Try to relax! Try to think of pleasant things. Imagine dat da war is already over and ya're back in Mambusao with yar old friends. Imagine dat ya're playing a game dat ya really enjoy! Now, tell me, what is da game ya like to play?"

"I like to play basketball."

"Den, imagine yarself playing basketball! Imagine making fantastic shots and every shot goes in. Imagine dat yar team is winning!"

"Thank you uncle Pepe. I'll try to follow your advice."

"Ah hope ya feel better next week!"

Chapter Thirty Two
At the Edge of a Breakdown

As usual, Taling and Junior were scheduled to return to the shore in the evening of the following day. Once again, getting caught in the crossfire the day before was particularly traumatic to the severely traumatized boy. Thinking that the war might be over, he had lowered his guard. The unexpected guerrilla attack was particularly traumatic!

He couldn't tolerate any more hostilities! His headaches were getting more severe and his hearing in the right ear was also getting worse. The loud noise caused by the shelling nearby must have punctured his right eardrum.

Overall, he felt that he had become more fragile! His general health seemed to be crumbling! The combined effects of the traumas he had sustained for months were approaching a breaking point! He could feel his brain tighten as if his skull was shrinking! His nerves were more frayed than ever before!

When they were a few kilometers away from the shore, he talked to his mother about his deteriorating health.

"I don't know *uh* ... how you feel, *nanay*," he said haltingly. "I'm really *uh* ... sick of making these dangerous trips. The past *uh* ...five months have really been very hard on my nerves. I think they're *uh* ...*uh* ... shattered. I'm incapable of *uh* ... making these trips any more!"

Taling turned around and said, "Oh, no! I'm really shocked to hear that, son! I didn't realize you're in such a bad shape. I thought, as a child, you're more resilient than I am."

"I've been feeling this way *uh* ... for months now, *nanay*," he said meekly. "Every week, I feel my nerves are *uh* ... becoming tighter than ever. The skin on my forehead feels very tight. My emotions just seem *uh* ... flat, as if I no longer feel anything. I've never felt this way before. I'm really scared of *uh* ... becoming completely paralyzed in my emotions!"

"I might be close to that condition too," Taling said, looking really worried. "You know, son, I was really more nervous than you were when we started these missions. These worsening war situations only make matters worse for me.

"Still, the Custodios told us that the war is definitely coming to an end at any time soon. Can you just be more patient until the war finally ends?"

The Child Daredevil Hero

"*Nanay*, uncle Pepe also said that *uh* ... the allies might have to invade Japan. If they do that, *uh* ... the fighting could last for several more months.

"Remember what he said about the *uh* ... *bushido* code? The Japanese are so fanatical *uh* ... they might fight until all of them are dead! To surrender is against the *uh* ... *bushido* belief."

"He did say that. Nevertheless, I don't know who can take your place."

"Why not Mabini? Or, *uh* ... Paterno? They should have *uh* ... undertaken this responsibility, in the first place."

She thought about his suggestion and seemed reluctant to answer him. After a while, she said, "Son, for the last three years, I've resisted the temptation to tell you the *true story*. Now, that the war is almost over and because you're asking for a replacement, I might as well reveal the *secret*!

"Right from the beginning, your father asked Mabini and Paterno to make these trips for the family. But, Mabini refused. Paterno used Mabini's reasoning to also refuse the assignment.

"Both used the same argument that they'll be easily mistaken for adults. They feel that the *Japons* will kill them, if the enemies should catch them.

"That's why I volunteered to go with you because someone had to take the risk."

"*Nanay*, now I understand why you have taken this dangerous assignment with me. When tatay told me that you volunteered to make the dangerous missions with me, I could not believe that you would do it!

"Now, I also know from your revelations that uh ... my older brothers are real cowards!"

"Son, I want you to understand one important thing. Your dad can't really force your brothers if they refuse to obey him. They are now grown up. They can physically challenge and disobey him!

"If he really uses his authority as a father, he'll have to threaten them with physical violence! And, if they refuse to obey him, then he'll have to follow through on his threat. And, that could result in a serious physical violence and injury! I was afraid of what could happen!"

"*Nanay*, if he really uses his authority and *uh* ... order them to obey his command, will they challenge his authority?"

"It's possible. But, he never invoked his authority because I intervened!

"I was afraid that Mabini would defy his order! I feared that he might use his martial art and hurt the boy badly!

"There was another reason why I intervened. I was frightened that if your father insisted that they perform this job, they might *run away and leave* the family!"

"Where would they go?"

"They can go to other villages and stay with some kind and charitable strangers for awhile. If your father pursues them, then they might just hide in the mountains or join the Filipino guerrillas. Son, I feared that I might never see them again!"

"Now, I understand why we were stock with these life-threatening missions. We had to do them even though I was just a small child and you were a frail woman. Nobody else would do it!"

"You're essentially correct, Jun."

"Still, *nanay*, please ... bring up with *tatay* about my immediate replacement. The teenagers might *uh* ... think differently today. After all, the war is almost over. The likelihood of their *uh* ... being caught by the *Japons* is now very slim."

"I'll bring it up to him but I'm not sure whether he'll do anything."

"*Nanay*, you must really help me! If I don't get a *uh* ... relief soon, I'll have a nervous breakdown!"

"Junior, I've already promised you to bring it up with your father. He'll have to do a lot of convincing to get those boys to relieve you. I don't know what he'll do."

"Thank you, *nanay*, for taking my message to *tatay*."

Junior left the village for the swamp somewhat disappointed. Still, he was also grateful for having the courage to tell his mother about his mental condition.

He was also glad to know that his dad didn't single him out to be sacrificed to the Japanese. He became the 'logical choice' to risk his young life only after the teenagers had refused to obey their father.

As he reflected on the revelations made by his mother, he concluded that part of his problem was that he hadn't yet learned how to disobey and get away with it. That was exactly what his older brothers were doing. They disobeyed and got away with it!

He became even more resentful of them for exploiting his innocence and vulnerability. They could dodge their responsibilities because they knew that their parents would then dump those responsibilities on poor Junior. They forced their father to make Junior his 'logical choice.' That was exploitation of the worse kind! It was closer to blackmail!

For the present, his immediate problem was his mental frailty. He thought he must be more assertive about his personal needs and rights. He must protect his own health and life. Nevertheless, he didn't know what else to do if the changes he had requested didn't happen. He didn't have any alternatives because he knew he could never disobey his parents!

On August 14, Trinidad and Ruperto showed up at the cabin. Junior's heart seemed to stop upon seeing his younger brothers. He knew immediately that nobody was replacing him. The younger boys were just following the usual pattern.

If there was any change, the boys wouldn't have shown up. He naively expected Mabini or Paterno to take his place as he had requested. Again, he felt that his parents just ignored his request. He cried in frustration!

He felt very disappointed that he had to keep on doing something that might ruin his mental health or kill him. He intended to talk again to his mother about his replacement during the trip. Maybe, he should talk directly to his father.

From his own observation of his mental condition, he knew that he was mentally damaged. But, he didn't know just how severely!

He needed at least three month's rest to allow his nerves to heal. His brain needed even a longer rest from all the emotional pressures and traumas. He had already reached his limits. He could sense that something drastic was about to happen, like a mental breakdown!

As he looked at his brother, Trinidad, he noticed that the boy had grown bigger and stronger. He became more muscular during the past three years. If the teenagers still refused to do their obligation to the family, then perhaps Trinidad could replace him.

He knew that Trinidad had just turned nine. He was only a year older when he started doing the dangerous errands for the family.

He thought that at age nine, Trinidad was better prepared to make those trips than he was at age ten. The muscular brother was almost as tall as he was. But, Trinidad was a more skillful canoe navigator.

He decided that, next week, he would talk to his parents about Trinidad as his replacement.

In order to prepare the boy for the dangerous ordeal, he would warn him about getting caught in crossfires. He would share with him everything he had learned about the deadly missions. He intended to teach him how to elude the Japanese guards, how to deal with the deadly whirlpools, the vicious rapids and the hungry crocodiles!

However, he was already feeling guilty about exposing his innocent brother to near-death types of experiences! To him, it wasn't fair to destroy his brother's precious innocence! Innocence was among his greatest loses in the war. He'll never be the same simple boy again. He didn't want to deprive his brother of his natural simplicity.

He was feeling guilty about his proposal!

When he reached the shore, he greeted his mother with a kiss on her forehead. She immediately took him aside and said, "I'm sorry, Junior. I spoke to your *tatay* about getting one of your older brothers to replace you. But, again they refused to obey him. He even tried to shame them into compliance! Still, they refused!

"You told me how sick you are. I'm sad and frustrated that I can't be of any help to you."

"Don't feel badly, *nanay*. You did your best and ... I'm grateful for that. Perhaps, I'll try my best to be more relaxed! And, *uh* ... hope that my mental health will hold up. Uncle Pepe gave me some pointers on how to relax. I believe his advice will help me greatly!"

"I'm glad you feel that way, son. It is true, you can now afford to be more relaxed! Since the *Japons* are clearly losing the war, you don't have to be afraid of getting arrested at this time.

"I don't know when the war will end. But, I know it will be soon. Just put in the least effort until the war finally ends!"

"Yes, *nanay*. I thought about Trinidad as my replacement. But, I've already changed my mind about him."

"Trinidad, you said? He is too young! Please, forget the thought!"

"Yes, nanay. I'd rather suffer a nervous breakdown than *uh* ... rob him of his natural innocence!"

Chapter Thirty Three
New Beginnings, Lucky Endings

On August 15, 1945, Taling and Junior left for their usual weekly trip to the Custodio farm. Junior was surprised not hearing any fighting anywhere, not even in town. It was an eerie feeling especially since he had expected even worse hostilities! He expected the guerrillas to use even bigger guns, like ten-inch canon balls, if they had such ammunitions. He wanted the guerrillas to really flatten the Japanese garrisons and expel them forever!

When they arrived at the Custodio farm at around five in the afternoon, Magda came out running and yelling, "*Mabuhay*! Da war is over! Alleluia!"

"When did it end?" Taling asked.

"Only yesterday! According to an underground radio, da emperor surrendered his country, without any conditions!"

The atom bomb that ended the war!

Junior couldn't believe what he had just heard! Even though he also expected the end to come at anytime, it was still surprising when it really happened!

He thought that the allies would invade Japan itself. He personally hoped that the allies would retaliate for what the Japanese had done at Pearl Harbor. He also wanted to punish them for invading the Philippines and the other Asian Countries.

He also wanted to penalize them for the destruction and atrocities they committed during the war, especially in the Philippines. He felt extremely angry and vindictive!

The dropping of the two atomic bombs by the United States on Hiroshima and Nagasaki and the Russian invasion of the Japanese-held Manchuria finally convinced Emperor Hirohito and the military leaders that it was pointless to go on fighting. They had already lost virtually everything!

Of course, Junior was very happy, just the same, that the senseless war had ended! Perhaps, his dreaded mental breakdown was prevented. He would no longer be making those dangerous trips! And, his mental traumas could start to heal immediately!

Alleluia! The war was finally over! It was the final liberation of the Philippine Commonwealth! The bombs finished what the guerrillas almost succeeded in doing!

The Japanese were completely obliterated from Makato. Most of them committed hara-*kiri,* upon learning of their country's surrender. The guerrillas and the civilians massacred those who refused to commit suicide!

There were rumors, however, that some of the Japanese soldiers may have escaped to the jungles and the caves in the neighboring mountains. If they did, the guerrillas would hunt them like wild pigs until they eradicated them completely!

In fact, some of the Japanese soldiers didn't surrender until more than ten years later. Some of those who surrendered later on didn't even know that the war had already formally ended.

Junior knew he was a 'walking wounded' because of the psychic traumas he had experienced. The last eight to ten months of the war were extremely harmful but he survived! He could have mentally broken down like some shell-shocked soldiers who became 'basket cases' and couldn't function normally in society. Some ended up in mental institutions. Others became street people or committed suicide to end their own miseries.

In a sense, Junior and his mother were veterans of WWII. They had their psychic scars to prove their claim!

Junior was lucky that the war ended before he had a severe mental breakdown. He felt that he was just days away from a mental disaster!

Finally, it was time for healing and rebuilding whatever was still left. He was fortunate to survive and to move on in his life!

After the war, everyone tried to resume the life they had left in suspended animation. They had to overcome tremendous inertia that had developed like rust on machine parts. For over four years, their academic faculties had been left virtually unused.

Nobody said anything about the war that could only reopen wounds and deep psychic traumas. The war experiences were like bad dreams, buried in total oblivion. There was a strong taboo that prohibited anyone from saying anything about the war events.

Some pupils who had only minimal schooling had completely forgotten whatever academic lessons they were presumed to have learned. Junior, for example, had only two and a half years of rudimentary schooling when the war disrupted his education. He discovered that he had become completely *illiterate!* Therefore, he was non-functioning in the postwar classroom.

Instead of sending him back to first grade to learn his alphabets, the dysfunctional school system promoted him twice within a period of one year.

Incredibly, he found himself in fifth grade and completely incapable of reading his textbooks.

To make his situation doubly worse, he could not understand the new medium of instruction, which was English.

Before the war, the media of instruction were the vernacular languages. There were eighty-seven different dialects throughout the 7000 islands of the Philippine Archipelago. In his island of Panay, the medium of instruction was *Ilongo*.

In his fifth grade class, *Ilongo* was completely prohibited. There were 'language spies' who could report a pupil for speaking *Ilongo*. And severe fines were strictly imposed.

He went through academic hell! Despair completely replaced hope as he flunked every subject at every grading period!

His illiteracy and ignorance of the medium of instruction left him no viable alternative except to drown himself in the Mambusao River. The water velocity, however, was not strong enough to strangle him.

While recuperating, however, an instructive dream showed him how to teach himself literacy and English.

In his dream, he was playing with wooden blocks, which contained the letters of the English alphabet. He had thousands of letters to play with.

In the beginning, he played randomly with the letters. Slowly, he combined the letters into syllables. Then, the syllables became words and later became sentences. The sentences became paragraphs. And, unbelievably, the paragraphs became stories!

In the dream, he could spell and read the words he had formed.

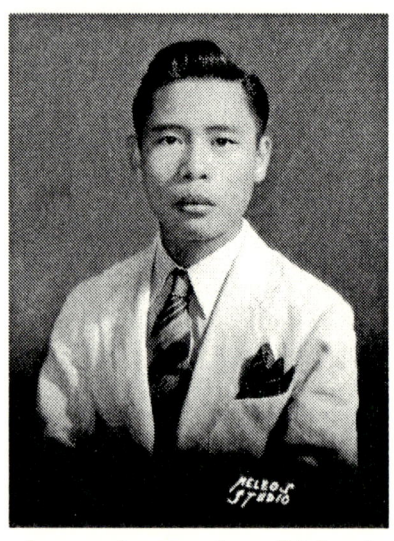

Junior graduating from high school

Upon awakening, he immediately put the dream lessons into practice. Slowly, he acquired literacy and learned English on his own! To his surprise, he passed some of his subjects but only barely!

Encouraged by his improvements, he worked extra hard to catch up with all his classmates. His extraordinary progress gave him a bright ray of hope! Goaded by his passing marks, he worked even harder to pursue what his dream had implicitly promised him: academic competence and excellence! In time, he excelled way beyond his own expectations!

By the time he graduated from high school, he had successfully made himself the top student! He graduated as the valedictorian!

He won a coveted scholarship to a prestigious college in Manila and graduated *summa cum laude*! Eventually, he acquired a doctorate in philosophy and became a college professor!

Epilogue

Junior was among the few who thought that there was something mentally unhealthy about the collective silence regarding the war. He believed that *healing* could be quicker if the wounds were aired and exposed to the sun. There were gaping psychic wounds that needed to be medicated and closed.

There was no natural *closure* to various psychic momentums created during the war. There was no proper *ending* to the plans and projects initiated during the war times.

There was no review or accounting for whatever had occurred during the World War. An inquisition could have provided important lessons. The lessons, insights and conclusions drawn could have served as the solid foundation of postwar life.

Everything abruptly ended in August 1945. And life resumed based on hazy memories and false assumptions. For instance, the administration wrongly assumed that the pupils had retained most of what they had tried to learn in school before the war.

If there had been an objective review and testing after the war, the teachers and administrators would have known that some pupils retained little or nothing in memory after over four years of disuse. The administrators and teachers would have discovered that some pupils, like Junior, were completely illiterate. They could have handled the situations more humanely. And, Junior didn't have to suffer utter shame, ostracism, ridicule and complete lack of self-esteem! He would not have attempted suicide!

For years, he wanted to write his memoirs to create some closure to the loose ends left dangling after the war. He didn't find the time to write until the year 2001. In fact, he completed his memoirs only at the insistence of his American born wife, Ruthe.

It was ironic that after his Memoirs was published in 2002, one older brother finally said, "Thank you!" The brother put a belated closure to his own personal debt of gratitude.

On May 12, 2003, his brother, Hermogenes, wrote, "On May 7th, I received a package that contained your new book. I immediately began reading it from cover to cover for three days. Admittedly, I was excited reading it as it enlivened my thoughts … recalling some events that were unforgettable…

"At any rate, until I read your memoirs, I was never aware that you lived a hermitic life in the swamps of Makato, sacrificing your life and limbs for the sake of the family, coupled with your hazardous trips to Makato procuring food. Congratulating you at this point in time would not be necessary. However, I felt deeply obligated to thank you for this heroic life. I was a recipient of the economic benefits as a member of the family. ...."

While this letter was heart-warming and expressed a belated sense of gratitude, Junior still wondered that if Hermogenes wasn't aware of his life in solitude during the war, were all his other brothers and sisters equally unaware of his prolonged absence from his family? He had solicited more in-puts from his other brothers and sisters. As of this writing, there were no other materials he could use.

Perhaps, this non-awareness of a brother's absence was normal in a large family of ten siblings. Junior, however, found it still unbelievable!

It is no wonder why he was *the unknown child hero*. If his own family didn't know or didn't realize that he was a true hero, then others couldn't be expected to know his existence either.

Perhaps, this is a *truer heroism*, which nobody knows or acknowledges! The hero himself took his own heroic actions as commonplace.

After sixty years of anonymity, however, his American born wife refused to concede! Ruthe believed that the heroic story must be told to celebrate the greatness of the human spirit. When forced to survive, under impossible conditions, some people become heroes while others perish!

After twenty years of gentle wifely nagging, she convinced him to tell his unusual heroic story! He was a hero not just once or twice. In fact, he was a hero a hundreds times or more!

Every time, he and his mother left the safety of their hideout, they had to perform heroic acts just to survive the trip! The most difficult obstacle was finding their way in the dark as they navigated through whirlpools and rapids! And, they made those death-defying trips every week for three years!

She wanted children throughout the world to know that young children, like themselves, can be great heroes!

Some readers might wonder what happened to the child hero after college.

On a scholarship, he pursued a master's and a doctorate degree in philosophy. He taught philosophy in Notre Dame College in Cotabato City for five years.

In 1966, he immigrated to the United States and taught philosophy at West Chester State University in Pennsylvania.

In 1971, he obtained another doctorate, this time in Foundations of Education, from Temple University in Philadelphia. He taught Foundations of Education courses at Temple University until he decided to change careers in 1980.

In 1979, he married Ruthe Paul in Philadelphia. Together, they started a new business in real estate investments and management. By 1985, they had accumulated sufficient assets to move and retire in Cape Coral, Florida. There, they continued investing in real estate as their primary source of livelihood.

He became a well-known visionary artist. In 1999, he wrote, 'My Taoist Vision of Art.' The book explained the principles and symbols that he used in his artwork. In 2003, he wrote, 'Everyone Is An Artist: Making Yourself the Artwork.' He continues to write books on several subjects.

Today, the couple are 'snow birds' who commute to Boone, North Carolina, in summer, and to Cape Coral, Florida, in winter. Both continue to create art and write books.

For a more complete story, read his memoirs, *Surviving WWII As A Child Swamp Hermit*. (1stbooks Library, 2002). The book is available at Amazon.com and from local bookstores.

The writer wanted to end this book on a poetic note. In May 2004, he woke up asking himself, "If I were a poet, how would I give this book a poetic ending?" He responded, "Simple! Just write a poem."

So, here is a poem entitled, ***What Does It Take To Be A Hero?***

Just do heroic deeds!
I did them many years ago when I was only a child.
When I was only ten, I navigated a canoe through a
    Flooded river to find food for my family.
I paddled under the glare of thunder and lightning
    To prevent my family from starving.
My mother and I steered our canoe through whirlpools
    And rapids at night,
    To prevent the Japanese sentries from killing us.
We defied the crocodiles that wanted to eat us for
    Breakfast, lunch or supper.
I gouged a crocodile's eyes to force it to release my
    Mother's thigh.
I performed these feats every week for three years!
    And, I was only a child!

The end!

About the Author

Sal Kapunan is a philosopher, educator, artist and writer. He has a doctorate in philosophy and in education.

He is a practicing artist who has decorated both of his homes in Florida and North Carolina with pathways and large outdoor sculptures. In 1999, he wrote *My Taoist Vision of Art*. In 2003, he wrote, *Everyone Is An Artist: Making Yourself the Artwork*

He is a bonafide and prolific writer who wrote four wonderful books in the past four years. In 2002, he wrote *Surviving WWII As A Child Swamp Hermit*. In 2004, he wrote *The Child Daredevil Hero*.

Kapunan is a 'snowbird' who, with his wife, Ruthe, flies to Florida in winter and flies back to the Appalachian mountains of North Carolina in summer.

They have three children and two grandchildren.

Printed in the United States
25013LVS00004B/58-105